"THE POWER SUIT! CHRIST, WE'RE DEAD!"

Zelde saw a monster—a metal and plastic giant—facing the mutineers from the edge of the passage landing. She knew what power suits were—no way she could cut into one to the man inside. And *heavy*, they were. . . .

She didn't think about it—she just jumped. Both feet, legs stiff, caught the power suit square in the chest. She bounced back and landed curled up. The thing—it was falling, waving its arms as it toppled over the edge.

It pinwheeled, crumpled a railing, caromed out to graze a wall and come back again—and crashed to a dead stop far below. Sparks came from the jerking mass, then smoke and flame. The shrieking seemed to last forever.

The Latest Science Fiction from Dell Books

Denotes an illustrated book

ZELDE M'TANA

by F. M. Busby

A DELL BOOK

To Bubbles, who
spots the glitches
before they hit print.

Published by
Dell Publishing Co., Inc.
1 Dag Hammarskjold Plaza
New York, New York 10017

Dell ® TM 681510, Dell Publishing Co., Inc.

ISBN: 0-440-19906-9

Printed in the United States of America

First printing—March 1980

Wrists handcuffed behind her, she lay in the dusty van and felt it jounce along the rough street. This was bad. Oh, the Kids would manage—the others had got away, and Horky could take over for now. But . . . herself? They had her; that was all. Fear wouldn't help; she knew that much. Gradually, breathing as little as she could because of the dust, she relaxed and let time pass.

It could have been worse—she'd *expected* worse. But except for the man she'd bitten—still trying to fight, she was, even with the cuffs on—no one had hit her. Panting, one of them laughing but sounding scared, they'd boosted her into the van. "Never mind the rest now—this one can tell us. Let's get out of here!"

The jouncing eased—must be in *their* territory, she guessed. She smelled fumes and heard other motors, and was sure. A time came and went; then the van stopped, and two of them took her out and walked her into a building. She knew the look of it—she'd seen plenty of them, at a distance. But never to go into one—that had been her hope.

Blue-gray halls and then a room—a desk, no one behind it. Three people, standing. When two came to hold her, the men who had brought her turned away and left. She heard and felt her fighting nails clipped; then the cuffs came off. She turned—the woman with the nailclippers looked, frowning, and shook her head. The two men watching—no choice. "All right. I'm not for fighting." She saw the woman relax.

So they stripped her and in the next room scrubbed her—and seemed surprised that except for what the scuffle had done, she wasn't really dirty. Then the woman gave her a short robe to put on and motioned for her to sit down, and where.

The questions began. And because no one had hit her besides the man she bit, and because she had clothes on and was clean and nobody'd tried to rape her, she changed her whole way of thinking and decided to answer. She didn't decide that right away, but the woman was still sounding patient when the first answers came.

She couldn't give her age because she didn't know it. Maybe six or eight years ago, her first recalls began—before that, there was something she couldn't remember and mostly didn't want to. They looked at her a lot. She was taller than the woman and the short man—nearly head-level, both standing, with the taller one. But she knew she was skinny, breasts newish and small yet, and the bleeding curse only three years with her.

The woman asked of that, and she told. The woman said, "About fifteen, I'd call it—and a bit of a late bloomer."

The short man chuckled. "Blacks don't usually bloom late." The woman frowned at him, and went on to other questions.

Her name? She wasn't superstitious—or not very—so she gave it. "Zelde M'tana." And she was close to sure it was her *real* name, though she couldn't remember for certain. But it didn't sound like the Kids'-given names—Horky and Squatcheye, all those. Horky had a Kid name and no other; Arlycharly was really Arlen Charles and everybody knew it; her name and Fred Schroeder's were real because they *sounded* real. All right?

She didn't worry about saying names because by now the Kids wouldn't be anyplace near where she'd been caught, anyway. And if ever she got her hands on Fred Schroeder, she wouldn't need her fighting nails. That copping son of a Utie . . .

Now the woman asked questions she couldn't answer, or wouldn't. About the Kids—"Wild Children," the woman called them—names were no snitch, but numbers and places and ways of doing things—those weren't for Uties to know. Even if they weren't beating or raping her, she was still in the hands of UET, with its Presiding Committee and its Total Welfare Centers. The Kids knew about that stuff.

They didn't know what all happened in there—but Zelde purely didn't want to find out, either.

Finally she shook her head. "No more. I tell about me, 'cause you got me anyway. Help you get somebody else, I *don't* tell. That's how we are, the Kids." Didn't they even know *that* much?

The tall man nodded. "You see? That's why they're dangerous. Autonomous groups—their own strange code of ethics, opposed to ours, left alone to grow . . ."

The woman frowned. "I know that, Gerich—that's why I'm here. What's your own suggestion?"

With a shrug, Gerich said, "Just what we're doing, I suppose—catch them and Welfare them, the best we can."

Total Welfare. Without thinking, Zelde said, "You mean . . . ?"

Grinning, the short man waved a hand. "What did you expect, Skinny? A goldplated appointment to the Presiding Committee?"

Before he finished, she was across the room and onto him—hitting, biting, one slash before she remembered her fighting nails were gone. But when Gerich and the woman dragged her off him, the short man still lived.

Gasping, he blinked blood away and squinted at his fingers, which stuck out at odd angles from the hand. He coughed blood; his voice barely husked through his battered throat.

"Kill this one—or slice her brain, fry it with shock—I—" Coughing stopped him, and then something jabbed into Zelde's neck. She lost strength, first, and then all knowing.

The cell—eat, piss, shit, sleep—lasted a long time. In between, sometimes she thought. She had plenty of time for it, and it helped ease the panic of being cooped up so tight.

I wish we could of talked more. Before she'd yanched out—but *Welfare!*—any Kid would of; Welfare was being dead without lying down for it. But still, the woman was *telling* stuff and she could use it, to know.

Well, she didn't have it, was all, and now she wouldn't get it. There'd been something—thinking back, she rubbed palms over the new stubble growing on her scalp—pretty soon nobody'd know her for a fighter, would they? Something, though—she hadn't listened close, but the woman said like, "When the terrorists nuked the old U.N. building—remember? A festival upstate, for a lot of the Embassy children—with all the confusion, nobody ever found out what happened to them. She could be—" But the short man had snorted, interrupting, changing the subject and leaving Zelde hanging on questions with no answers.

Here, naked in the cell, fighting her fear of the damned box, it didn't matter. Except that—who *was* she? What was it she could never quite remember? Well, what she didn't know, she couldn't tell. And what she did know—from now on, she *wouldn't*.

"Zelde." Warm voices had called her that. "Zelde M'tana," and hearing inside now, she felt less warmth but still some of it. The—no, nobody was really there. But the something—explosion sounded in her head and she flinched, cringed, curled up tight—no, she couldn't ever quite get that, so *quit it*.

Vaguely, the time with the first Kids—cold and wet and bad smelly, all of them. Dragged staggering along with a dirty rope around her neck. Sleeping with the big ones each side of her, all warm stinking together.

Then into something, lying the same only it all swayed and rattled a long time. She was really sick. Getting off, she couldn't walk, and they kicked her until she got up. After that she had the flat blanks until the fever left her, and there was somebody new taking care of her. Terelda, the name was, and the first Kids were gone and she was with— well, it was Stud's Cruds, then.

Stud was big Porlanter who never hit anyone who listened the first time. That was one nice thing; the next was that these Kids weren't dirty. Where her infested skin had been raw so long, Zelde healed up.

Stud—Porlanter—died of something that swole up inside him, for months, and wouldn't stop. Well, it looked silly for Terelda to call herself Stud, so she told lanky ol' Sentenerl he should do that stuff. But she still ran the Kids, because she knew how.

For Zelde, it went along not so bad, then. How many years? They'd asked her, those Welfare catchers, but she couldn't say for sure. Three–four years, there, she was little. 'Way too young for fighting or screwing, either one— but she trained for the first and grew her nails for it, and saw enough of the other to know what it was about. And when she got tall, it was all in one summer.

The Cruds lived, mostly, in the parts of towns where the Welfare roundups had cleaned everybody out. Well, not quite everybody—always, some way or other, a few hung on. Some of them liked the Kids, traded favors and stuff—and trading was one way the Kids stayed alive. Others acted scared, wouldn't talk, mostly stayed locked up inside. That's the kind to watch, Terelda said—the kind that's on the snitch for Utie.

True or not, sometimes the Uties did raid. Welfare roundups, usually—and for those, seeing strangers around and figuring them for advance spooks, the Kids just spread out of town and lay low 'til it was over. Some got caught—not many, though. But twice it was the Committee Police their own damned selves. And *those* peacefuckers the Kids didn't mess with—it was pull stakes and go crosscountry the slow, hard way, out of sight where wheels wouldn't take anybody. Find a new town and start over.

It was after the second move, they had the war. The town they went to, there was already a gang of Kids. Plenty of pickings, room for everybody, no problem—except that Red Ear's patrol, all with knives, met the Cruds and said to move on.

That wasn't how it worked. Remembering, Zelde chuckled. Oh, they pulled back, all right, past the ruins and slagpiles, clear into the woods. Except Zelde and Horky split off out of sight and cut around to tail Red Ear's bunch back to their diggings—talked out a mind map and kept it straight between them while they got back to where the Cruds were camped. Then Terelda drew the map down, got it just right for all the Kids to study, while they waited.

Three days is when people's guard lets down, was Terelda's idea—and she hadn't been wrong yet that Zelde knew of. Terelda—she'd been a fighter herself. On her forehead, below the hairline, part of the tattoo still showed. But these days, with two little Kids of her own to look after, she only fought when she had to—like now.

The afternoon before Move It Day, Zelde made up her mind. Still too skinny, maybe, but she was tall; she knew a lot and her nails were right. So without asking Terelda she borrowed the sharpest knife she could find, and lathered up her head and started scraping away. Part of it she couldn't reach very well, and was cutting herself, so Horky helped her finish it. Then she went to Terelda.

The older girl looked up; her grin showed a broken tooth. "Who the hell scalped *you*?" Then: "You think you're ready, Zelde?"

"I got to be. There's so *many* there in town." When Terelda didn't answer, Zelde said, "So, could you give me my tattoo?"

No grin now. Terelda said, "Not just like that, I can't." Zelde felt her face change, and the other said, "These things take *thinking*. What I give you, it's got to be right for you. But I tell you—sit down here. What we'll do— *everybody* gets the circle, and the dot in the middle, and the spokes of the wheel, to build the design on. So I give you that much now and the rest of it later, with time to think on it more. All rights?"

Zelde nodded.

"How many spokes? And pointed how?"

She thought. "Make it five. One pointed down front, the rest spaced around even."

"Sure." Zelde sat, and soon the pigment burned and the needle stung the scraped skin up above her forehead and toward the top of her head. She felt blood ooze—but less, probably, than from her own slips, shaving. And when it was done, Terelda said, "Tomorrow, going in town with us, wear a cap."

"But why?"

"So they won't see you're new."

The war was bad. That first day the Cruds hit fine, and had surprise—but Red Ear got his Kids together so they didn't give up or run off, and Terelda had to pull back finally. But this time, not out of town. Red Ear, for that day, couldn't make his bunch follow and fight any more.

They were ready, though, for Terelda's next try; it didn't work. So things settled down some, both gangs staying around, pulling raids on each other and deadly little fights when scouts or work parties met. It surprised Zelde how they all got used to it—even Kids getting killed sometimes. But it was no good way, really—fighting their own kind instead of both sides staying braced for Uties.

What broke it was when Red Ear's patrols tore up the Crud's plantings not long before time for first harvest from the patch. Terelda got the maddest Zelde ever saw her. Before, she wanted "live and let live around here" with Red Ear. Now she said, "Any time you meet some of them, cut one out from the rest and *kill* it." And two days later, still boiling, she decided to stage an all-out raid.

Zelde hadn't ever killed anybody, and she didn't this time, either. Not for want of trying—she just didn't have the skill of it yet. Later, though, she never liked to think on that raid. It wasn't the blood so much—she'd seen plenty of that, and a lot of it her own. She lost some that time, too. She guessed it was the guts that bothered her most, sticking out of a Kid that hadn't died yet. And Terelda having to cut Sentenerl's throat when he asked her, because blind and one foot gone, he wouldn't be any good now. He made six for the Cruds, and nine of Red Ear's, all lying still now, for keeps.

Red Ear and ten more were taken live; the rest got away. The war was over, all right. Terelda, dark blood running down from the bandage on her side, walked to where Red Ear was staked out. Naked and spreadeagle, he blinked up at her as she said, "You give yourselves all up to me?"

He shook his head. "Not to no gunch, I don't."

Terelda's laugh turned to coughing. "The hell you don't."

"You heard me."

Saying nothing, Terelda nodded. Wearing only the bandage, she squatted astraddle of Red Ear, facing his feet. She made a slipknot in a piece of cord and drew it tight to tie off his balls. Then she pulled.

"What you *doing*?"

"Gonna rape you—then I own you."

"Can't—*aah!*—can't be done."

"Learn different." She pulled harder; Red Ear shrieked, but his hardon came up. Terelda settled down onto it, moving only a little but jerking on the cord in time to her moves. Red Ear sobbed and moaned; then of a sudden he screamed again. Terelda stood slowly; she reached to touch herself, and showed what her finger collected. "He came— see? I own him now."

But she staggered, and shook her head. "Gotta go lie down." She told who was to watch for the night, and what order, and went into the nearest hut. Whoever had it before, it was hers now.

Zelde and Horky had third watch. After a while they heard Red Ear groaning. He was unstaked now, just tied up, with a cover over him. Zelde drew back the cloth and looked. His ball sack was blood-swollen bigger than his head—maybe twice as big. He made one more noise and then she saw him die.

In the morning they found Terelda dead, too. So she never gave Zelde the rest of the fighter's tattoo.

The Cruds couldn't decide who should run it now. Red Ear's Kids walked away together; nobody tried to stop them. Zelde saw Horky looking to her, and nodded. They collected their own stuff, and some things lying around loose, and left.

Nobody said good-bye.

It was a long move, Zelde remembered, but finally they came to this town—the first real big city she ever saw. Scouting, they saw that several gangs shared the whole place, with hardly any real fighting between them. Spying to see which group looked like a good bet to join, one day they got caught and taken underground to face "Honcho." Zelde didn't feel as scared as she figured she probably ought to.

Stripped and guarded, they stood while Honcho sat. He was short and wide, solid without fat; white teeth grinned in his dark brown face. "What we got here? You two chickies from anybody special? Anyplace I know?"

Zelde shook her head. "Never been here 'til just a couple days ago. Been walking a month, maybe—in from the coast. And then, just looking around—you know? Trying to pick a good bunch to tie in with." It wasn't easy to do, but she grinned back at him. "You think we found one?"

Honcho's brows came down together, but he didn't look mad. "The coast, huh? That's a ways from here, all right. Maybe I believe it—'cause nobody trying to raunch me much, around here, 'cepting Rover Boy and the Duke. And neither of they's smart enough to set you up for ringers. So maybe—" He looked from Zelde to Horky and back again.

"How come, tall chickie, you got your hair sliced off and she don't?"

Zelde touched the week's stubble. "This—it's for, I'm a fighter, just got to be one a while back."

He pointed to Horky. "What's you, then?"

Horky blinked. "Nothing special, I guess—just work, and some scouting. And screwing, sure, when I grow to it."

Honcho beckoned; both girls stepped forward, and he looked. Then he shook his head and grinned. "You neither of you ready for that. So nobody bother you here." He looked around, and his voice rang deep. "*I* said that. See the word's spread."

Honcho didn't run just a gang; he had it split up in sections and divisions—people in charge of doing different things and they better get done or Honcho he'd want to know *why*. The other gangs—he didn't take them serious but he had patrols keeping track, just in case. And for Utie raids, he had plans, too—"all you troops break up in itty ol' gangs and play like that's *all* you ever was—then you do your hideout stuff on you very own. See?"

Zelde saw. Welfare roundups caught hardly any of Honcho's people—lots less than out of the other groups—and even the Committee Police their own damned selves didn't do much better. Honcho had a rule about Police: "Nothing in this world I rather see killed—but don't you ever do it in *our* piece of town."

And nobody did, either.

Hassling with other gangs and playing hideout with Welfare roundups, Zelde turned into a real fighter. In two years she had a squad of her own to lead. The Duke tried to move into South Sector and Zelde covered one flank while Meatwagon took the other—Honcho had the middle himself. The Duke got away, and a few with him—but the rest, dead or alive, were Honcho's.

Honcho called her in to see him alone. "You pretty good, Zelde." She didn't say anything—standing while he sat, she felt wide open to something and didn't know what. "*How* good you think you are?"

"Don't know what you mean, Honcho."

"Good enough to take over, maybe? Don't need Honcho any more?" When she didn't say anything—couldn't think of anything that fit—he said, "You about the age to get that itch. I hate to see you try it, hate to lose you. You get me?"

She shook her head. But now she knew what he meant—twice while she was here, people in good shape working up had got in a hurry and tried to kill Honcho. Only it worked the other way around. She said, "You think *I* want to try run all this? You think I'm crazy, Honcho?" She felt tears moving, and tried to blink them away.

Not much, just a little, his hand moved. "Awright—calm you self now. I figured you good in the head, Zelde—just had to know it." He reached and beckoned her to sit beside him. "One other thing. You screwing yet? And anybody special?"

"No." She hadn't, either. She'd had the bleeding a few times so she knew she was ready enough—if what the Kids said was true and not a big pile of Utie shit. But any time some stud made the signs she thought about Terelda and Red Ear, and didn't want to.

"I gonna check." His finger moved on her, and probed; he nodded. "You ready, Zelde. You know that?" She looked at him and didn't say anything. "You want to?" She just blinked. "Come on back where I stay." He had hold of her hand, and she didn't argue.

In his own room where she'd never been, there wasn't any special fuss to it. Clothes on or off, she was used to, and he had her lie down and then he played around a lot, the way she'd done with other guys or with Horky sometimes. So she played around right back, and Honcho grinned. "You all right, Zelde."

The funny thing was that when he got to the new part, what she'd never done before, it was just like she'd been expecting it.

"Hey, Zelde—you, I *told* you you was ready."

"Yeah. But did you tell me I still am?" It was all right; she knew that guys had to wait a while between times.

Screwing was fun, but after that first two days with Honcho she never did much of it all at once. He told her straight out, *he* couldn't see her more than a month or so between: "You fine, Zelde. But you got any idea how many *other* fine chickies in line with you?"

Well, all right—maybe there was a lot of fine studs, too.

Except they didn't seem like it much, to her—or turn out so good, either, if she did try with them. She didn't know why.

Meatwagon, say. Hell, they'd *die* for each other—and a couple times damned near had. But with her legs around him she wished they were both somewheres else—different places.

For a while she tried it with any guy who was all right for not pushing, either way—so that there wasn't too much boss or bossed, by how their jobs were. Honcho was different. . . .

It never worked enough so she wanted more with anybody. She wished it would—especially with two she liked pretty well—but it didn't. Hell with it. When Honcho said now was when to clean Rover Boy out, before he got to be a real nuisance, Zelde waited—so as not to be pushy—long enough to see if anybody spoke up. Then she said, "Nobody else wants the work, I'll try it." That got her a night with Honcho, and a little more. Then she moved her team out.

Arlycharly had the backup squad. Zelde didn't know him very well; he'd had outlying duty mostly; they hadn't mixed much. He was a big guy and looked fat, but moved pretty good. Pale skin and dark curly hair—Zelde thought maybe he smiled a little too much but didn't worry on it.

Second day out, they stopped in the afternoon. From here the move was all heavy push—so give it the full day tomorrow. With everything all set up—it took a while, that—she looked at Arlycharly and said, "Let's talk how it goes tomorrow. My tent."

Inside there, he put hands on her. She said, "That's not what we got to do."

"Sure not. But lots of time, isn't there?"

Smiling, he was. She looked at him. "You saying I have to? You better not be."

He moved back from her. "Nothing like that, Zelde—Arlycharly, he's not crazy. I just thought you might like—but all right. What's about tomorrow?"

"Yeah, Arlycharly." She frowned. "First off—you told everybody, did you, okay to *pick* stuff from Rover Boy's plantings but don't wreck nothing?"

He nodded. "Sure I did. Don't tear up what's going to be ours. Right?"

"You got it. Now, here's how we take it in from here . . . "

The way Rover Boy defended was to send half his people the long way 'round to outflank three times as many. By the time those got to where they could do any good, the main fight was over. Half of them gave up on the face of things and the rest turned and ran; nobody chased them. Zelde talked with Arlycharly and set out how Rover Boy was going to give up. She'd said about all this with Honcho—Terelda, she'd been too rough, was all.

Only two Kids held Rover Boy down. Zelde had to grin—somebody'd painted him up pretty cute after he got stripped. The bull's-eye target—as if she needed it—was sort of funny.

So she straddled him. Before she touched him at all, she said, "Rover Boy, we *got* you. So you got to tell your real name and give all you selves up to me—to Honcho." He shook his head. "You think not? I prove it now. Rape you, so I own you. Want to bet?"

She looked at him—his eyes bulged, and spit drooled from the mouth corners. "Don't shit yourself, guy—you gonna do what you got to. But I don't kill you." It didn't seem to help; he was still too scared to make sense. She added, "I don't nut you, either—don't even hurt you, any more than I got to."

He wouldn't say any word at all, so she reached under one ball and pinched the cord, and felt him rising under her. "Your *name*, man!" And she squeezed harder, and pulled.

"Fred Schroeder!" Like all the air came out of him at once.

"That's starters. Now say when you give up." She got her hand around both balls now, pulling and gripping in quick jerks. He came erect and she squatted and brought him off without much work, too quick to ask more questions. She had to push it. "I own you now—you know that?"

Looking up, Schroeder's face was blank. "You do?"

Her hand clenched. "Want to argue?"

He yelled once, then shook his head. "No. But what do you *mean*?"

"I belong to Honcho, you belong to me, *you* belong to Honcho. No more pissing around on your own, Schroeder. You part of us now."

After a minute, he said, "What do I get out of it?"

She squeezed. "You get to keep these. That's the first thing."

They put Rover Boy—Fred Schroeder—in a pen with the rest of his captured people. Tomorrow was soon enough to sort things out. Now Zelde and Arlycharly ate in her tent. Then she said, "Yesterday you had some ideas. You still do?"

He looked at her. "Like you did with Rover Boy when we had him down?"

"No. Just together. And partly to get the taste of *that* out of my head."

It wasn't bad, but she knew once was enough with Arlycharly.

Honcho's turf got too big for a one-man show. He farmed parts of it out, where he could trust people. Meatwagon ran the part the Duke used to have, and Zelde took over Rover Boy's old country. Fred Schroeder—not called Rover Boy anymore—did small jobs, not far out of Zelde's sight. She didn't want to bother deciding to trust him or not.

Zelde was operating bigger than Rover Boy ever had, but she didn't feel that way. She was working for Honcho and liked it. She hardly ever went in to Honcho Central to see him—but when she did, she got the best kind of welcome. Once he said to her, "Don't it ever bother you, I'm the top dog?"

Grinning, she looked down to his hot, sweating face and said, "It ever worries me, I'll tell you, Honcho."

A year, the best she could figure it, she worked that job. Then it all stopped. The shockwave woke her; she pushed up over Horky to get to a window and look out, and saw the firecloud still rising above Honcho Central. She heard herself say, "Good-bye, Honcho," soft-voiced—before her mind screamed "PissfartshitdamnUTIES!" and shut down to burning, simmering embers, dealing only with what the hell she had *left* in her life.

All right—play it like Honcho would of. They'd be looking for big action, so break it up into small stuff—everybody scatter out and don't know nothing about nobody. They'd sure's hell practiced it enough.

Might have got away with it—should have. Maybe it was Zelde's own fault that she didn't, herself. She knew to leave Welfare roundup flunkies alone on their big sweeps, not to rouse up any local push on you. But one day she saw a Committee Police mask. . . .

You killed Honcho! She had the sense to follow the police jackal alone, with only two trailers working behind her. and to send everybody else the hell away. And she knew to wait until she had the angle where nobody seeing the kill could look and see *her*. Then she let loose the harpoon.

The gun knocked her back, almost down. She struggled up to see the man's neck pinned to the wall, and the blood—*the blood*. And then she ran.

And if Fred Schroeder had stood his ground and left sign for her, how to get out fast and go find the others, she'd have got away, too.

But he didn't.

In the cell she woke, hearing them outside, and backed into a corner. Two guards opened the door, but one stayed by it and held his gun ready. The other carried a gray-blue jumpsuit, a pair of sandals—and handcuffs. He motioned to her; she shook her head and stayed where she was. He said, "They want to see you—Mr. Gerich and Ms. Laina Polder. You have to put these on."

"No."

By the door, the other laughed. "So leave 'em here for her. No food or water 'til she does it. Then she can holler and wait for somebody to decide to notice."

Clothes and cuffs dropped to the floor; that guard stepped back. Zelde thought, but there wasn't any other way out. "All right—I guess I have to." In moments she had the clothes on; she picked up the cuffs.

The armed man said, "Put 'em on yourself. You can do it." She snapped one cuff on her left wrist, but not tight. She began to fit the other; the man said, "No. Behind your back." Fumbling, it took her a while; then she had it. The second man moved fast, grabbed her shoulder to turn her, and squeezed both cuffs down as tight as they'd go. When she faced him again, he grinned. "Now then—let's see the great fighter do something."

The way he was standing, she could have, easy—but there was the other one, and the gun. She said nothing and made no sign. He took her shoulder again. "Come on. Let's go."

They walked her a distance, then into a cubby-closet; the door closed and the floor pushed at her, then stopped. The door opened into a different hallway. She looked around. "Never saw an elevator before, dummy?"

He seemed to want an answer, so she said, "Never needed one." The other—the armed man—laughed, and they walked some more. The room they took her to— maybe it was the same one as before, maybe not. Gerich and the woman—Laina Polder?—sat there. The unarmed guard took Zelde to sit in a chair; the two men left.

Polder said, "You shouldn't have attacked Friesch. It was stupid of him to taunt you with Welfare—especially since the decision hadn't been made yet. But I'm afraid you've pretty well ruined your chances, Zelde."

The woman didn't look angry; Gerich had no expression at all. None of it made any difference. Zelde said, "His mistake, I pay for it; right? No surprise, Utie."

Polder ran fingers through her short dark hair. "Is that what you call us? Do you know what it means?"

Sure—being chased, hunted, and killed. Zelde said nothing.

"UET is short for United Energy and Transport. Did you know that? It's the corporation—conglomerate, really—that's made the winning bid to govern North America in the last three elections. The Presiding Committee is its governing instrument, and its enforcement arm is the Committee Police. I suppose you—"

"You a policebitch, are you?"

Gerich laughed; Polder's face got red. She said, "I wouldn't advise you to use that term again. But no—I'm not Police. We here—we're in Rehab. Rehabilitation— trying to bring all you Wild Children back to civilization so you can live better. You see—"

"That why you took a bomb and killed Honcho? So he could live better?"

Gerich's brows raised. "So we got him, did we? Well, I'm afraid the problem there was a little difficult. Honcho—and we didn't know whether the name meant a person or a group—was just too well organized. While he was operating, we didn't have much luck trying to pick up the rest of you, to help you. So we had to—" Looking at Zelde, his voice stopped.

"Help, huh? Like you're helping *me*?" She pulled at the handcuffs and was going to say some more, but there was no point to it. She shrugged, and waited.

Polder spoke. "Friesch wants you lobotomized first and then Welfared." The first thing, Zelde didn't know what it meant, but *Welfare!* Her face must shown how she felt, for Polder went on. "Maybe I'm a misfit in this operation, but I don't agree." She turned to Gerich. "Let's put her on consignment to ship out on the *Great Khan*. It's not much of a break, but she's got guts and shows signs of having brains, and maybe *off* Earth they'll do her some good."

Off Earth? Zelde had heard of starships, sure—but she'd never seen one, let alone. . . .

Gerich looked surprised. "Friesch won't like that."

"So what? We're two to his one and he's still on sick leave."

Now Gerich grinned. "And I owe him one in the eye, at that. All right, Polder—you're on." He looked at Zelde. "I doubt that you'll thank us for this, before you're done. But at least you'll have a whole brain left to hate us with."

Hands free now, Zelde sat alongside while Laina Polder flew the aircar. The woman had told her, "I'm taking valuable time to save your mind for you. If I can't trust you, it's not worth it; if I need the cuffs on you to avoid trouble, you're not worth saving. So which is it?"

"Don't worry; I won't hurt you." Zelde thought she'd said it nice, but Polder got mad.

"*Hurt* me? I'm not Friesch. I may look soft, but I'm trained in moves you can't possibly know. What I'm asking is this—will you go with me and do what I tell you? Or not?"

Zelde looked at her. "All right. You know, if you wasn't

a Utie, I'd like you." The woman laughed—then looked
hard at Zelde, shook her head, and called the guards in.
The cuffs came off, and Zelde followed Polder outside to
the aircar.

Now, looking down as the ground passed below, she
said, "I never before rode in the air. It's a good thing to
see."

The sound Polder made wasn't quite a laugh. "Too bad
you won't see space from where you'll be riding. It's im-
pressive."

Then she slanted the aircar down, and Zelde saw the
ships. What surprised her was when she could see how tall
they stood.

Walking across pavement, Zelde looked up at the great
towers. They all looked much alike so big and high, each
standing on three legs with the ramps slanting down from
farther up the ships. A couple had patterns of things sticking out, up high toward the tops, but most didn't—
including the *Great Khan*, that Polder led her to. Zelde
asked what the difference was, and Polder said, "Those two
are armed ships; you're looking at projector turrets." Zelde
was still curious—but now they started to climb the *Great
Khan*'s ramp, so she didn't ask anything more.

At the top, just as they went inside from bright sunlight,
a man met them. Taller than Zelde he was, and wearing a
cap with bright metal at the front. His left cheek was tattooed, a design like a round pie with the upper quarter
missing—was he a fighter, maybe, with the Uties? Polder
said, "One for cargo, First Officer."

Zelde looked him over. Tall, long-faced, with a lot of
sandy hair showing gray at the sides—and restless, the way
he moved. He said, "Yes. I'm Ragir Parnell. Captain Czerner's not aboard yet. But . . . cargo, you say." He looked
at Zelde. "This *kid,* you're sending to the cribs on Iron
Hat?"

Polder looked across at the tall man, as though they
were the same height. "Don't tell me my job, spacer. The
alternative was worse." She handed him some papers. "Authorization. Sign it, and I'm done with her."

He looked at the yellow forms. "Sure, it's legal enough."
He scribbled on the top sheet, and then on two more. "I

can't leave here at the moment—and I'm short a runner. Do you know where to take her? There's someone on watch at the hold, to check her in."

Laina Polder said, "I do know. I've been to space once, Parnell—I have two ages, even though they're only twelve years apart. Which hold is it?"

"Portside, Upper." He paused. "Who'd you ship under?"

"Rigueres, on the *Tamurlaine*. I heard—that ship Escaped. If so, it's the first armed ship that ever did. You know anything?"

"If I did," said Parnell, "I couldn't tell you. So forget it." He frowned—not looking mad, though. "Do you remember who the officers were on your trip?"

Polder nodded. "The First was Monteffial. Farnsworth, Second—*he* was a cold fish. And the Third—the only one who ever bothered to talk with us first-trippers, but he was strung so tight he scared me—his name was Tregare."

Parnell shook his head. "I don't know that one—met him once or twice, but we were in opposite cadres at the Slaughterhouse." He cleared his throat. "The Space Academy, that is—I'm sure you've heard the old jokes?"

"Enough to know they're not jokes, Parnell." Polder looked around her. "Even if this area's not monitored, I think we've said enough. Now—Hold, Upper Portside, I think you said?"

"That's right. And if you'd like coffee or anything before you leave, tell the galley I said so."

"My thanks; maybe I will." She nodded. "Let's go, Zelde."

"Just a minute." Zelde looked at the tall man. "What's Iron Hat—and what's a crib?"

With his hand, he covered a cough. "It's her decision; let *her* tell you."

He turned away. With Polder tugging at her arm, Zelde followed the woman on into the ship. They went down two levels—steep stairs, almost like ladders—to a broad corridor. A few meters along it, beside a door, a guard sat. She had a gun but didn't raise it. Polder said, "Here's another one for you. First Officer Parnell signed her in." She showed the paper and the guard nodded. With a quick touch to Zelde's shoulder, saying, "I wish you better luck than you're likely to get," Polder walked away and climbed the ladder, and was gone.

The guard stood. Zelde looked at her—medium height and stocky, with a round face; straight brown hair hung to her shoulders. Zelde couldn't guess her age—except that she was some years past being a kid. The guard said, "Put the suit and sandals on the floor. Then you can go into quarters." When Zelde didn't move, the other moved her gun a little, not quite pointing it. "Come on—don't play games. You won't need clothes in there—nobody else does." Zelde shrugged, and obeyed.

The guard opened a peephole and called, "Clear for admission. Inner door closing." She looked and nodded, then opened the door and motioned. Zelde moved past her into a small entry-way with another door barring the other end. The first one closed behind her; the second opened, and she walked forward. Seeing "Portside, Upper" for the first time, she hardly noticed when that door, too, closed.

The place was painted a dingy light brown, and was less well-lit than the corridor. The ceiling was a little higher than she could have reached, standing, and she guessed the central open area at about twelve paces long and eight wide. Along each side were rows of four-decker bunks; she didn't count them. What caught her eye was that the place was full of women, all different ages and sizes and colors. The guard hadn't lied; none of them had any clothes.

None of them had much hair, either—just stubble, about like Zelde's own head. Looking at the nearer ones, she saw no sign of fighters' tattooing.

There was some low-voiced talking among several, but Zelde couldn't make out the words. The women closest to her moved aside and a big woman came through the group. Two steps away, she stopped, and looked Zelde up and down.

She wasn't as tall as Zelde, but built heavy, with a lot of muscle to her arms and legs. The stubble of her head was a faded reddish color. Her breasts, too small for the rest of her, sagged almost flat.

Zelde waited, wondering if she ought to speak first, and then the woman said, "Another extra—that's all we need. There's nearly sixty of us and only forty bunks—so you'll have to move in with someone. If nobody volunteers, I'll assign it. You got any questions?"

Yeah—she had several. All women and no studs, was it?

But the first problem, maybe: "You're boss, are you? How come?"

The woman grinned. Somewhere along the way, she'd lost some teeth. "Want to fight me for it?" She shook her head. "No—don't bother trying. That's not the way it works. I'm boss because I'm top person here from the Underground. So if I was so skinny you could bite me in half, I'd still be boss. Is that all right with you?"

After a bit, Zelde grinned back. "Sure. It wasn't—I'm not the kind has to be tops, can't work for anybody. Just wanted to know, was all." She held out her hand. "I'm Zelde M'tana."

The woman stepped forward and shook hands. "Turk Kestler. Real name's Roseanna, but Turk's been my code name so long, it's all I answer to." She looked closer at Zelde, and reached to run fingers over the short hair above her forehead. "That looks like tattooing under there—the kind the Wild Children along the coast put on their fighters. Is that what you were?" Zelde nodded, and Turk Kestler said, "Damn all! I wish we could have got together while we were both on the loose. There's so much the Underground needs to know. How long since UET caught you?"

"I don't know; I was locked up. Two weeks? Three, maybe?"

"Then you haven't had time to learn much, have you? About how things work under UET. I—"

"Going off Earth, I won't need that. But—" She asked the questions Parnell wouldn't answer.

Without sound, Kestler snarled. "The bastards! Lied to us—said we were consigned to Farmer's Dell, where they treat women right!" She shook her head. "Iron Hat's not a real colony, just a mining outpost. Cribs—they keep us shut up someplace, and when a miner makes his quota or whatever, he comes in and one of us spreads for him."

Zelde frowned. "You mean, screwing because we *got* to?" She thought of Red Ear and Rover Boy, and laughed. "First one tries that on *me*—"

Turk didn't smile. "You're being stupid. Think they'll give you any kind of *chance*? Not more than once, they won't."

Looking, Zelde saw she meant it. All right—things were worse than she'd thought. That didn't mean she gave up, yet. She said, "How long are we in here? You know about that?"

The answer confused her. Six–eight months, Turk said, except it'd really be maybe ten–twelve years. So close to light speed, whatever that was, the *Khan* rolled up time at nearly twenty to one.

Finally she nodded. "What it comes to, Turk—we're stuck here half a year or more? Just—just *us?*"

Turk squinted at her. "That's right. Why?"

"I'm kind of used to—well, with guys around, more."

The older woman shrugged. "Doing without—you'll get used to that, too. One way or the other." She turned and walked away.

Feeling like a strange Kid in a new gang, Zelde moved quietly around the room. Some nodded to her or said hello; most didn't. It made her nervous, staying ready to speak back or not—this wasn't like the Kids at all. Toward the back of the place she met fewer women; now she looked to see what kind of setup she'd be living with.

In the left corner, the three shitters were squatovers, not seats. Next were two spray-bathing closets like the one the Rehab people had put her in; a woman came out of one, walking away still wet, and the line moved forward. Alongside, next—four basins, each with a two-way washing/drinking tap. No towels. A broad opening in the wall, only a hand's-width high with a flap covering it, behind. She pushed the flap back and looked in. No light—a trash chute?

And then a big shelf, waist-high, with a raised edge. And just above it, three openings in the wall. She looked, trying to figure it out.

A hand touched her arm; she turned to face a slim, fragile girl not much older than herself. "That's where the ration packets come out." The voice was soft. "Twice a day, just exactly one for each of us." For a moment the girl smiled; then her face went solemn.

"Thanks. I hope they got me counted in." Zelde gave her name.

"And I'm Tillya—Tillya Ormetir. You—I heard what Turk said when you first came in. You can bunk with me, if you'd like."

The girl's face—pale—scared, or just natural? She had delicate, little-girl features, and her light brown hair was longer than most here, nearly two centimeters. Well, there was something Zelde could ask about. She did.

Tillya's hand brushed at her forehead. "It's Welfare haircuts—isn't yours? Once a month, and I just missed mine when they took me out to come here. I expect the ship will do it the same, but they haven't yet."

"I wasn't in Welfare." Zelde explained, and the girl's eyes went wide.

"With the *Wild* Children? But I thought—they said you were savages, maybe cannibals! I—" Her teeth worried a knuckle.

Zelde laughed. "Maybe some are, at that. And I tell you—we do some things, might scare you."

"And you were a *fighter* with them?"

"Yeah. You sure you still want me bunking with you?"

Now both of Tillya's hands went to Zelde's shoulder. "Oh, yes! You can protect me—and I'll be nice to you!"

Protect, huh? Yeah—always some liked to pick on what couldn't stick up for itself. Zelde never liked seeing that. And Tillya, now—the only one to step up and explain anything, after Turk walked off. And she looked a little like Horky had, before Horky beefed out so fat. And there weren't any studs, and there weren't *gonna* be any.

Zelde patted the small hands. "Sure, Tillya. We'll work it out—no big hurry. And thanks for the bunkspace."

When the bell rang, Tillya said, "That's chowdown." Lying back to back on the bunk just wide enough to hold them that way, now she and Zelde got up to join the line forming. Turk came over and thumbed at Zelde. "Back of the line. All the way."

Zelde stood her ground. "You telling me to be hind tit in this place?" She shook her head. "I don't take that shit, me. You in front of me—some others, okay—not *everybody*."

Turk gestured peace. "Not for keeps. Just until we know they added you on for rations, is all. Then you line up when you get here, like everybody else."

Tense, Zelde still stayed put. "How I know somebody doesn't take mine and say I ain't got one?"

Turk pointed toward the head of the line. Two women stood there, one to each side; they were big, like Turk. "You're looking at my enforcers. You think anyone messes with them?"

Tillya pulled at Zelde's arm. "Come on—I'll go to the back *with* you."

"Don't need to." Zelde patted the girl's head. "Get on up there, get fed. I be along when I get to it."

As Zelde moved back, Turk called to her. "Nothing personal—it's just the way we do things here."

"Sure." And maybe things might change around a little, too!

There was food for her, all right—a flat, oblong packet, hot to the touch but not too hot to hold. The cover came off in two pieces; one was a tool to eat with. The food inside was a brown, mushy paste with grains and chunks in it. It smelled good enough, but didn't have much real taste. A little better than what they'd fed her in Rehab, Zelde decided. When she was done, she put the empty packet down the trash chute and went for a drink of water.

Then she stood in line for a spray-bath. When the lights dimmed, not quite dark but close to it, the women in front of her left the line and headed for the bunks. As she stood, hesitating, one said, "Water's turned off now." So Zelde went and lay beside Tillya.

The girl said, "You—do you want anything?"

"Yeah. Some sleep. Good night—okay?"

"Yes. Good night."

Zelde couldn't sleep, though. She found herself sweating, a cold sweat, and breathing fast. After a while she figured what was doing it—being boxed in, like the cell again.

This was bigger, sure—but a lot more crowded, too. No real room to move around, and *no way out*. Well, thinking had helped her before, so she thought back. Sure-damn she'd slept crowded before and never jittered by it. But she'd always been outdoors a lot, when she wanted, and here there wasn't any outdoors. And if there was, no way to get there.

Figuring it out seemed to help, some; pretty soon she was breathing easier. Then she must have dozed off, because hands and voices woke her. She sat up. "What . . . ?"

Tillya said, "I don't *want* to go with her. And you don't have to leave, either. Zelde—you *don't*."

"Wait a minute." Zelde shook her head. "What's going on?"

The strange voice said, "Tillya, come along—you hear? And you there—it's none of your business, so stay out."

Is that right? Zelde grinned, and reached for the hand that gripped her shoulder. The unknown woman made a shrill, muffled noise—as Zelde stood, crouched, twisting the arm she held to bend the woman forward, off balance. "Say me that again, why don't you?" She pushed; the other fell sprawling. Zelde moved to stand over her. Her foot nudged more than kicked, but the woman groaned. "I don't hear you."

"Let—let me alone!"

"Sure. I was doing that. Now, though—" She wanted to see the face. By habit she grabbed the hair—too short, it slipped out of her fingers. She reached again and got the neck. "Sit up where I can see you," and in the dim light she looked. Wide eyes, pudgy cheeks, a hooked nose—easy to remember.

"You got a name?"

"Cleta. Cleta Parrin. You—"

"You ain't hurt, Cleta. Not yet. You want to keep it that way, I guess you know how."

"Yes." A nod, violent. "I won't—I'll go now."

Zelde let her loose, and Parrin scuttled away. Zelde flexed her arms, stretched, and lay down again. Then Tillya was all over her—hugging and kissing, making little crying sounds. "Oh, Zelde—Zelde!"

Zelde caught the girl in her arms, held her quiet. " 'Sall right, Tillya. Let's sleep now."

"No! I want—"

"Not tonight. We talk about it tomorrow." And after a few minutes, when nothing more happened, this time she went to sleep right away.

When Zelde woke, the lights were still dim, but she saw women lined up for the spray-baths. Without waking Tillya she got up and joined a line. Faster than she expected, it moved; she mentioned this to the woman ahead of her.

"Well, it's timed," the other said. "So you can't stay in there too long and keep everybody waiting. The water goes off, you have to come out."

A little later the lights brightened; not long after, the

chowdown bell rang. The women ahead of Zelde left the
line and moved to get their rations. She thought about it,
and stayed; when the one in the spray-bath came out, Zelde
took her place and washed clean. Then she went to the
rations shelf; one packet was still there, and Tillya stood
with a hand on it.

"Zelde—I was afraid you wouldn't get anything to eat."

"Turk's enforcers don't wait around, right?" Zelde
laughed. "Thanks, Tillya. I missed a lot of meals and lived
through it, but thanks anyway." She opened the packet.
Breakfast was pretty much like dinner—color and flavor a
little different, but not enough to make a real change. Zelde
ate fast, then dumped the empty packet.

She turned to go—where?—back to the bunk, maybe,
because where else did she have? But a group blocked her
way, and Tillya's. Looking from one to another of them,
Zelde paused.

In front was Cleta Parrin. Behind her, two other
women—one was young and fattish, blonde and red-faced.
Older, the second one—a pale coffee color, and skinny but
with muscles showing; Zelde decided she was the one to
watch. And at the side stood Turk Kestler—the one to talk
to.

Looking straight at Turk, Zelde nodded. "Morning. I
know Cleta Parrin here. She a friend of yours or something?"

Turk shook her head. "Don't get smart so early in the
morning. I've got nothing against you, Zelde, but Cleta has
a complaint. We have to talk about it. I—"

Zelde cut in. "Let's hear what she got to say—*herself*."
Like always—watch out for that in-the-middle shit, was all!
She stared at Parrin and the woman couldn't seem to break
loose from it. "Well? Say your say!"

Parrin licked her lips. "You—" She turned to Kestler.
"This one—I just asked Tillya, like you know we do, and
this one beat me up for it. Are you going to let her get
away with that?"

Turk looked at Zelde. "Is that how it was?"

What choice? "No."

"Then how was it?"

No good at this. "Said, Parrin did, Tillya *had to* go with
her. Said, me, stay out of it, none of my business." Zelde
frowned, and motioned toward Cleta Parrin. "Had a grab

on my shoulder, leaning." Looking at Turk now, she kept her face straight—no grin. "Tillya, she'd gave me half her bunk, said she didn't *want* to go with Parrin. So I took care of it—that's all."

Turk looked from Zelde to Tillya and then to Cleta. "Zelde, she says you hurt her."

"Where's the marks, Parrin? *I* hurt you, you'll show it!"

Before Cleta Parrin could talk, Tillya said, "Cleta, you've kept me slaved and scared for a month, you and your two wolf bitches with you. But now Zelde's with me, and I'm *done* with you."

Beside Parrin the fat woman chuckled. "A real tiger, aren't you, Tillya? Maybe Zelde isn't with you forever—you think of that?"

Tillya went pale. Zelde reached and touched Turk Kestler's hand. "You heard that! You need any more answers?" Then, to the fat woman but looking at Parrin too: "You want to try something, I'm here right now. Turk? You got rules or anything?"

"Stop it!" Kestler got her voice down from a shout. "Cleta, your complaint's dismissed. I don't know what all you've been up to, but whatever it was, you just-now stopped. You and your bunch lay off these two. Now, Zelde—don't *you* take any license to run a feud, either. You hear?"

It was all a mess. Zelde looked around the group. "Anybody leaves me alone, I leave them, too. They don't, I don't. All right?"

For a moment, Turk Kestler stood silent. Then she said, "In the situation we're stuck with, I guess I have to settle for that."

Parrin and her sidekicks didn't try anything more; after a while, Zelde quit worrying about them. The days went all the same; she settled into enjoying the occasional gentle love of Tillya Ormetir and hearing from the girl about the ways of UET's world that Zelde had never known. The day the ship lifted, Zelde first knew about it because after standing in line quite a time, she got cut short on her spray-bath. A little later there was a lot of noise and vibration, and the floor felt funny—like pushing up or dropping away, only not really. Then, when it steadied, she was no-

where as heavy as before. Turk said that was spaceships for
you, so why worry?

Space wasn't so different. The worst thing, just as before,
was having to stand in line for everything—to eat, to get
clean, to shit. The next worse thing was there wasn't ever
anything to do, except eat and sleep and the next best thing
to screwing.

A lot of the women sat around and talked about how it
was to live outside of Welfare. At first Zelde was interested,
but they all seemed to be bragging how good they'd had
it—trying to top each others' stories—and after a while she
decided they were mostly lying. Even if they weren't, none
of it was real to *her*.

Except the stuff about UET; to that, Zelde listened close.
United Energy and Transport hadn't always run North
America, she learned; Turk even remembered before the
"conglomerates"—whatever those were—bid for the job of
governing. "And until UET got in," Turk said, "it wasn't
really so bad. But once they had space travel. . . ." She
shook her head. "Too much power there. Nobody else had
a chance again, so UET got *all* its own way."

"Well, you have to admit they earned it." Zelde squinted
over at the smallish woman, sitting back in a dim corner,
who said that. The woman always stayed on the edges of
things, seemed like, and had one hand or the other up to
her face a lot. Hiding something? A big scar, maybe? Zelde
couldn't see her very well, but got the impression her face
was lopsided. "Any group who could get the human race
off Earth—" the woman began, but then Turk cut in.

"Bull poop! Maybe *you* believe that UET invented star
drive about the same time they invented Total Welfare, but
the Underground knows better." Snorting, Turk waved the
other to quiet. "UET *stole* it, is what."

"Who from?" Now Zelde was really curious. "I mean—"

"Aliens," Turk said. "Nonhumans, and from God only
knows where. UET's Committee troops went to meet them
where they landed, and killed them. Then UET copied
their ship; it took 'em a year or so."

"You don't *know* that." The hideyhole woman again.

Turk laughed. "I know UET's nervous enough to main-
tain a fleet of ships on a fortress planet—Stronghold, it's
called—in the opposite direction from any *other* explora-

tion they've made." The woman said nothing as Turk nodded. "Think about it."

Every day after dinner now, Turk sat and held meeting. You didn't have to join in if you didn't want to—but Zelde figured if anything was happening or going to happen, that was where to hear about it.

One day, first thing, a skinny woman stood up. "When this girl—" She pointed at Zelde. "—when she spilled it that we're being shipped to Iron Hat, not Farmer's Dell, you said you'd see about it—for us to wait and you'd report. Well, you haven't done it."

Turk shrugged. "I've passed word by the guards every chance I get, that we want to talk to somebody with some authority. They keep stalling."

"And that's all they'll do!" The woman had bulgy eyes with reddened lids; she squinted to left and right, then said, "Well, if you won't do anything, we will! I—"

"Who's we?" Turk kept her voice flat.

"Our committee—I'm chairing it. There's six of us. We've made up a petition, and—"

"Let's see it."

"See it? There's nothing here to write on; you know that. But I can tell it to you." She took a deep breath. "First, we demand that the officers of this ship meet with us and consider our grievances. Second, we insist that—"

Turk clapped her hands together once, loud; she stood. The woman stopped talking, and Turk said, "You demand; you insist. Next, I suppose you threaten. You damned fool—what do you think I've been trying to do? Get somebody to listen to us, that's what. And if I do—that's *if*, not when—you'll keep your big mouth shut. Because I don't know if anybody can do us any good—but if there is, it's the captain. And our only chance is to get him to *want* to help. We won't do that by putting his back up. You hear me?"

"But I only—we wanted to—"

"Sure. But there simply isn't any way you can help." Turk looked around; her gaze fixed on Zelde. "What the hell are *you* grinning at?"

Zelde hadn't known she was smiling; she stopped it. "I—just at her, Turk—talking silly, like you said. That's all."

Turk glared. "On Iron Hat I bet you'll laugh right out loud." She turned away. "Meeting's over."

Zelde went to her. "Hey, I'm sorry—didn't mean nothing. It's only, the way she—*you* know."

Turk's face relaxed. She put a hand to Zelde's head, fingertips around the back and palm over the ear, and squeezed gently. "Sure. A kid your age—if you can't see the funny side, what the hell? Maybe I just wish *I* could find something to grin about."

"Well—" Zelde thought. "You're out of Welfare now, anyway. That's something."

Kestler looked at her. "That's right—you were never in a Center, were you? What do you think they're like?"

Zelde frowned. "Like in cages, right? They push you around—go here, go there! Send you out in work gangs, only you don't get paid. Can't call your soul your own, is what they say. Welfare—that's what really scared me!"

Turk's shoulders moved; she breathed in snorts and her face went red. Then her laughter bellowed. Finally, wiping her eyes, she said, "You can't believe how I needed to do that! Look, kid—you know what you said, that's so funny?"

Zelde shook her head.

"Welfare's everything you said it is, and more. It's legalized slavery, with UET as the slaveowners. I was in it for over ten years, so I should know. The only thing is, Zelde—what we have right here is *worse!*"

After love and before sleep, Tillya explained. "There's dining rooms where you sit down to eat—three meals a day, and the food's better, sometimes. Seat toilets. Showers every day you go out to work, and once a week, anyway. There's a gymnasium, you can exercise or play games—a room where you can watch Tri-V in your free time. And you wear jumpsuits, not naked like this."

She patted Zelde's hand. "But it's still hell, in Welfare—it really is hell, all the same."

One day the guard called in a message. Turk went to the outer door to hear it; Zelde followed and listened. "After dinner tomorrow, everybody get in your bunks and hang on. It's turnover coming up—and the skipper's in a hurry about it, so the move could get rough. You got it?"

Turk said yes, and asked again about meeting with the captain or with someone who could speak for him. The guard answered, "I haven't heard anything. We pass your word up, Kestler, every time—but that's all we can do."

Back in the main area, Turk repeated the announcement. Zelde asked what turnover was, and Turk said, "Most of the trip we're speeding up, pushing. Then they swing ship to point backward, and the rest of the way we slow down."

Well, that made sense. But what stuck in Zelde's mind was that whatever Iron Hat would be like, she was close to getting there.

In the middle of that night the bunk lurched and Zelde hit the floor. Dazed, not awake much, she rolled over and saw the lights go bright and then fail completely. Green spots danced against blackness—the deck moved under her—she reached and found a stanchion to hold onto as she got to her feet. *What the hell?*

Somebody bumped into her. Now people cried out; someone screamed. Zelde shook her head, blinking; she couldn't see anything, and didn't know which way she was facing.

Turk's voice, shouting: "Everybody stay put and hang onto something!"

Zelde said, "This—is it the turnover thing?"

Turk again. "I don't know—it shouldn't be, not yet. All of you shut up now, so we can listen."

Everything moved again, jerking. All Zelde heard was the ship creaking under strain, then something like a shout, but so far away she couldn't tell for sure.

The lights came on again—dim, for nighttime. Turk came past, heading for the door; without thinking, Zelde followed. Turk beat against the closed peephole. "You, outside! What's happening?"

No answer; she shouted it again. After a time the tiny peephole opened. "Pipe it down in there! We've got trouble enough!" The ship made a jarring plunge; Zelde barely kept her balance.

Turk cursed. "If the drive's freaking, we don't have a chance here—we're right next to it. For God's sake, let us out!"

"It's not—" Then the man's voice came again, but not talking into the peephole. "You—get back—I'll—" Zelde heard gunfire, then a scream and a thud. Turk peered out but shook her head; she turned and saw Zelde.

"They're fighting out there. What . . . ?"

At the peephole, part of a face showed. A woman's voice said, "It's mutiny—Escape! Parnell's leading us." The voice rang; Zelde heard no fear in it. "It's touch and go—we may lose—but if any of you want to bet your lives along with ours, come on out!"

The door opened. Before Turk could move, Zelde gave a war whoop and dashed past her—but Turk came right behind.

The woman outside was the same guard who had first let Zelde into the hold; now she wore a green armband. Zelde grinned at her and reached to pick up the dead man's gun. While she was checking it, Turk grabbed her arm. "Do you know how to use that thing?"

"A little. I have, a few times."

"Better let me take it. I got halfway through Space Guards training before I figured out who I'd be supposed to shoot." Zelde hesitated, then handed the gun over. The dead man's knife was still sheathed; she took that instead.

Others came out now—about half the naked women. Turk took a quick count, then turned to the woman guard. "There's three ways upship, right?" At the other's nod, she said, "Then we split into three squads—and up our chances, maybe." In a hurry, she divided the group and set one of her "enforcers," Marty Cogan, to take the first squad. The other enforcer hadn't come out. "All right—I'll take you-bunch there myself. But who the hell—"

"Me!" said Zelde. "Let me, Turk! I've *done* this stuff."

Turk looked doubtful. Someone said, "She's good enough for me." Surprised, Zelde saw it was Cleta Parrin.

"But—"

"Sure," said Parrin. "We haven't liked each other—but here we're on the same side, and you sound like you know what you're doing. And you've got the guts for it."

Turk Kestler nodded. "All right. One thing first." She touched the gun the guard held. "If you're not coming with us, this is. All right?"

"Of course I'm coming. Why do you think—"

"Okay, okay. You go with Marty, there." She assigned
routes—her own group up the main central passages, Cogan's to climb the bypass from drive level to Control, and
Zelde's to take the emergency ladders betwen inner and
outer hulls. "Mainly you block them, keep them clear, so
nobody gets past you to catch us from behind. If you make
it all the way, though—" She turned to the guard. "I imagine the fighting's mostly around Control?"

"Between the galley and there, I expect. We've got the
Drive—they can't blow it, or threaten to."

"But we could." Turk looked thoughtful, then shrugged.
"All right—let's move out. And remember—green armbands are on our side." Her group went one way along the
corridor, Cogan's the other. Zelde followed the latter for a
few meters; then Cogan gestured to a side-turning and nodded. Zelde started toward it; then, behind her, she heard
the sound of running feet. She glanced back and saw Tillya,
face contorted and tearstreaked. The girl ran to Zelde and
clutched her arm.

Zelde looked, and shook her head. "No, Tillya. You go
back. This—you don't belong in it."

"But I can't—I've got to be with you. Don't you see?"

Zelde gripped one thin shoulder. "You can't take care of
yourself where we're going—and I got no time for it." She
gave a gentle shake. "I want you safe. So get your ass back
where it don't get burned off—you hear me?"

Crying, but not making noise at it, Tillya let go her hold.
Zelde kissed the girl's cheek, and turned away to lead her
group toward the emergency route.

Up through the first few levels she didn't see anybody.
Behind her the others were noisier than she liked, but—she
decided—not bad for beginners.

When she saw a man on a landing above, she paused.
He'd spotted her, all right—and he had a gun. Behind her
back she wiggled a hand in the "Stay put!" sign. Then,
keeping that hand on her hip so the knife was out of view,
she started up the ladder.

His voice came high and strained. "You, down there!
How did you get out? What do you think you're doing?"

Zelde smiled. *It can't hurt.* She tried to keep her lips
from trembling. "They said—the ones that let us out—you

could use some help. That right?" Now she saw him better—no green armband. A Utie. . . .

"You want to help in the mutiny—is that it?" All right,
so he wasn't as dumb as she'd like. Play it his way.

She said, "And get in worse trouble than we got *now*?"
She kept on climbing—not fast and scaring him but not
stopping, either. When she could look over the top, see the
deck he stood on, he stepped back and motioned for her to
stay where she was. But she looked down, pretended she
hadn't seen his signal—she saw his feet move, a slow side-
step and then forward. Her own feet reached the landing
and now she did look up—to him and past him—and
gasped.

"Behind you!" For long enough, he swung to see the
empty landing. She jumped—the knife caught his neck and
went in.

Then the others climbed to join her.

On the narrow landing there wasn't room; some stood on
the steps below. In the dim light, Zelde couldn't make out
all the faces. She tried to get her breathing—and her fear—
under control, but she didn't have enough time. She said,
"On up, then," and turned to climb again.

The next two they found, several levels higher, were already dead. The man, big and wearing a green armband,
had half his chest burned away. The woman lay with her
neck twisted out of life. "They got each other." Zelde
picked up a heavy gun; she'd never seen one like it up
close. "What's this? How you work it?"

Someone said, "It's an energy-bolt weapon, is all I know.
You just aim it and pull the trigger switch."

And someone else: "Don't keep it turned on, though,
like spraying water. You could burn through and blow the
whole ship. And when the charge runs out, all you've got
left is a club."

Puzzled, Zelde asked, "How I know it ain't dead *now*?"

"Point it away from everybody and hit it just a touch."
For a moment the deck flamed. "Okay—it's live. There's a
way to check how much you have left, but I don't know
how." Zelde waited, but nobody spoke up.

"Yeah. Whatever, it's got to do. Time to move some
more." Up she went, and still up. When she heard shouts
above, and some gun noise, she moved faster. Then she

came to a landing with no more ladder above, just a door. She paused, panting, while the rest caught up to her.

"All right. Now I crack this door a little and look out there. Don't know what we do, 'til I see. What I say then, everybody do it *right now*—we got only the one chance."

"That's right." It was Cleta Parrin. "Any other way could get us *all* killed."

Slow, real slow, Zelde moved the door. What she saw out there was a siege. Metal desks and toppled equipment made a barricade guarding a room with its own door lying bent and burned. She couldn't know who was inside—but the ones shooting at the barricade, lying behind other furniture or just plain wreckage, didn't have armbands. So she knew whose side she was on, and passed word back to the rest.

"Outside is Uties, and we're behind them; we go out fast and just plain kill, the best we can. No noise 'til they see us, then *everybody* yell—they get shook up some, maybe. I count three—then we go."

She went in fast, off to the side where she could get cross-fire, and braced to shoot. A Utie turned to face her; she cut loose with the energy gun and saw his head char black and fall away. Then no time for thinking. She shot and ran and dodged, shot again and nothing happened. She swung the gun and hit a woman square in the mouth—something caught her across the legs, and she fell. Rolling, then up again—the fight was out of hand to try giving any orders—a man raised his gun at her and she kicked it to one side and dove at him behind her knife. *Got him!*

Why wasn't she scared now? Maybe just no time for it. Above all the other noise she heard a shout: "Don't shoot those women—they're fighting for *us*." She'd heard that voice before!

She was too far forward now—in the middle of it all, where she couldn't guard herself. Backstepping, looking to the sides—she saw the clubbed gun that hit her, too late to dodge all of it. On the deck again—somebody stepped on her—she grabbed an ankle and the stepper went flat, too. Starting to get up—a flash of bright heat went past from behind, and swung toward her—she dropped. *Pain*—she smelled her own hair burning and slapped at her head. Two people, struggling, fell on her. She pushed and rolled out from under, away. There wasn't time for it but she couldn't help feeling of her head—it didn't sting so much now, couldn't be burned enough to matter. . . .

A bellow—louder than any real voice. "Give yourself up, Parnell! You've got nothing that can crack this armor!"

The barricade was down. In the doorway, cradling a gun in one bloody arm, stood the man who had signed her aboard. Opposite, facing him from the very edge of the main passage landing, she saw a monster—a metal and plastic giant. Someone said, "The power suit! Christ—we're dead!"

Maybe. Zelde knew what power suits were—the Police used them sometimes—no way she could cut into one, to the man inside. And *heavy*, they were. . . .

She didn't think about it—she just jumped. The overhead light fixture held her weight long enough. As she swung forward, bullets whined. Both feet, legs stiff, caught the power suit square in the chest. She bounced back, landed curled up and somersaulting backward. The thing—it was falling, waving its arms as it toppled over the edge. She scuttled forward and looked down.

Part of it hit the landing below and the rest didn't. It pinwheeled and fell again, crumpled a slanted railing and caromed out to graze a wall, and back again—how it was *bellowing!*—and crashed to a dead stop, finally, far below. Sparks came from the jerking mass, then smoke and flame. The shrieking seemed to last forever.

She couldn't feel or think; she walked, but didn't listen to anybody. She saw Cleta Parrin, sprawled with half her head gone. She felt herself start to shake, and gripped her hands together, pulling at her muscles to steady them. She wanted to say something, but words wouldn't come. *What's wrong with me?*

For an instant she felt ghost-arms holding her and thought she heard a voice. "It's all right, Zelde." Who? Terelda—but Terelda was dead! And then bigger arms—or was she smaller?—and a softer voice. She stumbled, and almost fell.

And then Zelde shook her head and came back to herself. But when she got to the man she wanted to see, she couldn't remember his name. On her second try, she could talk.

"You all right there?"

He sat now, legs outstretched, back against the wall. She heard him mumble, "Terihew dead. Dopples down in Drive. All up to me here, but—" Then, looking up, he said, "All right? Not very. But—that power suit—thanks anyway, kid."

"Zelde M'tana—you signed me in; remember? What you got wrong with you?" She went down on one knee, to hear him better. Somebody pulled at her, but she brushed the nuisance away.

The man said, "Too much. I don't suppose you can get me a medic? No one else seems to—"

She turned, and said it loud. "You heard him! Get a medic," and didn't watch to see who did what. A hand clasped her shoulder; she looked around and recognized Turk Kestler. "Hey—you made it, too. You know anything about medics on here?"

Turk patted her shoulder. "They're looking for one—his people—don't worry. Zelde? How many did you lose getting upship? My God—Marty's squad, *all* wiped out! And only three got all the way with *me*. You?"

She had to try to think; she looked around, standing again, and couldn't decide who she ought to recognize. She shook her head. "We got *up* here good—then, except for Parrin, I don't know. You tell *me*."

But then she had to notice something else. A woman with a gun and armband brought a man who had neither. "Here's your medic, Parnell—the only one we have left. But he's not one of ours, you'll notice. Can you trust him?"

Parnell, sure—Ragir Parnell. Now Zelde knew him. She pushed her way back to him and said, "You got a problem, Parnell?"

Pale-faced, he tried to grin. "If I don't get medical help, I die. But maybe I die even more surely if this man gives it."

Maybe. Zelde squinted her blurred eyes into focus and looked at the Utie medic. He was nothing special—nobody you'd pick out of a crowd and remember. She said, "You need to go with this one, Parnell?"

"She said—nobody else left." That was all; his eyes closed.

Zelde was stopped. Then she thought: *like with the Kids—this is no different.* Again she looked at the Utie, and she knew when somebody was straight on the outside and grinning inside.

Parnell had dropped his bullet gun; she put her foot on it. Her knife, she pointed at the medic's gut. She didn't touch him with it but once, and then not hard. She said, "Utie medic, you listen. What's your name?"

"Fesler."

"All right, Fesler—you fix Parnell up. Hear me?"

Now the man did grin, and shrugged. "Well, I'll try, of course. But you know how it is; I can't guarantee anything."

Zelde shook her head. "You don't have to. I will."

"I don't understand—"

"He dies, so do you. That clear enough?"

"But you can't—"

The knife reached again. "You want to bet?"

When it was done, Parnell still breathed. People that Zelde didn't know began asking her questions and telling her things. She had to answer. "All right. Lock this Utie—Fesler—up someplace. Keep him fed—we might need him some more."

And Parnell, knocked out with dope, snoring, nose still seeping blood a little—they said he was captain now and should sleep in captain's quarters. She nodded. "Good. I'll stay with him. You carry—and you, there."

The second man she picked, he started to argue. But the other said, "Do what she says. She earned the right, I think."

And when they'd settled him down in the big bed, and Zelde knew where to get food and water in this place, she said, "Fine, now—thanks, and everybody please get the hell out." And for a wonder, everybody did.

When they were gone, she looked around and shook her head. She wasn't certain just what she'd done, let alone what to do next—but this was sure better than Hold, Portside Upper.

She did remember to lock the outside door.

She heard noises and woke up. Parnell was groaning, but not loud. She went over to him. "You need anything? Can I help?"

He tried to smile but he looked like death warmed over. "Thirsty—any water?" She brought it, and steadied his hand while he drank. Then he said, "I hurt worse than you'd believe, but maybe I'm going to make it. You did something about that, I think. What?"

She tried to tell it, but got mixed up and stopped. "You make it—that's good enough."

Now he did smile. "The ship—what's the situation?"

"Captain's quarters, they say this is. So you're Captain."

He nodded. "Yes—but who's running things?"

"Don't know. Somebody has to?"

"That's right." He pointed to a panel with lights on it, and buttons. "Push the red one, down in the corner, and ask to speak to the watch officer."

She did. When somebody answered, Parnell said, "Captain speaking—Captain Parnell. Report." Zelde listened to what they said but didn't catch most of what it meant. When the talk stopped and the panel light went out, she said, "Working right, all of it?"

"Good as can be expected. I should be up there. . . ."

"Something I could do, maybe?"

"You've done it, Zelde. You're still doing it."

First she couldn't figure it; then she did. She nodded. "Sure, Parnell. I take care of you while you can't. Now then—when you can again—you look out for me, on here?"

Parnell smiled. "That's the way it works. You own my life, you know. Maybe someday you'll collect it."

She couldn't stand that look on his face. So that she wouldn't have to see, she bent and hugged him. Then she heard his breathing go toward sleep, and after a while she let go and straightened the covers over him.

She didn't know how, exactly, but things were all right now.

The panel buzzed and a light blinked; she pushed at the light and under the push of her finger, it gave a little. A voice said, "Zelde? This is Turk."

"Hey—you know how to work all this stuff?"

"Somebody showed me. It's not all that hard to learn. Listen, though—there's a bad thing."

Zelde listened.

The hell of it was, if you looked at the girl's face, it was like she was just asleep. But down below on her, she was cut damned near in two. Dead in only seconds, Zelde knew—but why did it have to *happen*? She'd already said that, out loud; now she did, again.

Turk said, "She came after you, only up the main passage—she couldn't help it. Way back, it should have been safe enough. But that Utie in the power suit, the one that would have retaken the ship for UET if you hadn't got him—one of the landings he hit on his way down, Tillya was on it."

Her hands clenched, and her jaws. *Honcho—Tillya—they get everybody I love.*

And Parnell?

That was the first she knew, that she loved the man.

Parnell wasn't fit to get up, two days later, and Zelde knew it—but he said he had to. "We have to choose our new course, quit coasting, and we have to make the divvy. If I'm not there, they'll do it without me—and maybe rename the ship, too. My new authority—right now, it's use it or lose it."

While she helped him dress and spruce up a little—not easy, with one arm strapped across his chest—he called Turk Kestler in. Turk wore a faded jumpsuit, too tight on her. She made a half-salute. "Help you, Captain?"

"With information, I hope; Zelde tells me you were in the Underground." Turk nodded. "All right—how do we get to a Hidden World? Do you know any of the coordinates—or even where we can go—what colony—where it might be safe to ask?"

The woman looked at him, then said, "You're sure you've got this ship solid now? No chance of a surprise takeback?"

"Very few are alive and running loose who weren't with us actively—except a few of your women who stayed below, where it was safer. *You* guess."

Turk made a kind of smile. "Those women don't want back under UET; that's certain. All right—what's your course now? Not the coordinates—they wouldn't mean anything to me—but for where?"

"Still aimed near Iron Hat. Not slowing for it, though."

"And you were next for Terranova, I heard." Parnell nodded. "You have in mind to go there?"

"If we must." He scowled. "Terihew claimed to know

data on some Hidden Worlds, but he's dead. So if you can't help, we have to chance a UET colony and hope for Underground contact. And Terranova's the straightest shot we have."

Zelde just watched; Turk said, "I don't have any numbers; sorry. But why Terranova especially? And what's a straight shot?"

Parnell's smile went a little sour. "Riding up near light, as we are, do you know how much energy it takes to change course?" Turk looked blank. "A right-angle turn costs the same, in fuel, as slowing to zerch and climbing back. When it came to grounding, we'd be out of margin and go splat. UET's fueling isn't planned to give us choices." He said more, about slighter turns and sines and cosines; Turk didn't seem to get it any better than Zelde did. He paused. "Except for Iron Hat, Terranova's our best chance to sit down safely, with a little leeway. But I wish I knew more about our chances of getting Hidden World data there."

Turk hawked a cough. "Something, maybe still good and maybe not. Before UET boarded us on here, word hit the staging area. Sources I can vouch for. The one running Terranova's Underground, code name Horsehead. Young, they said—though not by the time we get there, of course. And if that's where we do go."

Like stone, Parnell looked. "Given a better choice, I'd take it."

Turk blinked. "Well. Risky, taking an Escaped ship into UET country with fudged papers and out again safe—but we all know it's been done, and more than once." Turk scratched her head. "I remember something else about Terranova. There was word—a second spaceport planned for the big island there, at Parleyvoo settlement. By the time we'd get there, it should be in business for some years."

The man smiled. "Yes. At a secondary base, less chance of UET ships groundside with us—and armed ones, especially. It's a good thought."

He made to stand; Zelde moved to help him. He tried to wave her away, but she said, "Just while we're getting you there. Going into meeting, you walk it by yourself; sure."

"All right." And with one woman bracing him on either side, they went out and along the corridor.

Zelde knew she looked a mess. Parnell's old coverall suit

hung loose on her except where a belt cinched it at the waist; she had the legs turned up so as not to scuff, and the sleeves rolled. Where the energy beam's side-losses had burned part of her hair, she had some scalp blisters—didn't need a bandage, but she could smell the salve that soothed the burns.

She shrugged. What difference did it make?

Just outside the galley Parnell stopped, looked to each woman, and drew free of them. Then, as they followed, he walked in. He went to the one vacant seat at the end of a long table. At his gesture, Zelde and Turk brought other chairs and sat flanking him.

Zelde recognized a few of the people, the ones who'd visited Parnell or she'd taken messages to. Mr. Adopolous, the Second Officer—Dopples, Parnell called him sometimes—spoke first. His cheek tattoo was only half the pie—the bottom and lefthand quarters. The thin-faced man, bald at the front with a big fluff of curly black hair remaining, talked fast and loud. "Well. Are you finally ready to do business—Captain?"

Parnell's cheek twitched but he kept his voice quiet. "We're here for that, aren't we? I have an agenda ready. Unless you have a priority item in mind, Dopps, can we go ahead with it?"

Dopples opened and closed his mouth, swallowed and then nodded. Parnell said, "Start recording," and at the foot of the table a young rating turned switches and made a go-ahead sign.

Parnell cleared his throat. "Now then—meeting of surviving Control and engineering officers, and senior ratings, of the Escaped ship the *Great Khan*. Ragir Parnell presiding. First item—unless a majority overrules, I am confirmed as Captain and Cyras Adopolous as First Hat. Your vote?" He looked around the table. "Done. After this meeting, the ratings present will caucus to nominate four of you as candidates for the Second and Third Hat slots; Dopples and I will make the final selections. All right?" Again he scanned the group; no one said anything.

Parnell sighed. "We can't change the paint job—our ship's insigne—until we're in and out of a colony for fuel and supplies. But for ourselves, I propose that this ship

now become *Chanticleer*. Any other nominations?" Silence.
"Then be it so recorded."

Adopolous fidgeted, and started to raise a hand. Parnell
said, "I'm coming to it, Dopps, I think. Where we go
next—right?" The balding man sat back, and Parnell explained their limitations and outlined Turk Kestler's
suggestion. "A new port—just *having* two ports on one colony—gives us better odds against running into UET muscle. We can get a look at both, going in, and take our
choice."

"You have in mind," said Dopples, "that if you're wrong
about Terranova, we won't have fuel to go anywhere else?"

"Of course. But do you have an alternative you like better?"

The motion passed.

The next few items, Zelde couldn't follow. Bored, she
daydreamed, until Parnell said, "All right. What's left to do
now is the divvy." Around the table, one and then another
nodded—leaning forward, intent on what came next.

"I think you've all heard of the Agowa formula for di-
viding ownership after Escape. Even back in the Slaughterhouse, smuggled copies were passed around. I propose we
take that as a basis, with modifications if the majority here
so votes."

A heavy-set senior rating—Zelde wasn't sure of his exact
rank—raised a hand. "Not meaning to sound grabby, sir,
but I don't see what's wrong with one person, one share."

Two or three others made supporting noises—but shut
up when Parnell thumped his good hand on the table, not
very hard. "Because, Declennter, that's not the way it's
earned. How much risk, and for how long, did you have in
this Escape?" Before the man could answer, Parnell continued. "Not until five days ago did you have to put it on the
line—when Dopps and I and poor old Terihew decided it
was time to move, and got around to asking you. You
know how long *we'd* been working it out, with our necks
on margin every time we took a chance on talking to the
wrong party? More than a year, that's what. No offense,
Decko—when the time came, you did a good job. But you
don't get the same share I do, because you didn't earn it."
He paused. "Comments?"

The man shook his head. "No, sir. I was asking, was all.

I'd never thought about it, the way you just explained. No more argument."

"Good. Anyone else?" No one spoke. "All right. Basic Agowa divvy is half—in descending scale—to the Control officers, twenty percent likewise to the Engineering officers, the reminder to the crew in shares, with ratings getting double. Any case that needs a vote, Captain's vote breaks ties. I move that this system—and I'll quote individual percentages in a minute—be adopted, subject to amendment by majority vote here."

A fattish, sandy-haired man Harger, Chief Engineer— spoke up. "Officers, yours and mine. Do you mean just we survivors, or including the replacements? I lost my Second—Wanela moves up from Third and I have that slot to fill. So my new Third—and the two Hats you and Dopples pick—do they get officers' shares, or ratings'?"

Blinking, Parnell rubbed his eyelids. "That's a good point. It does make a difference—I hadn't thought." For a moment, he bit his lip. "In truth, they haven't earned officers' cuts. On the other hand, Dopps and I—and your people—we'd look pretty greedy, splitting dead men's portions." Frowning, he drummed fingers on the table; then he smiled. "Compromise—surviving officers take the shares of our new ranks only. The rest goes into the crew's pot, to increase *all* the other shares." He looked around; no one answered. "Vote?" And then: "All right; passed. I think it's the fairest choice."

Dopples said, "With the casualties we took, the crew shares were pretty good-sized already. But I agree, Parnell—your way gives everybody a better stake in the ship."

"About half again what it would have been, and a little more." As Parnell gave the numbers, Zelde listened; working for Honcho, she'd had to learn those things. What she understood of it—from Captain's twenty percent down to just over half a percent for unrateds in the crew—was that Control and Engineering officers together held only a bare majority in wealth and voting. She wasn't sure how much voting there'd be, or why—but in it, to stay on top, Parnell was going to need his people behind him, solid.

"I think that covers most of it." She could hear how tired he was; she hoped nobody else could. "Anyone who wants off, any place we stop, the rest of us pool and buy them out." He grinned. "You, Dopps—you'd better stay on. I can't afford you!" More relaxed now, the man smiled back. Making slow work of it, Parnell stood. "Then we're adjourned."

He turned to Zelde. "My leg's gone to sleep. Steady me while I walk it alive again?" She went to him, and when he tried to move she held his arm until the rest of them left, most giving parting words or gestures. Then Turk took his other arm and the three moved along together. "I didn't fool them much, did I?"

"What matter?" said Zelde. "You been hurt; they know that. Easy now—not much more to go."

Back in his rooms, he sat on the bed and looked up at Turk. "I want to thank you." She nodded. "How are you quartered?"

"All right. With so many dead, and the Uties locked up, there's vacancies. Dopples let me put my people in them— issued what clothes he could, and fit us into galley schedules. Some of us have jobs to do now, and that's good." She waited, then said, "There'll be more than a few saying, when they hear, that we ought to have shares, too. What should I tell them?"

He began to shake his head, then squinted. "Starting with the fighting some of you did, and now working, you can earn credit toward shares. It'll take some figuring, but I'll handle that."

"You think fast, Captain—and good. That ought to hold them. Well—I'd better get back and see what's been going wrong. I'm straw boss, sort of, for my crowd—mainly to get them settled in, on here, without bothering *your* people any more than we have to. I'll see you."

Turk left, and Parnell said, "She'll be a help, that one."

"Sure. She was Underground—big in it, I think. Couldn't hardly be dumb, could she?"

Zelde got his jacket off him, then the shoes. She started to do more, but he shook his head. "That's enough. Just to lie down for a while."

"You hurting?"

"Some. I'll manage."

So it wasn't the time yet. All right—she could wait.

Parnell woke hungry. Zelde called the galley; it was one of a few places she knew how to get hold of, on the intercom. "Could somebody pile a couple hot trays for captain's quarters?" The man at the other end asked when she wanted them. "Oh, I'll come get 'em. Thanks." As she left, Parnell gave her a smile.

Going into the galley she felt funny. She didn't know anybody much, yet. They seemed to know her, though, and several told her hello, looking friendly. Not like down in the hold. She tried to figure it, and decided it was partly she was younger—sort of a pet, the way the Kids had been with little ones, sometimes. And couldn't hurt, either, that she'd knocked out the power suit. Anyway, having people act nice was a help, with everything so strange and a little scary.

She got the food down to Parnell and they ate. He did better than he had been, but still left some; she didn't let it go to waste. Drinking coffee, he looked pretty relaxed, so she said, "Some things I don't know." His brows lifted. "Like what's the ship going to *do?*"

First he didn't say anything. Then: "I think I know what you mean. We got clear of UET, but what happens from now on?" Zelde nodded. "Well, we're in business for ourselves. When we make connections with the Hidden Worlds, which is our prime concern now, we have to keep ourselves in fuel and supplies by giving service. Buying and selling cargo, carrying news and messages and passengers." He looked thoughtful. "Most of us are on here because we prefer space to groundhogging. Some will get off, somewhere or other, and there'll be people wanting on, too, so there's always some change. The difference now is that *we* decide those changes, not UET."

Zelde thought she had it straight but wasn't sure. She felt her frown tighten up. Parnell said, "Look at it this way. Our first priority is keeping the ship a working concern. The second is to be some help to other Escaped ships and to the Hidden Worlds. And the third is, any time we get the chance, to do UET one in the eye."

"Like how?"

"Escaped ships sometimes raid small colonies, just to hijack needed supplies. That's one way, but quite a risk for an unarmed ship." The armed ship Zelde had heard about, he didn't mention.

*   *   *

Parnell's hip and thigh healed fastest; the leg stayed stiff, a little, but he moved around all right. Fesler took the stitches out of his belly, but Zelde thought the gut wound still hurt him, inside. The shoulder was worst, though; when he tried to exercise, to make it move loose again, his face got gray. Then he'd take another pill and keep trying.

Zelde fetched and carried, stayed beside him when he took duty, slept in his quarters on a foldout cot. Hearing what she heard in Control and what he said back, she began to understand a little bit of how things were done on *Chanticleer*. She got really interested, and began to ask questions—but never when Parnell was busy, or more tired than usual.

When time came to change course and set thrust, aiming for Terranova, she watched like a cat at a mousehole. At first she couldn't follow it at all, couldn't see any pattern. Then she noticed something—the numbers Parnell said, and punched into the computer terminal, kept getting bigger. But not so *much* bigger, each one, as the one before had been. It was leveling off, whatever he was doing—and it did, and then the numbers got smaller and the dropoff kept getting faster, until the bright trace moving on a sidescreen went out of sight at the bottom, and Parnell said, "Curvature zero, effectively." And over the intercom: "Keep thrust as-is for now, Harger. We'll correct later."

Excited, Zelde had all she could do to keep her mouth shut—but until they were back in quarters, she did. Then, after they'd eaten, she said, "Parnell, I'm learning! Changing course, what you did—it started to make sense. When you—" She explained, words coming as fast as she could talk. Then she waited.

"Yes." He nodded. "You got that part straight. I rather thought you were bright, Zelde, even though you're obviously not schooled. Now the important thing is, if you want to train in these matters on a regular basis, you'll be a bigger help to me than you are already. Which also means, of course, that you'll be improving your own status." He paused. "I think I'll list you on the roster as—oh, apprentice navigator. Does that sound all right?"

She grinned. "Just fine, Parnell!"

So she began to study, not just watch, what happened in Control. First she had to learn what things were called and what they did—she was a long way, she knew, from know-

ing anything about how they did it. And she had to relearn
reading. She'd known how, a little, the earliest she could
remember—but except for keeping records for Honcho,
she'd never used it much.

She got tired sometimes, and discouraged at all the mistakes she kept making. Once when she'd tried three times
to call a star-sight bearing and come out worse the more
she tried, she went off watch feeling like something you
throw away, and back in quarters she curled up and looked
at the bulkhead. When Parnell came in and said hello, she
didn't answer. He walked over and sat down alongside her,
and put an arm around her shoulders.

"Something wrong, Zelde?"

"It's just—I'm no damn *good*, Parnell! All I do is fuck
up."

His arm squeezed her. "Now, that's not true—not true at
all. You can't get it right all at once; nobody can. But I've
been keeping track of your progress, and considering your
lack of the usual background—"

Eyes stinging, she sat up straight; his arm dropped away
from her. "Background, yeah! I don't know half what I
need to, and maybe I never will. Parnell, I—"

His finger to her mouth quieted her. He said, "I'm the
captain around here, and if I say you're doing well, don't
argue with me." Startled, she looked up to him, but he was
smiling. He nodded, and said, "It may be that you need
more help than I've found time to give you. All right; we'll
change that."

Briskly, for once, he stood and moved over to his work
desk. "Now tell me what happened, and we'll see where the
problems are."

For a minute or two she froze up and couldn't talk at all,
but then she shook loose from whatever it was and settled
down to work.

Probably she'd been trying to do too much on her own,
Zelde decided. Now she got easier about depending more
on Parnell to tell her things. "I guess I figured you had too
much on you already, without me pestering," she said
once.

"If you pester, Zelde, I'll let you know it."

Her official status on the roster meant she could ask
other people questions, too, in Control or off-duty in the
galley. Most were willing to help, to explain anything she

needed. Dopples, the First Hat, wasn't. His answers were curt—and, often as not, off the point. After a time she gave up asking him anything at all, and tried to avoid asking anyone else when he was there.

One question only Parnell could answer—but she couldn't decide how or when to ask. Either he was busy or tired or his face showing pain—when there was any time for personal talk, he wasn't in shape for it. So all she could do was wait.

She didn't know much about the way living patterns had been on the *Great Khan*. On *Chanticleer*, though, arrangements seemed pretty flexible. She knew that a lot of people were living paired-up, some for keeps and some not, and the pairs weren't always of both sexes. From what she'd heard of UET, that last part had to be new on the ship. She guessed it was about like it had been among the Kids— everybody free to choose.

Well, that was fine with her—but what about Parnell?

One day when Zelde and Parnell came off-duty together, he poured a short drink and sat down to look through some papers. For a minute or so she watched him, expecting that he'd take his usual pill and lie down, but he didn't. She opened the navigation manual to where she'd left off, and began reading—but now and then she looked aside to him. She saw him set the papers down and open a drawer, taking out a small folder. He opened it and looked—and sat, looking, for a long time.

Then, on his cheeks, she saw the tears.

Without thinking she closed the manual and went to him, standing and looking over his shoulder but not touching him. What he held was the picture of a woman—just the head and bare shoulders. Oval face, a strong smile, blonde hair long enough that the picture stopped before the hair did. Softly, Zelde said, "Real fine, that woman. Who is she?"

Parnell turned his head and looked up. She thought he'd wipe his eyes, but he didn't seem to notice. "She was my— we were together a long time. Until—" He shook his head. "It was her life or the ship—the ship, and all of us."

"Parnell—I don't know what you're saying."

"We'd already begun Escape. It was out in the open—

too late to stop. Plain bad luck, they caught her. She was on the job, right where she was supposed to be—someone else got signals crossed, I suppose. The same way I missed my try at Czerner, so that he got away."

Czerner? Oh, yeah—he'd been UET's Captain. Now Parnell's head moved back and forth—violent motion. Zelde bent down and held him to her. He said, "I can't even *blame* Czerner for using her as hostage—she was the only handle he had. But—" He looked up again and gripped Zelde's arm. "I couldn't give in, you see—give us all up to UET again. Not even to save her life, I couldn't do that!"

"He—he killed her?"

"Never mind who did it—or say that it was I, because my words triggered Czerner's order. I—" Now he cried freely, and Zelde crouched to hold him, moving to get her arms around better, and rubbing her cheek against his ear.

She whispered to him—not words, only sounds to comfort. A long time later he pulled away, wiping a sleeve across his face, enough to turn and look at her. She said, "Your woman gets killed—it takes 'til *now*, before her man grieves?"

"I—all this time—always busy—so tired. . . ."

"Yeah. Takes strength to grieve—to do it right."

His smile, not complete but starting, surprised her. "You know a lot of things, don't you? Thanks. I'm glad you're here."

"I'm not done yet." She got up, pulling on his good hand until he, too, stood. Very quickly she kissed him, then moved toward the big bed; he let her lead him. "You're ready for me now." She began to undo his shirt.

"Hold on, Zelde. I—"

"You're ready; you know it." He didn't stop her—but he didn't help, either. After she unfastened his trousers she stepped back and got her own clothes off, watching him all the while. With no expression on his face he undressed, also—*my God! the scars on him!*—and then sat down.

But still he shook his head. "Zelde—you're much too young."

"I been screwing for longer'n you'd likely guess. Missed it lately, too—same as you have, I bet. Now you just lie down there—that's it—and don't worry.

"Parnell, love, I'll do you right."

* * *

Now in the next days, Parnell had more life to him. Whether it was Zelde, or the grieving done, or just plain healing, he looked better and moved better and took no pills at all. They shared the big bed for sleep and loving both, and after the first time he needed no favors from her to save his strength. Not that she couldn't offer or that he didn't sometimes accept—that, Zelde thought, was part of the fun. But it was nice he didn't *need* coddling.

She'd had a sore thigh herself for a couple of days— because right away, after the first time, Parnell had Fesler, the medic, give her a contraceptive implant. Well, she'd never liked the ways the Kids had to use to keep from catching a baby.

Since the Escape fighting, a lot of damage-repair work had been held up, waiting for Parnell's inspection. Now he was in shape to move around—climb up and down ladders to look at things—and make his decisions. Zelde saw the change in how officers and ratings behaved to him. Before she hadn't known just what was wrong. Now she saw it— he was full boss again, and nobody talked a little bit to one side of him, the way they'd been doing. All right—she'd keep that in mind, signs of trouble to watch out for.

Changing course for Terranova, Parnell had had to guess, some. Good guessing, it turned out, but not right on the nose. He and Dopples made corrections; every few days they reviewed their sightings, fed the numbers into the computer with time-dilation adjustments that she still didn't understand at all, and made small changes to the Drive program.

The computer bothered Zelde. She'd got to where she understood, pretty well, what went into it and what came out—but when it came to operating the thing she was still shaky. Parnell was willing to answer questions, but she wasn't making enough sense out of the operating manual to know what to ask. So—keep trying, was all. . . .

One day Parnell came into quarters with a fresh scab on his cheek, where his tattoo was missing the top segment. At her look, he said, "Dopples and I have put our story to-gether, to use when we reach Terranova. So I need the full Captain's tattoo—and Dopps has his own upped from Sec-ond Hat to First."

"Pretty sore, is it?" She stopped her finger short of touching him there.

"Not much. This woman down in the maintenance shops—Henty Monteil—turned out to be an expert."

Zelde thought. "How about the new Hats—Tzane and Mauragin? Do they get the marks, too?"

He shook his head. "No. Promoted in space, the story goes." He scratched near the scab's edge. "I'll be glad when this stops itching."

These days she wasn't with Parnell all the time on duty—he didn't need it, and there was other work she had to learn. So until he called her to come to quarters, she didn't know about the accident.

He was lying down with his clothes on; by the looks of him, if he hadn't been taking the pain pills again, he should have.

"What happened?"

"Up on a ladder, pushing at a cable so the splicer could get a look at the bad section—nobody else seemed to know what to do. Something fell on my bad shoulder—knocked me off balance, and then *I* fell on it."

Oh, shit! "Anybody look at it yet?" Headshake. "So let *me*." Gently she got his shirt loose, and off him. *Double shit!*

The bruise, bad as it looked, didn't worry her. Something, though—something inside—was torn loose, because under and around one scar the flesh swelled and blackened. It had to be blood seeping in there. And at the back—she didn't know what stretched the skin, punching outward, but she knew it didn't belong there. Through her teeth, breath hissed.

"Bad, is it?" He might have been asking was it dinnertime yet.

"Not good. Parnell—that Fesler—you need him again."

"Then call him. And—he's all right now. I think we can trust him."

"If you say so." She called on the intercom. In a few minutes Fesler, carrying his equipment kit, arrived.

When she let him in, he nodded. "Ms. M'tana. The captain's hurt?" She gestured toward Parnell. Fesler moved over to the bed, set his kit down, and gently touched the

injured shoulder. "I'll have to open it up again. Captain—
for this, you'd better be out."

"Whatever you say. Go ahead."

Fesler injected an ampoule into Parnell's neck; Zelde
watched while the man's eyes closed and his breath slowed.
Now the medic took a spraycan and shot mist over all the
injured part; he handed the can to Zelde. "Get my hands,
thoroughly—then each instrument as I hold it up to you."
She nodded, and carefully did as he told her. Over the pro-
trusion, he slit the skin; metal showed. "Broke the pin
loose. I'll have to do the whole job over." What he said
next, she barely heard: "But this time, I'll do it right."

Until he was done—the wound bandaged and his own
hands clean—Zelde thought a lot, but didn't talk. Then she
pulled the bedcover up to Parnell's chin, and stood facing
the medic. "You said something." He looked at her. "That
this time you'd do it right."

She gripped her knife hilt. He said, "Out loud? I hadn't
realized." He didn't look scared. "I was crazy mad—bitter.
My best friend killed during Escape, and the only reason
we both weren't in on it was that nobody asked us. So we
were caught on the wrong side—Jerry killed, and me once
or twice damned near it. And the way I thought, just then,
it was Parnell's doing." He shrugged. "A couple of days
later, I saw reason. Too late. I just had to hope my patch-
work job would hold up, because I didn't dare tell anyone."

"You told me, just now. Why?"

"I didn't know I did. Maybe I had to, was all."

"Why aren't you scared? *I'd* be, in your shoes."

He shook his head. "If I've got it coming, I'll get it. But
now I *have* done the job right. It's a bad break—multiple.
He'll always have trouble with that shoulder, I expect. But
not by my doing—I swear it isn't."

She moved back, out of his way, while he packed his kit
and stood. As he walked past her, she said, "I'm not telling
Parnell—that's for you to do. But I'll be on hand to hear
it."

"Yes. That's fair enough. Thank you." And he left.

It was three days before Zelde figured Parnell was in
shape to decide things. Then, after Fesler changed the
dressings, she nodded to the man and he told his story.

Parnell looked to Zelde. "You don't seem surprised."

"He told me already."

"And what do you think?"

"That it's up to you. He wouldn't have had to tell, though."

Parnell smiled. "More to the point, apparently he *did* have to tell. All right, Fesler—the matter's done with. Except for one thing." With his good arm, he gestured. "The hell of it, man, is that you *would* have been on the Escape team—we wanted you. But you were too close to Jerry Schadel, and neither Dopples nor Terihew trusted *him*. If we guessed wrong, I'm sorry—but you know the risks we were taking. And I couldn't overrule a majority in council."

"Jerry was safe as houses! But, I know he *did* make noises, when Captain Czerner was around, as though UET was his mommy and daddy all put together. Well, he *had* to, you see—his brother was Welfared, and you know how they watch the family after that."

Fesler shrugged. "Well, it can't be changed—not any of it, now. I guess I owe you thanks."

"We're even." And when Fesler left, Parnell said, "Zelde? I'm surprised." She didn't answer. "I mean, Fesler told you what he did—and you didn't put a mark on him!"

"And not long back I'd of had a knife in him?" She grinned. "Maybe I'm learning a little." His laugh was easy, relaxed, so she said, "You feeling better, are you, Ragir?"

She saw him pause and consider; then he said, "Enough better, I think—if you don't mind my being very, very lazy."

This time, Parnell recovered faster—and, if Zelde could judge by the way the pill bottle held up, with less pain. Certainly he got more movement in the shoulder. But from the way he moved sometimes, she thought the gut wound still bothered him. During the first week he went back on duty, she stayed with him all through each watch. Then, as before, she branched out and worked with others.

The thin-faced, balding Dopples still puzzled her. She couldn't get him to talk straight with her at all, and even trying to get answers from other people made her nervous if he was there. It wouldn't have been so bad, except that he was First Hat, Parnell's next-in-command.

One day after he'd cut her off cold—and damn it, her question *was* in line of duty—she went off watch, headed for the galley, and found the new Second Hat, Lera Tzane, sitting alone at a table. Zelde stopped for a second, remembering what Parnell had said about the slim, quiet woman. "Lera's capable, well trained. I wish she had more confidence, though—more sense of command." Maybe so, maybe not—Zelde got coffee and went to join her.

She was met with a smile. She said, "I swear, I don't know what makes that Dopples tick!" Lera Tzane's dark eyes widened, but she didn't speak. "Won't answer a simple question—you'd think words cost him money."

The woman's hand smoothed the coil of hair—black, with the first streaks of gray—at the back of her head. She smiled. "You're not the only one to have that problem. Getting him to treat me like an officer instead of a rating is like pulling teeth. And Carlo's having the same trouble." Carlo Mauragin, the new Third, was a young man in his bio-twenties; Zelde found him friendly enough, but not much help to her learning. He seemed to have a hard time handling his own new job. Zelde said so.

Now Tzane grinned; around her eyes, laugh wrinkles showed. "In Carlo's old rating, he was bright enough to get by without any real study. He got lazy, and now it's catching up to him. But I expect that he'll make it." Over second cups of coffee they talked a little longer—but in the matter of Dopples, Lera Tzane had no advice to offer.

Asking Parnell, that was out. Somehow it would lose her the game—the game she had to play without knowing the rules. So she decided to ask Dopples himself.

To his face she'd never used the nickname—always it was "Mr. Adopolous." And when she knocked at his quarters, that's what she called out.

Opening the door he wore no shirt. He was scarred nearly as much as Parnell was. He said, "What do you want?"

"To talk with you, sir."

He frowned, then said, "All right. Come on in." Two women—both blonde, looking like identical twins, and neither fully dressed—sat on the big bed. He said, "You two go take a bath or something," then turned back to Zelde. "What is it, M'tana?"

She waited until they were alone. "It's—I'm trying to learn things—you know that. So I can do more, and work at different jobs. Parnell wants that and so do I. Everybody else, nearly, helps if they can. You, though—you don't even answer what I need to know, to do the job I'm *on*."

He said nothing. "At least you could say why."

He moved to the bed and sat, leaving her to stand. "You're all alike, you women who make your way in bed. First you carry messages for your man. Then you start speaking for him, and pretty soon you think you own a share of his authority. And the men—nothing against the skipper, you understand—they're flattered, and let you get away with it. Captain's doxies! More trouble, they cause. . . ." Then he shook his head. "Not all—I shouldn't say that. The woman he lost in Escape—she was different. But she held Chief Navigator rating before she ever met Parnell. You—" He looked her up and down. "You're a green kid—on your way in a hurry, I suppose you think. Well, I'm watching you—so don't get out of line."

He spread his hands. "Now I suppose you'll tell the skipper on me. Well, go ahead—he knows what I think and how I feel. You won't give old Dopples much trouble, M'tana."

"Wasn't figuring to." Breathing fast, she heard her voice come more shrill than she liked. "If I wanted Parnell in on this, I'd of went to him. I didn't. This is between us—Dopples."

His eyes narrowed. She said, "*You* just called yourself that. I never did, before."

"And don't again. But did you mean it—that you're not intending to run and hide behind Ragir Parnell?"

"Me? Don't hide behind *nobody*. Never did, never had to. You know what the Kids are? Wild Children, the Uties call us. I made my first kill before I had my first period." *Well, almost. . . .*

"Into threats now, are we, M'tana?"

She caught her breath, shook her head. "Didn't mean to, no. Trying to tell you, is all—what I do on duty is just *me*, not Captain's woman. I can keep it straight—why can't you?"

His brows lowered; under them his eyes glinted, looking up. "You make it sound good—maybe you even think it could work that way." She started to talk; he motioned silence. "All right! I'll give it a try. Any question pertaining directly to the job you're *doing*, ask and I'll answer. As long as you keep your place. I'll do that. Start using any of your man's authority, though—and I mean *any*—and captain or no captain, I chew your skinny ass right there and then. Do you understand me?"

"Just fine; we got us a deal. One thing, though."

"Yes?"

"Pretty rough, you put it." She frowned. "You say you'll watch me. Good enough—I'll watch you, too."

He looked puzzled. "For what?"

"To see, maybe, if you ever stomp so hard with your mouth, on anybody you *don't* have so damned much rank on. Sir."

She gave him plenty of time to answer, but he didn't. So she turned away and left.

Parnell glanced up when she came in. "Zelde. I looked around for you, but no one knew where you were."

He hadn't asked where she'd been, so she didn't say. "Something I had to straighten out, was all."

"Anything I could help with?"

"No." She shook her head. "Thanks—but you got to stay out of it."

Now he frowned. "That sounds as though it might be serious."

She went to him and kissed him—pulled his shirt loose, and moved her fingers on him. "Don't you mind, Ragir. You ever need to know, I'll tell you. Now you don't."

He smiled, and joined in her game. "I've ordered up a dinner I think you'll like. But it won't be here for a while."

"That's good. I'm not hungry yet, anyway."

But sometimes when he moved she felt him wince. It had to be the gut wound—and what could she do about *that*?

Dopples kept his word. He still didn't like her—Zelde could tell that—but now he didn't brush off her questions. All right, good enough. If she needed friends, there were other people around.

Like Turk Kestler. Coming off watch, Zelde met Turk. The woman looked a lot better in clothes than out of them, and the slight, growing bulk of hair over her head helped, too. Zelde said, "How's your strawboss job going?"

Turk's grin was the same; it still needed a few teeth. "Fine, Zelde. Oh, I had to stamp on some nids who thought they had a free ride coming, but it's all working pretty good now. Hey—*you're* moving up in the world, the way I hear it."

Zelde shook her head. "Not so much. I'm on apprentice rating in Control, is all. Trying to learn navigation, communications—maybe how to pilot, someday." She saw Turk's brows raise, and said, "One part, you could have heard wrong. Living with Parnell—that makes me no rank, Turk."

"If you say so; I'd have thought different." Then: "Hey—you want to come see something?"

"What is it?"

"I'd rather show you." Well, why not? So Zelde followed her friend downship, along past Drive, to a maintenance shop where a small, older woman worked at a bench. "Henty Monteil, Zelde."

The two shook hands. Zelde said, "I heard of you. Yeah—you're the one tattooed Parnell . . . and Dopples. Right?"

"Yes. If you feel like being decorated, come around." Zelde shook her head. "All right. Ready for the fitting, Turk?"

"Yes, I think so." Kestler fumbled at her left earlobe, taking out what first looked like a button earring. But the post was thick, nearly three millimeters. A moment later, Turk unplugged the other lobe.

Zelde stared. "How'd you do that? Punch it out some way?"

"No. just stretched it—bigger inserts every few days. Practically painless, but it took me over a month."

Henty Monteil opened a drawer, and Zelde saw several gold rings—open, with the cut ends separated a bit. Henty picked up a matched pair, sized for Turk's lobes and more than three centimeters arcross. "These are the ones you want, then?"

Turk nodded. Henty showed a heavier pair, not bigger around but a lot thicker. "I thought she was going to take these, Zelde, but she chickened out. Now I don't know where I'll find a customer for them."

Zelde put her hand out, and Monteil let her take the heavy rings. Using the shiny panel of an equipment console for a mirror, she held them up to her earlobes and liked what she saw. Handing the rings back, she felt as if she'd lost something.

Now Turk sat. "Here's what I want you to see—how Henty welds these closed without burning me." Monteil put a little grease on one of Turk's rings and worked the end through the left earlobe until the gap was farthest from flesh. On the other side she repeated, then used a tool to close both gaps.

"Now," she said, and held up two blocks of aluminum, grooved to clamp together over a ring, and snapped them into place. "See? They don't touch Turk, and they leave the juncture free for my torch. The heat never reaches her; the aluminum dissipates it." One hand moved the torch; the other fed gold wire to melt into the groove. When Henty's wet finger, touched to the weld, brought no sizzle, she removed the blocks and buffed the joint to smoothness. Then she did the other side.

Turk brought out a small mirror and looked. "That's really a tidy job. I'll be another month paying you, but it's worth it."

Henty smiled. "I'm glad you like it. Do you think your man will?"

"That's the general idea. But mainly—*I* like them."

Zelde made up her mind. "The big ones—how much would those cost me?" The answer was a lot more than she'd hoped, but she said, "You've got you a customer." She took out her own small button earrings—Honcho, a long time ago, gave her those. "Let's see how big a stretch plug I can take, for starters."

Henty's brows raised. "You realize these are nearly half a centimeter thick?"

"That's why I want to get started. Not planning on taking any month at it, either. I don't mind a little hurt."

Climbing back upship, Turk said, "Stop by, why don't you, and have a drink? Rooster should be off watch by now, and I'd like you two to get acquainted." Zelde had met Rooster Hogan, but not much more than that. So she agreed, and when Turk showed her into the tiny cabin, the little man gave her a cheerful greeting.

"Siddown, siddown!" He made busy, pouring spirits into three glasses, fussing until the levels were exactly even. He carried maybe sixty bio-years, Zelde guessed, but moved like a much younger man. He hadn't much of his gray hair left, and his face was deeply wrinkled, but aging didn't seem to cut his energy. He handed glasses around. "Okay—what'll we toast?"

Turk pushed short, bushy hair back from one ear. "You might notice something, Rooster."

He looked, then laughed and set down his glass. "So that's what you been up to! All right—give us a kiss first, *then* we drink."

He really worked at his kissing, Zelde thought and his hands didn't stay put, either. Finally Turk pushed him back. "Can't you wait until Zelde has her drink? I tell you, girl—you've got to watch these little old skinny ones. They'll fool you."

"I'll drink to that," Rooster said, and he did it. Sitting, he said, "It's this way, Zelde. Past few years, under UET, I got to where life wasn't any fun—nothing seemed worth the doing. Hadn't even bothered with women in a long time. Then—Escape! Twice I was damn near kilt. Once an energy beam missed me—" He held up thumb and finger. "—no more than that. And then a knife . . . but never mind. The thing is that the close calls made me think. And since then—well, I don't waste any day I've got!"

She thought about it. "Seems like a good way to be."

He swallowed the rest of his drink, and stood. "Something I have to do—promised I'd check the watch, down in Drive, and see how the new man's doing. Won't take long."

After he left, Turk said, "That little old goat—he makes me feel like twenty again! Doesn't mind that I'm built like a tank—well, a small tank maybe, but it's the shape that counts. Only not with Rooster, it doesn't." She looked in a mirror and pulled at the hair bushing behind one ear. "Hair grows out wrong. This ought to be trimmed back."

"You want me to try it?" Turk found comb and scissors, and sat down. Not too sure she knew what she was doing, Zelde snipped here and there until she had the ragged outline down to a fairly smooth curve. She paused, holding up a few strands with the comb, then shook her head. "I think I'd better quit. Take a look?"

Turk did, and nodded. "Hey—that's fine. Thanks." Now Zelde studied the mirror; her own tight-kinked hair didn't look very tidy, either. She pulled a bit of it out straight, frowned, and patted it back. Turk said, "You need a little work, too?"

"Hard to do, I think. With the Kids—you know, that seems like forever ago, but it's not so long, really—being a fighter I just kept it shaved off. On here, though. . . ." She thought of the tattoo, never finished, on her scalp. "No, it wouldn't fit. What I'd like, though—well, as if it was shaved about a month ago. But can you . . . ?"

"No problem—if you don't expect it perfect. Sit." She touched the place where the burn had been. "About even, all over, with this that's just growing back?" Zelde nodded.

This job took longer; then Zelde used the mirror. No, it wasn't perfect—but she liked the look, a tight cap above her face. "Nice, Turk. I'd forgot what my ears looked like—and *they* forgot the feel of fresh air."

She finished the last of her drink, and left.

When Parnell came into quarters, Zelde was standing naked at the big mirror, seeing herself from one angle and then another. She went hipshot, taut belly pushed forward, head back and tilted. She put circled thumbs and forefingers to her earlobes, half-closing her eyes, imagining how the heavy gold rings would look against her black skin. Then she heard the door close, and looked past her image to see him behind her.

He smiled. "Got a haircut, did you? Not bad at all—nor is the rest of you, by any means. You—whether it's the hormones in your implant, or just nature, you're developing."

She faced him. "The tits, you mean." She cupped her hands over them, and laughed. "Sure—just little bumps, they were. Now, rounding out more. I noticed, too. You like it?"

"Surely I do. Though you didn't hear me complaining before, did you? But yes—it's more comfortable not being reminded how young you really are."

"Sixteen maybe, by now. Don't know exactly, I told you."

He came to her kiss; against her back his hands moved. "It doesn't matter, Zelde. Sixteen's legally adult—and in many ways you'd grown up before we ever met."

"And others I still don't know from a bowl of beans. Lots to learn yet, Parnell—I know that."

"You'll get around to all of it; you have time." Through his shirt she could feel, in his muscles, how tense and tired he was—and not the way she could help with.

She said, "Get your shoes off and sit. I'll make you a drink. Then you lie down a while, take a nap. Right?"

In his face she saw his thanks, before he said them.

More and more, now, the Control room made sense. Zelde learned how to feed the computer and to figure the meaning of what it fed back. She still made mistakes, but not as many. What she still didn't understand, was *why*— and near the end of one watch, she asked Lera Tzane. "I can mostly get along with the computer now, I think—but I don't guess I'm ever going to know how it works."

Tzane smiled. "*I* don't understand how all the little electrons and their exotic relatives scuttle around in there. I merely know a number of things that the metal mentality is supposed to do on command. If it doesn't—if I *think* it hasn't—I call a technician to check it out. And that's all that *most* deck officers can do."

"Really? No scut?" Suddenly Zelde felt as if she'd won a fight. Well, she thought, maybe she had.

Parnell seemed better. He drank more than she liked to see, but never to getting sick or mean or passed-out. And the pill bottle sat with the same few at the bottom—no change. He wasn't tired so much—never skipped duty, and hardly ever gave her to know he didn't want her when she was ready. Once in a while she'd see him lean forward a little, with his hand to the hurt side of his gut, and not say anything right away. But that was the only way she could tell he still had troubles.

And for sure, he had *Chanticleer* under control. Just listening to the people she worked with, she could see that.

One thing she couldn't figure—so one day, the two of them lying a little sweaty, still, she asked him. At the meeting right after Escape, the talk of voting. "So what's to vote on?"

He sipped at his drink, swirling it so the ice cubes clinked. "It's not out here, Zelde—not in travel. Here, I'm Captain and what I say goes. But the ship's a business, too, now—owned on shares, as you heard. It has to make its own living. And the best way to go about that—starting with what we buy and sell at Terranova, and choosing where we go next—all the shareholders have a rightful voice in those decisions."

"But what if you *know* what's right to do, and they vote to do something else?"

Either he laughed or coughed; she couldn't be sure. "Well—if I couldn't swing the vote *or* put up with it, I could demand to be bought out, and get off. That's happened sometimes, I've heard. I don't expect it to happen on this ship."

She hoped he was right, and she thought he was. Still, the idea bothered her—if the captain didn't have full say-so, there was a lot more chance for things to get screwed up.

Working for Honcho, there hadn't been any of that crap.

Dopples had to test Zelde himself before he'd approve her for a real rating, not just apprentice. He didn't look straight at Parnell when he said it. "It's my job to certify promotions, Captain."

"Or mine, if I choose—though I'm not overriding you, Dopps. But you have Lera Tzane's evaluation there. Isn't that good enough?"

Zelde sensed the First Hat's anger. She said, "I'm not asking for anything more than I've got coming. Mr. Adopolous—when's it handy for you, to run me through all of it?"

He told her, and when the time came, she was ready and waiting. She knew he wouldn't make it easy, and he didn't. But he wasn't going to scare her, either—get her to freeze up and make mistakes.

She did a good job and she knew it. One time he said she screwed up. She thought he'd told her wrong, but all she said was, "Two out of three? I'll go on it if you will."

He looked at her and she knew he'd make the two re-runs as hard as he could—and the way they went, he did just that. But now she felt her blood moving, and a little extra sharp edge on everything she saw and heard. Almost before he had the problems set up, she was guessing close to the answers—and then *solid* on them, soon as she had all the figures.

At the end of it he looked like somebody biting on a

sour rock. He said, "You rise well to challenge. I'm not greatly sold on that quality. Sometimes it works—but when it doesn't, we're all in trouble. I prefer people to be dependable on a steady level. Maybe you are, M'tana—but you haven't proved it."

Why answer? She didn't. Finally he signed the paper and gave it to her. It granted her ratings of Second in navigation, First on the comm-boards, and as watch monitor in general—and approved her for pilot training at the apprentice level.

She said her thanks with a straight face. Dopples didn't speak at all; he only nodded.

Parnell, when he saw the paper, grinned. "Well—you've upped your share aboard here, more than double. Not that it's terribly big, even yet—but, Zelde, in case you're interested, you are no longer dependent on me in any way."

She saw how he meant it, what he said. And most likely she didn't need to show him about the part he wasn't saying. But why not?

More testing, she had to work through—and some things she wasn't so good at as she'd thought she was. Fighting without weapons, she was nowhere near to being a match for Turk, who practice-fought with the big earrings taped flat to her neck. Zelde caught a lot of bruises before Turk told Dopples, "For now, she's as good as she can get until her weight builds up more." Saying no word, the man looked at both of them, then nodded and signed the paper.

Knives, though, nobody could show Zelde much—and sometimes she showed *them*. With the blunt, rounded practice weapons, she gave more marks than she took. Dopples didn't say anything.

Guns were something else. Sure, she'd shot bullets and she'd sprayed energy bolts around—but not enough to learn much. Parnell took over and showed her the difference—holding a bullet gun on target and then firing, but then with the heavy energy projectors, swinging the beam *across* the target. For some time she had trouble doing it all the way he wanted. But then it began to work for her, and when Parnell handed Dopples the signed paper, he didn't ask whether the other man liked it or not.

* * *

Any morning her earlobes didn't hurt, she went to Henty Monteil for a larger pair of stretch plugs. She'd made the down payment on the rings with her apprentice credits; now she signed for half her present earnings to pay off the rest. She was pushing to get those rings as soon as she could—and as she'd said, didn't mind a little hurt along the way. The plugs looked like ordinary button earrings; until the job was done, Parnell couldn't notice anything. Which was the way she wanted it.

On watch one day, she saw a blip in a screen that hadn't shown sign before. She frowned, then remembered what it should mean. "Mr. Adopolous! We're getting signal from off-ship."

He looked, and nodded. "Call the captain."

She did. Sooner than she expected, still buttoning his shirt, Parnell came in. "Move over one, Zelde—I'll take the comm." She watched as he tuned the equipment. "Can't make out what ship it is. Too much hash, at this distance."

"Course?" said Dopples.

"Crossing ours on a skew—small angle. Closest approach, maybe a thousand kilos—but we'll be in talk range for some time."

"So close? Out here, that just doesn't happen." His mouth curved downward. "Except on purpose."

"You're too suspicious, Dopples. More than one route goes through this volume."

The First Hat worried his hair behind one ear. "The thing is, Parnell—could it change course and intercept?"

Parnell's hands moved on his computer keyboard. After a time, he said, "Possible, if they started in the next few minutes. But why should they? They've got their own trip to make."

"UET? If *they* get suspicious? We're not where we're supposed to be; you know that."

"Of course I do—but do they? That course doesn't come straight from Earth—or from Iron Hat, either. So how *could* they know?" He leaned toward the screen, looked closer. "And it's not an armed ship—even from here, I can tell that much. So what could they do if they did follow us?"

Dopples still talked worried. Finally Parnell said, "Don't fret, Dopps; I'll play it safe. We hold off opening visual

contact until the last believable second—plead bad signal
and distort our own enough to make the complaint sound
reasonable. And keep our cover story straight while we're
talking, of course. I'm no more inclined than you are to
give UET the news, any sooner than we can help."

Zelde spoke. "What if it's another Escaped ship?" Then:
"Do we have any scut about what UET trips are scheduled
through this part of space?"

Dopples waved a hand. "Not between colonies. We can't
have—the time lag's too long. Remember—we're maybe
fifteen years out from Earth, planet time."

That silenced her. She knew in a way—she'd been
told—how the ships ate time without seeming to. But she
kept forgetting. To her, the time she'd *lived* through was all
that was real.

On the screen the signal changed. "Almost close enough
for talking," said Parnell. "Zelde—call down for some coffee, will you?"

"I'll go get it." The truth was, sitting and waiting, nothing to do, was getting her nervous. Glad of the chance to
move around, she went to the galley and brought a fresh
pot and clean cups. Lera Tzane had joined the group, and
Harger from Engineering. Zelde was glad she'd brought extras. She poured for Parnell and herself and sat again beside him, letting the others serve themselves. Dopples
looked at her—but now that she was rated, fetch and carry
wasn't her job. What she'd done was because she wanted
to.

Turning a knob to put his outgoing signal a little off proper tuning, Parnell winked and switched on a speaker. The
voice came: ". . . read your beacon, but won't pass close
enough to make out your insigne, most likely. This is the
Hoover, calling the *Great Khan*. Come in, please. Come
in. . . ."

"We'll give it a couple more minutes," said Parnell.
Again the waiting got to Zelde; she tapped fingers on her
chair arms. When Parnell punched the "Send" switch she
leaned forward, but still he paused. Then he cleared his
throat and spoke.

"First Officer Parnell speaking for the *Great Khan*. Second Officer Adopolous, here with me, sends his respects
also. Captain Czerner—well, he's busy, if you understand

me. Says he can be up in twenty minutes, no sooner. But sends his greetings."

After a time—Zelde knew she should be able to guess the distance from it, but she hadn't noted the seconds when Parnell first spoke—the other's call stopped and a new voice came. "Hello, Parnell. I think I remember you from the—uh, Academy. First Officer Bernardez here, bringing you the great good will of the *Hoover*. Captain Durer, now—you'll recall him also, I do believe. But the poor man's having a bit of a fever, just at the moment, and he's full of enough sedation to keep half the ship drowsy. But I'm sure he'll be pleased to have your regards and I do think I'll take the liberty of sending you his own."

"And Captain Czerner's," said Parnell, "to all of you on the *Hoover*." He cleared his throat. "And what news from other friends?"

In the delay, Zelde heard the silence crackle; then came the voice of Bernardez again. "You'll recall Raoul Vanois, from the backwoods planet? Well, he had a thing to say of Terranova. Being there a time, staying offship in the town, he found it cold sleeping. But quite warm, that odd man said, when under enough covers." A laugh came. "And doesn't it just sound like him, though?"

"Yes," said Parnell. "I know Raoul, all right." Brows raised, he looked at Dopples; then both men nodded. Zelde started to ask what it was all about, but Parnell shook his head.

Bernardez may have chuckled; with the background noise, Zelde couldn't be sure. Then he said, "And now where might you be heading, this fine year? We were out of Far Corner for the Twin Worlds, but hardly clear of atmosphere when the *Attila* passed us going in and messaged a change of plans. So now, instead, we're for—" The signal crackled and, for a moment, failed.

Parnell silenced his own sending to say, "I swear he did that on purpose." Then, with his "Send" switch live again, he said, ". . . and naturally we'll give word of you when we get there." Dopples winked at him and grinned.

Watching the blips, Zelde saw that the ships had passed their closest and were moving apart. Bernardez' voice came weaker. "And it's been a good meeting, Parnell and Adopolous—we don't get so very many, do we now? Perhaps, some decade from here and groundside together, we'll have the chance to buy each other a great untidy lot of drink."

Parnell swallowed. "I'd like that, Bernardez." But incoming signal was gone; maybe the other had heard, and maybe not. Parnell turned to Dopples. "You know what I think?"

The balding man nodded. "You think he's Escaped, same as we are—and didn't dare *say* it, same as us. Isn't that it?"

"Yes. I wish—" He shook his head. "But no—we couldn't chance it. Bernardez, though. . . ."

Zelde cleared her throat. "You know him, do you?"

"How well I do. And if anyone had been voted 'Most Likely to Escape,' my vote would have gone to Kickem Bernardez." He shook his head. "No—that's an old story and not for here. But you know *why* I think he may be Escaped?—a reason that didn't come to me until afterward?"

Dopples made no move or sound; Zelde shook her head. "All else aside," said Parnell, "did he sound like a man talking for the benefit of his captain's recording instruments?"

"But one thing he did tell us," said Dopples. "On Terranova, the Underground is alive and well."

Maybe they'd missed the chance to find an ally, but at least the meeting had gone without trouble. Consensus, when Parnell reported to Ship's Assembly, was better safe than sorry. Zelde wasn't so sure—but no point in arguing. The chance was past.

Leaving the group, Zelde checked the way the stretch plugs felt in her lobes and decided it was time she got the rings put in. Below, in the maintenance shop, Henty Monteil disagreed. "One more step first, Zelde. You've got a little swelling there—do it your way, you may have a lot." Zelde felt herself pouting; Henty grinned at her. "You want these to look good, don't you, the first time Parnell sees them?"

So Zelde shrugged, and went away with another set of buttons showing—but those, she decided, would be the last.

Next day, Parnell called a meeting of Control officers and senior ratings. The subject at hand was twenty-two-year-old Carlo Mauragin, recently promoted from his

Navigator-second rating to Third Hat. Zelde sat back in a corner, hoping no one would notice she didn't rightly belong here. She liked Carlo well enough; his temper wasn't too even, and sometimes he didn't answer on-the-job questions too good, but he was mostly friendly.

Dopples read off the list of complaints. "These aren't charges, Mauragin; we're not sitting as a court here. But you make too many mistakes—and the same ones, too many times. So the skipper has us here to talk it over, see what's to be done about it."

The young man was pale; without his usual color he looked sallow. His mouth twitched, and Zelde saw how his hands gripped his knees. "I try to do my best."

"But you heard the record, didn't you?" Mauragin nodded; Dopples turned to Lera Tzane. "You said he's asked you to speak for him. Go ahead."

The woman stood, slim but not looking fragile. She moved to stand behind Mauragin, and put her hand on his shoulder. "Carlo's new aboard, this trip. He's had less training than his brains deserve. His job before Escape was too easy for him; he could coast. Third Hat—well, it's a big bite, all at once."

"A big chance for him, too," said Parnell, "if he'd lived up to it."

Tzane looked at him. "On the record, I grant you, he doesn't fill the job yet. You could relieve him on your own authority, Captain, if you wanted to—but instead you've brought the matter up for vote. My vote is to give him the rest of this trip—to Terranova, I mean—to see if he can handle things."

Parnell nodded. "Defense noted. Now, vote." Seven to two, one rating siding with Tzane, the vote went against Carlo Mauragin. "All right. Carlo, you're not being punished here—merely relieved from this job at this time, without prejudice to possible future promotions. Before Escape you held—let's see—a Second rating and in line to try for First. I think you've learned enough that we can better that, for you. I recommend you now revert to First, with option to test for Chief rating when we reach Terranova." He looked around. "Vote? Including the recommended rating." Only one did not raise a hand, the same who had sided with Mauragin before. "Passed. Carlo, you can move out of Third's quarters tomorrow—no rush. And you'll stand Third's watches until your replacement's named and confirmed."

He waited, and Mauragin swallowed and then spoke. His normal coloring had come back. "It's a hard thing, to fall flat when you get your biggest chance. But I guess you're right—I'd had it too easy, not used to hard work, hard study. Somehow I couldn't adjust to it fast enough." He tried to smile, too, but it didn't work very well. "Maybe, taking it a little slower, I can get there again someday."

It was Dopples who said, "And we all wish you luck at it." Then he turned to Parnell. "Do you want the ratings to caucus again, to nominate for a new Third?"

Parnell frowned. "No—that's a popularity contest, I'm afraid. We're lucky that one out of two worked this time. I think—Dopps, let's hear *your* recommendation. Yours, too, Lera."

For a long time Dopples didn't speak. Then he shook his head. "You really put me in the grinder—you know that?" Parnell said nothing; Dopples shrugged. "You know how I feel about these things. But, Ragir, there's only one recommendation I can make. Your best bet, out of this lot, is Zelde M'tana." And Lera Tzane nodded.

Hardly able to hear, let alone think, Zelde sat through the vote and heard herself named Third Hat. Walking back to quarters, not quite stumbling, she thought: *Why did he do that?*

In the galley, first chance she had, over coffee she talked with Carlo Mauragin. "Look—what happened—it wasn't—"

Seemed to hurt his face some, but finally he smiled. "I know that, Zelde. At first I thought, maybe, you know—you living with the captain and all. But not when *Dopples* put your name up." Now he looked serious. "It might pay you to be a little extra careful, though, when our First Hat's around." He finished his coffee and left.

Well, she'd thought about Dopples already—about the chance that he might be setting her up for a fall. All she could do was watch herself and double-check her work. She knew about crossing people up—she was braced, if Dopples ever passed her an order that sounded out of line, to make sure it went on the record. And, if she could manage it, with witnesses.

He didn't, though—he gave her, in her new job, the same chilly courtesy he gave Lera Tzane. As near as Zelde could figure it, he was playing a straight game.

So—she kept her guard up.

Turnover was due soon, but Zelde didn't know when, exactly. If it happened on her watch or Lera's, she was pretty sure Parnell would take over—but still she wanted to know as much as she could about it.

The manual wasn't much help. It said that in theory a ship would push ahead—accelerate—for half the trip, then turn over and push backward to slow down. "But in practice . . ." and then the text went off into a lot of equations, and lost her. So, deciding she couldn't work it out on her own, she asked Parnell.

"You learn so well," he said, "that I keep forgetting you simply don't have the math. Well—" And he explained how any ship, just to *hold* up near light speed, had to keep its drive pushing so the resistance of the interstellar gas wouldn't slow it. "It takes about a month—*our* time—to cut from near-light to zerch. The screens and the computer tell you when the distance is right for it. Next time we're in Control, if you like, I can show you the numbers. But you won't need them—twelve hours ahead, the turnover clock lights up and starts your countdown."

He raised one eyebrow. "Is it clear to you, from the manual, what you do from then on?"

"I think so. But I'd still just as soon watch somebody else do it the first time."

He laughed. "I think we can arrange that."

Paying off at the rate of half her Third Hat's earnings, Zelde's debt to Henty Monteil was almost cleared. When the final pair of stretch plugs—the same thickness as the rings themselves—sat comfortably with no swelling or redness, Zelde went to collect.

Monteil helfted the gold rings on her palm and handed them over. "You're sure you want to pack this much weight around?"

"They don't feel so heavy."

"Over three ounces apiece. Sorry—I mean ninety grams. I grew up in one of the last places on Earth to use the old measures, I guess, and still think in them, if I don't watch myself."

Zelde didn't care about that. She removed the stretch plugs and waited while Henty slipped the split rings into place. She nodded her head, shook it, tilted it. "Heavy, sure—but I like it. Go ahead and close them—okay?"

Henty pressed the rings' ends together; over the left one she clamped a pair of her aluminum blocks. The welding took a time. Zelde felt heat at her earlobe, but only after the blocks were off did she say, "Maybe that didn't work right. My ear got damned hot."

The woman's mouth tightened; she looked close. "Yes— it's red there. Why didn't you say something?" Zelde shrugged; Henty said, "True—not much I could have done, by that time." She paused, then nodded. "Bigger cross-section—it changes the ratio between the heat conducted through to you and what's dissipated by the aluminum. Just a minute." On her desk calculator, she punched keys. "All right—the other one I'll do in two sessions, letting it cool betwen times. Could have, on this one—next time, for heaven's sake speak up!"

Zelde grinned. "What next time? Two ears is all I got." And Henty laughed with her. A few minutes later, when the second ring was finished, Zelde spoke her thanks and left for quarters. First she made a stop. Then, at home, she made her preparations.

What she saw in the mirrors, she liked. This time, Turk had cut her hair more evenly—so short, it looked like a cap of thick felt. Her body gleamed with the scented oil she'd rubbed over herself. And those gold rings. . . . She sighed. *Want to look the best there is, for that man!*

When the door opened, she turned to face him. "Parnell?"

He stopped; his eyes widened. "Zelde—"

"You better shut the door." He did, but still stood there.

"Parnell—" She gestured at her body. "You like this? Me?"

He nodded, but stayed where he was.

"Come prove it." When he finally moved, she laughed. Because for a minute there, she'd been worried.

* * *

The funny thing was that until things started getting better, she hadn't noticed anything was wrong. Just the week since she got the rings, Parnell was more man to her than in a long while. And he seemed stronger, all ways—less tired. Well, she'd known, already—when the screwing goes good, so does the other stuff. Or maybe, sometimes, the other way 'round.

She didn't know why the rings made a difference—to her, or to him either—but they did. Okay, using the oil, too—and maybe the tight haircut and a couple new things she did now. Or just showing him—pushing her own self at him more—how she really wanted him, not waiting around until he said first. All right—whatever, it helped him, with her.

She wouldn't forget again.

One night the ship jolted and the alarm rang. Parnell got up, half asleep, fumbling around getting dressed. Zelde dressed, too. He looked at her. "You don't have to go; it's not your watch."

"I want to. All right?" So they went to Control—Dopples had the watch—and heard the reports.

From the drive room, Harger was talking. "I have it back in balance, for now, and I *think* we have enough spares to get us to Terranova. But one landing, Captain—that's all it's good for. Without an overhaul—a new Nielson cube, at least—where we land is where we stay."

Not talking, Parnell nodded. In his face Zelde saw the lines deepen. Finally he said, "All right, Harger. Good work—stay on it. And—none of this is your fault. We both knew they stretched our maintenance skeds on Earth, skimped the repairs." He paused. "I'll be thinking what we need to do on Terranova." He cut the circuit.

Dopple beat his fist against his knee. "Thinking? What *can* we do? All respect, skipper, but half our money cargo—those women—they're crew now. Not that Terranova pays for such, anyway. And—"

Parnell laughed; Zelde heard the effort it took him. "Dopps! I've thought of all that, and past it."

"So? Past it, to *what?*"

"To figuring what we *can* afford, all shares willing and given a favorable situation, if Terranova won't issue us a cube against Space Service credit. Meanwhile, First Hat, you start training combat teams."

"I don't see—"

Ragir Parnell grinned. "The hell you don't. On Terra-nova, there'll be ships. Ships have drives in them. The only question, if it comes to that, is do we gut one for its drive? Or do we hijack the whole thing?"

For once, Dopples had nothing to say.

Compensating for the weakened drive, Parnell announced early turnover. "More time to slow—so that if we have periods of failure, we can still keep from overshooting." Zelde understood that part, all right. It was the mechanics of turnover, how to do it, that she was still studying.

When the turnover clock started, she saw that the actual work would begin on Dopples' watch, not long after the next time he relieved her. So this time, before leaving, she asked in advance if she could observe turnover.

Narrow-eyed, he looked at her. "You don't need my permission—not with Parnell in your pocket—and you know it. So why ask?"

"It's your watch, Mr. Adopolous—and I hear that turnover can get tricky. So if I'd be in the way—bother you any—just say so now, and when you relieve me I'll get my ass out. But I really want to see how you do it—*if* it's all right."

After a moment, he nodded. "M'tana, I don't mean to pick on you. It's—well, I told you how I feel, early on. All right. Considering how much you don't know, you do your job. And, so far, you stay inside it. Yes—hang around for turnover."

"Thanks."

For once she smiled at him freely—but then he said, "Don't get any ideas. I still watch you."

She shrugged. "Whatever you say. Thanks just the same."

Waiting, the next twelve hours, got under her skin. For the first time since she couldn't remember, in bed with Parnell she couldn't make it. He looked bothered; she stroked his cheek. "Not your fault, Ragir—it's mine. Got my thinking all into turnover, I guess. Not enough left over, for *us*."

"Turnover? Why that, Zelde?"

"Dunno, Parnell—I really don't. It's just—maybe I'm making more out of it, learning how it goes, than I should ought to."

He laughed and held her tighter. "Then we'll wait and see how things are with you tomorrow." She could grin at that, and she did.

Turnover countdown—tighter and tighter it wound her up. Dopples came on watch—*the* watch—twenty minutes early. Having him see and hear everything she did—that didn't help her any. Once she glanced sidewise at him, saw his eyes directly on her, and didn't look again.

The end-of-watch chime rang. On the beat of it, Parnell came in. Almost, she started to say him welcome—but she had no business doing that. She turned to Dopples. "Relief acknowledged, Mr. Adopolous. Your watch." He nodded and quickly checked the log. Zelde picked a seat, not in anybody's way but close enough to see what went on, and moved to it.

Dopples looked to Parnell. "Captain?"

Parnell nodded. "Proceed, Dopps. I'm just here to observe." He found a seat, on the far side from Zelde's. She looked toward him but he faced the screens and instruments, so she did, too.

The clock counted down. On ship's broadcast, Dopples said, "Fifteen minutes to zero-gee. Everybody—last chance to see that your duffle's stowed properly, then strap in!" Zelde knew—Parnell had told her—that some didn't take this order seriously. Stuff would be left loose to bounce around; couples would try screwing in the air, free-fall, and a few might get hurt. It generally happened, he said, so why worry about it? She didn't—but checked her own seat straps and watched the indicator boards.

Finally Dopples said, "Harger, cut drive and swing ship." All Zelde felt was no seat pressure on her butt—and some way, she was *turning*. She gulped back from throwing up—not really sick, it had to be some reflex—and watched harder. Nothing happened.

She was starting to get used to it when she saw how tight Parnell's face was, watching Dopples. She couldn't figure it—now she saw that the First Hat looked scared, too. Then came Harger's voice. "The drive! Pilot stage cut out with the rest and didn't start again. I've got to recycle from scratch, and hope *that* works!"

Parnell strained against his seat strap, then shook his head and leaned back. Dopples looked over at his captain, nodded, and opened the intercom again. "We read you, Harger. Go ahead with it—take your time—advise progress when you can." He cut the circuit.

Parnell said, "Good, Dopps! Taking the pressure off him; you did right."

"What else could I do? But now—what if it doesn't work soon enough?"

Parnell shrugged. "Either we have fuel to loop back if we overshoot, or else we don't."

Adopolous stared at him. "You *mean* that, what you just said?"

"Why not? It's true, isn't it?"

For Zelde, time dragged. Nobody said anything and Parnell wouldn't look at her. Dopples scratched fingernails on the comm-panel but touched no switches. She felt like yelling, but of course she knew better.

She wanted coffee, or a drink—but damned if she'd move when nobody else had to. Wishing somebody would talk, she sat there.

It couldn't have been as long as it seemed before the intercom squawked again. Harger's voice. "I think we have some gees coming up in a minute. Get braced."

Nobody answered—but then the seat hit her butt and she knew, from Dopples' relieved gasp, that things were all right.

For the moment. Then came a bounce feeling and Parnell said, "He doesn't have it steady yet." Nobody else spoke. Finally the push came solid again. After a minute of it, Parnell unstrapped and stood. "Harger's got it now, I think. All right, Dopps—with all that jittering, our time's off. Run the readings through Tinhead and integrate for corrections; right? Set decel to hit zerch a week before we need it—we can ease off at intervals to use up the difference, and we may have to. Agreed?"

"Right, skipper. Will do." On his computer keyboard Dopples set up patterns, punched activation, frowned and began again. Parnell beckoned to Zelde; she stood and joined him, and they walked back to quarters.

* * *

Inside, he pulled her to him. One slow kiss, then he said, "We're in trouble. You know that?"

Looking at him, she grinned. "I sort of guessed. How bad?"

"Harger's already said he can get us to Terranova but not off again—not without at least the bare guts of a new drive. I believe him." He stroked her shoulders. "Zelde—we could all die on that world."

"Could of died in Escape, too—but we didn't." With narrowed eyes she squinted at him. "Parnell—what you up to?"

To gesture, he had to let go of her. "Terranova—it's UET, with *maybe* Escaped ship contacts. I—and *Chanticleer*—we may get in and out safely or we may not—the odds aren't good. But you, Zelde—you're not tied, not labeled, one way or the other. You could jump ship, if necessary, and melt into Terranova with whatever story we fix up for you. You're not stuck—"

Her palm covered his mouth. "And leave you, Parnell? Don't you ever say like that again!" She made herself smile. "You said once, I own your life. Sneak off, leave you to take care of it by yourself—what kind of way is that, to own something?"

She reached down at him; the same moment, his hand found her. She hadn't thought she was in a hurry, but getting to bed they left clothes wherever they happened to fall. Then her body *urged* at him—no taking it easy, no slow delight, no rests—and Parnell stayed with her all the way. Afterward, when she got a hand free to wipe sweat—his and hers, both—off her face, she said, "Parnell, we just screwed my *brains* out—you know? Same time, though—part of my head, where I didn't notice, thought other ways." Mouth trembling, she looked up at him.

"What ways?" He didn't have much breath yet for talk.

"Suchlike, we're in hard on Terranova—could be maybe I *act* like you said—run off and hide, all that. *Look* like I'm on my own, but be finding stuff out for you, is what." How he looked, it didn't change. "Oh—I can't *help* what my head does!"

His face twitched; then he grinned. "Zelde—my God, girl! Do you think I'm hurt?" His hands cupped her face.

"When your mind works to help me, how could I possibly feel slighted?"

She had to laugh. "Parnell, sometimes I don't understand all I know about you!"

Then he tickled her, and she fought back—and if it hadn't been so late, and so soon again, both, they might have started all over again.

Harger kept his promise; the drive—except for a wiggle once in a while—stayed solid. Every time Zelde came on watch she checked the computer tapes; the time and distance figures stayed close to what Parnell had said he wanted. For now, she quit worrying.

The day the power suit was ready for testing, Parnell told her about it. They were having breakfast. "It's not the one you smashed—and praise peace that you did! This is a newer model. Its power unit failed, and no replacements. So your friend Henty Monteil has been jury-rigging to use the power supply from the wrecked suit. Harger did the circuit designs, but it's taking a lot of handwork, too. Nothing much fits, without modifications."

Zelde swallowed the last of her scrambled eggs and poured more coffee. "A lot of work, you say. Is it worth it?"

Parnell grinned. "Because of the way you knocked one out? Well, not to belittle the very brave thing you did—but I don't think you know how many kinds of luck you needed, to do it."

She listened while he ticked off points. The man in the suit wasn't trained—barely checked out in its operation. Standing with his back to a long drop—that had been foolish. And the suit's gyros couldn't have been revved up to standard and balanced right, or no lunge of Zelde's could have toppled it; she might have slid the whole thing back slightly, but that's all. But most important—although it was unheard-of for anyone to tackle a power suit barehanded, no trained operator would have been taken by surprise.

She frowned. "What you're saying—you mean I ought to take this gadget more serious? What for? Me, I mean."

"Because I want you trained to use it. All right?"

"Sure, Parnell—whatever you say. Ready to go?"

"If you are." They stood, and he led the way downship.

* * *

In the equipment staging area just above the drive room, they found Dopples arguing with Henty Monteil. The man stood encased in the lower half of the power suit. Spread behind him like a partly shed carapace, the upper half lay sprawled over a workbench. Nodding to Parnell, the First Hat looked over his shoulder and continued his raised-voice complaint. "All right then, Monteil—what *else* can't this thing do, that it's supposed to?"

Before the woman could answer, Parnell said, "More problems with the interface circuits?"

Straightening up from the suit-glove she'd been adjusting, Henty stood only shoulder-high to Dopples. She pushed gray hair back from her forehead. "That's it, Captain. The circuit redesigns, between this suit and the one that got smashed—several of the interfaces between suit and power pack are at different levels, one from the other—even different frequencies, sometimes. I've done what I can, but even Chief Harger admits that we have to scrap a few functions. There's no way out of it."

Adopolous made a snort. "You managed the gyros—took the exciter feed ahead of the shifter and then used the shifter to handle the dark-sensor input. So why can't you—"

For a second or two, Henty looked like shouting, but the small woman's voice came calm. "Sure. Harger and I rigged this and shifted that and shuffled the other thing. And a good job, too—if I do say so myself. But what I'm trying to get through your stubborn head—*sir*—is that I've used up all the angles the equipment has to offer. I *won't* hang interface units outside the suit where anyone could smash them with a kick or a beer bottle, or where they'd go sour in vacuum work near zero-Kelvin. I—"

Moving with precise restraint, Parnell's hand cut air. "Let's talk about what we have and what we don't have. Maybe we can make some tradeoffs."

Henty Monteil nodded. Dopples began climbing out of the suit, and said, "You take it then, skipper—maybe you can get some sense out of her. I'm due on watch." Parnell waved a hand, and the man left. Then the captain looked to Monteil, and she began to explain.

Listening, Zelde understood most of it. The basic power extensors—the part that made someone in the suit stronger

than anybody and maybe faster—all of that worked. Seeing
with light or without it, hearing in ranges humans don't
hear naturally, the use of reflected sound and radiation—a
few problems, Henty said, but mostly okay. And the gyros—the balancing units that had to disconnect and then
hook up again fast when you bent or turned or did much
of anything except straight-line movement—those controls
were in good shape.

Going outside in space—that's where it got itchy. You
had to hang on, Henty said, because the magnetics weren't
reliable—and stay tied to a line, too, for safeties. All
right. . . .

"And there's no way," she said, "to derive a power feed
for the emergency projector that's built to *mount* on this
suit, as part of it. That's mainly what pissed Dopples."

Parnell had explained about projectors, the big guns that
armed ships carried. "Two convergent lasers," he'd said,
"operating above the visual octave and heterodyning in the
peak range for heat energy." The energy guns she already
knew of—they worked the same way, he said. But pea-
shooters by comparison. This one, that they couldn't use, it
had to be somewhere in between.

"Well," Parnell said now, "if we can't, we can't. What
else?"

Henty shrugged. "That's most of it. Some of the fancy
stuff—ratio circuits for null-gee operation, all that—Harger
doesn't know it very well, and Dopples couldn't make it
clear to either of us, so why try?"

Parnell waved her scowl away. "Then good enough, I
think. Are you finished with the modifications you *can*
manage?" She nodded. "All right. I'll take it from here—
and you get a bonus." She tried to protest; he said, "Don't
argue with the skipper; you can't win." Henty Monteil
grinned, and left the area.

Now Zelde followed Parnell to a side room. He opened a
cabinet and brought out a skeletal contraption that slid
along an overhead track. "This is a suit trainer." Not sure
what she was agreeing with, Zelde nodded. "It has all the
basic servo-circuits of a power suit, and simulates the iner-
tia without the actual weight—lots cheaper to operate, and
safer for the student. You strap into it, and I'll feed you
enough juice so you can begin learning how to use it."

He showed her how to adjust the harness; not saying anything, she did as he told her. But just before he could push the power switch, she said, "Parnell—why? Why is it you want me doing this?"

Lopsided, not moving the shoulder that still bothered him, he shrugged. "All officers and top ratings should have this training." Now, and still only on one side, he grinned. "If Czerner had stuck to that rule, we wouldn't be here now. But he didn't."

"I see what you mean. All right, what do I do next?"

Long after the simulator's balky response had her untrained muscles aching, she kept practicing. At the end of it, before their late lunch, Parnell said she was doing pretty well.

I'll do better.

On the screen, Terranova's sun grew. "About five days out, Dopples," Parnell said. "If they had Earth's facilities, we'd have been detected by now. Here, though—"

Adopolous straightened up from the computer keyboard; he stretched. "Maybe they have here, too. Do you want to check the log again, skipper?" Zelde, in Control a little early to relieve the First Hat, knew what he meant. The *Great Khan*'s entire trip log had been replaced, so far as normal access codes were concerned, by a faked version.

"Sure." From his auxiliary position Parnell punched for access. "If anything's suspicious—any real investigation— we're in the soup. Lucky for us, UET isn't given to checking up on underlings. But *we* have to have it all down pat."

As the readout came, Parnell mumbled under his breath. Zelde listened; she'd heard it all before but she wanted to know it by heart. All right—Captain Czerner promoted to a groundside command on Earth, Parnell upped to skipper with several other promotions entered as retroactive to Earth, and thus official. About half of Turk's women were now on the books as crew from the start, and the rest scheduled for Farmer's Dell, not Iron Hat. Those last, they'd have to move back into Hold, Portside Upper, before the landing.

No hiding the period of drive failure, so use it: Terihew and the dead Engineering officer listed as accident victims. And the *Khan*'s UET-assigned schedule now read Earth to Terranova to Farmer's Dell, where further orders might be waiting—or if not, at the captain's option, return to Earth either directly or via the Twin Worlds.

There was more—a lot of details that Zelde wouldn't be expected to know. Those she let go by, listening with only half her attention. At the end of it, Parnell said, "Good work, Dopps. You covered everything that any of us have been able to think of. The only trouble is—"

"Yes," said Adopolous. "I wouldn't believe it, either."

Now, getting ready to land in UET country, Parnell was busy all the time. He called meetings and lectured groups on the version of ship's history they had to know and keep straight. He set quotas of who could go groundside and who couldn't. "Folks who talk when they drink, they drink aboard, where they won't speak to the wrong ears." In Officers' Council, nobody argued with his choices.

He was thinner, Zelde noticed—and he looked tired again. She knew he was worrying—how the hell not? On the job, that was his business. But off duty she tried to get his mind relaxed.

It wasn't easy. He was off the pain pills now but used stimulants a lot. Nothing she said, helped—but booze did. So—not liking it at all—as the least of the evils, she didn't fuss when he drank more than he should.

The second time, after he'd okayed the fake log, that they had off-watch time together, she got him out of Control and back to quarters right away. Once his shirt and shoes were off and he had a drink at hand, she said, "You just stay put now. I'm going to fix me up some." His brows raised, and she grinned. "Lately, Parnell, you've been screwing like it was a training exercise or something—when we get to it at all. And me, I let you get away with it. Not today, though. You just wait there, see? And build your strength—'cause I aim to see that you need it!"

Preparing, she took her time. Turned out, it was worth it.

Three days short of Terranova, groundside hailed the *Khan*. Hearing the scratchy signal as it rose and fell between noise bursts, Zelde wasn't surprised when Parnell didn't answer yet. "Ionization," he said. "Flares, and the radiation belts from the two big gas-giant planets—it's be-

lievable that we couldn't read them from here. Zelde—put
on the loop tape."

He turned to the comm-board tech. "Off-tune your signal.
Overload the mixer stage for plenty of peak distortion, but
run your final output at half power. Once we're past the
two biggies—and we're lucky they're both on this side of
the primary—we'll have to talk. But not until then. Meanwhile we *listen*."

On a side-screen he had charts of Terranova; on another
the planet showed in direct view, at top blowup. Standing,
using a pointer to indicate surface features, he said, "None
of us has been here before, so this is all we have to go on."
Zelde saw Dopples shrug as Parnell's voice went into his
lecturing tone. Personally, she liked to hear him explain
things. . . .

". . . with that much axial tilt, the northern continent's climate is all extremes. Except for mineral-search
teams and the like, it's uninhabited."

"Was, you mean, the last we heard," said the Chief Engineer.

Parnell smiled. "Right, Harger—but the odds say it still
is." He moved the pointer. "The other continent, here—
same name as the planet, is it?—I'm not sure. Its north
coast hugs the equator, nearly halfway around Terranova,
but none of the landmass extends south of it more than
about a radian. And most of the main colony push, that we
know of, has been near the west end of it."

Now he pointed—on the chart only, since in direct view,
the feature he wanted wasn't showing—to the large island
that was Terranova's only other major piece of land. West
and north of the southern continent it sat—in the planet's
temperate zone, Parnell said.

He wiggled the pointer. "We don't know the name of
this, either. Only the settlement on it—Parleyvoo—and
that we got from the Underground. Doesn't sound like
UET's style of naming, so maybe the colonists are getting a
little independent—or were, for a time." And again Zelde
realized, this time-rolling thing the ships did, it was something she didn't understand very well.

Parnell set the pointer down. "You've heard before, we
have the two choices—main port, at Summit Bay on the
southern mass, or the new one, if it's really there, at Parleyvoo. Now here's something important."

He frowned. "When we start talking with groundside I want to be here at all times. I mean, no one else gives the planet any answers. Understood?"

Dopples said, "No problem. Calling for you won't add enough time-lag for them to notice—not early on, when you're getting things settled."

"Right." Parnell nodded. "It's not that I don't trust and depend on all of you. But this decision—putting the facts together—it has to be in one set of hands. And right now, it's mine."

Leaving Control with Zelde beside him, he seemed less anxious. Tired, yes—but more relaxed than he'd been in a while. She said, "It's set now, how you do it?"

"I think so. The decision still has to be made, but—"

"But either way, Parnell, it goes on course. *Your* course."

At fifty hours out, Parnell decided he had all the info he was going to get, and quit playing coy with Terranova. The planet's beacon—its hailing tape—came clear now, so gradually Parnell had his comm tech tune and strengthen the ship's own signal. When it brought a response, Zelde followed him to Control.

On the screen a world loomed; on the speaker, volume shifting with the solar current, its signal blared. ". . . from the *Great Khan*, acknowledged. Greetings and welcome. Please advise estimated time of landing and specify your designated landing site. We are now ready to record any priority messages you wish to send in advance." The voice continued. When it began to repeat itself, Zelde knew she was hearing another loop tape.

Parnell, at the central control position that duplicated the major functions of every console there, didn't answer directly. He spoke onto tape, played it back and edited it. Then he signaled for transmission. Zelde listened.

"To Terranova from the *Great Khan*. Ragir Parnell, Captain, brings greetings from Earth. Our ETL, slightly under fifty hours, Earth standard." He'd been sounding like some kind of ceremony; now his voice changed. "If I may be a little less official for a minute, who's *there?*" He paused a moment. "I mean, what ships, which of my old friends? The years, they're so *long* out here." And Zelde saw that he wasn't acting; he meant it. Then he went back to official talk, finished it and waited for an answer.

Eventually it came. After some more ceremony, a voice came that sounded halfway like a real person. It named ships and captains, three groundside at Summit Bay just now, then said, "There's a message here for you, Captain, left by Aloysius Malloy of the *Charon*—First Officer, I believe—yes, that's right. It doesn't bear privacy seal, and—why, it's quite short. The text reads, 'Congenial place, this. Though likely there'll soon be a pig in the parlor.'"

A pause, then an embarrassed laugh. "I was waiting for your answer; I forgot the time lag. Well, Captain, I'm sorry, but you've missed your friend. The *Charon* lifted from Parleyvoo, leaving that port empty now, about nine days ago. For Short Haul and then Franklin's Jump, if that's any help."

"Not much," said Parnell, but his voice switch was dead. The groundhog may have forgotten time lag; Parnell hadn't. When the port's message ended, he answered. "Thanks for all the information; it's logged. Awfully bad luck that I missed Malloy, especially since Parleyvoo's our designated landing site. But that's the way of it sometimes, when you have two ages." He said more, but nothing that caught Zelde's attention. Then he cut the circuit and said, "Malloy's saying he found local Underground contacts and his ship's making ready to Escape. *Pig in the Parlor's* what he plans to name it. Well, I wish him success. But to us, another vital factor is that Parleyvoo is free, just now, of UET ships."

"So that's where we land?" Seeing Dopples' look, Zelde knew she'd talked out of turn.

"Right." Parnell looked around, nodding, a smile almost breaking loose but not quite. "Better than I thought—a *lot* better. We go in, the only ship on the place."

Harger asked, "What about the drive cube we need?"

"An aircar can bring that from Summit Bay. And with no other space personnel at Parleyvoo, under normal protocol, nobody has the authority to breach ship's security on us!"

But Zelde thought, *how can it be so easy?*

When the planet's rotation next brought Summit Bay into view, transmission lag was small enough for direct conversation. Now, unable to edit his words, Parnell talked directly with Port Commandant Horster, his staff, and the captains of the three ships at groundside. Zelde watched him check readouts of the faked log, making sure not to cross up his "facts." "When I do this," he'd told her, "I have to sound chatty about it. If I act at all secretive, they'll know for sure that from UET's viewpoint, something's wrong." So now she watched him play his deadly game.

Horster wasn't much trouble—it came clear that he had little interest or experience in space itself. He talked mostly of administration and possibilities of promotion—and Zelde knew a politician when she heard one. Parnell told gossip about politics in Earth HQ—whether he sprinkled any truth into it, Zelde had no idea.

Two of the captains and their ships were, to Parnell, only names on a list—and vice versa. The third, Fahrquar of the *Cortez*, was an Academy classmate of the late Captain Czerner, and wanted full details of his friend's promotion. When that talk was done, Parnell wiped his forehead. "Damned good thing, Dopps, that you worked out all the background you did for our story, not just the bare bones." Dopples grinned and shrugged, and for a moment Zelde almost liked the man.

Now a lot had to happen in a hurry. Zelde tried to keep track, but she knew she missed a few things.

Maybe Horster wasn't much of a spaceman, but he could shuffle more than paper. The new Nielson cube, the heart of a ship's drive, was on its way to Parleyvoo and vouchered for the *Great Khan*. "It's not exactly the same model we have," said Harger, "but the specs and modification kit sound right. No problems."

"Or so we hope," Parnell said. But he didn't look worried.

He called a meeting of Turk Kestler's women and explained why twenty-five or so of them had to move back into Hold, Portside Upper, for as long as the ship was groundside. "I can get away with some of you being listed as crew from the start, but not all. And I have to choose on the basis of the jobs you're doing. We'll upgrade the food, certainly, but you get no clothes—because the setup has to look like what UET will be expecting." Zelde saw a few scowls; then Parnell said, "While you're in there, you'll draw work credits double what your present jobs rate. All right?" The scowls cleared. *Parnell, he knows what he's doing.*

Now Zelde had to memorize her own background as Dopples had invented it. Seeing the faked readout, she laughed—then looked to the First Hat and said, "What's funny is, none of this ever happened, but you did it up so *real.*" Just for a bit she thought he might smile, but no chance. All right; she began to learn it. . . .

When and where she was born, her folks' names. Went to school—ha!—took beginning Space training at Academy South Branch, shipped out as a Second rating. On another ship, of course; came onto this one as a Chief. Which made her—with all that travel—well, about fifteen–twenty years older, by planets' time, than she really was. Someday she'd have to get Parnell to explain that "two ages" stuff so she could really understand it.

But right now, going through the fake log things a few more times, she figured she was set for any UET snooping, all right.

She just hoped Parnell was, too. And the whole ship.

Landing time came up during Lera Tzane's watch. Knowing that the woman wouldn't object, Zelde went in with Parnell to see how it was done; she sat off to one side, out of the way. Dopples, she saw, sat right behind the watch officer and looked over her shoulder. *He would!*

With maybe a half hour to go, Tzane got the fidgets. She looked around, and finally said, "Captain? Mister Adopolous? Are you sure you want me to land us? I've never done it. . . ."

Before Dopples could speak, Parnell did. "We all have to begin sometime. You have a long string of perfect runs on the simulator; I checked." Well, so did Zelde have a good string, for that matter, but in Tzane's shoes she'd feel the same way.

Now Adopolous spoke. "If she's not sure, skipper, then maybe one of us should relieve her. We don't want to bet the whole ship on someone who's afraid to bet on herself."

"It's not that!" As soon as she opened her mouth, Zelde knew she shouldn't have. But now they were all looking at her; she had to explain. "If this was my watch, now——" She

had to think—to see what was right to say. "If I was all on
my own, I'd land it and not think twice about trying. And
if I was told to, I'd do it right now, too. But with both of
you here who've done it already, I'd ask first, if you'd
rather do it yourself. It's only polite."

Parnell looked at her, and then to Lera. "Is that how it
is, Tzane?"

No pause at all. "That's how, Captain."

Parnell grinned. "Then land us, Second Hat. Land us."

And about twenty minutes later, she did. If there was
any jolt, Zelde didn't feel it.

Cutting ship's power down to standby, Tzane took her
time. Then she turned and said, "We're groundside, skipper. Orders?"

Already standing, ready to leave Control, Parnell said,
"Finish out your watch, Tzane. And log yourself a com-
mendation—mine—on your first landing." As he walked
out, Zelde followed him.

Parleyvoo, the way Parnell told it when they were back
in quarters, had started as a freelance settlement. "UET
owns the planet, of course, but just as on Earth, a lot of the
economy has to be free enterprise—people working on
their own, for themselves. So a number of those left the
main colony to look at the possibilities here on the island."
Mining, temperate-zone fishing, and some different kinds of
crops to harvest, it sounded like. "After a while, a second
spaceport turned out to be a good idea."

Back in Control, later, scanning the town on direct
viewscreen, Zelde saw what he meant. In the flat, down by
the bay, the older part of Parleyvoo was mostly a shack
town—even the bigger buildings. Wood frame and slabs a
lot, with some stone and brick used, some scrap sheet
metal and plastic—stuff left over from other uses. Up
around the port here, things were different—concrete all
over the place, and where there was plastic, it looked like
on purpose.

She decided she liked Old Town better.

Leaving the buildings out of it, the place looked a lot
like Earth. The sunlight was the right color, and the grass
and all. Except it wasn't grass, exactly; the ground cover,
when you came down out of the ship and looked close, was
built different. And the trees. The leaves looked right

enough, but there weren't any real trunks—big woody plants with every thick limb growing up from the ground by itself. Overgrown bushes, really, she thought. But big enough to give good lumber for building.

She wanted to get down to the bay and look around Parly-voo for herself. But being Third Hat, she had to stay on ship while all the red tape happened—stand watch while Parnell and Dopples talked with the local UET ramrods, that sort of thing.

"You don't want to have too much to do with these people," Parnell said, "in case you need to jump ship, as we discussed, on your own." Well, she didn't have to hide out, either. When she showed up in the bushy wig, wearing "fat clothes," Parnell laughed. "All right. Keep the disguise consistent—and in their company, talk as little as possible. But it might very well pay for you to know them without their knowing you."

With the rings taped to her neck as for combat practice, the wig covered them well enough. In the galley Zelde sat to one side while Parnell talked with Eldra Siddenour, just in from Summit Bay. This fat woman, with bleached hair straggling around her sagging cheeks, was third in command on Terranova. She outranked the local Port Commandant—but on the civilian side, not Space Arm. In UET, Zelde knew, women could be second or third in line but never first.

Maybe that was what made fat Siddenour so hard to get along with. Or maybe she was born that way. Whatever, Zelde didn't like her much. At least, though, she'd had the tact to leave her Committee Police escort outside the ship.

Now she was arguing, shrill-voiced, about the Nielson cube. "Just why, Captain, have you ordered a new unit when the one you have hasn't been thoroughly tested?"

Parnell shrugged; Zelde saw him work at being patient. "My Chief Engineer says the cube can't be trusted to lift us off safely, let alone land us again. I have to go with his word; he's the best I've got. And a complete overhaul takes considerably more time than our schedule allows." He spread his hands. "Coordinator Siddenour—you'll appreciate my position. Outside our own areas of direct competence we must both rely on experts. Agreed?" He waited for the nod that merged her second and third chins. "Well, that's what I'm doing. All right?"

Again she nodded, but her voice sounded grudging. "What you say is true, of course. Still, a little more deference to established procedures . . . it's hard enough keeping the colonists in line, without you spacers taking shortcuts, setting them a bad example."

Parnell made a quick grin, maybe with Zelde's own thought that not many colonists were apt to hear of the hurry-up Nielson cube. But he said, "Actually, of course, it was Commandant Horster who took the shortcut. I told him our problems and he said a unit would be on the way when we arrived. That's all."

The woman shrugged. "I suppose it's all right. Still, we don't like to have equipment shuttling around with no requisition to justify it." *Red tape—nothing's real without paper to prove it.*

"Yes." Parnell nodded. "Well, you have the requisition now. It's in the packet with the other reports." Her frown eased; Parnell looked at his watch. "By ship's hours I'm now entitled to a drink. How about you, Coordinator? All our stock's direct from Earth, of course," and he named several types and brands.

Siddenour chose Scotch whisky; she drank it straight and within two minutes took a refill. Parnell had his bourbon over ice, and Zelde was glad to see he was nursing it.

By her third glass, the fat woman's face was red and her voice loud. Her fleshy hand moved to squeeze Parnell's wrist. "Your name—it's Ragir, isn't it? So call me Eldra."

"Of course—Eldra." He got his hand free to refill her glass; then she recaptured it. To herself, Zelde grinned; she'd never before seen Parnell really embarrassed. Talking again, now the woman was plainly making a play for him—dropping hints that everyone could hear, while Parnell pretended not to notice. Peace up a pipe! Was she going to rape him right here?

Siddenour leaned over, talking to Parnell in a raucous mumble. All Zelde heard was, ". . . and we can talk priva'lly—*privately*." Lurching, she stood and hauled at his arm. Brows raised, Parnell looked once at Zelde. Then he shrugged, and let the woman lead him away.

Well. Zelde guessed she'd need a place to sleep tonight. Her own official Third Hat quarters were empty, except for a few things stored there. She got some fresh bedding, and made do until it was time to get up and go on watch.

When Dopples relieved her, Parnell hadn't shown up in Control. Gesturing at the wig, the First Hat snickered. "It doesn't do much for you, M'tana."

"Not supposed to—sir. Just has me looking different. You know why."

"Yes. Well—" He read out the brief watch log. "No problems, I see. All right. Relieved." She stood, and he took the watch seat.

Her training work these days gave Zelde a good appetite. In the galley she took seconds, and then sat with one cup of coffee after another. When she got tired of coffee, still she sat—she wasn't sleepy, and she had no place else to go.

Carrying a tray, Turk Kestler joined her. UET's tabling of officers, ratings, and crew separately had broken down a lot; friends sat together where they wanted to.

Turk said, "Seen the skipper this morning?" and from her sidelong look, Zelde knew the story was all over the ship. Well, her own feelings were clear enough—but how to get them across without saying too much?

"Not in Control, or here." Nothing more, yet—figure this out as it went along.

If Turk felt easy, it didn't show on her. "Look, Zelde— with the authority that cow has, he couldn't help it!"

"I know that. Wasn't sure you did, though."

Then they both grinned, and Zelde said, "Hey—where'd you get the teeth?" For the gaps in Turk's smile, all but one of them, were filled. On a real close look, the new parts wouldn't fool anybody—but who *looked* that close?

"The medic, Fesler," Turk said, "and Henty Monteil. She can build just about anything, once somebody tells her how it's supposed to work. And he figured which way these things had to be braced." Exposing the new teeth again, she smiled. "One more to go. Tomorrow, Henty says."

Again Zelde congratulated her friend; then Turk stood to leave for work. "One more thing," said Zelde. "I don't own Ragir Parnell. He says I do, but I don't."

Nearly an hour later, Parnell brought Eldra Siddenour into the galley. Zelde pretended not to watch. Moving slowly, the woman hung on his arm. Face puffed and slack-featured—*I've seen some hangovers in my time, but . . .*

When the two were done eating—Siddenour picked at her food, no appetite to notice—Parnell led her out. Twenty minutes later he came back, got a cup of coffee, and sat across from Zelde.

"Good morning." His voice didn't tell anything.

She nodded. "Morning to you, too, Ragir. You look healthy enough. Not cheered a lot, though."

"Zelde! Do you think—"

She couldn't reach his mouth but her hand moved as if to cover it. "Nothing you need to say. Except—if she's coming back any, I'll want some clothes kept In Third Hat's quarters."

He shook his head. "No. She's back to Summit Bay—in the air by now, I'd guess—and we'll be off-planet before her next inspection here. But, Zelde—"

"But, Zelde, nothing! I saw how you looked, being dragged out of here last night; that's all I need to know. If you'd seemed happy, now—well, that's still your own business. But I'd of thought your taste stunk."

He spread his hands. "I tried to feed her enough booze to pass her out." Zelde didn't speak. "Don't you want to know if it worked?"

"Not for me, no. For you, if you have to say about it."

Like machinery running out of oil, Parnell laughed. "Do you know what the worst part was?"

"Not hardly. I wasn't there."

"No." What his mouth did, then, wasn't any smile. "You'd think—but physically, age and fat and all of it, her body doesn't shame her. Any man who wanted to be with her, she could delight him. And she's a cleanly person—in the shower I had to keep her from falling down, but that's what got her awake again, damn it. No—it's none of those things."

"Then what, Parnell? I wouldn't want her picture on the table, to look at over breakfast."

He shook his head. "It's not even that. Lying back, looking up with her face relaxed and smoothed out, her bones are too good to let her look ugly."

She waited, and he said it. "But I couldn't forget—I was in bed with that goddamned UET *mind*."

Seeing the hurt in his face, she reached to touch him.

"Poor love." And then he smiled.

* * *

Nearly a meter each way, the Nielson cube came in a box twice that size. Helping to unpack it, wearing heavy gloves that shielded her against stray discharges from the untamed device, Zelde saw that only the rough outline made a cube. The eight corners were beveled off to make space for connector interfaces—capped now, but Parnell said they were all identical. The center of each face was sunken, and these six connectors were larger than the eight. And at the center of each of the cube's edges was a flattened part making room for a smallish terminal; each of these twelve leaked a steamy vapor.

"Eight, six, and twelve," Parnell said, during a pause in the work. "The eight—well, the prime diagonals of a cube are as close to a set of four-dimensional axes as we can get in only three. It's—well, Zelde, it's hooking mere space into space-*time*." Knowing he really didn't expect her to understand, she nodded.

"The terminals on the six faces do their pulsing in *our* three dimensions," he went on. "And the twelve on the edges—they monitor and modulate, and basically keep the whole thing from turning into a big puff of nothing. And the ship with it."

He raised one eyebrow. "Do you know any more than you did before?"

"No." Zelde grinned. "But you do tell it good."

"All right." He turned to the entire work gang. "Come on—let's get the old cube out and this one in, before it warms up enough to go sour." And after another forty minutes the two were exchanged, each safely back into the grim chill that kept such a unit in one piece. Parnell looked for his Chief Engineer. "Harger? What do you think?"

"It'll take a while, skipper. The new cube's fully charged, of course, and more evenly than the old one. But I'm getting into the adjustments now—and this cube checks out solid. Which, I might say, is one hell of a big relief."

"Good. Take your time; we've only begun refueling, and there's still all the cargo unloading and loading to do. No hurry."

And Parnell, with Zelde following, left the man to his work.

* * *

On the *Great Khan*'s sixth day groundside, local commandant Delvin Trask visited ship. Refueling was complete; Trask came, he said, to take Parnell's receipt for the fuel ". . . and do my courtesy inspection at the same time." He arrived, Zelde noted, without Police escort.

A tall man—stooped and, except for a pot belly, thin— Trask apologized for not appearing sooner. He said he'd been down with a local virus—but the way Zelde heard it, the man was a lush who needed drying out pretty often.

"His wife, acting as his secretary, does the real work," Parnell had said. "He keeps his people happy by spreading the graft around, and a number of them are his relatives, anyway." He grinned. "In this case, nepotism pays. But the son-in-law—Cort Verrane—word is that he's the hatchet man, in case anyone gets out of line."

Verrane boarded with his father-in-law. The plump, smiling man—who said little, and combed his thinning blond hair often—stayed close to Trask, to one side and a step behind. Watching his eyes, Zelde decided the smile might as well be painted on a mask. *Look out for that one!*

In the control room, Parnell offered the commandant a routine scan of the ship's log. Trask didn't show much interest; he punched a few codes, looked briefly, and nodded. Verrane nudged his elbow and whispered. The older man scowled and shook his head, but Verrane whispered again; the commandant moved aside and let him to the keyboard. Zelde looked to Parnell; his face showed no reaction as he said, "Commandant, if you're delegating your authority to inspect the log, will you please do so in writing?"

Verrane turned; his smile didn't change. "No need to be quite so formal, is there, Captain?"

If Zelde hadn't known Parnell, she'd have thought he looked friendly. "Just sticking to regulations," he said. "We don't want to show the *next* inspector any irregularities. Right?"

Verrane shrugged and turned away. Trask said, "But don't you want . . . ?" and the younger man shook his head. "Well, then." The commandant faced Parnell. "It all looks shipshape to me, Captain. I assume you'll have the usual summary tape transcribed for me, complete to your liftoff countdown, before you leave?" Parnell nodded. "Good. Then my staff can analyze it at leisure."

"Yes, sir." Parnell signed the fuel receipt and handed it over. "Would you like to join us in the galley? Coffee, a drink—whatever you like?"

Trask started to nod, but Verrane jogged his elbow. After a moment he said, "Thank you, Captain, but I have a conference coming up, and wouldn't like to be late."

So after handshakes and the usual chat of taking leave, the commandant and his shadow left the ship. Parnell went to the galley, and Zelde with him. After one sip of fresh coffee, she said, "I guess we know who's boss at this port."

Parnell made a flicking gesture. "Maybe. We haven't met the commandant's wife yet. *Or* Verrane's, the Trask daughter."

Zelde wanted to go down to Old Town, and finally Parnell said she could. "And be on the lookout for any clue that might lead us to the local Underground group. Be very cautious, though."

"Glad you told me." She snickered. "What I thought was, Parnell, I'd just go up to one of the Committee Police their own damned selves and ask if they seen Horsehead lately." For a second his eyes went wide; then they both laughed and she went downship.

The ship had the use of some of the port's groundcars, but Zelde hadn't ever learned to drive one. Never had the chance. Well, it wasn't more than four kilos, and she wanted to go in town alone, so why not walk it?

Morning was chilly; she wore gray tights, fairly heavy cloth. No badges of rank, naturally. A hood, dark goggles attached, covered her hair and ears. In that outfit she didn't figure to be recognized.

Past the port, the land dropped off fast. Heading down toward the lower plain, Zelde saw that the rough-paved road made two switchbacks. At the top of the first, she stopped and looked. Then she nodded and left the road, walking directly down the steep hillside. Where the road next crossed her path she came to the top of a high bank; she eased herself over the edge and slid down, landing sprawled. Rising, she brushed loose, tan soil from her legs and seat. Probably there was some on her back, too, but she couldn't see or reach it. Oh, well. . . .

At the next crossing the bank was vertical, perhaps even undercut. She followed it downhill to the left until she came to a washed-out portion, and climbed down. Crossing the road again, she set off at a diagonal, toward the lower switchback's end. When she reached straight road—and here, on nearly level ground, no high bank—she turned and looked back up the hill. Yes, she'd saved considerable time and distance.

Closer at hand, Old Town looked bigger. Well, she knew it held nearly ten thousand people and was home base for about as many more, spread out through the surrounding country.

The first shacks, at the outskirts, sat haphazardly back from the road; footpaths went past the nearer ones to others farther away. Then she came to the first cross-street— bare dirt—running about a hundred meters to either side. Two more dirt streets—each a little longer than the one before it—and then she reached a group of larger buildings. Two and three storeys, these, and here the cross-street was graveled. Yes, definitely she was coming to the downtown district.

Until now she'd met, walking, only a few people. Some paid her no attention, some looked but made no sign, and a few spoke or nodded. Clothes varied from new, tailored fabric all the way to makeshift cloaks of animal hide; Zelde could see no rhyme or reason to the differences.

Near the intersection, though, there were more walkers. At the corner Zelde stopped and looked around, standing off the pavement beside a ramshackle wooden building; its sign read "Rooms to rent." To her left, across the road, a stone structure looked more prosperous. Offices, mostly, it looked like—"Doctor Ras Tarrasogan, no app't needed," "Independent Miners Exchange," and at ground-floor corner, a shop: "You Need It, We Have It." Shrugging at the last one, she looked across the intersecting street.

Straight ahead, a building of wood and plastic—no signs, and the windows boarded up. Across the corner to her left, some kind of bar—maybe food and rooms, and could be other things, too. She looked—no groundcars in sight. She'd seen only two, both with UET markings on them. And people seemed to amble across the road however they wanted to. So Zelde crossed cattycorner and went into the building.

The door was partway open; she turned sidewise and got in without moving it. Darker, inside, than she expected—

dirty windows, and only a few dim lights. A bar at the back, and tables here and there across the floor. Not many people, though. She looked around the room—some were watching her, some not—and went to the bar.

The woman behind it, hefty in a pink dress, had a lot of fluffy blonde hair, and a chubby young face that didn't look quite right. Zelde hitched up onto a stool and grinned at her. "Morning." The woman smiled back, and what looked wrong was that she had no teeth. Zelde tried to act as if she didn't notice; she said, "I got a thirst."

The woman nodded. "You want beer, trair, jash—or something fancy-mixed?" She talked plainer than Zelde expected.

Questions weren't a good idea. "Beer's fine," and she got it cold in a big glass. Trair, though—and jash? She wished she knew more about the town—but who was there to ask?

She took two big swallows. "Good." She paid out a UET credit slip and received a handful of plastic slugs in change.

"Barse—he's the boss here—got the cooler fixed just yesterday. Warm, that stuff tastes like you already drank it once." At Zelde's chuckle, the woman said. "My name's Soft Touch; you can call me Softie." Zelde felt her brows raise; Softie said, "My *professional* name, I mean." Then: "Well, I told you who *I* am. And where are you from, anyway?"

"All around." No thought needed for that. A name, though—she thought a long way back. "Horky, they call me." And was the real Horky still alive? And by now, the ship rolling up time, how old?

Lines pudging her brow, Softie frowned. "What's it mean?" Zelde shrugged, and the other said, "If you'd rather not say, then don't. Mine's no secret, for sure."

At a table, someone called for service. Zelde finished her beer, and when Softie came back, was standing to leave. The woman began to speak, but from the foot of a flight of stairs at the far end of the bar, a skinny, bearded man whistled.

"Hey, Softie!"

The blonde hair jerked with the quick turn of her head. "Yeah, Barse?"

"Clients, lovey. Get your trained yap upstairs." As the woman hesitated, he said, "I'll cover the bar. It shouldn't take you long. Before I was out of the room she had his pants down—and he was groping hers."

I don't like this. Zelde turned toward the door, but the man Barse said, "What's your hurry, blackie? Stick around and have one on the house."

Blackie. Sounded like him calling her a name or something, and she wasn't used to that. Not since the Utie she damn near killed—how long ago? Whatever—she paused, and Barse reached across the bar and grabbed her arm, just above the wrist.

"On the house—okay?"

If he was strong, he wasn't using it; she could have pulled loose, easy. But she was here to find out stuff, right? So she stayed put and looked at him, and grinned. "Sure. I'll take a free drink any old time."

His own grin showed a lot of tarnish—brown, mostly—and one gap. "Name it and you've got it."

She wanted answers without having to ask real questions. "How's the jash here, and the trair? You like them yourself?"

First he looked insulted; then he said, "Hell, yes—I own this place, do my own buying, drink my own stock. How else?"

"Then serve us up both the same. Jash or trair, whichever."

Leaning toward her, he laughed. His breath smelled of rot; until he moved back again, she held hers. "A little of both, love—a little of both." He stood. "I'll get it. Sit easy."

The trouble was, this way she didn't know which was which. The stuff in the plump little tumblers was apricot-colored, and the tiny thimbles—on stems—held a bright green liquid.

He was looking at her, waiting. *Does he know I'm just fishing? And does it matter?* But the rule was, all her life, never tell the bastards anything they don't know already. So she made up her mind. "Barse, I think the trair first."

His eyes moved then, and he held out the larger glasses. No difference between the two; she reached with her left hand. And setting both glasses down, with his own left fist he hit her.

She fell back off the stool, landed rolling, and came up to see him vault over the bar. He reached for her—his hand slipped off her hood, then off her shoulder. "You don't know jash from trair! What is this, you're trying to pull?"

And what makes it so all-hell important?

He was still attacking but he wasn't very good at it. She heard sounds behind her, though; maybe the customers could be a problem. Shoving Barse away she grabbed a barstool and flung it, without looking, backward over her head. Jumping up onto the bar, in the act she stepped on Barse at the shoulder and felt him start to crumple under the force. She turned. People at the tables were standing, but only one came at her. She grabbed up a bottle and threw it, and that one ducked away.

"What the *hell*?" Barse was getting up again—but she had no time for Barse. She ran along the bar and jumped to nearly halfway up the staircase at its end, and in long strides climbed the rest of it. At the top, in a short hall, sat a bench. She heard footsteps behind her. The bench was almost too heavy, but she tumbled it down the stairs. Someone below screamed—outrage, it sounded like, more than hurt.

Panting now, Zelde looked. The hall—one door on each side and one at the end. To her left she heard sounds. Should get out of here—but she opened that door, anyway.

She saw. Softie writhed between a woman at one end and a man at the other. Zelde gasped—*I ought to stop this!*—but on the stairs behind her, footsteps clattered. Slamming the door, she ran for the end of the hall—*just so I don't puke now!*

That door was locked. She kicked the latch; it broke and the door opened onto a slanting roof; she ran down it and jumped. Landing on a pile of loose dirt and cut, dried plants, she turned and ran again—off the hummock and downhill. At the corner of the next building she swung into a narrow alleyway. Where it reached the main road she strolled out slowly and joined the people walking along it. By that time her breathing was slowed down to usual. Pausing, refusing to think about what she'd seen in that room until she had time for it, she looked back up the road to see if anyone followed.

Nothing she could spot. The only UET uniform in sight was going the other way and not in a hurry. As for others —she peeled the hood back partway, off her forehead and the front of her hair but still covering her ears, and put the goggles in a pocket. Then she turned downhill again. After all, she did want to scout the town all the way to water. *Do one thing at a time.*

The buildings weren't too interesting—"Warehouse Brokers" and such. The people, now—she looked—some were different, but she couldn't see any pattern. She kept walking. Two cross-streets were paved; then she came to the great road that ran along the bay.

The docks, across it, varied—some ramshackle, some well-built—and warehouse buildings the same. A lot of boats—fishing gear on most of them, but two carried mounted guns. Some kind of patrol? Police, maybe? Well, she wasn't going on the water.

She walked along a vacant dock and looked to each side, then to where both shores curved back together and made a narrow opening—far out from her, and with sun-glint making it hard to see much. All right. Outside was the sea, and she'd already decided that was none of her business. She turned and began walking back, up through the town again.

She'd walked through only the middle slice of Parleyvoo's Old Town; she knew she didn't understand it much, yet. But now, like it or not, she had to think back to that upstairs room. The blonde, Softie—with the woman sitting on her face, she couldn't scream much, though the man had his hand in her up past the wrist, and his forearm muscles indicated a clenched fist he was pumping there inside. Zelde hoped he hadn't seen her at the door. Because remembering the wild eyes, and the mouth stretched out tight to show all his teeth, Zelde decided she'd never seen anyone look so insane mean as Cort Verrane.

Well short of Barse's place, Zelde cut over to the parallel street on her right—bare dirt, rutted. Three blocks farther on, she went back to the main, paved road. Looking back, she saw nothing to worry about, and kept walking.

Now the day's heat reached her—and she realized she hadn't eaten since breakfast. Another thought—it was a good time to hood herself again, so she did. And speeded up her pace.

When the groundcar passed her and stopped just ahead, she pretended to ignore it. But sidelong she saw that one woman, alone, sat at the controls. And when the woman beckoned to her: *What else can I do?* Slowly, she walked to the car.

"You're going to the port? Hop in." The voice was deep for a female, but not harsh. Squinting against sun glare, Zelde saw a heavy silhouette—not fat so much as strongly built. Then, climbing in, she got a better view. This woman was black-browed but pale in skin and hair. Strong, bulky features—her jaw, Zelde thought, could bite your arm off. Not ugly—just strong looking.

"The port, yeah," she said. "Thanks for the ride."

"No shake," said the other. She pushed at the pale hair coiled at her crown. "Except—when I pick up a rider, I want to hear a name."

Name? Not Horky—Barse or Softie might have tipped that one, or still might. Hmmm. . . . "Honcha."

The woman either laughed or coughed. "What kind of name is that?"

"It goes back a way—too long to explain quick." Now, though—leave it one-sided, or ask? Might's well try it. "Do you tell me yours, too?"

The car had begun to move; now it stopped, and the woman frowned. "You don't recognize me?"

Headshake. "Afraid not."

"Then you don't live here, do you? Well, I'm sure you've *heard* of Amzella Trask Verrane."

Zelde blinked. Cort Verrane's wife? And *not* the woman who'd been upstairs at Barse's. So put that mess out of mind, and concentrate on *now*. She wished she'd turned down the ride, said she was only going another block or so. No—she'd been alongside the last batch of shacks and still going straight ahead.

She nodded. "Yeah, sure." What to say to this big stuffed ego? "I—hey, it's a real honor."

The heavy face relaxed; the car moved again. "And where do you come from? What's your business at the port?"

Good question. To stall a minute, she faked a coughing spell. All right—admit to being off the ship, because she couldn't make anything else stick; she didn't know enough. "The *Great Khan*—you know, the ship up there. I came groundside, to look around Old Town. Now I'm due back."

Verrane didn't look convinced. "And aboard ship, what's your job?"

"Comm tech, second rating. Just made second a while back."

"I see. What's it like, riding a ship?" *Bought it!*

Zelde shrugged. "I don't know. I mean, it's all I'm used to, by now. Like if I asked you what's it like *not* being on a ship."

Amzella Trask Verrane laughed. "Yes, I see what you mean." Then her brow wrinkled. "But I still want to know. My father was in space for years, before I was born, but he won't tell me anything of how it was—living in a steel bottle and spanning years without living them. And when we came here from Earth, I was too young to remember much of it."

Zelde couldn't afford to like this woman, but she found herself beginning to, anyway. "That last part, the ships rolling up time—I don't hardly understand it. Never been back to the same place twice. I guess that's when you find out." Now they reached the first switchback; Verrane's jaw clamped as she steered the sharp corner. Zelde said, "The ship—well, I guess it's like a town all to itself and nothing outside. You have your job—everybody has—and if you're late for it, you cheat the watch you relieve."

Past the first turn, now. "The people—what are they like?"

"Like anybody else, I guess."

"Cooped up that way, I mean. Don't you have problems?"

Problems? "Sure, I guess—like anyplace else. But you got the rules and you got the Captain, see? Get out of line and it's your ass—so you don't, if you have half sense. Not more than once, anyway."

Here, not for long, the road climbed straight. Verrane said, "Not too different, really. It's more complicated here, of course. That is to say, our authority system is much more complex."

She seemed to want an answer, so just before the switchback ended, Zelde said, "Yeah, I suppose so. Wouldn't know about that."

Loose gravel littered the tight curve; Verrane wrestled the car around and straightened out for the last leg to the top. "I have the feeling, Honcha, that you're overplaying your ignorance. People tend to do that—or try to—with someone in a position like mine. Well, I don't have time today to pursue the matter." Now, completing the final turn onto level ground, she turned eye to eye with Zelde. "But if I ever do decide to take the time, be assured that I'll get correct answers."

What the hell? Zelde made a smile, not big, not long. "Ms. Verrane—there's any time you want answers, you'll get the best I have." As she thought, *This one didn't take long to fix it so there's no way to tell any truth at all.*

Now the car slowed. Verrane pointed toward a concrete building to the left, opposite the ship's direction. "That's where I'm going. You don't mind walking the rest of it?"

Mind? This way, going aboard, no chance anybody'd call Zelde by name and Verrane hear it. "Just fine. Let me off where you turn, up ahead?"

"Surely." And she did.

Zelde got out. "Well, thanks for the ride, Ms. Verrane." For seconds she wondered how much the woman knew about her husband—but then decided that was none of Zelde's business. The car moved on; Zelde walked to the *Great Khan* and climbed upship.

She found Parnell, just off-watch, in quarters. "Want to hear where I been, and all?" He nodded, and she began.

When she was done, he frowned. "I did something wrong, maybe?"

"No." He shook his head. "It's Verrane—Cort Verrane—that bothers me. When it comes to sex I'm widely tolerant, but outright sadism—it would be none of our business, except that perhaps he carries it into other areas. And we have to deal with the man."

He shrugged the matter away. "You, now, Zelde. Plastering the town with two false names in the same costume is a bit clumsy, I suppose. So, simply don't wear that outfit again."

He paused. "The bartender's reaction when you didn't know the—what was it, again?"

"Jash—or trair; one." She thought back. "I took the pink stuff for trair, that's it. So it must be jash, and trair's green and comes in little thimbles." Deciding she had the answer, she nodded. "I guess he just got sore because I tried to bluff."

"Any stranger might do that. So it must be *because* you're new."

"Nobody else off here had trouble in town, did they?"

"No." Carefully, Parnell set about cutting and lighting one of his rare cigars. "But the others went in groups, and wearing ship's insignia. Identifiable. So it may be that Parleyvoo is nervous about strangers they *can't* peg down. From Summit Bay, for instance."

Zelde thought. "Terranova having a bad case of politics, you think? But locals from the continent, they'd know the booze."

Parnell gestured. "Different areas, different specialties, perhaps. But why else wouldn't the man simply *assume* you were off the ship?" Zelde didn't have an answer. Parnell frowned. "If we've landed in the middle of some kind of ferment, we'll have to watch our step. And nose around a lot. I've never heard of a UET colony rebelling but that doesn't mean it never will." He looked like he was tasting something sour. "Well, time to go check on hull maintenance."

After he left, Zelde lay down for a nap. Before her watch came up, she could use some rest.

Next time Zelde visited Old Town, she rode. Lera Tzane was driving, and behind sat Turk Kestler and Rooster Hogan. Zelde and Lera were dressed as officers, though Zelde wore "fat clothes" and the bushy wig. Brushed forward, it shielded her face pretty well. The other two were in clean worksuits with rating emblems at the collars. They left ship at mid-afternoon, all but Tzane freshly off-watch. The Second Hat's next duty began at midnight. She said, "Anywhere special, that anyone wants to go first?"

They'd already talked on that, Turk and Zelde and Parnell. It was getting urgent, to find a handle on some Hidden World they could get to; they couldn't hang around here forever. Zelde knew what Turk's first idea was, but the other didn't speak up, so Zelde guessed she was supposed to carry the bucket herself, for now. She cleared her throat. "Maybe it's dumb, but I'd like to check out that bar where I had the trouble. Find out right away, if this outfit I got on fools anybody. Use my own name this time—and everybody remember, I'm new there. All right?"

Slowing the car, Lera turned to look at Zelde. "But why

take a risk like that? I should think you would avoid that place."

Behind them, Turk spoke. "To go there, might be a help. To me, that is. I'm supposed to be looking for Underground contacts; remember? Well, first thing—I nosed around a little, talking to groundhogs at the port, and this Barse's place has a funny smell when anyone mentions it. It just might be worth checking." So she'd had to say it herself, after all.

Tzane coughed, then said, "And the second thing?"

Turk smiled wide, no gaps in her teeth now. "If I make a mistake and say the wrong words to the wrong party, I can tip Zelde to pull the wig off and feed it to Barse. .Sometimes a diversion helps." Until Zelde gave an elbow nudge, Lera didn't seem to get it that Turk was kidding, that last idea. But then she nodded, and brought the car up to speed again for a while, and as they came into the town, Turk said, "This Underground thing, it's all mine, here. Don't any of you try to guess what I'm doing, or listen if I say anything odd, or even think about the problem. We're here in town to have some fun. And to stay out of trouble." Then Zelde knew why Turk hadn't wanted to say anything; she'd wanted the others relaxed, not jittery. Oh, well . . .

So Lera Tzane parked the groundcar alongside the blankwalled building across from Barse's place. The four crossed the main road and went in; at this time of day the room was nearly filled. Slouching, trying to look shorter, Zelde looked around and pointed to a vacant table, halfway between door and bar, and a little to the right. In four of the table's six chairs, they sat.

Skinny Barse, scraggly beard and all, came to take their orders. His left cheek bore a bruise. *Did I do that? Don't remember it.* Zelde shrugged; in Barse's line of work, fights likely weren't all that rare.

He showed his brown-toothed grin. "Off that ship, aren't you? What's your pleasures?"

The others looked at Zelde. All right, it was her show, this part. She'd check out Parnell's ideas. "Some drinks. What-all you have?"

"Local, you mean? What little I've got from offworld, costs heavy." On his fingers he counted names. "There's beer and jash and trair, mainly, for straight drinking. Lots of different things I could mix up for you, too, if—"

"Beer I know, but not the other two. What are they?"

In his professional friendly look, no change. "Trair has the most wallop—doesn't taste strong, which fools some." He laughed. "Jash, now, it gives you more leeway. Peach-colored, you'd expect it to be sweet but it's not, very. And the beer—well, beer's beer, isn't it?"

Rooster and Turk ordered beer; Lera Tzane chose jash. Barse looked at Zelde; she said, "Trair with a beer chaser."

He blinked at her. "It's your head," and he went to fetch the drinks. Tzane paid for the round. Barse said, "Enjoy yourselves. Want more, just holler," and went back to the bar.

Turk grinned. "Sounds as if Parnell was right. Strangers are okay if the people here know where they're from."

Zelde nodded. She sipped trair, and decided its strength wouldn't fool anybody who paid attention. Not much taste at first, but after she'd swallowed, a tart glow filled her mouth; it grew for some seconds and then faded. When it was gone, she took a mouthful of beer. She felt the urge to drink more trair—but decided not to, just yet.

"This stuff," she said, "This trair. You got to watch it, all right. Good, though—damned good."

Turk's brows raised. Zelde handed the tiny glass across for a sip; Rooster took one also, but Lera shook her head.

Rooster pursed his lips. "Something more than alcohol in that."

Turk stared at him. "Doped, do you think?"

He smiled and shook his head. "Not the way you mean; the stuff's a regular part of the drink."

"What kind of stuff?" Asking, Zelde *did* feel a little odd—her coordination seemed too fast, and everything she saw was sharp at the edges.

"I forget what it's called." Rooster squinted at the green trair. "If it's the same thing I ran into on Far Corner—and it could be, for that's not much of a jump from here—" He paused. "Anyway, the barman's right—be careful of it. Because the other stuff in that drink, it lets you get happy as hell on the booze part without being drunk. But it wears off a lot faster than the alky does. So if you've taken on any kind of a real load, all of a sudden there you are—bombed flat!"

"All right. After this one—and a jash, to see what that's like—I'll stay with beer." Still, she found she finished the trair faster than she meant to. She had a jash—Turk and Rooster tried one each, too, and Lera had a refill—and paid that round.

The talk lagged. Hard to find a subject—nobody seemed to be listening to them but still they couldn't speak of the real situation on the ship, and so far there wasn't much to say about Terranova or even Parleyvoo. And Earth, now, hardly seemed to exist.

Zelde liked jash—it was something like a dry wine, but stronger. But as she'd said, after one glass she went to beer. Actually she was ready to leave—she didn't think there was more to learn here—but nobody else was in a hurry so she waited.

Rooster bought the third round; Lera, with duty coming up, had coffee. The fourth was Turk's, and this time the blonde woman Softie brought the tray. She showed no sign of recognizing Zelde, or of hurting from Verrane's games two days earlier, and Zelde hoped she'd controlled her start of surprise when the woman smiled—with teeth. *False ones, sure.* But as soon as Softie went back to the bar, Zelde said, "After this one, let's go."

No one objected. Rooster said, "Excuse me a minute," and walked off toward the end of the bar, then around a corner, out of sight. When he came back, he said, "Real chummy, the facilities. Just one room—two squatters and a trough."

Half-standing, Lera Tzane sat again. "There'll be somewhere else."

Turk laughed. "I'm not waiting. Zelde?" And the two went to the room—it wasn't dirty, anyway—and paid no more attention to the one man present than he did to them. Well, the Kids had never bothered much about being private. . . .

Outside the bar, they walked down toward the docks. About halfway they came to a newer-looking building, a restaurant, and decided to eat. Lera Tzane nodded; the place had two toilet rooms. When she came back, a man brought menus.

He was short and wide, with a big nose; Zelde hardly noticed his other features. She looked at her menu and didn't recognize much that was on it; she said, "We're off the ship. Tell us what's really good here, will you?"

The man smiled; he showed small, spaced teeth. "If you're Earthers, let me say, our native land beasts are mostly red meat—not far off what you're used to. From the sea, now, my own favorite is stooger—either the end joint of the foreflipper or else a rear haunch, which feeds two. As to what the animal is, in your terms—well, more like reptile than fish, I'd say."

Turk and Rooster chose red meat; Lera and Zelde shared a stooger haunch. Zelde found it tangy, and firm to chew but not tough. She sampled the mixture of vegetables from the steaming bowl in the middle of the table. Also they had a big pot of coffee; Turk took a sweet dessert with hers, and Zelde decided she could manage another glass of trair.

And now, knowing the effect ahead of time, she wasn't bothered by it.

They walked to the waterfront. Standing at a gap in the row of buildings where a warehouse had burned, they looked seaward. Straight out across the water, slightly north of west, the sun neared setting. At the horizon a slight haze gave a pink tinge to the light blue sky; above, one bright strand of cloud glowed brilliant scarlet. As they watched, the reddened sun slowly moved to touch the line where sea met sky, then quickly sank.

"Nice that there's a good long twilight, this time of year," said Rooster. Lera Tzane nodded, and moved off to the left, looking at ships and smaller boats. The others followed. After walking about half a kilometer, they turned back and reached the main road again.

Going upslope a little now, they strolled. The walking, Zelde found, eased the overstuffed feeling she had from dinner. Behind them the sky gave light—not like day, of course, but enough for clear seeing.

So when the tall woman stepped out of a bar, half a block ahead, Zelde recognized the uniform. Even without the blue-and-red plastic mask—which now, she saw, swung at the woman's belt—she knew it.

Turk, stopping, spoke first. "Policebitch!"

Before Zelde could answer, tugging at Turk's arm to get her moving again, Lera Tzane said, "Of course there'll be Committee Police here. I'm surprised we haven't seen any before, here in town." Then: "Come on, Turk. Do you *want* to look suspicious?"

Kestler nodded and began walking. Rooster winked, and muttered encouragement. Nudging Zelde with her elbow, Tzane laughed; after a moment Zelde understood, and laughed also.

A mistake, maybe. Because now the Policebitch—and that was the only way Zelde could think of her—turned to look at them, and stopped.

They kept walking. Zelde mentioned how the light shone off the windows of a pink stone building; Lera gestured toward a flagpole in the vacant square across the road. Rooster laughed.

As they came closer, Zelde saw the woman better. Tall—a strong-looking person with a dark, lean face under close-cut black hair. Indian, maybe? American Indian, she meant. Not smiling or scowling, just giving them an intent look. And standing in the middle of the path—so that when they reached her, the only natural thing to do was stop.

"You're off the ship?" The quiet voice gave away nothing.

Lera Tzane was senior; she answered. "The *Great Khan*. Yes."

"And you have your papers, of course."

Quickly, Tzane produced hers, and gave her name and rank. Gesturing toward the others, "They're with me." And before the woman could ask, gave their names and ranks. Yes, that was right, Zelde thought—to UET, it's who's in charge that matters. Nobody else counts.

Looking at Lera Tzane's ID, the Policewoman nodded. "Promoted on this trip, right? How did that happen? I see this is only your third time out."

Tzane gave a quick summary of her space career. Best part, thought Zelde, was that except for blaming Second Officer Terihew's death on a drive room accident, it was nearly all true. *Good thing it's not me, having to do this spiel!*

Tzane got her papers back. "All in order, Second Officer. One thing, though—do you go in for this sort of outing much? Officers and ratings together, I mean—socializing."

Lera made a tiny shrug. "Off-duty rules have eased quite a lot, even at Headquarters—Newhausen Port—on Earth.

Captain Parnell didn't like it at first, but then he found it didn't affect shipside discipline. And here—with our one lone ship groundside and only a few on leave at once—he decided that segregated liberty tours weren't practical. Too lonesome, with no other spacers around."

The Policebitch actually laughed! "All right. Have your-selves a good evening, and stay out of trouble."

"Of course—and thank you." As they walked away, Zelde felt relief. For one of the Committee Police their own damned selves, the woman hadn't been half bad!

As if reading her thoughts, Lera Tzane said, "They're not all ogres."

One side of Rooster's face twitched. "No. It's just that you shouldn't forget—any time they want to, they *can* be."

Here was the widest part of town; the cross-streets were longer, and the group strolled along one. Away from the main road, the orderly row of buildings gave way at street's end to a hodgepodge gathering—close-packed, here, with narrow alleyways running in no regular patterns.

The sky had darkened. Lera Tzane looked at her chrono; Zelde squinted at her own, trying to apply ship's time to the Terranovan day. "We'd better start back," Tzane said. "There are a few things I need to do aboard ship, before I go on watch." So they went back to the main road and walked toward the groundcar. As they reached it, two more cars—neither filled—came down the road and passed them. Several of the riders waved and shouted greetings.

"That was Dopples," said Zelde, "driving the first car. Anybody recognize more of them?"

Rooster nodded. "Harger drove the other one. The ones with him are his First, Juvier, and a Chief rating in Drive."

"In for their own spree," said Turk. She sighed. "Fact is, I think I'll stay a while longer, myself. May have spotted a possible contact; like to have a shot at following it up."

"I'll stay with you," said Zelde. "All right, Lera?"

Tzane nodded. "Surely. There's no need for you to go back, just because I do. You can get rides with the others."

Zelde chuckled. "Or walk it, if we had to." She put a hand to her belt. "Yeah, my handlight's here."

Rooster shook his head. "Not me. Hard day on watch, I had. Harger found what was wrong with the adjustments on the Nielson cube. Little dent in a waveguide elbow—

probably what knocked the old one out of balance. Anyway, we had to take loose half the fixtures to get it out—and then put.'em all back." He shrugged. "But at least now it's fixed. Anyway—you two go raise all the hell you want, but I'm going back to the ship."

He and Turk kissed, and he got into the car with Lera. Turk and Zelde waved after them as the woman drove away. Then they turned and walked downslope.

Turk said, "Zelde? Remember what I said before, about this contacting thing being all mine?"

Zelde nodded. "Sure. Why?"

"Because with just the two of us, it's even more important. You mustn't *notice* where I'm looking, or who at, or what little moves I might make, or they might. Because if you notice, somebody else may spot you doing it. The *wrong* somebody else."

It took Zelde a minute to figure how this had to work; then she grinned. "I think I got it. It's not I don't *know* you, woman; it's just, I don't pay you much heed."

Turk squeezed Zelde's arm. "That's close. Closer is, you don't heed anything that might strike you as unusual, if you did." Another squeeze. "Try not to forget that, Zelde."

She nodded; fair enough. Now she thought about it, this wasn't much different from one time, early days with Honcho's Kids, he'd had her sit decoy. It had worked, too.

And anything she'd done before, Zelde figured, she could do again.

They found the two cars parked in front of a bar; the place looked a little better than Barse's. Turk nodded toward it. "Want to go in, say hello?"

Zelde was thinking about it when someone hailed them. "Hey, Zelde—Turk! Come on in." Carlo Mauragin, holding a glass of jash, stood at the door.

Zelde shrugged. "Might as well, Turk." They joined him, and all three went inside. Carlo got a load on fast, Zelde thought; he drained his glass and put an arm around each woman. Heading for a table toward the rear, he called, "Hey, team! Look who *I* found."

Looking up, Adopolous didn't seem too pleased—but then he smiled and said, "Pull up some chairs and sit down." Young Mauragin took two chairs from a vacant table and fussed until everyone had seats.

Zelde looked. Drinks scattered all around the table, with a big pitcher of beer and a smaller one of jash. Several extra glasses; she took one. Mauragin poured her beer, and Turk's.

After a quick scan of the place—it was clean, well lit, not really crowded—Zelde paid more attention to the group. Of the Engineering people she knew Harger and his first, Juvier, who called himself black but had light tan skin. The young redhaired Chief rating, she didn't know.

Dopples had his arm around another redhead, this one female and slim, probably in her bio-thirties. Zelde remembered her from the hold, but hadn't known her to talk to. She wondered what the First Hat's two blondes would say. Well, that was none of her business—and as though he read minds, Dopples was staring at her.

"Where's Tzane?" Now he looked at Turk. "And your man? I thought you all came in town together."

Was he drunk already? No—just being feisty. Zelde said, "They went back to the ship. We all were, but when you came past, Turk and I decided to stay a while. Figured we could ride up with you, if that's okay."

After a moment the man nodded. "Sure. Sure, M'tana. If it's all right with Parnell, it is with me, too."

"With Ragir?" Zelde frowned. " 'Course it is." Parnell, as a matter of fact, had told her he was going to bed early—and for her not to wake him if she got back and found him asleep. She thought for a moment, and decided she'd said enough.

A waitress brought more drinks—trair, mostly. The woman's black dress, skin-tight, covered her from chin to ankles—except for a cutout that exposed most of her left breast. From the pierced nipple hung a tiny bell that tinkled when she moved. Her face was made up in dead white; her pale hair, cut all around exactly at the hairline, was lacquered flat to her scalp.

When she left, Zelde said, "They go in for fancy getups here, don't they?" Then she turned to Dopples and told him, quoting Rooster, what she knew about trair.

He raised one eyebrow; then he grinned. "Far Corner, sure—I remember now. They called it something else there—something-*vine*, I think. I barely tasted it, myself, but my buddy went ape-rape on the stuff. No fun getting him back to the ship." Dopples nodded. "Right. Let's all watch it with the trair."

The redhead blinked and looked at him. "How 'bout *me*?"

His hand moved on her thigh—then out of sight, under the table's edge. "Don't worry about a thing, Darlene— you, *I'll* be watching." Again Zelde wondered about the twin blondes. *Coming on like a real stud, Dopples is!*

The place got noisier. Feeling her own drinks some, Zelde looked around to see how the others were doing. Well, Darlene was getting soggy and didn't care, but she was Dopples' problem. And Carlo Mauragin was flying with one wing over his head, for sure. But she noticed he'd pushed his glass of trair away and was back to beer; he'd make it, probably. No one else seemed out of shape. She nodded; it was going along all right.

She sat, not talking much or noticing what was said, watching folks at other tables and the odd getups of the women who brought drinks—and now and then, food also. She felt the stay-sober part of earlier trair wearing off, and decided the remaining booze load wasn't all that bad. She took one of two neglected glasses of trair to sip along with her mug of beer.

Over at the far side, a fight started, and they all watched while the bartender sent three heavies to break it up.

Two beers later, Zelde admitted to herself that she was bored to hell and gone. "Whyn't we blow out somewheres else?" Only Turk noticed; she nudged Zelde's elbow and nodded toward the entrance. Zelde grinned. "Sure. Let's go." But when the two worked their way between crowded tables and stood just outside the door, the others had followed. Darlene, with Dopples' arm around her, sagged a little. And nobody was saying anything. Without any special purpose, Zelde pointed to a side street. "Let's go that way."

Dopples said, "Taking charge, M'tana?"

She felt her face go hot. "No. Just suggesting, was all."

After a moment he said, "All right. Why not?" And the group, not walking very fast, set out along the graveled street.

On the main road, a lamp hung above each street corner. Here, there was only light from buildings. Terranova's biggest moon, smaller than Earth's and not as bright, wasn't up yet. Zelde tried to remember when it should be rising, and couldn't. In the dark, on the rough footing, one or another sometimes stumbled.

Here the buildings were separate, not making a solid front. They came to a vacant area to their right; just past it, light came from an open doorway. As they got closer, sounds came, also. "Drink stop, everybody!" said Carlo Mauragin. He stepped forward and led the way inside.

Peering in, Zelde said to Turk, "This makes Barse's place look good." But she shrugged and followed the rest into the dingy room. The low ceiling trapped smoke, which didn't help what lighting there was. Spread out at four of the room's tables, less than a dozen people sat.

Mauragin moved to the far right corner, and found a table larger than most. The others followed, and now Zelde noticed that there were only six of them; Dopples and his redhead were missing.

She looked back to the door, then to the others—and saw Carlo Mauragin grinning. "The First Hat? He and Darlene took a little detour, back alongside the building. I expect they'll be along after a while."

Not my idea of a good place for it, Zelde thought, *but none of my business, either.*

A woman—beefy, red-faced, with dark hair hanging in a greasy braid—brought drinks. In this place Zelde ordered beer in a sealed container and ignored the streaked glass set beside it. Most of the others did the same, but Carlo drank jash.

The original customers didn't talk much; the noise Zelde had heard from outside was absent now. She looked at the occupied tables more closely.

Everybody in old clothes, for one thing. Work outfits, mostly—worn a lot and not too clean, either. Except for the couple at the far left—clean and neat, with the woman's hair in fussy little curls, they looked out of place. And as Zelde thought this, the two stood and left.

The three men and one woman at the table nearest the bar—they could have been sitting there for a week. And the rest—the other two tables—well, the light was too dim to see much. Zelde got another beer, and wondered when Dopples would come in, so that maybe she could suggest leaving this pigpen.

Carlo Mauragin stood, weaving a little, and wandered across the room and out a door. After a while he came back and sat again. "Anybody has to go," he said, "it's outside."

Not really needing to, Zelde decided to take care of the chore anyway. She went out the door and found that when Carlo said "outside," that was exactly what he meant. And a light over the door—she could see all around for maybe ten meters. Back over that way, though—past the corner of an unlit shack. . . .

Once around that corner, she couldn't see a thing. She took two more steps, heard something behind her, started to turn—and from both sides, unseen hands grabbed and held her. A heavy body against her on the right—no clue how big the other was, but the grip was strong.

She braced to move; anger drove out the haze from drink. A shadow moved in front of her; something caught at the wig and pulled it, to the left and over her eyes. She shook her head and kicked to the right, raking her heel down the shin to stomp the instep. Impact and gasp told her she'd guessed the stance right; the hands loosened.

Now, then—but before she could follow through and break the other's hold, something tore at her right ear. Pain! She moved with the brutal tug and tried to shake free; she heard another gasp, but more like surprise than hurt.

The pull wrenched her ear again; she slammed an elbow into the one at her left and tried to—*No!* At her ear, sharp stinging pain—then again, and the terrible pull was gone. Warmth wet the side of her neck, and she knew she bled. With her right arm free, she pulled the wig off and threw it down—and now, only a little in the dim light, she could see.

The bearded figure ahead of her held a knife—and in the other hand, her severed earlobe, gold ring and all. He came at her again, reaching. Still held from the left, she braced against that hold and kicked out—both feet—the knife flew loose and the man bent double.

The one to her right still pawed at her—the left-hand one was only hanging on. *Why, these can't fight!* And with a shout—half scream, half roar—Zelde attacked.

Within seconds, two were down and not moving. But the third, the one with her flesh and her gold ring, was up now and scuttling away. Panting, she scrambled for the dropped knife and threw it. She heard a *thunk* and no clatter, so she knew she hadn't missed, but the figure reached the corner of a shed and disappeared around it. From the darkness at her right a new shape came, running, and followed the first. Pulling out her own knife, she ran after. But rounding the corner she saw only darkness—and, stifling her own panting to listen, heard no sound of movement. Belatedly she reached for her handlight, but it was gone—knocked loose in the scuffle, likely.

Well, the sumbidge had got away clean—but who had followed him? One of the other two? But she'd thought— she went back to see.

No she hadn't botched the jobs, either of them. One man's clutching hands hid his crushed throat. The other lay face down, so she couldn't see the ruined eye that had shocked him out of whatever defense he knew. The *sound* of her chop to his nape had told her he was dead, and he was. All right—but that didn't give her back the ear. She sheathed her knife.

Now, pulse calming, she had to take stock. Her ear throbbed, pain burning. Blood still ran down her neck. She wadded a piece of cloth and held it to the wound, then found the wig and pulled it on, so that it held the dressing in place. Nothing more, for now, she could do about that part.

She looked at the two dead men. Robbers—maybe she wasn't their first pigeon, tonight. Then she shrugged—any loot they might have, she didn't want it.

She started back toward the tavern, then realized she hadn't done what she'd come out for. So, first on one man's head and then on the other's, she did it.

A light flashed at her; against it, she squinted. "Now what's this?" She knew the voice but couldn't place it. Standing, she shaded her eyes and tried to see past the light.

"Who . . . ?"

"We met this afternoon. Your Second Officer vouched for you, but now I'm not so sure. I asked you once—what's this all about?"

The Policebitch! Now Zelde regretted her moment of

petty spite against dead men. What to say—what *could* she say? At least she hadn't been found looting the bodies!

She wet her lips, and winced; somewhere during the fight, she'd bitten the lower one badly. "I—they jumped me. Three of them. The one that cut me, got away." She turned the bloody side of her neck to the other's handlight, then gestured toward the ground. "These two didn't, though."

She took a step forward; the light jerked. "No—don't move, you. I'll have a look." The light came closer. "You're cut, all right." Then the light and its holder moved to the corpses. A hand turned one over, to show the face. Yes—she'd got that eye good and proper, Zelde had.

The Policebitch straightened, and stood a pace from Zelde. "You were alone in this?" Zelde nodded. "In this part of town, by yourself?"

"No." She pointed to the tavern. "We were in there. I came outside for a minute, to—"

The other's comment was part snort, part chuckle. "Yes. I saw. Couldn't figure out what you were up to. What's your name again?"

"Zelde M'tana. Third Officer—promoted after the drive room accident, behind Lera Tzane. I—these robbers—am I . . . ?"

"In trouble? For *those two*—and you ship's personnel?" The voice dropped to a lower pitch. "I know those men—who they are, I mean, and who their gang is. The one with the eye—there's a reward on him. Not big, but I'll see you get half of it. Just come to Police Headquarters and ask for Torra Defose."

Half? But I—and then Zelde remembered; it was UET she was dealing with. And, go to Police base? "I don't expect I'll get leave again, Ms. Defose. So you better keep all the reward." Compliments—that was how to go, here. "The hours you work, you earn it."

"What? Oh, I see. No, I'm off duty now, since midevening. I was walking home and heard someone yell, and it sounded bad, so I came to see what was happening."

"That was me, I guess—when I got cut."

"I'd forgotten! We'd better get that seen to. Let's go in the tavern first, and then I'll call—"

"It's all right. Thanks, but ship's medics can handle it.

No hurry." The pain was dull now, and she felt no new blood trickling along her neck. "Time we all got back to the ship, probably. Thanks for your help, though."

But when Zelde walked back toward the bar, the other followed.

Inside, she saw that one table had emptied and a new quartet sat at another. Not much change—they all looked like the bottom of the bin. The ship's party, now—Mauragin was close to passing out, and the young Engineering rating wasn't much better off. He had one arm around a woman, nuzzling her neck, and to all seeming, she *was* passed out. And the woman was Darlene—so where was Dopples?

She walked to the table. Turk stared at her; Zelde spoke first, low and in a hurry. "The Police one—she's not trouble. Not yet, anyway. I was jumped, robbed. She got there later." Behind her, the woman approached. "Tell you when I can."

Plump Harger spoke. "Should be getting back, I think. There's three here who can't walk too well, and—"

Do it fast—get it moving. "You and Juvier bring the cars." She saw him look—startled, as if asking who had the rank here. "I haven't driven one of those things, or I'd do it. All right?" And Harger, and then Juvier, stood and walked out, each nodding at Torra Defose but not stopping.

The woman said, "Is this all of you, then? From the *Great Khan*?"

Zelde waited, then realized she was in charge. "First Officer Adopolous. He should be here in a minute." She paused, hoping someone would give her any hint, what to say next.

Turk cleared her throat. "Mr. Adopolous hasn't joined us in here. Yet."

Now what? "Well, I guess we can wait a little." Zelde sat; a tray of drinks was brought and—the hell with dirty glasses—she took a jash. "You like a drink, Ms. Defose?" *I hope not.* But she had to offer. . . .

"Sure. Thanks." Suddenly the woman's strong features had a vulnerable look. "Ship's people—usually you don't have much time for us groundhogs."

No answer, Zelde decided, to that. "Drink up," and De-fose did. And then had another, while Dopples didn't come in, and didn't come in—and then he did.

Holding his side with one hand—and below it, Zelde saw blood on his jacket—the First Hat sidled, crabwise, through the door and across the room. Bent forward, his pale face grinning on one side, he came to the table. Easing into a chair—Harger's—he sat across from Zelde, then extended and opened his free hand. "This is yours, I think."

The gold ring still pierced the bloody flesh. The cut, she noticed, was jagged.

Everybody talked at once. Then Torra Defose slapped the table; the impact brought silence. She pointed to Dopples. "Gut-stabbed, are you? I'll get an aid car here."

"No." The man shook his head. "On the ship, I'll get treated. Standing orders—but thanks just the same." He smiled, but Zelde saw the effort it took him.

Defose nodded. "Police routine, then. What happened? Just briefly, for now."

Dopples drained a glass of trair; in seconds he looked more like staying alive. He reached for another and took one sip. "Report, sure. Well, I heard this holler and it didn't sound good. So I went to find out, and—"

The timing wasn't right. Zelde said, "You go by way of the ship, did you?"

Dopples laughed; the trair was hitting him fast. "You ever try to run with your pants down?"

He'd better not talk too much, she thought—not here. "But that was you, ran past just as I threw the knife after the one that cut me?"

"None other, M'tana."

"And you caught him?"

"Sure as hell I did that. Not all good to it, I suppose you've noticed. Faster than I thought he'd be, and I slipped, too. But—" As if he'd forgot what he was saying, Dopples fell silent.

Zelde frowned. "But why—you've never even *liked* me!"

He shook his head, and now his voice was faint again. "Makes no difference. Saw the mucker, knife out at a *ship-mate*. Had to go for him. And when I saw what he'd taken . . ." His left hand searched a jacket pocket and

came out again. "I collected some interest." On the table he
laid a matched set of bloody ears.

The Policewoman spoke first. "Did you kill the man? If
so, where's the body?"

He shook his head. "Damn if I know. I went dizzy when
he holed me. Soon as I had him stopped, I did what you
see and came off away. Got lost—not sure exactly where it
was. Alive or dead, *I* don't know." His mouth twisted; he
drank more trair. "If I owe the law anything, I expect I'll
pay it." His head slumped forward, chin on chest, but his
eyes stayed open.

Torra Defose stared at him, then looked around at the
others. "Let's get one thing straight. UET doesn't put up
with lawlessness—*anywhere*. If you were local citizens, the
two of you'd sit in jail until we got this thing cleared up.
But ships are different; they have to be. And I'm keeping in
mind that you were the victims, most likely. So I'm parol-
ing you—Adopolous and M'tana, both—back to your captain. And—"

Harger came in, Juvier following. "We have the cars
here. Can we—" He looked at Defose, and stopped.

Watching Dopples, Zelde saw he wasn't in shape to manage anything. She said, "Yes. Let's get to the ship now."
The gold ring, with its bloody tag, she put in her belt
pouch.

She helped Dopples outside. Juvier came out with Darlene slung over his shoulder; Harger guided the young rating, and Torra Defose gave Turk a hand with Carlo Mauragin. Then they were all in the cars, and the Policewoman
stepped back. "I'll call your captain tomorrow," she said.
"If I need to question any of you further, he'll tell you."
Then Juvier started the car.

The ride seemed like close to forever; at shipside, Zelde
was pooped. She climbed upship and rousted the watch to
bring the rest up; she and Harger and Juvier had done
enough carrying for a while. Waiting, she sent a galley
standby to wake the medic, Fesler. He arrived as Dopples
was brought in. "Gut wound," she said. "You ready to handle it?"

"Oh, my God!" Barely awake, Fesler tried to understand. "Cup of coffee—time for that?" She nodded, poured

a cup full and handed it to him. "Give me a minute. I'll be all right." Aides came and took Dopples away. "Anything you can tell me?"

"A knife, is all. About an hour ago, maybe."

Sipping the hot black stuff, he looked at her. "You're bleeding, yourself."

"Nothing big; it can wait."

"Maybe. But prepping the First Hat—that'll take a while. Just a minute." He went to the intercom, spoke, listened and spoke again. Coming back, he said, "I can't do anything on him for several minutes yet. Let's go to the infirmary. If yours is minor, as you say, I can handle it there."

Too tired to argue, she followed him. In the white room, she sat and took off the wig. He used a wet sponge to soak the wadded cloth loose from her wound. He looked, pursing his lips but not whistling aloud. "Dull knife—on your neck there, it's more scrape and bruise than a real cut."

"Sharp enough to slice my ear. How's *it* look?"

He was still dabbing at it. "Messy. It'll heal ugly—ragged, with an odd nubbin at the front. I'd better—"

"Just a minute." She brought out the ring with the severed lobe. "Could you sew this back on?"

He took it, held it to the light, and squinted. Then he shook his head. "Too late, I think. I'd be afraid to try. With the dirt ground into the raw edge, I could give you gangrene. In town, earlier, maybe a real doctor could have done it."

In town? Police Headquarters, maybe? She shrugged— the hell with it. "All right. You said something?"

He blinked. "Oh. Yes—that I'd better trim away these tatters. Do you want to see first, and decide?"

"No. You want to make it neat, go ahead."

He nodded. "I'll give you a pain shot. Then in a few minutes, when it takes—"

Hell with that, too. "We don't have time. There's Dopples, waiting." She outscowled him. "I didn't have no pain shot when the pisser cut me!"

Now Fesler shrugged. "All right. Just hold still, then." He took surgical scissors from the steamer, unwrapped them, and began.

Because he was being slow and careful, she had more pain than she expected. But she took it; she didn't even let it make her tense up. Until he said, "Brace yourself. Antiseptic." Then she came half out of her chair; Fesler's hand on her shoulder eased her back to sitting down. "Easy does it," he said. "It's all right, Zelde." Then of a sudden, as he dabbed the stuff on her neck—it didn't sting much, there—and put on a light bandage, she couldn't hear so good, or talk at all. He said something she couldn't catch; she looked at him and he blurred on her. Zelde shook her head, and put her face down in her hands for a minute.

Fesler was still talking; she could hear the noise but it didn't make words to her. *This shit got to stop!* She bit her teeth together and squinched her eyes shut, hard. Then she heard him say, ". . . just shock—have a drink." She sat up, took the glass and gulped raw spirits; even with her eyes watering, now she saw better. She tried to grin; the medic said, "That should do it." For *shock?* The man wasn't thinking—but what the hell. . . .

One deep breath, and then: "Yeah. Thanks, Fesler. You ready for Dopples now? Can I come along?" And she could stand up, and put herself back where she was supposed to be; she looked to Fesler.

He nodded, and she followed him. Two doors along the corridor, they entered the small surgery. Dopples lay with a sheet over legs and hips; on his belly he held something wrapped in a towel. A young woman, one of Fesler's aides, stood at one side.

The medic pointed to the towel. "What's that?"

Adopolous grinned; his voice was a husky whisper. "Icebag. Don't know if it's kosher but it feels good. I bullied her into it; all right?"

Fesler shook his head. "It doesn't matter. But, sir—*why* didn't you get treatment in town? I've been taught to go inside, as I'll have to, here—but I've only done it on animals, and that was more than five years ago. You should have—"

"Hold it." The hoarse voice came stronger now. "In town, you say? They give me a shot, right? And it's babble juice, it has to be—and there I am, talking my head off in front of UET staff? And so they get Police troops up here and retake the ship." He shook his head; it barely moved. "No. Get on with it, Fesler."

The man's nod looked reluctant. "All right. I'll have to cut extensively, to make sure I find all the damage. Don't worry about that—anything that can be patched, I have the materials to do it. Organic sealer where that's sufficient, and organic tape to put over the stitches if I have to sew— to avoid adhesions. And plenty of anti-infectants, organic and inorganic both. So you see—"

Zelde barely heard Dopples' laugh. "I see that if talk counted, I'd be healed now. Fesler, trot out your stuff."

The medic and his aide began laying out apparatus. Zelde paid no attention; she said to Dopples, "But if we didn't have Fesler, what would've happened?"

"We do have him. What's bothering you, M'tana?"

"He's not a real surgeon but you put your life on him. I—"

"You heard what I said. I can risk *me*, but not the whole ship. The ship comes before my life—and before yours, too. Don't ever forget that!"

"I—I won't." Gently she touched his shoulder. "First a shipmate, then the ship, you risk yourself for. Mr. Adopolous—"

He tried to frown. "Just learn the lesson, that's all." Fesler signaled that he was ready; Dopples said, "All right, M'tana; you'd better leave now." She turned to go. "Oh— stop by my quarters and tell Hilde and Helga where I am, will you? And that I'm all right, and not to come looking for me until I send for them. Got it?"

"Yes, sir." Outside, closing the door, she thought some more about Cyras Adopolous.

A little way down the hall, Turk stood. Zelde went to the stocky woman and put a hand to her shoulder. "It's a damn shame. All that trouble, and we got no place. We didn't do shit!"

Turk gave a quick hug, then moved back. "Not your fault, Zelde. It's a disappointment, sure; we're so hellish short of *time*. But I think I spotted a sign or two—old emblems, little stuff, twenty years out of date so it could be coincidence. Or might be just right, for our time-lag from Earth. But I'll hit Old Town again and try some more." Turk made a face. "Maybe I should take the loan of your wig, look different next time."

"Sure, if you want." From the look of Turk as she turned to walk away, Zelde couldn't tell if she'd been joking, or not.

But for now, Zelde had a job to do for Dopples. She went downship to do it.

She could never tell the two blonde women apart. The one who opened the door this time had bangs now—but so did the other, standing behind a little. Both naked, hair mussed, a little sweaty and out of breath—were they having somebody else in here? No—not on Dopples; they wouldn't dare that. Must be playing together, just by themselves. That figured—for two women, one man had to be on short rations.

She thought they weren't going to speak, but the one behind finally said, "Dopples isn't here."

That gave her a lead, how to tell it without shaking them too much. "I know. He sent me to explain why." So right off, they'd know he wasn't dead or anything. "We ran into some trouble, see, down in Old Town." She told it, the bare bones of what had happened. "And Fesler's patching him up right now."

At Dopples' final instructions they pouted, but had to agree. Then the one in front said, "Come on in and get comfortable. Three's company sometimes."

"No, thanks." Her hunch was, Dopples wouldn't like that. "Thanks anyway, but I'm bushed."

Back in quarters, though, undressing quietly so as not wake Parnell, she wasn't so sure. It didn't help, lying beside him, feeling sticky-skinned but putting off a shower because of the noise—it didn't help that Parnell was snoring enough to keep her awake for quite a while.

She woke early, though, and got up and showered. The bandage on her neck got wet; she peeled it off and decided she could do without it. In the mirror she looked at the clipped ear—Fesler had trimmed a good neat line. If the other was the same, nobody'd even notice, once it healed.

Now, moving her head to see herself from different angles, she felt the unbalanced weight of the other ring. She frowned; the thing put strain on her neck; if she didn't pay attention she tended to hold her head not quite straight. Well, maybe she'd get used to it. For now, she taped it to her neck as if for combat practice; that way she could ignore it, mostly. *If I'd done that last night*—but she hadn't.

Looking for fresh clothes, she opened a drawer. It

squeaked; Parnell groaned, turned over, and sat up. He
blinked at her. "Well. Did you have a good time in Old
Town? Lera said—I couldn't sleep, and went up to Control
for a few minutes—she said you and Turk decided to stay
later and come back with Dopples' party."

She found she was holding a hand to her neck and ear,
covering the hurts. Deliberately she took the hand away
and turned to show him. He sucked in breath; she said, "A
little bit of trouble—bandits, three of them. I caught this,
and Dopples got gut-stabbed. We better call Fesler and
make sure he fixed it all right." Then she shook her head.
"No—if anything was wrong, he'd of called here."

Parnell only looked at her. She said, "I guess I was
dumb," and told how it all happened. "I killed two, right
enough, but some late. And Dopples thinks he got the third
one. I—"

Parnell stood, and came to her. He cupped a hand over
her hurt ear. "I'm sorry, Zelde." He kissed her, then turned
to the intercom.

Fesler reported that First Hat Adopolous was repaired
as well as could be done, and was sleeping. "I think he'll be
all right, Captain. But not up and around in a hurry. I had
no idea that one stab could cut a man's insides up so
much!"

No—Dopples hadn't eaten yet. A little water and some
juice, at his first dazed waking. Food later in the day, certainly. Yes—the captain would be informed of any
changes.

"Thanks, Fesler. Good job." He turned to Zelde. "I'm
due on watch before too long. But I could wait, and have
breakfast brought to me there."

She went to him, and felt his hands move on her. "Sure,
Parnell. I'll bring it myself."

After he left, she lay there, thinking. No two ways about
it, Parnell wasn't his old self. Tired more, and hurting and
trying not to let on—he'd had his "stitch in the side" again,
and couldn't pretend it didn't bother him a lot. And screwing didn't seem to help him now. She frowned. Was it *bad*
for him, even? How could she ask him, something like
that?

I can make it easier, that's what. Work on top more.

She went to look at the pill bottle. Bad news—it had

been less than half full; now it was a lot more. Meaning a refill, and a lot taken since she'd last checked. *Hell.*

She dressed and went to the galley. Lera Tzane sat with Carlo Mauragin; she joined them. Lera said, "I've heard what happened. I'm sorry it did."

"My own fault," Zelde said. "One thing, though—when Dopples went past me, after the third robber, and then got himself stabbed, I didn't know it was him. Winded and runny-eyed, and so dark and all, I couldn't see much—and he didn't say anything. What I thought—a fourth prowler, maybe. So—"

Mauragin touched her hand. Except for bloodshot eyes, he looked healthy enough. "Nobody's blaming you for Dopples. You didn't know where he was; none of us did." He shook his head. "I'm just sorry I got so tanked—couldn't help or anything."

Zelde made a face. "What difference? None of the sober ones were out there, either. Being polite—waiting 'til I came back in, first. You got to blame something, blame the scrungy bar!"

Then the truth of it hit her, and she had to laugh. Carlo gave an unsure grin, but Lera's forehead wrinkled. "What in all the worlds do you find *funny?*"

Zelde caught her breath. "Well, *you*—for one! But not just by yourself. I lost part of my ear, and Dopples got his guts ripped, because people have a twitch about peeing in company!"

Tzane looked as if somebody knocked the wind out of her. "Don't worry about it," said Zelde. "Hell, you weren't even there."

She took a breakfast tray to Parnell, on watch. "Hope I didn't keep you waiting hungry too long."

He pushed back from the console and clamped the tray to an armrest. "No—I'm not very hungry, really."

She touched his shoulder, staying away from the sore part. "Eat up, anyway. Good-tasting stuff this morning; you might as well enjoy it." As he ate, she talked to him—about what she'd seen down in Old Town before the trouble started. And telling of Torra Defose—who, Police or no Police, behaved "—why, halfway like a human being, Parnell!"

Swallowing—and she was glad to see he'd finished

nearly all the meal—he looked up at her. "That's the hell of it, you see. Even among Police you'll find decent ones. But one thing you can't afford to forget. Their loyalty— admirable in itself—is to something obscene."

She thought about it, and nodded. "Yeah. Yeah, Parnell—I see the difference. But it sure makes things tough."

"No one ever said it didn't, Zelde."

His tray was empty now, or near enough. She kissed him—with Dopples away, she could do that—and took it to the galley.

The gold ring. Back at quarters she tossed it in her hand. No use for it, now. She went downship and found Henty Monteil at her workbench, showed her what had happened. Shocked, Henty offered to pierce cartilage and weld a link to the ring so the two would hang level. But Zelde didn't feel like doing that; the whole thing had gone sour for her. And finally Henty agreed to take back the ring at twenty percent discount. "That's my labor." With the credit assignments made out, Zelde left. Somehow, with that settled, she felt a lot better.

She had duty, starting at noon, at the cargo port; after a quick, early lunch, she reported. The port faced west, so she put on a visored cap to shade her eyes; against rising breeze she wore a light jacket.

Unloading was finished; now all traffic was incoming. Everything came already packed. Zelde knew nothing about the cargo items in detail. What she had to do was check container numbers against Parnell's list and make sure each piece was initialed by one of the ship's own inspectors. And check the item number off the list. The job didn't take much of her attention; it gave her plenty to spare for daydreams—and worries. *Parnell . . .*

Between loads, she noticed activity at the foot of the main ramp. The way the ship curved, most of that area was out of view. Hearing a voice get louder, she leaned out to see.

What it looked like, a man and woman wanted to board and the guard wouldn't let them. From this angle she didn't recognize anybody—the guard wore a helmet—then the woman turned to one side and Zelde spotted the heavy jaw of Amzella Trask Verrane. The plump man beside her, then—no standout to be recognized at a distance—yes, it was Cort Verrane, all right. He was the one being loud, too. *Trouble?*

Her intercom to Control wasn't working, so she couldn't alert Parnell or ask advice or get relieved, here. She saw the guard—he wore only Second Rating marks—shake his head again. With these people, that one could get in bad—and probably just for sticking to orders, at that.

Leaning out, she gave a piercing whistle. The three looked around, up at her. Motioning, she whistled again, then had to wave the guard back when he started to come along. The Verranes walked along the curve of hull, detouring a landing leg—and stopped, looking to where she stood, two and a half meters above ground.

Neither spoke up, so Zelde did. "You got a problem? Maybe I could help."

Red-faced, showing no sign of recognizing Zelde, Cort Verrane gestured. "That stupid guard—he should be put to dumping slops! I *told* him we have business—that it came up suddenly, with no time to go back to Admin and call in for clearance—but he refuses to let us board." Crazy, his eyes looked. "If I had him under interrogation for twenty minutes—"

"Interrogation!" The wife turned on him. "That's your answer to everything, these days, isn't it, Cort?"

"It's a way to get answers. These ship people, they're getting away with murder. Literally—those two that left three men dead, and Defose turned them loose instead of sending for me. I've talked to her about that, and I may again. What does she think she's in—public relations? Buttering up offworlders—"

"Doing her job, perhaps," the woman said. "The Police carry a bad image, always have; anything she can do "

"Oh, a lot *you* know!" And then they were just plain yelling at each other, like Zelde wasn't there to hear, so she kept shut up and listened.

Until Amzella Verrane cut the man short. "Enough, Cort!" Voice icy, she said, "We do have some business here; remember?" She looked up to Zelde. "You called us over here. What for?"

Zelde thought fast. *Smokescreen, a little.* "The guard. You have to realize, he don't have authority to change the port's rules, on his own." *Your turn.*

The woman frowned; under the floppy hat that hid her

hair, Zelde barely saw the forehead wrinkle. "Do you know who we are?"

Good question—did she or didn't she? All right, she did—but keep it loose. "Sort of." She nodded toward the man. "Mr. Verrane, isn't it? From the commandant. And you must be Ms. Verrane."

Amzella Verrane smiled, not warmly. "The commandant's daughter. Did you know that?"

"Heard it, yes. Now then—wouldn't the guard pass word of you, up to Control?"

The man began to speak but his wife cut in. "You didn't ask, did you, Cort? Just tried to bull your way through, as usual."

"*I?*" Verrane's voice came shrill. "*You're* the one who—"

Not letting herself laugh, Zelde said, "Shouldn't be any problem. Just a minute." Under the cargo listings on her clipboard was a scratch pad. She tore a sheet loose and wrote on it, then folded it so the breeze wouldn't take it, and dropped it to Cort Verrane. He missed the catch, and had to step over and pick it up. "Show that to the guard and he'll call upship for you, all right. Should take care of it."

Saying nothing—*a little thanks wouldn't hurt*—Verrane turned to leave. His wife didn't. "Let me see that, Cort. If you're not curious as to what it says, I am." He came back; she took the paper, read it, handed it back. "Go ahead, then." He stared at her but she didn't move; finally he walked away, toward the main ramp.

The woman stood, looking up at Zelde. "Take off that cap. And move forward, where I can see you better."

"Hey, what's this?" But the commandant's daughter made her motions clear enough, and Zelde did what the woman asked. Cap off, looking face to face at less than two meters, she waited.

Finally, Amzella nodded. "You're the one, all right." Nothing else to do, Zelde decided, but look blank and see what happened. It didn't take long; the other said, "You sign yourself Zelde M'tana, Third Officer. Now, according to the Police report of your little fracas last night—I keep up on these things—you must have had a haircut and lost twenty pounds, this morning."

Now the smile looked predatory. "But that's not all. Hood or no hood, I know you. Honcha, you called yourself." She nodded. "Now—one step at a time—explain these things."

Keep it simple—and flighty, like a kid. "The other day— and thanks again, for the ride—I was out looking around on my own, not being official like Third Officer. Which I'm new at, you'll have heard." Grinning, she shrugged. "Honcha? Nickname, when I was a kid, is all. And handy, off duty. Y'see?"

Verrane shook her head. "If that were all—but let's hear the rest."

"Oh—last night, you mean? Gets chilly, evenings, they said. So I dressed warm. Some clothes borrowed, and too big around." What else? "Oh, the wig—that's for dress-up. I like my hair short, but not *all* the time."

Zelde paused. Over by the ramp, Cort Verrane shouted and waved for his wife to join him. She nodded, looked at Zelde a moment, and said, "It's not a bad story. You think fast, don't you?" She turned away, then looked back. "I'll even buy it, for now. Two reasons. I can think of *no* way that anyone in your position could be a threat to this ship or this port. And I appreciate your helping to straighten out our little mess here." Zelde said nothing, and this time the woman did leave. The guard stepped aside and let the Verranes go up the main ramp.

And then the next load of cargo needed Zelde's attention.

An hour later the Verranes came out again, and walked toward a groundcar. The woman paused, looked around in Zelde's direction, and waved. Zelde waved back—why not?—and went back to her checking.

As the day's last load arrived, her relief appeared. She showed the man—a Chief rating—the status of her list, and turned the job over to him. Parnell would be off watch now; she went to quarters and found a note from him:

> Meeting in Dopples' quarters. Come along, but no hurry.

So first she showered and changed clothes. She wanted coffee—but they'd have some there, wouldn't they? Sure.

Hilde or Helga—clothed, for once, and with the flamboyant hair tied back—opened the door and motioned her to come in. The other blonde—whichever—was pouring coffee. Zelde sat on the broad arm of Parnell's chair and accepted a cup.

Dopples, propped up on pillows in bed, looked better than she expected. Beyond the bed sat Harger. Lera Tzane was absent—on watch, of course. Zelde said, "You look healthy, Mr. Adopolous. Glad to see that."

But his gesture had no strength. "I'll live, they tell me. But I won't be up and around for a while. That's what we're discussing."

The question before the house was whether to make temporary promotions while the First Hat was out of it, or fill the watches unofficially. Harger, the Chief Engineer, leaned forward. "In my experience you don't put someone under the gun to decide things—even minor ones—without the authority to make it stick. The title, too, so people listen without asking a lot of questions."

So after more talk, not much, Lera Tzane was promoted to Acting First Hat and Zelde to Acting Second. For Third, Dopples suggested giving Carlo Mauragin another try. He chuckled; it turned into a cough, but not for long. "He needs to train some in groundside drinking, I'd say, but his work on ship is coming along well."

Face blank, Harger shrugged. Zelde said, "Lera was ready to give him more time, before, so she'd agree. Unless you got somebody better . . ."

"That's it, then." Parnell's grin lasted only seconds. "Now—we had some company today. Zelde, I'll talk to you later, about your part in that."

She looked down to him. "Blew my cover all to hell, yeah."

"It doesn't matter. We're past the situation when you might have needed to hide, groundside. At least you got the Verranes aboard without a major blowup. These people—I swear—"

"He's the one made the trouble, you might guess. She—when I asked did the guard refuse to pass word, she said he never asked, just pushed."

"That fits, yes. Anyway, it's the woman who's most curious about you—and also the one who appreciated your help."

"Yeah—I noticed. But what did they want, here?"

Parnell brought out a cigar, then looked at Dopples. The

First Hat said, "It's below the waist I got stabbed, not in the lungs. If the cigar bothers me, I'll say so."

Taking his time, Parnell lit up. "The Verranes. They were touchy when I asked after the Commandant, so I suppose the old boy's getting his liver wrung out again."

No ashtray. Parnell scowled, looking around, and one of the blondes brought it for him. "Now—what they wanted, those two. Well, there's another ship coming in, landing here in a few days. The *Bonaparte*, under Chalmers Haiglund."

Zelde squirmed. "So? I don't get it."

Parnell grinned, not for long. "Neither did I, at first. They asked a lot of questions about that ship—naturally enough, since it's coming here. But then the woman—she's smart, all right, but an amateur at intelligence work—she let it slip that they'd be correlating everything I said against the captains over at Summit Bay port."

Zelde shook her head. "You still don't see? It means that before we arrived, they did the same kind of questioning about *us*."

Now she understood, but Dopples spoke first. "You mean, it's a good thing we faked our log in such detail—right, skipper?"

"That *you* did, Dopps—most of it's your work." The First Hat nodded—not looking smug, just taking his due.

Harger leaned forward. "We're in the clear, aren't we, Captain?"

"I'd say so—or the Verranes wouldn't have come to me to do their asking. We're fueled and they know it. We could lift off at any time—the emergency checkdown takes twenty minutes. Some of the remaining cargo, we're only taking aboard to look good. No—we have no official problems here. Yet."

Zelde knew she looked startled. Parnell said, "I don't know about the Verranes, but the talk set *me* thinking." He butted out the cigar. "The *Bonaparte*—Haiglund's a book soldier, never made a decision in his life, if he could ask Headquarters. At least, that's his reputation; I haven't met him. His First Officer, though—there's another story."

"Somebody you do know—right?"

"At the Slaughterhouse, Zelde—the Space Academy. And he was Second Officer on the ship Lera rode, her first trip, as a rating. Except to get more dangerous, he doesn't change much."

Dopples spoke. "Anyone I ever heard of, do you suppose?"

"You might have. If you'd met him, you'd remember. He's a fox, Jimar Peralta is—and *all* ambition. In fact, I'm surprised he doesn't have command by now—through normal UET backstabbing or Escape, one or the other."

Stretching, Zelde stood. "Seems as how it's his captain, should worry. Not us."

Parnell reached to touch her arm. "Wrong. There's another way to command—fast, and sure. Only happened twice, that I know of. One man went straight from Third to skipper."

"How—?"

"Alongside a ship like ours, groundside, he guessed it was Escaped, and finked to the port. Before it could lift, that ship was retaken—and he was its next captain. I don't imagine Peralta's forgotten that story, any more than I have."

He looked grim. "And given the alarm, Summit Bay could intercept us."

With all cargo loaded, the *Khan's* lift clearance waited on the *Bonaparte's* arrival. Nearly a week now, since that word had come. But it was standard practice, Zelde learned—don't, to save a few days, waste the chance to exchange news across the lightyears.

"Or so the Port sees the matter," Parnell said. "For myself, I want off this world so bad I can taste it—but not, I hope, before Turk gets us some Hidden World coordinates." Kestler had made two contacts, who didn't appear to know of each other. "The cell system," said Parnell. "It's old, but it works." But so far, neither of them had told her the things *Chanticleer* needed to know.

In his second try at Third Hat, Carlo Mauragin did a better job. The log showed no complaints about him. And checking back, Zelde found that he'd passed for his Chief's rating, all right. By the date of it, she guessed that was what he'd been celebrating, the night she and Dopples met trouble. Well, it looked like he'd learned to settle down to business.

Dopples took a setback—something about drainage and

infection—and had to be moved back to "hospital." When Fesler got the fever down again, Dopples came back to making sense—but he'd lost weight, and his voice was weak, like his gestures.

The Verranes visited aboard again. Parnell surprised Zelde by inviting the two to captain's quarters—since they weren't in the line of Space Command, she knew he didn't have to do that. By the looks of them, they knew it, too. Then, his head turned so the couple couldn't see, Parnell winked at her. All right—sure—give them something they couldn't get by demanding, they'd think he trusted them.

In quarters, Parnell saw his guests seated, and poured drinks. "It's more relaxed here, and I feel like relaxing." *Fat chance.* "Now then—how can I help you?"

They wanted to know more about Parnell's friend Malloy—and the way plump Cort kept peeking at his notepad, Zelde figured he'd got his questions from Summit Bay headquarters. Mainly, somebody was curious about "a pig in the parlor."

Parnell put on a good act—Zelde could see the tension in him, but near as she could tell, the Verranes didn't notice. Sipping his drink, he lolled back and told long, rambling stories of himself and Malloy, long ago in the Space Academy. And to this audience he didn't say Slaughterhouse. Innocent pranks, he told about—things that boys would do, skirting the edge of trouble but meaning no real harm. She wondered—maybe some of the tales were true, even!

". . . and the cadet captain, no one liked him, had to lead the graduation parade in boots two sizes too small—and never did find out how his own came to be frozen solid, full of ice!"

Cort Verrane laughed; his wife gave a polite chuckle, and said, "So the message he left for you—that referred to some similar lark?"

Now Parnell frowned. "Probably so—but I don't know what." As Cort sat up, brows raised, Parnell waved a hand. "A year behind me at the Academy, Malloy was. And he's never had the worlds' most precise memory—which may be the reason he hasn't made Captain as yet. So I think—" And now he nodded. "I think he must be joking about something that happened during his final cadet year—and he's forgotten that I wouldn't know about it."

Cort's eyes narrowed. "So the message was a total waste?"

Parnell laughed. "Oh, no—it's always good to hear from an old friend. And now, when we do meet next, I know he has a good new story for me."

Well. He'd cut *that* subject off, neat as all hell. The Verranes looked at each other. When Parnell, rising, offered to freshen their drinks, Cort started to accept—but Amzella shook her head. "No, thank you, Captain. We should get back to our dull routines. Right, Cort?" The man drained his glass, stood, and shook Parnell's hand. Good-byes were quick; Amzella said, "Don't bother to escort us, please. We know the way."

Parnell nodded. "I'm sure you do. But the forms of courtesy—were you to leave ship unaccompanied, some might think I'd slighted you. Can't have that, can we?" His movement, as Zelde saw he intended, swept the Verranes along with him. Amzella looked as if she wanted to change something but didn't know how.

Parnell wasn't gone long. He came in, poured himself a strong drink, then sat. Zelde said, "You really did a job on those two."

"I hope so—for peace knows, the doing took it out of me!"

She saw his tension, and in his face the unhealthy color. "Drink half of that, Parnell, then lie down and rest. I'll put the other half to stay cool for you. Or would you rather. . . ."

His face twitched. "I'd rather, yes—but I need the rest more. I'm sorry, Zelde."

She went to him. "Don't you be sorry about anything. You do so much, so good. Just rest up and get healthy—and once we're off this world, that'll come easier, too. Now do your drinking quick and your resting slower."

He took one sip, then handed her the glass. "Put it away—I'll have a pill instead, and save this for when I get up." She frowned, but he didn't seem to notice. When he lay down she pulled a cover up to his chin, and kissed his forehead.

"You could use it darker, maybe?" He nodded; she walked over and dimmed the lights. "All right. I'll be back and wake you for dinner, if you need waking."

Going out the door, she looked back. His eyes were open.

Fesler wasn't with Dopples—the First Hat lay asleep— or in the infirmary. She found him in his office. After the small talk—her ear was doing okay, and Dopples was coming along slow but making it—Zelde sat one buttock on the edge of the desk and leaned across. "I got to know what's wrong with Parnell. And what the hell to do about it." She explained: him tired all the time, nervous and having trouble sleeping—she didn't say about there being damn' little screwing lately—too many pills, not much appetite. "And the booze, is that good or bad? I try not to worry, but always he gets *worse*."

The man frowned. "If we had a real doctor. . . ." He shook his head. "We have to do with what's available. All right—talking from hindsight, and I admit it . . ."

When Parnell got hurt so much at Escape, Fesler said, he was already worn down a lot. The months of plotting and keeping it secret, stretched him too thin. "He's not a natural worrier like Dopples—who thrives on it—nor yet a go-to-hell type like Terihew. The balance wheel between those two, I expect he was. Then when all of it happened— instead of being able to relax, finally, as he needed to— well, he lost his woman and damned near got killed, himself. Low ebb, Zelde—and he's had no chance to come back from it."

Her clenched hands hurt. "I try—"

"Sure, I know. Now then—the pills. I know I should ration them to him." He spread his hands. "It's the rank, I guess—the status. He's the skipper. My actual rating is Second—he's upped it to Chief for pay purposes, but I've never even passed tests for First. Nobody to give me them. And he and I, we both know that. So when he said, don't bother him with drawing pain pills and peppers in small amounts, I—"

She reached and gripped his shoulder. "You tell me what the ration ought to be, and *I'll* see to it. If I can talk him into going along—or maybe even if I can't. And what about booze?"

His forehead wrinkled. "Pain pills—three a day should be tops but I doubt he could manage on less than four. The uppers—one's the safe limit, but it's the same again; he'll need two. And booze? With that other stuff, he shouldn't have *any*—but he will, we know that. Just so he doesn't get really drunk, I guess."

He gestured to her. "This is lousy medical practice. If Parnell were a rating, I'd slap him into infirmary and make my orders stick. But he's *Captain,* and we need him functioning. Especially groundside here, and with Dopples out of action. So I just hope his liver and kidneys can take the punishment he's giving them."

Sure—too much booze and not enough good eating curdled your liver. And Fesler's hunch was that some of Parnell's inside pains from Escape were a kidney; the location sounded like it. And any kind of pain dope shut your body down partway, to boot.

No—to his question—Parnell didn't have to take a leak any more often than anybody else. No getting up in the middle of the night, that she knew of. But Fesler still thought his guess was right.

Nothing more to talk about; Zelde stood. "All right. What I do, Fesler, is try to hold down on the pills. And see he eats right, if I got to stuff him with both hands. Not worry about the booze much, long as it stays about like now. Right?" He nodded. "Good. And thanks—I sure hell *had* to talk with somebody as knew something." She started to leave.

Fesler smiled. "That's all right—any time. I owe you, Zelde, remember? And the captain, too."

Thinking back, Zelde stopped. She held thumb and first finger close together. "I came *that* close to killing you, then." She grinned. "Sure glad I didn't."

Prowling, feeling that it was too early to disturb Parnell, Zelde went to Control. Going in, she heard Carlo Mauragin talking, then saw him facing a man's picture on the viewscreen. "But, sir, I *told* you—the line to captain's quarters is redlighted. Which means—"

"Yes, I know—don't disturb except for emergency." The pictured head nodded—a thin, intense face under sleek dark hair. The mouth tightened. "Well, far be it from me to interfere with Parnell's pleasures in bed." *You're not. I wish you was.* "So tell him, when he has time to listen, that his old friend Jimar Peralta congratulates him on achieving command so soon. And that the *Bonaparte* lands tomor-

row, your time, so I'll be shaking his hand in person." The
man grinned. "In my other hand, of course, I'll carry a
bottle. It's the custom."

"Yes, sir." Carlo sounded relieved. "And if it's all right,
sir, I'm sure the captain would want me to thank you for
him."

"I'm sure—and acknowledged. First Officer Peralta signing out." The screen went dark.

Zelde walked to the control console; Mauragin looked
around to greet her. "Whew! Did you see that, Zelde? This
Peralta—I didn't know what to do—he acts like he thinks
he's an admiral, or something."

"Polite enough toward the end there, wasn't he?"

"I guess—but that man puts pressure on you, all the
way."

And Parnell was worried about him, too. Zelde nodded,
started to say something and then didn't. Finally: "Maybe
up close he's not so tough. We'll have to see, I guess."

When she went into quarters Parnell was sitting up, two
pills in one hand and a drink in the other. Not the one
she'd put away for him; this was darker. She said, "Just
hold it right there! Parnell—before you get any more of
those damn pills in you, we got to talk."

Looking up, he glared at her; then he set the pills on the
bedside stand. "What's got into *you* now?"

"A little sense, and I hope it's catching." She went to
kiss him, and sat with one arm hugging tight and holding
his free hand. "I been talking with Fesler. You got you a
problem, Ragir—and I need to help at it."

He took a deep breath; coming back out, it sounded ragged. "Say away, Zelde. Say away."

She did—awkward and stumbling at first, and then with
a fierce bite to her voice. "I'm not *letting* you wreck yourself! I know you hurt and I hate that—but hurt gets well if
you hang in through it. This dope, though—it drags you
down sicker. Parnell—if I want your life to stay with mine,
I got to do what I hate to!"

When she was done talking, he said, "All right, Zelde.
Take charge of the pills, as you said." He gave her the two
he held. "What's my ration?" She quoted Fesler; Parnell
shook his head. "I can't function on three a day—not until
we're safely away and Dopples is fit for duty. Then,

maybe—but I've been taking five, some days six. So I—"

They compromised. Three pills a day, he'd get without question. For anything more, he'd have to ask specially. And the bottle went into Zelde's locked drawer, out of bounds to Parnell. She looked at him—was this going to work? But he nodded, and said, "Yes. That's best. But every day you put the ration out for me; I can't be bothering you for each one separately—when one of us is on duty, for instance." He smiled. "And certainly—nag me to eat, if that's what it takes."

Sitting again, she squeezed him tighter. "For sure, I'll do that, love."

"Yes. Now don't worry about the liquor unless you see it getting out of hand. I've had no trouble that way since my first trip out of the Slaughterhouse—when every time I went groundside, someone had to carry me back aboard. All right?"

"Sure, Parnell." She slid free of him, to look at him directly. "Now, something else. This Peralta, you said about. He called us."

As she told it, the bare facts only, his frown deepened. At the end, he said, "And what's your impression of the man—the *feel* of him?"

"Wound up tight. Pressured, and putting it onto everybody he comes against. He had Carlo about ready to drop his pants and squat to pee."

"Yes." Parnell's cheek twitched. "Well, I'm not Carlo."

"He's young, Ragir."

"You're younger. But I think it'd take more than Jimar Peralta to jeopardize your toilet training." She laughed, but stopped when she saw him rub his side and wince. "No getting around it—I tore something there, in the fight, and it's healed wrong. If it healed at all. Maybe when Dopples is back in shape, I can get Fesler to take a look into *me*. I don't know what for—some kind of adhesions? I'm certainly no medic. . . ." He looked at his drink, the little that was left of it, pale from melted ice. Then his gaze went to Zelde.

After a moment, she laughed. "For peace' sake, Parnell! Your second *drink*, you don't have to ask. Here—" She made it for him, and one for herself, and sat again.

Glass between his hands, he wiggled it, clinking the ice. "Peralta. He's served notice he'll be coming aboard, to snoop. Haiglund won't come here—he'll stick to protocol, where the junior captain does the visiting." He paused. "Zelde?"

"Yeah, Ragir?"

"Maybe there's no danger—but as long as I've known Peralta, everywhere he goes, he pushes. Landing tomorrow, you said? So now we phase out groundside leave; if we have to lift fast, we'll leave no one behind for Committee Police questioning. See to it, Zelde?" She nodded. "And tell Henty Monteil to drop whatever she's doing and fix that damned intercom at the cargo port. Fine thing, if we need to scoot and there's the ramp hanging open."

"Won't it close from Control, too?" Then she remembered. "No—safety interlock, in case somebody's on it. All right—I'll go start on that stuff." She gave him a quick kiss, but when she tried to stand he still held her.

"It isn't that urgent. And I'm not hurting, right now—and it's been a while. Zelde?"

She grinned. "Sure." As they undressed, she said, "You just lie back flat for once, so you don't have to hump your guts up in a knot. And let me—"

Any time he started getting too active, she shushed him back to quiet—and not a single time did he wince, the way she'd come to hate. At the end, she lay forward and held him, so he couldn't see her tears. But she was smiling. Not real good yet, Parnell—but this was the best he'd been in quite a spell.

First in Control and then in Henty's workshop, she carried out Parnell's orders. She looked in on Dopples; he was eating, and griping about the food. "Well, sir—I don't notice you leaving any."

"Starve to death, if I did—but that doesn't mean I like this bland pap." Finished, he pushed the tray aside. "Now what's been happening? Fesler tells me nothing—if he knows what's going on, he's good at keeping it secret."

"Not a lot to tell. You know we're done loading cargo, and refueled." She shook her head. "I keep meaning to ask Parnell, how he knows we got enough fuel when we don't know where to go yet." Because Turk, trying to get to the Underground group, wasn't having enough luck to wet a fishhook.

Dopples looked surprised. "You didn't know why we

picked Farmer's Dell for our next stop, in the faked log?" She didn't; she waited. "Because from here to there takes as much fuel as any two average, normal hops. It's not the distance—" He was getting interested in what he was saying; he hitched up on the pillows and bore down with his voice, more. "—expanding gas nebulae, from old supernova explosions, and it takes two abrupt course changes to avoid them. So UET, stingy as it may be, had to dole out enough fuel to leave us with some flexibility." He'd talked too much, too fast; a coughing fit doubled him over. Until he sat up and wiped his eyes, Zelde stayed quiet. Then he asked about Parnell's plans for liftoff, and Zelde said it was set for three days after *Bonaparte*'s landing. "Leastways, if Turk finds us a good place to go, by then." Of Peralta, she told only that the man had called. Dopples made no comment, and Zelde left to meet Parnell in the galley.

He looked cheerful; as she sat across from him, he smiled. "Good eating tonight; we loaded more meat than there's room to freeze, so everyone gets big helpings for a while." But when the food came he didn't seem too interested, and she had to nag him to finish most of it. "Oh, it's fine," he said once. "It's just—I'm not—" She patted his hand; he picked up his tableware and ate some more.

He never lost his taste for coffee; he was into his third cup when he said, "I'm going to have a try, tomorrow, at short-circuiting Peralta." At her look, he grinned. "Simple enough—I'll pay captain's visit to the *Bonaparte* as soon as Haiglund will allow, before Jimar can get loose to come calling, himself. Then if he's mentioned it in his skipper's hearing—the business of toasting my new command— Haiglund may think to have him haul his bottle out then and there, so as to have a share of it." He shrugged. "Well, it's worth trying."

Zelde nodded. "You're thinking good, Parnell. And even if that don't work—"

"Yes. We'll assume that Peralta will get a look around this ship if he really wants it. I've no excuse to keep him out of any part except our quarters—and of course he hasn't the authority to inspect our log, directly. Haiglund does, but he'll go through channels and ask for the transcript we gave the port."

Zelde knew what he meant. "Which is solid on tape and

can't answer any second-guess questions, like our computer could."

Parnell filled his cup again. "You've got the idea. And that's why, while I didn't mind Commandant Trask searching the log directly, I was glad he didn't delegate the privilege to Cort Verrane!"

Parnell had one more idea about Jimar Peralta. When Rooster went down to Old Town to pick up the final liberty party, he brought back six bottles of trair and a case of jash. Plenty of the stuff in cargo, Zelde knew—but in sealed crates. More work to break it out, than to bring up some extra.

When she went on watch, she spent as much time as she could in going over the ship's faked log again. She'd thought she was done with needing to know that stuff—but now, considering Peralta, maybe she wasn't.

When Parnell got up next morning, Zelde woke, too—a little short of sleep but not missing it. First she lay there, relaxing; then she heard the shower start, and got up and joined him there. He shook water out of his eyes, off his face, and grinned at her.

Standing close beside him, under the spray, she said, "Feeling good this morning, are you, Ragir?"

He handed her the soap; she began lathering. He said, "Yes. For a change, I am. The pressure—the *Bonaparte* landing—for once it's building me up instead of wearing me down. I don't know why."

For a moment the spray hit her face and she couldn't talk. Then, away from it, she said, "Maybe you turned the corner."

"Maybe." He kissed her. He tasted soapy, and from the face he made as they moved apart, so did she. Then he moved the control—water came cold and hard—she pushed her head into the main force of it to rinse her scalp well. Almost too soon, he cut the flow entirely.

She looked at him. He said, "Aren't you done?"

She felt her hair. "Yeah, I guess." Then they toweled dry, dressed and went to the galley. *Right now, it's business.*

They joined Lera Tzane at breakfast. Waiting for his meal, Parnell said, "As soon as possible, after the *Bonaparte* lands, I'm visiting there. As my senior available officer,

Lera, you'll come along. Captain Haiglund's very strong on
protocol. So be ready."

She turned her head sharply, to look at him. Her hair,
worn loose today, fell forward across one cheek; she
pushed it back. "No!" When he didn't speak, she said, "I
don't want to see Peralta any more than I have to. Not at
all, if possible."

Parnell reached to touch her hand. "Easy, Lera. What—"

She interrupted. "I have the watch, anyway. So techni-
cally I'm *not* available. Parnell—" She turned her hand
palm up, to grasp his. "I could never hide anything from
that man. What if I still can't?"

Ahead of Parnell, Zelde said, "He had a handle on
you—that it? None of my business, what kind. But—" To
Parnell, now: "If she feels like that, maybe she's right, and
shouldn't go."

"Maybe. But I think, Lera, under the circumstances it
might be *my* business. What sort of hold Jimar had on you,
I mean."

Tzane squeezed his hand, then let go. "It's nothing
much, in the telling. He's always been quite a man for
women, you know. On that trip he was living with a Chief
rating, Hilaire Gowdy—but that didn't keep him away
from others. Well—I was one of them, and totally infat-
uated. When he ignored me for someone else, I pretended
not to notice—several of us learned how to do that, I'm
afraid. And eventually he dropped me."

Her hand clenched. "But still—any time he noticed me
at all, I'd tell him anything he asked. Just on the chance,
you see, that it might help me with him." She shrugged. "It
never did, of course. And at trip's end I had the good sense
to request transfer offship—and the luck to get it."

Zelde frowned. "And you think you still might—Lera,
how long ago was all this?"

"Planets' time? I have no idea. About eight years bio, for
me. For Jimar, probably less—I had two years groundside
between my second ship and this one, and I think he's been
on continuous space duty except for normal stopovers.
But—"

Parnell cut in. "You were right, Zelde. If Lera feels uncertain, she shouldn't go. So you get ready, instead."

"Me?" She thought about it. Well, why not? "Any reason to dude up special?"

"What? Oh, no—don't bother with a cover disguise. There's no point in complicating things any further."

Near mid-morning the *Bonaparte* landed. On screen Zelde saw the great hulk—balancing, it looked, on bursts of blue flame—as it came down. "That's ionization," said Parnell, "off the drive nodes." The blue glare reached ground, and dust erupted to hide the final touching. A dull thump came; the *Great Khan* shook a little. Then the dust thinned and blew away; the other ship sat quietly, close to midway between the *Khan* and the port's Admin building.

Leaning over the comm-panel, Parnell searched ship-ground frequencies and found the *Bonaparte* talking with the commandant's office. Listening, he nodded. "All very formal, very official—that's Haiglund, all right." When the exchange was done, he hit his own "Send" switch. "The *Great Khan* calling the *Bonaparte*. Captain Parnell requests Captain Haiglund's permission to come aboard and pay respects." He repeated the message once, then waited.

After a moment, a voice came. "Acknowledged, Captain. Please hold?"

"Right."

About two minutes—then another voice, deeper. "Captain Haiglund here. Request granted, Captain Parnell. Will you and your ranking officer do me the honor of joining us for lunch? We sit at noon sharp, but report a half hour early, if you will."

"Surely, sir. We'll be honored."

"Confirmed, then. Haiglund out."

Cutting the circuit, Parnell grinned like a wolf. "Good. That bottles Peralta up, for now. Zelde, we have nearly an hour to spare. Anything particular that you need to do before we go?"

"What kind of clothes, Ragir?"

"The outfit Turk tailored for you—it's the nearest you've got, to a dress uniform—is it in shape to wear?"

"Sure. But it's not really official—won't this book-soldier Haiglund get his tail in a knot?"

"You're a shipboard promotion, remember? And you could hardly wear poor old Terihew's leavings; you're a head the taller and only about half as wide!"

"All right; I'll wear it."

"Fine. Now—anything else on your schedule?"

She caught the look in his eye, and hated to disappoint him. "But—I ought to look through my fake record again—be sure I have it all down pat. Don't you think?"

For an instant his half-grin and raised eyebrow gave him a lopsided look. Then: "Afraid you're right. Well—it's just that I hate to waste feeling so good."

"Then *stay* feeling good. We won't be there all day."

Walking with Parnell across the port, Zelde knew she looked fine. She'd filled out some, since Earth—not to match her height, maybe, but enough to show off Turk's job of tailoring. She had a haircut only a few days old, and a little spray on it so that under lights it shone. She was used to the one lone earring now; the mirror told her she held her head straight without having to think about it.

She'd brought a clipboard, for taking notes if she needed to. Her free hand clasped Parnell's, swinging back and forth in rhythm as they walked. Today he was setting a good pace. . . .

And over her shoulder slung a pouch with two bottles in it—one jash and one trair.

Nearing the *Bonaparte*, they let go the handclasp. Parnell winked. "Right—let's look a little official, around here."

The ramp guard was armed and helmeted. She gave a quick "Present Arms" and reverted to "Ready" before Parnell could return the salute. "Captain Parnell?" He nodded. "Welcome aboard the *Bonaparte*. Go on up. You'll be met inside, and escorted to Captain Haiglund." She spoke, too soft for Zelde to hear, into the talk-set at her lapel, and then paid them no more attention. Parnell leading, they climbed the ramp.

At the airlock a young man, Oriental, greeted them with a silent nod and gestured for them to follow him. Inside, the ship was laid out exactly like the *Great Khan*—the escort, then, must be purely formal. Or maybe for security— though the man had no weapons Zelde could see. Well, neither did she—but she could get her knife out in a hurry, if she needed to.

A tall, broad man, gray-haired and smiling, admitted them to captain's quarters. He extended a hand to Parnell. "Welcome aboard, Captain, and your officer as well."

Zelde also got the handshake. "And meet First Officer Peralta."

This one, now—thin, dark, of medium height, Peralta moved like a cat on a tightrope. His hand, briefly clasping Zelde's, was hard—taut skin over lithe bony structure—its pressure firm and measured. Under a precise line of mustache, extending past the corners of his mouth, his quick smile gleamed white. For a moment his eyes met Zelde's—and looking up a little, for she had height on him. "Pleasure. Didn't get your name?"

"Zelde M'tana. Acting Second Officer."

Haiglund turned to Parnell. "Second? Where's your First?"

Parnell explained about Dopples' injuries and the temporary promotions. "And my Acting First has the watch." He smiled. "Captain, I know how you feel about disrupting schedules unnecessarily—so I didn't."

Haiglund nodded. "Right. I'll meet that one another time. What's the name, though?"

When Parnell gave it, Peralta said, "Tzane? Lera Tzane, by any chance?" Parnell nodded, and the other man grinned. "So Lera got her officer's rank, after all!" To Haiglund he said, "I knew the girl on her first trip. She was smart enough—knew her job—but a little flighty, I thought."

Haiglund motioned his guests to seats; Peralta began pouring drinks. No choices offered—Earth bourbon over ice for all. Parnell took the pouch from Zelde, and presented the two bottles to Haiglund. "Later I'd like you both to sample these with us. They're local products, and I think you'll enjoy them."

Then, accepting his drink and nodding thanks, he said, "Flighty? Lera Tzane? Well, eight or nine bio-years ago, on her first trip, perhaps. Cadets—new to space, excited—we expect a little foolishness, don't we? Not that we stand for any great amount of it, of course. But people do mature, and Lera certainly has."

"Good," said Chalmers Haiglund, and took over the talk with questions and stories about other ships and officers. Some, Parnell seemed to know; others he didn't. Listening, Zelde decided Haiglund had gone to space more than ten planet-years ahead of Parnell.

But she knew none of the people being talked about. Her

attention drifted. Mostly, she watched the man Peralta. The tension he showed so plainly—did it have to do with the situation, or was it just part of *him*? His eyes, never still, looked from one to another; now and then his head moved a little, barely enough to notice, as if he were deciding something. *All the time, he's waiting. What for?*

He made an abrupt, decisive nod; then he was still. *What was that about?* She thought back—who'd said what, just then? Then she got it, the thing she'd only half-listened to—Parnell telling about Captain Czerner being promoted to a groundside job. Then a pause, then Peralta's nod. She'd have to remember to tell Parnell; maybe he could figure it out. At least he'd know it meant something to Peralta.

Haiglund finished his drink; the other two men upended their own. Catching Parnell's look, Zelde followed suit. And thought, everybody even has to *drink* in step with this Haiglund.

Parnell spoke. "Now, if I may, I'd like to do the honors." Haiglund nodded, and Parnell moved to pour generous glasses of jash and smaller ones of trair, then serve everyone. Raising his trair, he said, "If you haven't encountered trair before, I must tell you that it should be drunk with caution. It's much more effective than its taste indicates."

Haiglund grinned. "That's fair warning," and he sipped. So did Peralta; then he shrugged. *Well, Parnell told you!*

The talk continued, now with Parnell and Peralta exchanging word of people they knew. For a time, Zelde saw strain in her man; then, again, he seemed to relax. A galley aide brought lunch; while they ate, discussion slowed, almost stopped. Then came another round of jash and trair— Zelde served it up, this time—and Haiglund took the lead again. Problems he'd seen at different colonies, how UET seemed to be handling them, and some ideas about how he himself, given the chance, might improve matters. The man's face was flushed, and he was talking louder and faster than before.

Haiglund and Peralta, both, were drinking ahead of Zelde's pace. Keep in step? She looked over to Parnell. He'd drunk most of his jash but hardly any trair. With his left eye, turned away from the others, he winked at her. *What . . . ?* He looked down at his two drinks and re-peated the wink. *Oh! I get it.*

Before Haiglund could finish either drink—his signal for all to do the same—she got up and made the circuit with both bottles, topping off full and near-empty glasses alike. And a little later, she did it again.

When she started up to do a third serving, Parnell made a quick frown. All right, it was his show. She sat back. Haiglund had a load on, for sure, but was handling it. Per-alta—he'd taken a lot of trair for his size, but all it seemed to do was make him quiet. His gaze still moved from one person to the next, and his concentration looked even more intent now. Zelde waited; she could feel the booze herself, but like Parnell, she'd gone easy on the trair. Now, though, he drained that glass. There had to be a reason, so she gulped hers, too.

Talking faltered and stopped. Parnell looked around, owl-eyed. Zelde knew he couldn't be drunk, not on *that* amount. He said, "Captain Haiglund, sir—want to thank you, your hospitality—think we'd better be getting back. That time of day—check the log and incoming messages—can't afford to skip captain's inspection. Right?"

Peralta was leaning forward, staring. Haiglund belched and grinned. "I like to see that, captain—stick to duty, yes. Fun's fun, but stay on top of the job. You're all right, Par-nell." He stood, steadier than Zelde expected. "See you out? Or grant freedom of the ship and let you find your own way?" He laughed.

"Freedom of the ship? Why, we're honored to accept." So Parnell and Zelde said good-byes and left without es-cort. But leaving the quarters, glancing back a moment, Zelde saw Peralta looking after them. His eyes were nar-rowed.

Groundside again and well away from the *Bonaparte*, Parnell dropped his drunk act. "What do you think, Zelde?"

"Depends. What was it you were doing, with us and them and the drinks?"

One quick laugh, then he said, "I warned them about trair, right? But they hit it heavy, early on, and we didn't until later. So for them, the sobering effect's worn off; they're *drunk*. We're not, and won't be for a good while yet."

She saw it, but: "What does that do for us?"

"Peralta, you see—he has to outdo everybody in everything. Outdrink, outfight, outfuck any man alive, to hear him tell it. He's drunk now and he doesn't know why. Coming aboard the *Great Khan* he'll be testing himself against me every way he can. But drinking trair. . . ."

"Yeah—you'll sandbag him again."

"*We* will. So that whatever he's looking for, he'll get too drunk to do much about it."

She thought to mention Peralta's reaction that she'd noticed. "When you said about Czerner's getting promoted, something clicked. I don't know what—but he looked like he'd just figured out an answer."

Parnell's own answer was more grunt than word. Then: "Maybe he knows something I don't, that puts a hole in our story. So far and long from Earth, it can't matter much—but I'm glad you spotted how it struck him. I'll be on guard."

They approached their own ship's ramp. The man on duty gave a salute, with his weapon, that was more comradely than official. As he returned the courtesy, Parnell smiled. He and Zelde went upship. After a quick visit to Control—no problems there—they went to quarters.

Parnell closed the door. "Zelde. . . ." He reached, and she moved to him. Kissing, undoing each other's clothes: "It's as you said; I do still feel good. So let's get to each other before the trair does its second trick."

How the booze part went with Parnell, Zelde wasn't sure. But she herself didn't start feeling drunk until afterward, dozing off with his head cuddled against her chin. And by that time, it didn't matter for hell.

If she had any hangover, she slept through it—and woke, feeling fine, in time to eat before taking the watch. Parnell was still asleep; she left without waking him.

She had a quiet watch. The last liberty parties were aboard, so she had no leave roster to check. Summit Bay had a few questions about cargo; Zelde consulted the computer and gave the answers.

She was bored; the watch went slowly. At last Carlo

Mauragin relieved her, and she headed toward the galley for a snack.

Parnell was there; she filled a tray—partly—and joined him. "Been sleeping all this time?" He looked tired again, but she thought she'd better make a joke of it.

He shook his head. "Up for several hours. I've been doing a little studying. On where to go next, mostly."

"You decide yet?"

"I think so. It's been a real worry, trying to get some kind of trustworthy coordinates for a Hidden World. Turk Kestler finally delivered the goods, a few hours ago. And explained what the delay was, with the Underground."

She swallowed a bite, then said, "Like to hear it."

Parnell made a savage face. "The contact she first knew of—Horsehead, the one in charge. He was caught, only a short time before we got here, and died under questioning by our friend Cort Verrane."

Breath hissed through Zelde's teeth. "They all blown, then? The whole Underground lot?"

"It wouldn't seem so. Still, that risk is another reason to lift, now, as soon as possible." He waved a hand. "But listen. Whoever took over from Horsehead fed Turk the coordinates for two Hidden Worlds, one through each of her contacts. Both of them coincide with sun-type stars on record, so that much is solid."

"Anyplace I ever heard of?"

"I doubt it. Refuge? Fair Ball?" She shook her head. "Well, both names are familiar to me," he said. "Refuge was a legend, in the scuttlebutt back at the old Slaughterhouse. Almost Earthlike, the story went, except for lighter gravity and less extremes of climate. Nice to know it really exists."

"That where we go, then?"

Parnell frowned. "It's a tossup. Fair Ball sounds good, too. Not a terribly long haul from here, for instance. The one hazard is, it's only a few months, by ships' time, from UET's colony on Johnson's Walk. That's quite a distance, mind you, by ordinary standards—but possibly close enough to give more chance of crossing UET traffic." He shrugged. "Not a major factor, though."

With nothing to say, Zelde waited. Finally Parnell smiled. "One thing about Refuge is its position—practically in line, from here, with Far Corner. You remember? The place the *Hoover* had last visited? So if Refuge didn't pan out, on a near look, we could go accel again and hit Far Corner with good fuel margin."

"UET, though, I thought it was."

"Yes; but a backwoodsy place; no garrison. It's known that Escaped Ships touch there fairly often." Now he chuckled, but waited a moment before he spoke. "And there, maybe we could nose around and see if the local Underground could tell us whether Kickem Bernardez was really Escaped, or not!"

She frowned, thinking back to the passage with that ship. "You think he did, then?"

"It wouldn't surprise me. Early years in the Slaughterhouse, before he was moved into my cadre section, Kickem was pretty thick with Bran Tregare. And once, I've heard, they shipped together."

Tregare—the name sounded familiar; she repeated it. "Somebody said that name before. Sure—when I was first on here. What about him, was it?"

Now Parnell looked puzzled; then his face cleared. "Yes—the woman who brought you; she'd shipped with him, and she hinted around, trying to find out what I knew. I couldn't trust her, of course."

She tapped her cup on the table; he poured it full, and said, "Stories differ. But if there's truth in any of them, Bran Tregare has the only armed ship ever to Escape. It's called *Inconnu* now, and scares UET more than all the rest put together. How he did it is something else; he was only Third Officer, and there are some nasty rumors of mutiny *after* Escape."

He shrugged. "Maybe someday we'll find out, maybe not." He finished his own coffee, and stood. "Time for me to tour Control, and maybe sit in for a while there. Mauragin's coming along somewhat better this time, but it can't hurt to quiz him occasionally—keep him on his toes."

"Sure, Ragir. I've got stuff to look after; then maybe I'll take a rest. Wake me up if you feel like it." After he was gone, she dawdled a few minutes before leaving.

She stopped off in quarters. Ready to leave, she looked into the big mirror and wondered, suddenly—How did other people see her? She knew her height gave her an edge; ever since the year she'd grown so fast—at fourteen, would it be?—she'd noticed that. Her face didn't look young *or* old; the strong features hadn't changed much, either. And her usual expression, she decided, had a challenging look to it. Maybe she'd better watch that; it could get her in trouble. Dopples? Could be. . . .

The tight haircut made her face look stronger, too, she thought. And the heavy ring in the one ear, and the other with no lobe—no two ways about it, they gave her a tough look. Grinning, she nodded to her reflection. *Maybe that goddamn bandit did me a favor!*

She went downship, hoping to catch Turk off duty, and visit. But beside the quarters door, the "Stay Out" light was on. There was no device, here, to take a message; she shook her head and started to turn away. Then, out of the corner of her eye, she saw the light turn off. She smiled and pushed to ring the entry buzzer, now connected again.

Rooster, opening the door, was closing fasteners on his worksuit. He grinned. "Come in. Just in time—which is to say, not too early."

Coming out of the bathroom in a robe, Turk said, "Oh, quit bragging, will you, Rooster? Hi, Zelde—use a drink?"

"Sure." They were drinking Parleyvoo beer; that was fine with Zelde. She sat and sipped at it. "Parnell says you got us a couple of Hidden Worlds. Tell me about 'em?"

Turk belched. "Lot of bubbles in this brew; doesn't pay to take it too fast." She swallowed some more, then said, "On the subject of Refuge, I didn't get too much scoop; that's one closemouthed agent. Just that it's very Earthlike—"

"Parnell said so, too. He's heard of it a long time."

"And several Escaped Ships base there. The man wouldn't say which ones—or, more likely, he doesn't know. Though he says Tregare's been in and out a few times." Turk shrugged. "Fair Ball, though—the woman agent gave me quite a rundown."

"And it checks," said Rooster. "I've heard the place described, you see, by a man who's been there."

Zelde stared. "But how——?"

"He was on a ship that Escaped, but he wanted to get back to Earth, to his family. So he jumped ship at a UET-colony landing."

Zelde had more questions, but Turk said, "Fair Ball, you

wanted to hear about. All right—the first thing is, it's smallish compared to Earth or here, but not very light on gees or air, so it must be heavy for its size."

Rooster said, "Whiter sun—so it has to be bigger, but farther away so it doesn't look it. Longer year, then. Pretty good climate at the settlement—a little hot and dry, even though the air's heavy enough with water vapor to haze the sky pretty much. They irrigate, there, out of a river that comes down from the mountains."

"The settlement, now." Intent, Zelde leaned forward.

Head tipped to one side, Turk looked away for a moment. "Trying to remember. Keep in mind, we're talking some years back, with more to go before we could get there. Last report, the town was only a few thousand. And not much offworld trade."

"Why not?"

Turk shrugged. "Because it *is* a small group, for one thing. And mostly farming and fishing—not too much to interest ships."

Zelde's eyes narrowed. "So we go there—you sure we can get fuel for the next jump?"

Now Rooster chuckled. "Not to worry. There's fuel ore—or nobody would have settled the place. Look—the first thing any ship does, scouting a colony site from groundside, is to set up the makings for a fuel refinery. Standard UET practice, and I imagine that Escaped ships do it the same."

"Yeah, sure." She nodded. "What else Parnell said, though—Fair Ball's awful close to a UET planet. How come?"

Turk shook her head. "Not that close. A lot nearer than usual, to be safe—but there's a gimmick." While she poured her glass full again, Zelde waited. Turk began drawing, with her hands, in the air. "Here's Johnson's Walk, see? And over here, Fair Ball. But in between, and blocking direct sight or travel, there's a gas nebula." Zelde didn't understand, and she guessed it showed. "Not a real nebula, like a whole galaxy. But—you ever heard of the Crab Nebula?" Zelde hadn't. "Well, it's an old blown-up supernova, is what. And you can't take a ship *through* it at much more than planetary speeds—let alone see across it. So—"

"So UET don't know that Fair Ball's there, you mean?"

Rooster cleared his throat. "Well, I suppose they have its

sun on their charts. But it's off their shipping routes—and not handy to get to, from the Walk, without a special reason. And must be at least twenty other stars in the general hunk of space around the Walk, that they haven't had time to check on, either."

"UET's cut back on exploration," said Turk, "since Escaped ships began raiding colonies. They're getting cautious."

"Raiding? This Tregare, maybe?"

Turk grinned. "You've heard about him? Yes—he's the number-one lobo, but not the only one. You don't need an armed ship to wipe a town by landing—or lifting off—across it, drifting sideways. Nobody actually *does* it, unless they have to—but everybody knows you can, if you decide to. Or you land peaceful, at some port with no other ships groundside just then, and storm off ship with your whole crew armed. Catch the locals with their pants down, and take what you need. If the scuttle has any truth to it, that's happened a lot, too."

"Then why—" But before she finished the question, Zelde saw the answer. "Sure—*we* couldn't do like that, here, because we needed a drive cube. And over at Summit Bay, three UET ships in shape to wipe *us* while we couldn't lift."

Rooster leaned to pat her shoulder. "You're getting it." He squinted one eye. "I keep forgetting, this is your first trip and you don't already know all this stuff."

Time to leave; Zelde stood. "So do I, sometimes. Hey, it's been nice, talking—and thanks for the beer."

Back at quarters she showered, then lay down to sleep a while. She woke to Parnell's touch. "Ragir? What time is it?"

"There's an hour before lunch. Then you're wanted, over at Port Admin. I took the call; Cort Verrane did the talking, but he's not the one who wants to see you."

She sat up; the covers fell away. "What's it about?" He didn't answer. "I mean—do I go, or not?" Why wouldn't he *say* something? "You're nerved about Peralta. You think this is part of it?" She gripped his shoulders; he winced, and she eased one hand. "What goes on here? What do I *do*?"

His hand touched her healing ear. "I'm still thinking.

Maybe we can figure it out together." Still, that told her
nothing; she waited. "This isn't Peralta; it can't be. What
Verrane said—do you remember Torra Defose?"

"The Police—" Policebitch. Except that—"Sure I remember. But she said she wasn't putting grabs on me."

"I know. And she's the one who's asking for you. That's
why I think it's safe, this time."

"You want I should go?"

"Not *want*—but I think you'd better." With one hand he
cupped her chin. "I swear Verrane didn't know what it's
about—and if it were big, he would know. So I don't think
it can be dangerous. If I thought otherwise, we'd lift right
now. A little inconvenient, but we could do it."

Deciding, she said, "All right; I'll go. Now, though—"
She reached to him. "An hour, you said, before lunch?"

The look he had, then, she hated. "I'm sorry, Zelde. Today I'm—today it's not good with me, at all."

She didn't let her mouth twist. "Not—not *any* way, Ragir?"

He looked worse, then. But all he said was, "Something
inside is acting up badly. I don't know what it is. But I
think—and this is the first time, isn't it, since our agree-
ment?—before you leave the ship, please issue me one extra pain pill."

She leaned and clung to him. "Oh, Ragir! Hell, yes—you
really need it, 'course I will!"

Silly, maybe, Zelde thought—but dressing to visit Port
Admin she tucked away two weapons. The knife was routine; the gun wasn't. A tiny monster—it shot needle-sized
pellets at speeds she didn't believe, and carried one hell of
a lot of them. Shooting it, she'd learned, near to took your
hand off. And if it hit you—pinhole going in, Dopples had
said, crater coming out. She stashed the gun where it
wouldn't show, cold against her thigh.

Push come to shove, she couldn't really shoot her way
out of Admin. But the chance to try, if she had to. . . .

Parnell lay still, eyes shut—but not breathing like sleep.
She kissed his forehead; he mumbled something she didn't
catch. She went downship, out into hazy sunlight, and began walking.

Passing the *Bonaparte*, she saw someone at the airlock.

Sun glare made it hard to see, but she recognized Peralta,
watching.

Which meant he wouldn't be at Admin. She'd settle for
that. . . .

The Admin building squatted—four storeys plus a penthouse cupola—gray concrete with beige plastic trim, dotted
with rows of small windows. Above flew the UET flag—
blue letters, black-bordered, on a red field. The three char-
acters made one shape; the right side of the U was the left
upright of the E, and the E's upper bar extended to top the
T. Not simple cloth, that flag—it read the same from both
sides. To one side of the parking area an open-topped
groundcar showed the same emblem, plus Police markings.

Climbing the main entrance steps, Zelde saw barred
basement windows looking out onto wells at each side. No
one guarded the double doors, propped open to the warm
day.

She walked into a small lobby, a little over five meters to
a side. At the back was an elevator; to its left rose a flight
of stairs. On the right side was another, leading down. A
lateral corridor led off each way; signs read "Odd Numbers
Left" and "Even Numbers Right." A few people moved
through the area, but she saw nobody who was obviously
on duty.

Beside the elevator was a Directory listing; she stepped
up and read it. All right; Commandant Trask's office was
500—penthouse—and Cort Verrane's 501. Verrane had
made the call—but wait a minute—how about Information,
in 103? She turned left and found that room.

The door was open. Behind the counter a man stood;
beyond were three desks. Two sat vacant; behind the third
was a heavy blonde woman. Zelde walked in; the man
looked up and nodded.

"Help you?"

"I'm off the *Great Khan*—Third Officer M'tana." Acting
Second, now—but why bother to say so? "Mr. Cort Verrane called. Ms. Torra Defose, with the Police, asked me to
meet her in this building. You happen to know just where
that would be?"

"One moment, please." The phone was a hush-set, so she
couldn't hear what he said. Then he nodded and put the
phone down. "The small conference room—five-oh-three,

next to Administrator Verrane's office. That's in the penthouse, you know."

I could of guessed. But she smiled, and thanked him.

The elevator took its time coming down; the indicator showed it stopping quite a while at each floor. Waiting, Zelde remembered her first elevator, and the Utie who made fun of her for not knowing what it was. How long ago, planets' time? If she remembered to, she'd ask Parnell.

Finally the door opened. Three people came out; one man entered with her. At each floor, some got on or off. One woman, small and elderly, rode with her to the penthouse. There the older woman turned left and went into 502. The door read "Conference," but while it was open, Zelde saw that the room was large.

503, the other way, had the same sign on it. Zelde walked past Verrane's office to go in, and saw a table with eight chairs. In one of them, Torra Defose sat. But not for long—the woman stood and held out a hand to Zelde.

"Come sit down. I've ordered up some coffee; we might as well be sociable."

"All right." The dark lean face showed no sign of what Defose might be thinking. As usual, she talked quietly. *What's it about?* But Zelde didn't ask.

For some reason of her own, Torra Defose nodded. She began to speak, but the door opened and a boy carried in a tray, with a coffee urn and six cups, plus "sidearms"— cream, sugar, and spicemix. He looked at the two women and cleared his throat. "I thought—I mean, will there be more of you, here?"

The Policewoman gestured; he set the tray between her and Zelde. "It's my mistake. I said, coffee to the small conference room, and forgot to say how many. Thank you."

When the boy left, she said, "I told you, you'd earned some reward money. You didn't come to collect."

Oh, is that all? Relieved, Zelde tried not to show it. "Yeah, but I *said,* then, go ahead and keep all of it. Remember?"

Torra shook her head; with the motion, her short black hair ruffled slightly. "You'd give up what's yours, before you'd go to Police HQ. That's it, isn't it?" Zelde didn't answer; the other sighed. "There's this *thing* between your Service and mine. I wish there weren't." She poured the coffee, adding sugar to her own. Zelde took the other cup, and sipped.

The woman said, "That's why I asked you here, rather than go to your ship. I knew I couldn't expect much of a welcome." Her mouth twitched—almost a smile, but not quite. Still, Zelde said nothing.

"How is your First Officer—the man who was stabbed?" Then, looking: "I see your ear healed nicely. Perhaps it's not much comfort to you, but the effect, now—it's striking."

Zelde had to grin. "Thanks. And Dopples—Mr. Adopolous—he's been slow getting his strength again. Cut up bad, he was. But he'll make it."

"I'm glad. And I have something here for him. The man he killed—that one bore a reward, too. I brought your officer's share of it."

"Mr. Adopolous, he'll thank you, I'm sure."

The woman handed Zelde two envelopes. "Both sums are in standard Weltmarks, not local scrip. Since you're leaving soon."

What to say? "I do thank you, for me and Dopples both. And 'specially for taking time to come way up here." She paused. "I suppose you're busy and need to get back, so maybe—"

Defose gestured. "I'm in no hurry. And we have lots of coffee left. So unless *you're* due back on duty—"

Thinking fast, still Zelde knew she'd waited too long for the lie to sound true. So she said, "Not right away, I guess."

"Good. Let's talk, then. Partly business, I admit." *Oh?*

"About that thing, happened in town—there's just not any more we know about it. Any of us."

"That's not what I have in mind." *Then what is?* "Part of my job is keeping tabs on the general climate of opinion— off this planet as well as on it. And the ships are our only source, really, for offworld information."

"The commandant—he's got our log, a copy of it, off the computer. I expect that's got all the news in it."

"Official news, yes. But what I need is the scuttlebutt."

Careful, now. "*Rumors?* Nobody can keep track of all that crap—anything you want to hear, and no two alike."

The woman's hand was on Zelde's—and nearly the same size, though the other wasn't as tall. "I'm not talking about content; what I want is flavor. You know what I mean, M'tana; you've had the training, or you wouldn't have your job."

"Not regular officers' training. I got promoted into a vacancy; you know that."

"Quit fencing—I'm not accusing *you* of anything. What I need to know is, is subversion a problem on the *Great Khan*?"

That one took some translating. Then: "Any place, there's griping—space, same as groundside. Bitchbitch-bitch—but still do the work, anyway. You know?"

Defose nodded. "Of course. Whether it's serious, though—that depends on the target."

Watch it! This was the Committee Police their own damned selves, and don't forget it! Zelde shrugged. "Target? Whatever. The job's run wrong, the watch chief plays favorites, the chow's lousy. You name it, you'll hear it. I—"

"Those things don't cause real trouble—you know that as well as I do. Tell me, Zelde—on the *Khan,* is there much talk of Escape?"

Sometimes truth was the safest lie of all. Zelde let herself smile. "Escape? Hell—I haven't heard anybody pushing *that* idea in maybe the last six months. Ship's time."

Torra's slight frown smoothed out. "Encouraging— because it's usually a favorite subject among the lower ratings. Your captain must be running a good ship."

"He's the best, Parnell is." Zelde spoke without thinking, then saw by the woman's face that she hadn't made a mistake.

Defose nodded. "That opinion—it's the basis of a sound ship. Or of any other stable operation. I've dealt with a lot of people in my work, including quite a few spacers, and it seems to me that if more of them had the knack your captain appears to have with his subordinates, then perhaps we—" The woman seemed to be looking past Zelde; then she shook her head. "I wish—well, some situations will always have more problems than others, I suppose. All right; I'm done with my questions. Do you have any, about things groundside here? Or must you return to the ship now?"

"I should, yeah. Maybe sometime else, we could talk." And in a way, Zelde almost meant it. Leaving the room, she thought, Why did the Policebitch have to make it so hard not to *like* her?

As she walked toward the elevator—Defose, making notes on a clipboard, had stayed behind—the door to 501 opened and Amzella Verrane beckoned.

"A moment?" Zelde stopped, then went to the doorway. No one else was in the office; the three desks were vacant. The blonde woman smiled, her big jaw moving slightly. "How went your interview with the high Police powers?" High? Maybe Zelde's surprise showed, for Amzella said, "Defose is second in command of Police here—fifth for the whole planet. You didn't know?"

Zelde shook her head. "She never said so. Anyway—all it was, she brought reward shares for those goddamn robbers. Mine and Mr. Adopolous', both."

Amzella's brows raised. "And that's all?"

"Asked about the ship a little, sure—how things are. Well, about like always, I guess—and better than most, she seemed to think."

"If that's true, you're lucky. The last ship here—well, never mind. Now—the *Khan*'s cleared to lift, day after tomorrow; is that right? I notice that leave parties have been stopped already. Why so soon?"

"If you know liftoff time, it's more than I do. But that's Parnell's way. He don't care for chasing down drunks and shackups, last minute, or else lose crew. Everybody's had liberty, anyway—and except for Dopples and me that time, not hardly any trouble. We—"

Verrane grinned. "Ships, people usually do take care of themselves pretty well. For your ear and your officer's wound, three dead—and we're glad to be rid of them."

"That's good." Time to leave. Shake hands, maybe? Yes. "Well, good luck, Ms. Verrane."

"And to you."

This time the elevator came fast, and made only two stops on the way down. Everybody on coffee breaks? Probably.

It was hot enough outside that Zelde worked up a sweat, walking.

"And that's all there was to it, Ragir." He sat on the bed, wearing shorts and holding a dark, strong-looking drink—

not drunk at all, but stretched out some way, for sure. The pills? No—she'd looked, and he was only the one over quota.

"That we know of, you mean." His voice came thin and strained, but he nodded. "You're right, probably. Defose seems to have taken a liking to you—if anything Police do or say can be trusted. And the other one—well, you made points with her when you eased the mess between Cort Verrane and the guard. So on balance, I'll go with your opinion."

She'd showered but hadn't toweled. She stood, sipping on a big mug of Parleyvoo beer, liking the way her skin felt as the water dried on it. "So we're all in clear now, you think?"

"With Parleyvoo, yes."

"Then what else?" Because he didn't look like off the hook.

"Peralta—he's coming here. Maybe for dinner, maybe later. I couldn't pin him down—*or* turn him away." For an instant, Parnell looked very old. "And I'm not *ready* to power-jockey with that man."

She set her glass down and began massaging his neck and shoulders, careful to be easy on the bad parts. "Parnell, love—you don't need to jockey that one none. You want, I'll take him out for you."

From his tired slump, he straightened. "What do you mean, take him out?"

She leaned to kiss him, then pulled back and grinned. "Fight or screw or drink him down—whatever. Just say the word."

He laughed; it turned to coughing; he fought it and won. "No. You can't fight Peralta. *I'd* have trouble with him, even on my best day, which this isn't, damn it!" Now he shook his head. "And I won't have you whoring for me— that's out. The drinking part—if that works as planned, all's well. But—"

Her free hand covered his mouth. "Now *you* listen." She let him push the hand away, but he didn't speak. "Ragir— if you was, right now, what you *really* are, you wouldn't need no help. But you're not—so I *have* to do stuff, maybe, that I don't like much. For us both—you see?"

She waited, but he didn't answer. So she said, "Dopples told me—*Dopples*. That the ship comes ahead of his life—

and mine, too. For me he took a knife in the gut, and he
don't even *like* me." Her eyes were watering; she shook her
head to clear them. "Now, if he can do that, I can do any
damn thing I need to do—for the ship, and for you. And
don't you argue!"

It was a long time he looked at her. Maybe, like Zelde
herself, he remembered Eldra Siddenour. Then he said,
"You're in charge of tactics, Zelde. You're in charge."

At the ramp she met Peralta. She and Parnell had waited
dinner for an hour and then eaten. Nearly another hour
later, Peralta called to announce his visit. In twilight now,
he climbed the ramp and shook hands.

"Evening, Mr. Peralta."

"And a pleasant one—Ms. M'tana, isn't it? Did you see
the sunset?"

"No. We was inside." She turned and led him upship. At
quarters she opened the door and let him go in first. Parnell sat at his study desk; before rising he put a hand to his
mouth and then swallowed coffee. *Pep pill—and held off it
'til the last minute.* Then he stood, his hand held out. Peralta went to shake it, and both men sat.

"Zelde, will you do the honors? What's your fancy, Jimar? We're still well fixed for Earth whiskies."

From under his loose jacket, the visitor brought out a
bottle. "First treat's on me—remember? To celebrate your
command—and of course Captain Czerner's promotion."
For a moment Parnell frowned; then his face relaxed again.
"This brandy, Ragir—it's special stuff. The last bottle I
have left from the time the *Bonaparte* visited Stronghold."

Stronghold—the fortress planet, where UET kept a fleet
of armed ships. The only other thing Zelde knew about the
place was that it lay on the far side of Earth from UET's
other explorations. As the men talked, she watched more
than listened. Peralta had his tension under better control
tonight. *Why?*

"No," he was saying, "Admiral Saldeen retired. Korbeith
runs Stronghold now, I've heard—Korbeith the Butcher."
He laughed. "In that job, he won't be throwing cadets out
the airlock, at least." He sipped the brandy, and looked to
Parnell and to Zelde. "How do you like this stuff?"

"It's excellent, Jimar. I thank you." And Zelde smiled,
and nodded; the tart, heavy liquor was really very good.

Parnell cleared his throat. "I didn't know you'd shipped with Korbeith."

For a moment, Peralta's eyes closed to slits. "Just once—and luckily it wasn't my first trip, so I was relatively safe." He leaned forward. "Do you know whose first trip it *was,* though?" Parnell shook his head. "Tregare's—Bran Tregare's."

Zelde saw Parnell looking at her. Waiting for her to speak? All right. "Is that the one they call Tregare the pirate?"

"Right. And do you know—Ragir, you'll appreciate this—Korbeith's *still* complaining that he should have spaced that man off the old *MacArthur* when he had the chance!" Again the visitor's eyes narrowed. What was he fishing for?

Peralta, Zelde decided, probably couldn't see past Parnell's relaxed pose. If you didn't watch close, the shrug looked easy. "No one guesses right every time, Jimar."

"What do *you* think, Ragir? Did you know Tregare?" And Parnell explained why his knowledge was at second hand, through Kickem Bernardez. Peralta hadn't met Bernardez. "He'd have been only a snotty, I think, my last year before spacing."

As Peralta poured a second round of brandy, the men sorted out the timing of various space careers—Parnell was two years behind Peralta, Tregare three and Bernardez four. They talked of others—Limmer, Quinlan, Hoptowit, Ressider, Malloy—and Zelde recognized only the last by name. Then, not heeding the words much, she concentrated on the sound of Peralta's voice, and the ways he moved. Whatever he wanted here, he was taking his own sweet time about it.

After three rounds, his gift bottle was empty. Again Parnell suggested Earth whiskey, but Peralta shook his head. "If you don't mind, I'd like another go at—what's the name of that green explosive you brought us?" He laughed, but his voice held an edge.

"Trair?" said Zelde. Peralta nodded, so she got a bottle and poured all around. Then jash, too, in larger glasses. Seeing Peralta's steady look on her, she said, "Just so nobody expects *me* to keep up with you two, on trair. It takes practice I don't have." And as if he'd spoken, she knew he took her words as a challenge.

Favoring the milder jash, she nursed her trair along. Peralta didn't, and Parnell's drinking ran about midway between the two. The way he held the small glass, Zelde couldn't see its level—and neither could Peralta. When he glanced sidelong at her, she took it as a sign to pour refills—and noticed he was taking trair about half as fast as Peralta was. *Good enough.*

Now Peralta did the talking—telling of his own travels and exploits along the way. He sounded a little drunk, but Zelde guessed he was putting it on. When the bottle of trair was gone, she said, "Afraid that's all we got here. Have to send down to the hold, for more. Maybe some bourbon now?" Peralta nodded; she poured him a fresh glass and added ice. She and Parnell weren't dry yet; she set the bottle on his desk.

The intercom sounded; she took the call—Carlo Mauragin, on watch. "Summit Bay's questioning a cargo discrepancy, and *I* can't find it. Could somebody come talk to these people?"

Draining his glass, Parnell nodded to Zelde; she said, "I'll be right up." Before she left, she poured another round.

In Control, on viewscreen she faced a whiny man with sagging cheeks. *This,* it seemed, was listed and shouldn't be—while *this* was missing from the vouchers and Saggy Cheeks was *certain* that . . .

"All right, just a minute. Flash those items on visual and I'll check against our readout." The man was no expert; two minutes passed before the listings showed. Without needing to check the computer, Zelde recognized them.

She tried not to sound mad but she knew it showed, anyway. "Somebody at your end hasn't caught up with Appendix E yet. That one makes these changes—and another one, I think. Hold it." She punched for the data, and nodded. "Yeah. Line-item twelve-seventeen, too. So when you come to it, be braced. That all, for now?"

The man looked half scared and half angry; anger won out. "Well—you *could* be a little more respectful of proper authority."

Careful? No—hell with it! "When it is, I am."

"What kind of answer is that?"

"It made sense to me." She put her hand to the switch.

"For the *Great Khan*, signing over and out!" She cut the circuit and turned to Mauragin; his mouth hung open a little. Her laugh caught in her throat. "Peace up a pipe! Can't find his ass with both hands, and he wants *respect*?"

His throat moved, swallowing. "Weren't you a little rough?"

"Maybe." Starting to walk away, she turned back. "And *you*, Carlo—why'n hell didn't you check that out yourself?"

"But—all that listing—I didn't know where to look. I—"

"Code the line numbers in and set up to scan. You should know—"

His face went sullen. "So it's that way again, is it? Only this time, *you* outrank me, too."

"I—" She caught herself. "Sorry, Carlo. I've been working with that stuff and I guess you haven't." She touched his shoulder. "It's just—right now you interrupted something, might be tricky as all hell. And I got to get back to it. But jumping you like I did—cancel that, will you?"

After a moment his sulky look cleared. "All right, Zelde." She squeezed the shoulder once, then walked out fast, toward quarters.

As she went in, Peralta was talking, but stopped before she could make words into sense. Both men looked at her; Parnell said, "Sit down, Zelde. Jimar, here, has an interesting idea."

He didn't say what it was. She sipped from her glass, still full but pale from melted ice, and he said to Peralta, "What makes you think so?" Suddenly alert, Zelde waited for the answer.

It didn't come right away. Then the man set his glass down. "It's simple, Ragir. You *have* to be Escaped—because it's not possible that Czerner was promoted as your log claims." Almost forgetting to breathe, Zelde watched Peralta.

He waited, but Parnell said nothing. "All right. You were on Earth about three years after I was last there." He talked fast, sounding less drunk now, but maybe too wrapped up in his argument to keep his act straight. So some of the drunk part was real. All right—he waved a finger. "I have connections, Ragir—everywhere I go. I keep track of seniorities, and who's in favor and who's out—to know where's the place to move, to be ready for a proper jump some day. I once thought the *Bonaparte* was it—but Haiglund's hanging onto that ship until he dies on it." Peralta coughed, and took more drink.

Parnell smiled. "Both eyes, always, on the main chance—eh, Jimar? I expected no less of you. But—about my ship—you say . . . ?"

Mouth full, Peralta laughed; his nose dribbled whiskey, and he went into a coughing spasm. *Oh, he's drunk, all right!* Finally, wiping his eyes and speaking hoarsely, he said, "My look-in at the records, last time on Earth, said Czerner was close to being eased out of the Service—that he'd be lucky to hold his rank, let alone get promoted. So—"

Parnell leaned forward. "But that, of course, was before we had completed our previous mission, before Captain Czerner's achievements on that mission went onto his record. You admit, Jimar, that despite your inside contacts you're still missing that vital *later* information?"

Peralta wiped the last tears from his cheeks, and cleared his throat. "No, Ragir—it won't lift. You're good, I grant you—best poker player in your class, I remember. But you forget—I've seen your log transcript. It doesn't show Czerner doing anything special on the previous jaunt. You should have shown him grounded—not for incompetence, exactly, but—without prejudice; that's the way they'd put it. And that story, I might have bought. I've got you cold, Ragir—and if we were on Earth, I could prove it."

Parnell looked worried; maybe this was time to push some. Zelde caught Peralta's gaze. "We're not on Earth."

Gesturing, Parnell shook his head. "Wait, Zelde. We don't know Jimar's thinking yet." *And we don't trust it, either.* He smiled at his guest, but Zelde saw the pain lines mark his face. "Just for the sake of discussion—supposing you were right, why would you tell *me* this?"

Yeah. The man came alone; if he had a talk-set hidden on him, it wouldn't work through the ship's hull. No—he'd have to be making a tape *and get out with it.* Zelde shifted her seating. Slowed by drink, Peralta was; no matter what Parnell said, she was faster now. Her knife. . . .

But Peralta said, "It's the only way I can get your help."

Parnell gestured for refills. Surprised, Zelde got up and obliged, and still stood when Peralta said, "I want a ship; I

170 F. M. Busby

deserve one. At least that much—and later more, with any
luck. But on the *Bonaparte*, Haiglund has me stymied—
and I don't have enough trustworthy people to take the
ship, in space. But here, if you provide me a boarding
party—"

Zelde saw what it cost Parnell to laugh. "Jimar—I'd sus-
pected a trap, but you've convinced me that you're sincere.
Because if you've guessed wrong, what's to stop us from
turning you in to Cort Verrane?"

Peralta sat up straight; his eyes widened, and Zelde saw
they were bloodshot. "Then I *am* right!"

Zelde moved between Peralta and the door. "Maybe.
Maybe not. Either way, none of it goes off this ship, without we let it."

"Easy, easy!" Parnell pushed a hand at air. "Let us talk
a little, Zelde." She nodded, but stayed where she was. "All
right, Jimar. Without prejudice—your own phrase—here's
why your idea couldn't work, in either case."

"This had better be good. Good, hell—*perfect!*"

Parnell gulped more drink than Zelde liked to see. "Be
reasonable. We're suspect here, ourselves. If you're guessing, then so is Cort Verrane, Summit Bay, the Police—all
of it. The only way we get off this planet is by keeping our
noses clean." He balled a fist and slammed it on his desk.
"And that's exactly what we're going to do." Before Peralta
could interrupt: "We're shorthanded, Jimar. Oh, we've
enough, weapons-trained, to defend this ship—I've seen to
that. But not trained in assault tactics. I saw no possible
need, and usually it's a rather suicidal move."

Peralta shook his head; he was losing ground, Zelde
thought, to the trair. Not tracking too well. "But I'd—I'd
get Haiglund as hostage. He's popular—a stuffed shirt but
a fair man. Nobody wants him dead." He smiled, and for
the first time Zelde saw a side of him she liked. "Hell, *I*
don't want him dead. But you see—with that threat I could
take the heart out of loyalist resistance."

Was Parnell wavering? *The ship comes first.* "You heard
the captain, Peralta. We can't do it."

She watched him. *Now?* Tension, a beginning—then he
slumped back. When he spoke, his voice was quiet. "I'll
hear final decision from Ragir Parnell, M'tana—if you
don't mind."

"I don't mind."

Parnell pushed up to sit straight. "And you're hearing it—the same as before. Regardless of your ideas about this ship—if you want to take your own, you'll have to do so by your own resources." Peralta started to get up; Parnell said, "Not to go just yet, Jimar. We need to know *your* intentions—considering your unfounded beliefs, you see."

Peralta's smile turned to giggle. *The trair's got him.* "Unfounded! All right, Parnell—don't worry. In UET, one ship's all I'd ever get. But Outside, maybe more—so that's where I have to go. Still think we could work it, right here—talk some more tomorrow, maybe—but someday I will, you wait and see. And then I'll want *you* there, too— on my side. Y'understand?"

Parnell frowned; Zelde moved to whisper to him. "Not lying—too drunk."

Peralta took the last of his drink; some ran down his chin. Parnell said, low, "Too drunk to go talking on his own ship, I'd say, at the moment. Have you thought of that?"

Peralta was slumped in his chair. Zelde whispered, "Keep him here tonight? Feed him a pill? What you think?"

Shaking his head, Parnell said, "Even drunk, no one dopes Jimar—unless the pill were dissolved in liquor, and I have nothing that would vanish in a hurry. So—"

All right. "He stays, then. Ragir, go someplace."

"But—"

"I don't think he's able. But it can't *matter*."

"Yes. I see." Parnell poured a drink and carried it out the door.

Zelde took bottle and glass, and went to sit on the arm of Peralta's chair. "Drink, Jimar? I'm having me one." She poured, and guided his hand to the glass.

"Where Parnell?" He got glass to mouth, and swallowed twice.

"Where he sleeps. We're alone now." Briefly, his face had purpose; he reached for her. She gave him the glass instead; he drained it and reached again; this time she took his kiss.

Drunk or not, he knows how.

He was urgent now; she dimmed the lights and walked him to the bed. Getting rid of clothes took a time—she remembered, in time, to hide her knife safely under the bed.

Now, want it or not, she began to arouse—and she mustn't try to stop him. But then, all a-ready, the train took him—still moving gently, to no goal at all, he began to snore.

She woke alert and turned to see; Peralta lay curled away from her and breathing heavily. *Good start.* Being quiet about it, she got up and dressed, and left quarters. In the galley she nodded to various ones, got a cup of coffee and went upship, to Control.

Parnell wasn't there, either; Lera Tzane had the duty. She hadn't seen Parnell and seemed surprised at Zelde's question. Zelde touched the other's shoulder. "Things happening, Lera—we had to be different places. But I need to know, where is he?"

At Tzane's headshake, Zelde said, "No problem," and squeezed the shoulder. "Don't call captain's quarters, is all, until Parnell or I call you from there first. Got it?"

"Not really—but I'll do as you say."

"Good enough." Zelde left—where the hell had Ragir got to? The Third Hat quarters she didn't use, maybe? And when she got there, she found him, up and dressing.

Tired, he looked, but not hurting especially. He said, "How's Peralta? What do we need to do now?"

After a moment he quit fending her off and let her hug him, then kiss him. "Last night he crapped out—no action. All right? Still asleep when I left, too. Want to go wake him up with a load of breakfast? *I'm* hungry enough."

He grinned. "So am I. Yes—let's do break in on Jimar's hangover—as good Samaritans, of course."

Wearing trousers only, combing his wet hair, Peralta came out of the bathroom. His arms and torso showed the scars of UET's Slaughterhouse. Aside from dark smudges under his eyes, the man looked well enough, but he moved gingerly.

Zelde smiled. "Sit down, Jimar, and eat with us." She sat with her own tray; Parnell offered one of the two he carried. Peralta gulped some coffee, sipped his juice, and took a bite of scrambled eggs.

Chewing slowly, he looked at them. "Where do we stand?"

Parnell spoke. "How much do you remember?"

Peralta's gaze moved to Zelde. "I—that is—"

He don't know. What was the best move? Parnell said nothing, so Zelde went with her hunch. "Then it don't matter—right? Either way."

Tension seemed to help his queasy appetite. For a moment he ate rapidly, then paused. "This much I remember. You're Escaped—you admitted it." Whatever Parnell started to say, he waved it off. "The exact words aren't important—don't split hairs. You're Escaped, but won't help me do the same."

Parnell frowned. "I *told* you, Jimar—"

"You did—and I have to accept it. But now you're worried about me, aren't you?" Again he gave Parnell no chance to talk. "Well, you don't have to be. I'll tell you why."

"You do that," said Zelde. "I'd sure admire to know."

The man certainly recovered fast; now he spoke with force, almost lively. "It's *because* of what I want—a higher place than I'm likely to get from UET—that I'm no threat to you, Ragir . . . Zelde." He refilled his coffee cup and drank from it. "Suppose—just suppose, now—that I took the informer's route to command. Turned you in, so that UET retook the *Great Khan* before you could lift." He cocked his head to the side. "What's the ship's new name?"

Parnell shook his head; Peralta continued. "All right—say I did that. Then, you might say, as Captain I'd be in prime shape, given a trip or two to reshuffle personnel to my own purpose, to make my own Escape. See anything wrong with it?"

"Quite a lot," said Parnell. "Do you?"

Peralta grinned. "Too right, I do! Because where would I *go*?"

Now Zelde saw it; she gasped, and the man nodded. "What Escaped ship or Hidden World would tolerate a man who got free by betrayal?" He shook his head. "And when Tregare heard—that armed ship of his would hunt me down if it took him the rest of his life. You see, Ragir?"

The way Parnell sat now, he looked more relaxed. "Jimar—I wish I *could* help you, because our side needs you.

You're a fox—what tricks you don't know, you'll invent when you have the chance. And you realize a basic fact—that good faith is best trusted when it's grounded firmly in self-preservation!"

"I'm glad you appreciate my reasoning." Done eating, Peralta moved to pick up the rest of his clothes and finish dressing. From a jacket pocket he took a package, and gave it to Parnell. "Almost forgot this—your courtesy copy of *our* log. Not as ingenious as yours, I'm afraid. Pretty dull stuff, mostly."

Parnell gave the routine thank-yous. Checking his clothing and apparently satisfied he was complete, Peralta nodded and held his hand out, first to Parnell and then to Zelde. "Hangover and all, it's been a pleasure. How soon do you lift?"

Parnell shrugged. "Day or two." *Hah! Today most likely.*

"Don't wait too long, is my tip. Nosing around a little, down in Old Town, trying to get a line on you—I heard rumors. Suspicion's building, Ragir—and my questioning may have added to it. I'm sorry, if that's so, but I think you understand what my problem was."

"Yes," said Parnell. "It could have been myself in your shoes." He paused, then said, "Once free of this place, my ship will bear the insigne *Chanticleer.*"

"That's good to know; thank you. And if, some landing, you hear of a ship called *No Return,* that one will be Jimar Peralta's."

At the door he made a half bow, then turned and left. Parnell looked at the closed door. "Jimar has his faults, but no one can call him stupid. If he were—with all that ambition. . . ."

"I know, Parnell. We couldn't of let him off here alive."

They went to Control, where Parnell set up a dual comm-watch, separating onship communications from the circuits to groundside. He gave the Port a schedule for lift-off two days later. The ship's own schedule, though, set the lifting at mid-afternoon that same day. The timing allowed an initial course toward the next destination shown in the faked log. But that course passed near the system's largest planet—out where a single ship couldn't be detected from Terranova. And the passage was close enough to use the massive, barren giant in a sling maneuver that would let

Parnell point the *Khan* toward either Hidden World he chose.

It sounded good. Zelde hoped it would work.

At noon, Zelde took the watch from Lera Tzane. Checking the "raw" log—it would be edited down to essentials before going into permanent record—she found a call from Cort Verrane. He'd asked if the cargo was complete, and Tzane had given him the planned lie that two essential items were still missing. And Verrane blew up—the items *had been delivered*, he said, and, "If you people would get your heads out of your ass, maybe you could see where you're going!"

Tzane had tried to soothe him, but he finished by demanding "a full investigation, before you leave this port!" Zelde frowned. Damn!—Lera should have passed this one to Parnell. The timing, though—yeah, the call came before she had clearance to call captain's quarters. But later, when she did have that go-ahead—this sure's hell wasn't something to forget about!

By intercom she found Lera in the galley, and put her questions.

"But I—it didn't seem to require any action. After all, we're lifting in—let's see—a little over two hours from now."

"If we're let to. A man like Verrane—he could still make trouble."

"What should I have done?"

"Told Parnell, first chance. Or me, at least, at change-over." Zelde stopped—hell, this was her superior officer she was chewing out! Was she riding Parnell's authority, the way Dopples said she would? She shook her head—no time for that stuff. "Kowtowed a little, maybe—promise you'd get right on it, give a full report by late afternoon, keep the spoiled brat happy 'til we're out of reach and off the hook. That's what I'd of done." *Would I, though?* Parnell never gave hindsight much points. . . .

"Let it go, Lera; I'll call Verrane's office, see if I can patch things." Tzane's apologies came fast; Zelde said, "It's all right," and cut the circuit. But it *wasn't* all right, not until she fixed it—if she could.

At the other comm-panel—for offship—she got Verrane's secretary first try. No, he wasn't in. Yes, Officer

M'tana could leave a message. Zelde thought, then said, "The cargo mixup this morning. I see by the log, Officer Tzane didn't make it clear she started a correlation search right away. Well, the mistake's here at our end, all right—somebody working relief at the freight ramp, likely. Hasn't found the items themselves, yet—but she'll report again before you close shop there. That's fifteen hundred; right?" With the *Great Khan* two hours into space . . .

The man confirmed. "I'll get your own report to Mr. Verrane as soon as possible, Officer M'tana. Thank you."

"Same here." She cut the screen and turned to see Parnell standing beside her, eyebrows raised. Quickly she explained.

He nodded. "Yes. Best way to handle it, I think. Too bad Tzane didn't do so this morning." At her look, he said, "In the galley, she was telling me. So I came right up."

"Ragir—you think we got trouble?"

"While we're on Terranova? Of course. We've had it all along, if you stop to think. Ever since we landed."

"Yeah—I guess." Then, slow about it because she wasn't sure what to say, she told of her talk with Lera Tzane. "Is that what Dopples meant? Was I getting too big for my Hat?"

"No—somebody had to move fast. Zelde, on this ship the only difference between Hats is precedence of command; basically you're all doing the same job. And you had the watch. Except—"

"What, Ragir?"

"You shook Lera down a bit. Rightly so—but I have in mind for her to lift us today, and I want her feeling ready and able." He looked at his chronometer. "It's time you had a break, anyway—I'll sit in for you. If she's still in the galley—well, you might. . . ."

"Sure, Parnell. If I can."

Going into the galley, she met Tzane just leaving. The woman nodded and started to pass; Zelde took hold of her arm. "If you got a minute, Lera—sit with me?"

A stiff nod. "If you wish." Zelde got coffee for both, then sat facing the other.

Where to start? Smiling, hoping to make Lera feel easy, she told about her call to Verrane's office. "So I think we're all right now. No point in worrying, anyway."

Face tense, Tzane leaned forward. "But it could have been bad, couldn't it—the mistake I made?" She shook her head. "I don't know *why*—"

"Too much stuff on your mind, like all of us—but not for long. Once you lift us off here, soon now, things'll clear up a lot."

It wasn't working; Lera's face stayed blank. "Lift ship? Me? I can't do it; I don't feel sure enough of myself."

"Parnell does. You landed us, didn't you? And that's fancier—a *lot* fancier. Liftoff, you just point us right, like the computer says, and pour it on. No sweat."

"Then if it's so easy, Zelde, why don't you do it?"

"On account of Parnell picked *you*. And you're rightly in line ahead of me, plus you landed us real good." She grinned. "I'll get my turn sometime; no hurry. Hell, I never *seen* a lift yet. Only one I had, I was down there naked in Hold, Portside Upper."

Finally the woman smiled. "All right; I'll be ready. After all, it doesn't take any diplomatic talent to lift a ship."

Zelde reached to grip her arm. "Now you got it."

When she got back up to Control, Parnell was slumped in his seat. Her footsteps made noise on the deck; first his head turned, then he sat straighter. Damn, he looked tired—face strained, and no good color to it. Standing, now, he said, "I'm going to take a rest. Call if you need me—and ten minutes before lift, in any case."

"Parnell, you all right?"

"I'll make it. I'm taking my next pill early, and may need an extra before I sleep tonight. We'll see when the time comes."

"All right." Quickly she hugged him, her cheek to his, before letting him go. Then she took the control seat.

The log, nothing new—well, she hadn't been gone long. Outside screens, all quiet. There sat the *Bonaparte*—and what was Peralta doing just now? Beyond, ugly as usual but no more so, the Admin building. Old Town, looking quiet enough—she wished she could have seen more of it. Farther out, where clouds hid the sea—some weather coming, seasonal changes on the way. Good thing to be away probably, before going offship meant slopping in mud and drizzle.

Not a bad world, though, Terranova. Except for UET. . . .

She shuddered, then. *Sure wish we was lifted already!*

The intercom sounded; she flipped the switch. "M'tana here."

"Drive room—Harger speaking. Sixty minutes to liftoff, and all green on the checklist board."

Sixty more minutes? But all she said was, "Acknowledged, and thanks."

"Report cleared, then. Short of a hitch, which I don't expect, my next call will be the five-minute alert." Then, not so formal; "Who's lifting us? The captain?"

"No. Acting First Hat Tzane. Being as she brought us down so nice and easy."

Harger laughed. "She did, at that. Well, tell her she's got all the punch she needs from this end. Harger out."

"Right." With the circuit killed, Zelde found herself wishing that Parnell hadn't streamlined the procedures quite so much. UET's liftoff routines called for almost constant reporting back and forth—wasted effort, sure, but something to do, to ease the nerves. She shifted in her seat—how could she take a whole 'nother hour of this?

She wasn't sure how long it had been, when on the outside screen she saw the vehicle coming up the road. Only at one place, where the slope was gradual, could she see any part of the lower road—the curve at the first switchback. That's where she saw it—just a quick look, not enough to tell what kind of car it was. Then it rounded the turn and was behind the cliff again.

Well. Now she sat up, concentrating. The road came in view over to the left of the *Bonaparte;* she watched to see what was climbing the hill—and where it would go.

And finally the car showed. It was closed over, not like the ones the Port used, and above narrow windows a thick bulge ran the length of it. And she knew what it was. The Committee Police their own damned selves!

When the car passed the turnoff to Admin and still kept coming, she flipped the switch and called quarters. "Parnell? I think you better get up here!" No answer. "Parnell!

Captain! Get woke up and come to Control. Don't stop to dress—*carry* your clothes. It's—"

"All right, Zelde—I'm on my way. But this had better be good."

I wish it was! When Torra Defose had talked to Zelde, over at Admin, she'd come in an open car. Not this combat job. Zelde hadn't seen one of these since Earth—since she was running a district for Honcho. But she hadn't forgotten.

On intercom to the main ramp: "That car. Anybody wants to come aboard, you *stall!* Quick as we can, we'll get help down." She couldn't order that yet—she had to wait for Parnell. "Keep this here circuit open, so's it relays up anything they say."

"Right—and no one's coming through *me*." She recognized the man's voice, remembered his face—but couldn't put a name to it. She shook her head. *Not now.*

The car passed the ship's safety perimeter, ignoring the guard's command—over his loudhailer—to halt. *If we had guns on here, like that Tregare!* But they hadn't.

At twenty meters out, Zelde's guess, the car stopped. She watched—*do your trick*—and the car did. Its topside bulge folded away and a gun raised out, to point at the open airlock.

A projector, an energy gun—bigger than the heavy thing she'd used at Escape, bigger even than the useless blaster that went with the power suit. Zelde waited.

"Ahoy, the ship—Police business! Request to board." The voice from the bullhorn, relayed by intercom, distorted so that Zelde made out only the bare words.

To the ramp guard, she said, "Don't answer 'til you have to—and don't shoot yet." The man acknowledged.

From the car came four armed Police, wearing the plastic hooded helmets Zelde remembered. Then one unhelmeted figure—and Zelde recognized Torra Defose. *Friendly, huh? I should of knowed!*

That one had the bullhorn, and now used it again. "Guard—this is not an attack, but you must allow me to board. Don't try to close your ramp; my gunner in the car would cripple you. His angle of fire, through the airlock, bears directly on the major circuits between your drive and control rooms. So, guard—will you be sensible? May I board now?"

"When topside tells me you can. No offense—but I have my standing orders." Zelde heard the man clear his throat. "It shouldn't take long." Nervous, was he? Well, who wasn't?

Time to take a hand—Zelde turned on her outside speakers. "The *Great Khan,* control room speaking. Nobody called ahead about this boarding. The captain, he'd like a little more reason than a gun and some uniforms. This ship's dealt civil here; anybody comes on us this way should show some paper about *why,* I think." Had she said that right? Now she listened.

She zoomed the screen view down, and saw Defose grin. "M'tana, isn't it?"

This here's the enemy, remember—so talk careful. Zelde said, "That's right. M'tana, Acting Second, on watch. But the captain, he'll be here in a minute and say for himself."

"That's not necessary—you'll do. Meet me at the airlock, top of the ramp. That's an order—on the commandant's authority, if you prefer it that way. I have the papers you seem to want. Come down and inspect them."

"As soon as—" A hand grasped her shoulder; she looked around to see Parnell. He cut the outside circuit. "Parnell, I—"

"I caught the gist of it, I think. You don't have to go down there, if I order you not to."

Almost too fast to follow, her thoughts went. Then she saw how it was, all this. "Her alongside me, I'm safe enough. Safe as anybody else of us, right now. So I better—"

"A moment." He made the speakers live again. "Captain Parnell speaking. And to whom, may I ask?" Out of screen view his hand pointed to the master chronometer. *Ten minutes to liftoff!* Zelde looked at him, and thought she understood.

Torra Defose identified herself. ". . . and presently, Adjutant and Executive Officer of Police for this settlement. Now—will M'tana meet me at the airlock, as I've asked?"

Parnell's look told Zelde nothing, but she nodded. To the woman outside, he said, "Yes. At this point, she'll do the liaison. Wait where you are until she arrives at the airlock."

"Very well, Captain—and thank you."

Zelde reached to embrace Parnell. First he flinched away; then he held her. "Be careful, Zelde. I wish I knew—"

"Me, too. But whatever this is, Ragir, seems like it's something I got to do." They let go of each other; she left Control and headed downship.

She recognized the airlock guard, all right—shorter than she was, red-faced, usually looking cheerful but not now. Left-handed, he made a welcoming gesture. His right hand was behind him, out of sight—and she didn't see his gun, either. She shook her head. "No. One handgun won't win this. Put it away." He looked as if she'd slapped him, but followed orders.

Zelde stepped to the ramp's head and looked out. Torra Defose stood at the foot of it. Beside her was one armed, helmeted member of the Police; the other three were spaced between the ship and the car.

Defose was looking up; Zelde raised her voice to carry. "Captain says, come up now—and bring the paper you said about. I'll look at it here—all right?"

Below, the woman nodded. "That far, I'll come alone. From there, regarding any problems that arise, I'll give the orders." And moving quick but not looking hurried, Defose climbed the ramp. Then, facing Zelde, the Policewoman held out a sheaf of papers and stepped inside. "You wanted to see these, I believe." Zelde took the packet, and looked at several sheets.

She couldn't concentrate; none of it made sense. She started to shake her head, but stopped herself from that. *Say something!* "I—your papers pass, for now, Subject to captain's review." She felt pressure at her armpits; sweat ran.

Defose put the folder back in her shoulder bag. She turned to the guard. "You're not needed here; you're relieved. Officer M'tana is in charge."

The man looked from one woman to the other. Zelde saw him tensing, and said, "It's all right. You go up and guard from the next landing. Nobody comes in through this airlock unless I say so—or the captain does."

The man left. Defose said, "You did that well—putting him out of my car's line of fire." Then she showed a small, thick-barreled needle gun. "But now *I* do the talking."

Zelde's hand twitched toward her knife. "Don't. You *can't* be fast enough."

Holding her stance, Zelde grinned. "Maybe not. This steel crate we're in, though, it's no place for shooting that thing. You miss, like as not you catch it right back, yourself."

Impatient, the Policewoman moved her head. "I know that; our risks are equal, here. Now let me speak to your captain."

"You have that pleasure." Parnell's voice. Over the intercom, the strain didn't show—but it had to be there. "I thought I knew Police procedures. With all due respect, do you suppose you might tell me what *this* is all about?"

As though he could see her, the woman nodded. "I'm bringing you a change of orders. Your Second Officer is hostage here, to see that you follow them."

Without sound, Zelde sighed. Did this one really think that any person weighed against the *ship*? She shifted position slightly—and hoped she was faster than Defose expected.

But Parnell kept talking, as though nothing was wrong. "Why couldn't the commandant—or Verrane, his administrator—simply call me? Are the circuits out of order? Perhaps I should check."

"No! Those orders didn't come through the commandant. And you will *not* contact Verrane, or else—"

Parnell still talked mild; Zelde couldn't see why. "I see no need for threats, surely. Why, I don't even know the situation as yet—what it is that I'm supposed to do."

"Then listen. My troops haven't been informed, either— I'll tell you all now." She unslung the bullhorn and raised it. "Sergeant Hallsey—squad—here's your mission. Orders, direct from Commandant Horster at Summit Bay. I'm taking this ship there, directly, as soon as it can lift. Sergeant—take the car well outside the safety perimeter. From this moment, no one enters or leaves the *Great Khan*. When the ramp closes, it stays closed—or you shoot. Two of you place yourselves to guard against outside intrusion—the car will shield you from liftoff blast. Any questions?" She paused; no answer came. Car and foot troops moved back. When they passed the marked perimeter, Defose said, "All right, Captain Parnell. Lift the ramp and close ship. And advise me of your soonest possible liftoff time."

Until the ramp closed, Parnell said nothing. Then he spoke. "Defose—you're cut off now, from outside."

"I know that. And—"

"And liftoff—scheduled *before* your arrival—is about two minutes from now. But not to Summit Bay. *Ship's* people, hostages?" His voice choked off. "Zelde, I'm sorry! I should have—"

Zelde glanced at the gun, then at the woman's eyes. "Parnell, love—I knew the chances."

Hoarse now, he spoke again. "Defose, you can't boss this ship—accept the fact. But if you harm Zelde M'tana—"

Zelde braced herself. *Now?* But watching the other's face—on a hunch, she waited.

Defose said, "You don't understand, Parnell. I—"

"Then tell me. Time's short—for all of us."

And the woman smiled. "It's simple. I wasn't sure, at first—but you're Escaped, aren't you? And now, *so am I.* Sorry about the pressure play, but it was the only way I could think of, to get aboard." And she handed Zelde the gun.

Liftoff alarm drowned out Parnell's answer. Zelde grabbed the other woman. "Lie down—*quick!*"

The deck was hard, but Lera Tzane didn't jar it much.

Fighting atmosphere, the *Great Khan* shuddered. The shaking had barely ceased when Parnell came in the airlock. When he saw Zelde holding the gun, he put his own away and dismissed the guard behind him.

Looking strangely uncertain, Torra Defose said, "Captain—"

He shook his head. "I'm not angry; I don't have time for that. And we're away free and clear, so no harm done. But you can't expect me to take your story at face value just yet."

She frowned. "Why—oh yes, I see. You think it may be a trick, that I'm infiltrating."

Zelde hadn't thought of that idea; now she did. "Well, you got us to admit we're Escaped, right? Now all you'd have to do is get the word out—which might be quite a trick, itself."

Defose looked as if she'd been hit. "Do you believe that?"

"Believe?" said Parnell. "Ms. Defose, we can't afford to believe much of anything. So we'll have to find out."

In her kit, Torra Defose routinely carried "truth" drugs; Fesler, though, preferred to use his own. "Not that truth's the right word," he said. "Nothing so cut-and-dried. The stuff knocks out inhibitions and reduces attention span, making it nearly impossible to stick to a complicated story consistently. But there's an art to the questioning—and some people are relatively immune to the effects. Or resistant, at least."

Strapped in a chair, Defose sat. Five minutes after Fesler gave the shot, her mouth hung slack and her eyes looked empty. It didn't *look* like a fake—Zelde shook her head; you had to assume *something*, or what was the point of this?

Parnell lit a cigar, sat, and began asking. Your name? Torra Marise Defose. Rank? None. Giggle. "Oh—*used* to be. Yes. . . ." Adjutant and Exec, for Parleyvoo. Age? Thirty-four bio, in Earth years. Born? Loose laugh. "Well, how *else*?" Born *where*? Calgary, Alberta, North America, Earth. And left Earth at what age? Twenty-six. For where? Here—Terranova. Summit Bay first, then—oh, two–three years ago—to Parleyvoo.

Leaning forward, Parnell was. Do you want to Escape? I *did* Escape, didn't I? Why? Same reason as you did. "Then I think you'd better tell all about it."

Strained now, the woman's face had a helpless look. She shrugged. "All? That's the reason—*all* of it. You know?" Parnell waited; finally she continued. And then, for quite a while, she kept talking.

It was the torturing. Not just watching it, but sometimes having to do it, too. Sure—something important, you knew they knew it, and couldn't get it any other way—routine, that was. But you judged weakness and worked on it— psychology—making the fear of pain worse than pain itself. It was still bad. . . .

Cort Verrane, though, *liked* it. Said he didn't trust drugs. Even her superior at Summit Bay, when she was there, hadn't been that bad. Bad enough, though. Which was why—but then she shut up, and Parnell couldn't find a question to keep her going.

Back to Verrane, then. Defose grunted; her face twisted. With him, you clear a suspect, and like as not, he tortured anyway. Did a lot of permanent damage, left some victims unfit to live. The face and crotch were his favorite targets.

Remembering Softie at Barse's, Zelde didn't doubt what she heard.

Defose went on. The Underground leader, Horsehead. Caught and interrogated not long ago. Plain crazy, Verrane was. The way he used the hacksaw. . . .

The woman tried to raise her head. "Ready to talk, broken, so I said, more babble juice. Mixed in half with killer-drug, though. Spilled only two names, and died." Parody of a laugh. "Heart failure. Traceless, you see. Would have thanked me, by then. Fooled Verrane, and the tapes. I—"

Zelde tried to figure it out. Defose had killed the tortured, ruined prisoner before he could give away his secrets? Why?

Parnell asked; head lolling, Torra Defose tried to answer. Her words made no sense; Parnell tried again. Then, eyes rolled up in her head, mouthing her words breathily, she said, "Because, you damnfool, I was Horsehead's *segundo*. Been in Underground four years, from Summit Bay."

Then it began to make reason.

They gave her coffee, and Fesler tried a counteractive shot; in a short time the woman was tracking better. "The two names Verrane had from Horsehead. I tipped one and he hit the boonies, dropped out of sight. The other didn't know anything. Verrane bent him, though, and used him."

"And at Parleyvoo, Verrane still holds the handle." Parnell shook his head. "I could wish—"

Still groggy, Defose bared clenched teeth. "Every week, Cort Verrane comes nosing through my office. Did, I mean. Today when he came I had my squad ready outside, with the car. He's still there, with the door locked. I killed him, and burned the Horsehead tapes. So the Underground at Parleyvoo, the rest of it's safe enough." The woman's face was flushed; her breath came too fast and her eyes glared. "You don't know! After Horsehead, with Verrane on the prowl, once he had the blood-scent, I couldn't last long. You plug one leak, there's another. Kill him and Summit Bay comes down and pins me. Run, and Verrane rips up the Underground. So I did both, and took care of *all* of it."

Parnell said, "I'm not sure I understand. What did Horsehead's successor, your new chief in the Underground, think about all this?"

Her harsh laugh rattled. "Horsehead—not a name, a *job*. All the time you were on Terranova, *I* was Horsehead!"

Parnell gestured to the medic. "Put her to bed. See that she gets some rest—and food, if she can use it." He turned to Zelde. "Let's go. My mind's balanced like a coin on edge, whether we go to Refuge or Fair Ball. I think we may as well call a quick executive council and vote on it."

"No!" Tottering in Fesler's grasp, Torra Defose shrieked it. "Not Refuge! No such thing—it's a UET trap!"

Getting it all straight took some time. Zelde got Turk out of bed, and Turk confirmed that her info on Refuge had come from a man called Jex. "Skinny. Hunched over to one side."

"Verrane's doing," Defose said, "and Verrane's finger. Always good with blackmail, Verrane was. Once he had the name from Horsehead, he broke Jex and used him. Until now, though, I hadn't known what that use was."

Being in Police she'd known about Refuge for a long time. Except for one armed ship kept there, painted with Tregare's insigne *Inconnu,* Refuge was a low-budget operation. The other three standing hulls were dummies, also disguised as known Escaped ships. For the rest, a plausible amount of land planted in crops and a scattering of buildings to simulate a normal Hidden Worlds settlement. But those buildings housed a UET garrison. A trap, all of it, for Escaped ships that knew no better.

"And to think," said Parnell, "that UET planted the myth so long ago that I heard it as a cadet in the Slaughterhouse. Has the place had any success, do you know?"

Defose nodded. "Two ships captured, at least; maybe more. Not a big return, over the years. But UET takes all it can get."

Parnell snorted. "Too right. Now—do get some sleep,

Ms. Defose. I think you've earned your passage on this ship." For a moment he clasped Zelde's shoulder. "Come on; I need a drink."

In quarters Parnell started to pour whisky. His hands shook; he set the bottle down hard, gave Zelde one quick look, and went into the bathroom. She made drinks and put one on his desk. She checked the pills; there should have been one left, of the ration she'd set out for him that day, but there wasn't. Well, he'd said he might need extras now; she brought out one more and put it beside his glass. Then, waiting, she sipped at her own drink.

Pale of face, he came out and sat facing her. The pill, he washed down with whisky. And said, "I threw up, in there."

She thought, then said, "Wasn't a very pretty story, Ragir."

"No. But I've heard worse. I'm just knocked out of shape, Zelde. Part of what I threw up, was blood."

Her voice came out a harsh croak. "You want Fesler?"

"Not yet. I have to go to Control. Tzane can't handle the course change, for the sling maneuver around the gas giant. When I've arranged for that—then we'll see."

She reached to touch him. "Ragir? I don't suppose—"

He clasped her hand. "It's been a while, hasn't it—since I've been much good to you." She tried to speak but he shushed her. "And I'd be no good now—even if my guts *weren't* threatening to leave home. Some of the things Defose told—they might sex some people up, I suppose, but not me." He drained his glass. "Time to get upship. Mauragin's due to relieve, so I can clue him as well as Lera, how we'll do the sling."

"Then saving everybody's time, I'll tag along, too."

In Control, Parnell tossed Lera Tzane a salute. "Good lift, Acting First." She looked like asking something; he said, "The business at the airlock—it's taken care of." Then he sat beside her. "Our destination is Fair Ball. Now, for the sling maneuver—"

Zelde stood behind them as Parnell explained the upcoming course change; beside her was Carlo Mauragin. Yes—she understood it, she thought—but wouldn't try it on her own, without running through the figures a few times first. Carlo shrugged, and said, "It beats me; I guess I missed something."

Over his shoulder, Parnell spoke. "Then rerun the figures until you catch it. And next watch, tell me how it works."

"Yes, sir." Mauragin stiffened. "I'll try."

Zelde said, "I need to do that, too. We can work on it together." Without answering, looking at no one, Parnell got up and left Control. On his face, Zelde saw the signs of pain.

But she'd promised to work with Carlo, so she did. For an hour, until he could duplicate Parnell's computer work. Then Zelde left, also—and in quarters found Parnell sleeping. She checked the pills—fine; he hadn't cheated. But on the bedside stand was a glass with dreg-drops of raw whisky. From the smell of it, Parnell hadn't bothered with ice.

Nothing she could do, for now. Zelde undressed and went to bed.

Out from Terranova, angling toward the gas giant, the ship drove—keeping that planet just enough off screen-center that the *Great Khan* could tap its gravity-well for the course change.

Big Mama, the Terranovans called it. It carried a girdle of flashing fragments—not like Saturn's rings in the home system, more of a belt of tiny, jagged moons. On her next two watches, Zelde ran the forward screens on hi-mag, to see all she could of this new thing, while she was here.

On the after screens, two dots hung. Ships from Summit Bay, they had to be—chasing after, but no way in time to catch up. Nothing to worry about, there.

The worry was Parnell—since the course change, he spent as much time in bed as out. Zelde kept him fed, gave him his pills and a little booze. She had Fesler checking on him—twice a day, at least. After the fourth visit, standing outside so Parnell couldn't hear even if he woke up, the man said, "I don't know what's wrong. He was doing fine, I thought. But now—"

"He said, maybe his guts is stuck together, from the hurts he took at Escape. Might be you have to open him, to fix it."

Fesler shook his head. "I hope not. Oh, I'll try if it's

needed—with Dopples I did, and it worked. But that
scared the hell out of me—and so does this."

And there was a time I hated this medic! She touched
his arm, a little hard but not to hurt. "Comes to need,
you'll do it—I know. Just your best, that's all you do."

He put his hand over hers. "If it's enough—that's what
counts. We *need* the captain." As Fesler left, she thought,
And I need him more than anybody.

Stretched between two kinds of pills—but no booze at
all—Parnell took control for the sling turn. Two hours of
it, with closest approach a little later than halfway through.
"Since we're on accel, not coasting. Of course, this is no
place to coast." Because only the drive field kept the huge
planet's radiation belts from feeding them a killing dose in
short order.

Not understanding, Zelde shook her head. "If you say
so."

He grinned. The pills, just now, were balancing well.
"Don't worry; you'll learn it. It all takes time."

On the intercom, Dopples' voice was steady but still
weak. "That's some planet! Have I thanked you, Ragir, for
giving me a portable screen in here? Well, I do."

"Any old time, Dopps. Besides, I might need your advice." They chatted a little longer; then Parnell said,
"Oops—time for the first correction check."

"Right. Later, then."

Parnell didn't look shaky, but he never turned a knob
without first bracing his hand or wrist against the panel.
Well, better cautious than not. . . .

He read off a set of coordinates, then another, finally a
third, pausing each time for Lera Tzane to punch them into
the computer. For a moment he hesitated, before nodding.
"That's good enough at this stage—maybe all the way, if
we're lucky." Stretching, he leaned back. "Second check in
twenty minutes—final, probably not needed but just in
case, after another ten. Then nothing more until we've
made the pass—when our course is back to zero curvature,
or as near as makes no difference."

Big Mama, growing on the screen, kept Zelde from being
bored. Parnell's second check went easily; he made one
small adjustment. At the third he touched a dial, then
shook his head and pulled the hand back. "It's so small a

difference, likely I'd overcorrect. We'll do it all after pull-out." But Zelde saw the tremor as his hand, unsupported, moved from dial to armrest.

Going by the screen only, she'd have thought the *Khan* was bound to crash—if not into the gas giant itself, then into the flashing necklace around it. For a time she thought Parnell might intend to pass inside that belt—though the angle was bad—but then their sidewise drift showed more clearly and she saw they had good safety margin. Good, that is, if you liked to cut things close!

Now the planet pulled aside to loom—*huge*, that thing was—and slide gradually away, until it was clearly behind and slowly shrinking. For half an hour, nothing more happened. Then, again, Parnell began taking readouts. "Curvature point-oh-one." And after a time, "Oh-oh-one," then "three noughts," "four," and so on—until finally he said, "Curvature off the board, no indication readable. Five minutes more, for luck; then we correct course."

And about time, thought Zelde. The pills must be wearing off. Parnell's voice was strained, his color bad, his hands twitching. He looked once to her, quickly, then away again. And when the readouts came he said, "Zelde—I'll call the numbers; you set those dials. That way, we'll have a double check."

On the intercom, Dopples cleared his throat. But the First Hat said nothing, so she answered, "Sure, Parnell," and moved within easy reach of the control panel.

He spoke the coordinates steady enough, and looked to check her dial settings. "That's good—that's *it*—we're pointed square for Fair Ball, if Torra's contacts knew their stuff. Now then—" He called the drive room. "Harger? You there?"

"Right, skipper. Do you have our course?"

"Correct as hell. So—set and hold accel at point-seven max. At that rate, if I have it right, turnover's at day one-oh-three from liftoff—give or take one, for luck. All right?"

"Acknowledged and logged. And congratulations for a clean pass. Anything else?"

"No—except, nice work, on the drive. It rumbles *solid*." Then, with the switch off, Parnell wiped his forehead. "You have it all logged here, Tzane?" The woman nodded. "All right—the watch is yours, then. Zelde—help me up, will you?"

So it was that bad, now—that he had to ask help in front of people. As if nothing was wrong—with no expression, she hoped, on her face—she gave him a hand up. And then support, as they left Control and went to quarters.

Once there, he sat heavily. "The pepper wore off—it leaves me without strength. And the pain pill, mostly, too. But if I take another so soon—ahead of schedule again—" He shook his head. "Booze, I think, for now."

She didn't have a better answer, so she poured it for him.

When he began to doze—and lately it didn't take much drink, for that—she got him onto the bed and took his shoes off. At least he'd got by without another pill—that combination, she knew, was dangerous.

She went looking for Fesler and found him with Dopples. Not stopping to make polite talk, she told how it was with Parnell. "Fesler, you got to open him and find what's wrong. If you don't—well, he won't be lasting long, is how it looks to me."

Head propped on a pillow, Adopolous nodded. "It's a risk, Fesler; we all know that. But if he's willing. . . ."

The medic's hands clenched. "If only he could have been treated on Terranova—with real doctors. . . ."

"You know why not!" Zelde's breath came fast. "Going under for the operation, coming out of it and maybe talking loose to UET people—it's the ship, *us*, he was keeping safe."

Fesler spread his hands. "I know. Well, now that we're on course, I'll talk to him. And if he wants it, I—I'll go in."

Dopples coughed. "No way you can build him up for it first?"

"Vitamin shots. He's supposed to have been coming in for them, but he misses more times than he shows up." The man shook his head. "I'll have him on IV first thing, before operating—with the pain drugs mixed right in with the nutriment. Those pills must be raising sheer hell with his stomach and kidneys. I tell you—I'm really worried about what I may find."

Zelde squeezed his arm. "I know you are. But if worry helped, he'd be well by now."

She turned to go. Dopples said, "If you get up to Control, look in on the side cubby, will you? I've assigned that ex-Policewoman—and we're keeping it to ourselves that she ever was one—to tape everything she can think of, about how her former outfit operates. How it keeps tabs on us, and all. I'm going through her tapes, organizing the information so it can go into the computer, where we can all use it." Awkwardly, lying there, he shrugged. "Gives me something to do."

For a moment, Zelde stood silent. "Mr. Adopolous—here I'm so worried-up about Ragir, I forget to ask how you *feel*, even. I'm sorry—and I do want to know."

Dopples smiled. "I understand, M'tana." Then: "Me? Too slow, healing, is the size of it. I'm allergic to two of the best anti-infectants—Fesler found that out the hard way. And God only knows what was on that knife. Anyway, I keep getting these damned little pockets of infections—and when the fever tips our medic off, he has to find and drain them. The upshot is that I haven't built up any strength. But I'll make it, don't worry."

"Sure you will." *But it was for me, he got stabbed!* "All right—if Defose has a full reel, you'd like it right away?" He nodded. "I'll see to that." And now she did leave.

In the cubby, wearing a ship's worksuit with no rating marks, Torra Defose didn't seem like Police at all. She turned her recorder off. "Officer M'tana. I haven't seen you lately." She grinned. "The last time, my head was looping with the truth drugs—and you, watching me like a hawk after a mouse. I can't say I blame you, either."

Zelde shrugged. "You'd put us through some jumps, then. Had to, like you said, to get on here safe. I guess you know, you took some chances."

Serious, the woman's face went. "I do know. I had no safe way to communicate—safe for either of us. And on—groundside, you call it—we don't know ships' ways. So I tried to plan how to get aboard without endangering the ship—and it worked."

"You did pretty good. But it took luck—mainly we was too much under the gun to think straight. If—" Then she thought, why was she bothering to second-guess?

Frowning, Defose said, "I don't see it. Would you have killed me out of hand? And what else could have gone wrong?"

All right, tell her. "The power suit. It's not in top shape but it does work—and I'm trained in it."

Still with a scowl, the woman shook her head. "I'm not familiar with those, but I do know their specs, from reading. Your suit projector couldn't match the one on the car—and neither could the suit."

"If I'd come out the main ramp, no." No point in mentioning that the suit's projector couldn't be used, anyway.

"But then how?"

"Freight ramp—let it down halfway, fast, and jump. In that suit I'd get to your car before it could turn to cover me. Then—do I have it, or don't I?" And as Defose nodded, Zelde said, "Or say I run and grab you before you get up the ramp. The hostage thing—would they shoot you to get me?"

"I—I don't know. With only a sergeant in charge—"

"Doesn't matter—the car was the best bet, anyway. I'd of gone for that." She had to grin. " 'Cepting, I didn't. Too much going at once, and me not in charge, really—waiting on orders, 'stead of making my own moves. Short of time, too. See?"

The woman nodded. "Yes. I think so. But what's your point?"

"Maybe, just that this ship here, it's not as dumb as you might think, from the way you foxed us up."

Torra Defose blinked. "I didn't think that. Your captain—your own man, isn't he?—is sick. Which I didn't know before I came here. And for what it's worth, I'm sorry he is."

No point to this; they were both on the same side now, weren't they? "Sure." Then, shrugging: "What I came for—you got any full reels put together now, for Dopples?" Blank expression on the woman's face. "Mr. Adopolous—he's the one asked you to tape all the Police stuff for us."

"Oh, yes. I'm completing a reel; then I'll take it to him."

"You do that." Starting to turn away, Zelde faced back. "Look, Defose, I'm not out to push at you. You Escaped, you killed that turd Verrane so the Underground at Parleyvoo has a chance now. You helped cover the agent that gave Turk Kestler the dope on Fair Ball. Hell, you saved this *ship;* you belong on here. It's just—"

"I know. Policebitch—that's your word, isn't it? I'm not

one, not anymore. But you'll be a time, won't you, before you can think of me in any other way?"

The lean face didn't give much away, but Zelde saw pain. Without knowing she was going to do it, she touched the other's hand. "Don't sweat, all right? First time we met you, down in Old Town, *before* any the rest of it happened—remember? Even that time you struck me too decent for—for Police."

Defose made a sort of smile. "And that's not the way you usually say *that,* either. Right?"

"No. How I always said it, is the Committee Police *their own damned selves.*"

Torra Defose laughed. And as Zelde left the cubby she saw the woman, face relaxed, still smiling.

As she went into Control proper, Lera Tzane was on the intercom. "All right, Carlo—this once, again. But make it fast." She cut the circuit and turned to Zelde. "He's got some little doxy with him; I heard her giggling. No problem, but they lost track of time. So he'll be late relieving me."

Zelde scratched her head. "You going to log him?"

"Oh, why bother? If he continues to make a habit of it, then—" She shrugged. "Incidentally, I tried to call Parnell. There's no captain's instructions logged for my watch or the next. And he didn't answer. What do I do?"

Think fast. "I thought he called it in—or I'd've brought the sheet myself." Stepping forward, she checked the previous entries, then nodded. "Same as before, it should be; no change. You can punch it in that way."

Tzane looked at her. "Over whose authorization? Yours?"

Impatient, Zelde waved a hand. "Parnell's, of course—same as if he *had* called it up to you." Frowning, she worded her lie. "Oh, hell—I forgot. I *was* supposed to bring the sheet up."

Without expression Tzane punched the data in, then answered. "If you say so. Zelde—"

"Yeah?"

"Be careful."

"Of what? Lera—something going on I don't know?"

The woman pushed back her hair. "Carlo's talking a lot. Says he's speaking for Dopples—which I doubt, but he does quote him, from back when Dopps was leaning on you. Pretends to talk for *me*, too—claims you're using Parnell's authority to take mine." She opened one hand, palm up. "I'm not in this with Carlo, Zelde—I want you to know that."

From narrowed eyes, Zelde stared. "Maybe I should talk to him—get some straight answers."

Looking down, Tzane shook her head; the hair fell forward again. "So far, he's just hinting. If you challenge him, he can say you have a guilty conscience. I—here he comes now."

Zelde looked around and saw Mauragin come in. She thought his step paused; then he smiled and came ahead. "Zelde—Lera—sorry I'm late." He looked at the master chrono. "Not by much, though. What's new on the log?" He scanned it. "Captain's instructions up to date now, I see. Did he punch them in himself, or call?"

Zelde looked at him until his grin stopped. "Sent them. All right?"

"Yes—sure—just asking." He turned away from Zelde. "Is everything else on the money, Lera?"

"Yes. You'll do your own full read, of course, before acknowledging acceptance."

He looked from one woman to the other. "Aren't we getting pretty formal here? What's up?"

Angry, Zelde tried not to show it. "Just reminding you, coming in late and all, to do things proper. You mind?"

Now she'd alarmed him. "Wait—I didn't mean—"

"That's good." And before she could say more than she should, Zelde walked, fast-paced, out of the control room.

Heading downship she passed by the galley. Lera would go there—and right now, it wasn't Lera she wanted to talk with. She went to Turk's quarters and found Rooster Hogan there alone, listening to a music tape. She accepted his offer of a beer—self-service, here—and sat with him. When the tape was done, she told him about Mauragin. "You heard any of this?"

Squinting one eye he took a sip of beer, then a larger swallow, and belched. "Some, maybe—and so has Turk." His story had more details than Lera's—Mauragin's way was first to mention how hard Zelde worked, then cite anonymous complaints about her and defend against them weakly, not convincingly.

"Like what, he says?"

"Like you're such a young-ass; younger'n him, even. And come up from cargo to captain's pet. All that idiot crap." Shrug. "So folks come away—well, you know— worried, sort of." Zelde snorted; Rooster looked up. "What's that for?"

"For being fooled, me—I thought we got along. But I guess he still burns at being set back, and I got his place." Rooster's glass was empty; she filled it for him.

"Thankee. What do you figure on doing?"

Her gesture didn't go anyplace. "Don't know. What you say, he's kept it so's I'd be in the wrong to call him out."

"Too true, Zelde. He knows you've got a temper—"

Her hand squeezed her glass. "And I got stubborns I never even used yet. Say I lean some, and *Carlo* flies off the handle—"

"And add fuel to his complaints? Not too wise, Zelde."

Scowling, she pointed a finger. "Hear it first. I been feeling sorry, leaning over backward, helping him look good. I just now quit." And she told how she'd handled him, being late.

"Thing is, Rooster, only jump him where there's witnesses, so he can't make up his own story. And stretch *his* temper."

Rooster's eyes widened. "And if he calls you out?"

She drained her beer. "Hadn't thought that far. He can't fight for moldy beans; I saw his qualification records. I could cut him too short to hang up!"

Rooster gave a startled laugh. Zelde waved a hand. "Thanks for the beer—and the talk." Out the door she went.

In Henty Monteil's workshop she found Turk, working by herself. "Hi, Zelde—what's going?" In a few words, Zelde told her. "Yes," Turk said, "I've heard things. Not much, though."

"Just keep a listen out, huh?" The other nodded, and Zelde looked at the workbench. "What you making? Some kind of big poster?"

Turk spread the sheet of plastic. About two meters by three, it draped off the bench to the deck, and spread a pace farther. Now, with most of the wrinkles smoothed out, Zelde saw what it was.

"Hey, our new insigne!" A stylized gamecock in bright colors—and, all in big capitals, the word CHANTICLEER.

Turk nodded. "Somebody in the drive room made the design right after Escape. Parnell okayed it when he was first up and around." So that's why Zelde hadn't seen it; they weren't so close, then. "But nobody got around to *do* it for a while."

Stroking the place where a proud wing curved, Zelde said, "Sure. We couldn't mount it 'til after Terranova, anyway."

"Right—but now we can. I'll have it done this afternoon." And Turk knelt to apply color to an unfinished part.

Puzzled, Zelde said, "How do we put it on the ship, outside? I mean—there's the power suit—but the shoes, the traction magnets, don't work. And the airlock—that's a hell of a ways to go on a safety line. Anyway—will that plastic hold up when we plow air, landing and lifting off?"

Turk laughed. "Last question first. Permanent electret, this sheet is—polarized, smooths on easy. Then spray on the sealer around the edges, and it's good for nearly forever." She set the color kit aside. "And the power suit isn't needed for this—*or* the main airlock. There's regular vacuum suits, too, you know—and an auxiliary airlock up near topside, for getting out to work on antenna systems if we had to." She frowned. "Rooster had better do this—he's used the suits, and the way things are now, I don't think you ought to work outside at all."

"Regular" vacuum suits—auxiliary airlock—Zelde felt like a new kid in a strange gang. *And how much else don't I know, that I ought to?* "Turk—how come you know these things and I don't? Maybe *you* belong wearing the Hat, 'stead of me."

The older woman put a hand on Zelde's shoulder. "Zelde—you've been busy learning your job, and doing it. Me, I've bounced from one job to another—first getting our bunch from the hold into ship's routine, then whatever else came up to do. So I've learned a little about things all over the ship, that you haven't had reason to meet with yet. But you see—all *you* need to do, Zelde, is ask. Me, or anyone else."

"Well, maybe. Anyway, thanks." She checked the time. "Hey, I've got to go. I'll tell Parnell the insigne's ready."

"Do that. And—about Mauragin. He's building a gang, I think. But Rooster and I—from the hold, and in the lower ratings—we already *have* ours. And you can count on it."

Zelde swallowed; she gripped Turk's arm. "I hope you can count on me, too."

Before the other could reply, she was out the door.

In quarters she found Parnell awake, at his work desk with a cup of coffee. He looked up. "Tomorrow Fesler wants to read the portents in my entrails. Is this decided, or do I have a vote?"

She paused, gazing—his face showed pain, yes, but he seemed less doped than he had for days. She went to him—his arms, at least, had strength. "Ragir, you've said it yourself—what's dragging you down has got to be looked at. And now we're on clear course for Fair Ball. Don't you think it's time?"

He kissed her—like old times, almost. "I suppose so. That's why I'm doing some work up ahead here—at best, after surgery, I won't be in working shape for a while."

"Anything I could do? Or help with?"

"I'm doing only the things you *can't* help with." He laughed—she heard, almost, the Parnell she wanted back again. "The rest of it I'm leaving to you and Lera. How else?"

A pep pill, it had to be. But why? And then his hand, moving on her, gave the answer. And he said, "Whatever happens, when that well-meaning amateur shuffles my insides like a pack of cards—we have something coming to us first, you and I!"

So she gave him—at the same time sparing him—as much as she could. *Oh*—it was so like before, but never quite. Once, drowned in her own sensation, she forgot his weakness—then she remembered, and saw to it that he didn't fail.

Lying back, stroking his forehead, she said, "Parnell, love—"

"Yes. You did me right, Zelde—you did me right."

When Parnell slept, she called Fesler. "M'tana here. He's agreed to be operated tomorrow. You ready for it?"

She heard his sigh. "As ready as I'll ever be."

"Don't think worried—you can do it. Now, I've got the watch soon. You take charge, personally—that he gets fed right, and those vitamin shots you said about?"

"I've given him two today. You were out, both times."

"Good—and thanks." Maybe that accounted for him being better. She nodded. "Talk to you later, then. M'tana out."

Going into Control she watched to see how Carlo acted. As she scanned the log she looked sidelong at him; he seemed nervous. She pushed the recording button. "All's well, Carlo?"

"You're early."

"That's right."

"Trying to show me something? Is that it?"

Was he this easy to bait? Zelde wasn't sure she wanted it that way. She cocked her head and looked at him. "Like what?"

"Well—I was late for watch today."

She paused. "I'd forgot."

He halfway stood, then sat back. "Had you?"

Zelde looked around —the whole duty watch was listening. She had her witnesses—*and* the tape running. All right—sink a hook! "Am I supposed to keep count the times you're late? That's for who you relieve, to log."

Now he did stand. "It hasn't been that often!"

"I didn't say it had." And when he didn't speak: "The log's all right. You're relieved."

He moved out of the command chair, but waved a hand at her. "Now wait a minute. You're saying—"

"I said the log's all right and you're relieved."

He'd been moving away from her; now he stopped. "M'tana—are you pushing something at me?"

She sat; now she had to look up and back, to face him. Again she said, "Like what?"

He stood almost in fighter's crouch—hands moving, clenching and then opening again. All at once, he stopped. "What are you *doing*?"

She waited until he gave up and turned away. "Just my job, Carlo; that's all. Not anything else. You think you can maybe remember that?" Before he could answer, she added, "Because I think you'd better."

He left without speaking. Turning back to her console, Zelde thought, *Well, Mauragin—that's for starters.*

Usually, in clear space, the watch was dull. This time, just after the two-hour mark, the screen caught a blip. Zelde's monitor tech ran mag and tracking up to max, but the thing lasted only a few seconds. She looked at the man. "How do you read it?"

He shrugged. "Not big, not fast—planetary speeds, a little more. If it's a ship, it's dead and drifting. More likely a cold rock, a few billion years from where it started." He tapped keys on his computer access panel. "And by now, it's a million kilos behind us—and losing ground fast."

She nodded. "Yeah. Thanks, Charvel. That kind of numbers—time and distance—they take some getting used to."

This chunky man, she knew, had been a buddy of Carlo's. Watching the freckled face, under wiry red hair, she wondered if he was on Mauragin's side right now. No way to find out—she couldn't afford to get edgy about everybody. Paranoid, they called that. So she sat back for another hour, watching screens and instruments tell her not much of anything. And then, just as if she trusted him, she gave Charvel the watch for her coffee break. She did say out loud, with her tape running, what everybody usually took for granted—that he should put all incoming signal on relay to the galley. He looked up when she told him that, but didn't say anything.

In the galley she got some bread and cheese with her coffee, and sat at an empty table. In the whole place were only a few people, at two tables on the far side. She ate faster than she intended, and was sipping her second cup of coffee when Torra Defose approached. "All right if I join you?"

Zelde nodded. The woman set down her tray—soup, a sandwich, and coffee—and sat facing her. Zelde said, "How's the taping going, for Dopples?"

"All right." Eating as she talked, Defose said, "That's not what I'm here for." She looked around; no one was within listening distance. "You recall I asked about subversion on this ship?"

"You think back, you'll see I didn't lie to you."

The lean, Indian features creased in a smile. "I know. In

making my decision to try to get on the *Khan,* I analyzed that interview. Using the truth to misdirect—it's a useful talent." Done eating, she wiped her fingers. "Now, though—do you know that you have a subversion problem yourself?"

"Carlo, you mean? How'd *you* find out?"

"Police work gives one an ear for such things. Of course, very few here know I was ever Police—and on Mr. Adopolous' orders, the fact's been kept quiet. So as a mere recruit, I get talked to—and I listen."

She leaned forward. "Zelde, you're very close to having a mutiny on your hands."

Shaking her head, Zelde sat back. "Me? Third Hat, Acting Second? Parnell, you mean—and do these lice think they'll mutiny on *him?*" One hand clenched; the other rubbed it. "They try that, there'll be some go out the airlock!"

Pushing her tray aside, Torra reached one hand to Zelde's two. "*Listen* first. The stories differ, but basically the cabal discounts the captain—because you and Doctor Fesler, being secret lovers, are planning to kill him." And before Zelde could explode her wrath: "Control yourself! Maybe we should speak more privately." Zelde caught her breath, and nodded. "All right. You have to know the worst, don't you? Needless to say, I don't believe any of it."

"You—you better hadn't. Look—at Escape, not even knowing Parnell yet, I saved his life. He says I own it—but I don't." She felt her mouth twist. "Wish I did, though—wish I could—so's I could keep it safe for him!" Her knuckles wiped tears away. "Tell me the rest, then. Like, how long's this been going on? And how come I'm only now finding it out?"

"Not long, I think. And you couldn't know until something happened. Now then—they're counting Mr. Adopolous out, too, while he's disabled. And you and Fesler get credit for that also." Unbelieving, Zelde shook her head.

"Oh, that's the story, all right. And the mutiny's against you, personally, because you're the one who stands in its way. Officer Tzane's totally loyal, I'm sure, but she's no fighter—and you are. And because you're so solidly tied to Parnell, you're the target. So that leaves Carlo Mauragin."

"For what? I don't see it. For *what?*"

"To be the figurehead, for whoever's organizing this putsch."

It made sense. After a moment, Zelde said, "Yeah. It didn't *feel* right—Carlo, all on his own, coming after my hide." And the thing *was* new; Zelde hadn't been as blind as she'd begun to think she was. Everyone Torra Defose listened to, told it the same—something that didn't start until after liftoff.

Zelde leaned forward. "How soon do they move? You know?"

The dark, serious-faced woman shook her head. "And neither do they, I think. Not the best-organized conspirators I ever heard of. A small group, I suspect, and working—as they must—with total amateurs." Her laugh was a quick bark. "Carlo Mauragin, for the love of peace!"

"Carlo, yeah—but what do I *do*?"

"Now, that's the right question. All right—I doubt that you like the idea of a security network. But that's what you need—and it's what I know how to do. Will you trust me to do it?"

Second thoughts—truth drugs or no, it was only after Defose came aboard that this thing started. But what *choice*? "Go ahead and start. I'll talk it over with Parnell."

"Of course. Can you recommend anyone to work with me, or shall I recruit my own people?"

That one was easy. "You know Turk Kestler?" A nod. "Good—you get with Turk, let her recruit for you. Anybody knows this ship, she does." Another thought. "And she'd better do go-between for us until this is settled."

Torra's brows raised. "You don't like my company?"

Impatient, Zelde shook her head. "Not that. But, Dopples or no Dopples, some of the wrong people will know who you are. So we shouldn't get together too often. One thing—if I'm a target, hanging around me could make you one, too."

She thought, but didn't say, that that idea worked both ways. Besides, still not able to be all sure of Defose, Zelde would feel better if her reports came through Turk. Because if there was anyone who could *read* people. . . . But all she said was, "On this ship, Turk's my oldest friend—oldest still alive, anyway." *Poor Tillya!* "So anybody sees her and me together, it's no new thing. Scan it?"

Slowly, Defose nodded. "Yes. We'll do it that way."

Zelde checked the time, and stood. "Peace up a pipe, I'm overdue on watch—and that's not something I need on the log just now. Look—soon as I can, I'll tell Turk you'll be in touch, and why." She paused. "And thanks. I appreciate the help."

"My pleasure." That was all, so Zelde went upship to Control, fast as she could without losing her wind.

Four minutes late. Hell with it; she logged it straight.

Nothing else new on the log except a routine drive room report. But she should have been here to punch it in herself. Oh, well. . . .

She switched her intercom to Turk's quarters. Then, to the side, she saw Charvel look at her and move a switch himself. Hold it!—if she used the hush set, he couldn't hear her, but could he record what she said? *Damn! I wish I knew this stuff better.* So for now, she switched off—contact with Turk would have to wait.

Idle now, her mind on other things, she was surprised when the watch ended. Lera Tzane relieved her; Zelde talked only of routine items, and left as soon as she could.

Turk would be sleeping now; Zelde realized she could do with some of the same. In quarters she found Parnell dozing, not quietly—covers thrown back, and sweating. She pulled one cover up, so he wouldn't take chill. Then, too tired to bother with washing up, she crawled in beside him.

In the morning, feeling better, she showered and dressed. Parnell began to stir; she called the galley and ordered breakfast brought. For a moment, no answer; then a voice said, "Just a minute." Zelde waited.

Switches clicked; Fesler's voice said, "Is that you, Zelde? In case I do operate today, the captain can't have any food; I left orders to that effect. Unless we postpone."

Behind Zelde, Parnell said, "Yes, that's standard. All right—Fesler, when do you want me?" Fesler set it at mid-morning; Parnell replied, "Then an hour before that time, I want a brief meeting of all Control officers—including the watch officer; this won't take long. And Harger, to represent the drive room. Dopples shouldn't be moved, so we'll meet there. Set it up, would you please, Fesler?" The medic agreed; Zelde cut the circuit.

"That's not his job, Parnell; you should of had me do it."

He didn't answer; looking, she couldn't tell what kind of shape he was in. Tense, maybe—the surgery and all—couldn't blame him for that. She went to him; his hug was gentle so she kept hers that way, too. "Ragir—you all right? As good as can be for now, I mean?"

"Ready enough to have Fesler plumb my unhallowed depths and see what he can fix." His grin was almost right. "Well—since I can't eat, I may as well bathe." He turned away, then looked back. "My stomach doesn't believe Fesler. So would you spare me the sight of food, Zelde, and eat in the galley?"

"Sure." Until the bathroom door closed, she watched his bare, scarred back. Then she went upship, to eat.

She found Turk and Rooster, and sat with them. As she ate, she told of the arrangement with Torra Defose. "She's level, I think. If she is, she's worth a lot to us. If she isn't—I expect you'd spot that, Turk."

Kestler frowned, then nodded. "I think so. And none of my other people are to know she's ex-Police, is that right?"

"Best not. It'll leak out, though, I expect."

"All right. All we can do, Zelde, is play it loose." Turk paused to sip coffee. "Now then—guess what Rooster's up to, this morning?" Zelde shook her head. "Mounting our new insigne, that's what! He's done suit drill with the airlock open, and it's all set." Rooster's grin was as wide as Zelde had ever seen it.

"Hey, that's fine. Does Parnell know? I'll tell him. But—" But when Rooster was outside, she thought, Parnell would be lying, unconscious, with his guts cut open.

Turk leaned forward. "Something the matter?"

"It's just—" She explained. "Seems so strange, is all."

"You tell him, anyway," said Rooster. "Give him a little something extra to wake up for."

They were trying to cheer her up, she knew—and after a few minutes she *did* feel better. And Parnell, when she told him, seemed cheered, also.

Dopples' room held only two chairs—by seniority, Parnell and Harger had them. Zelde, Carlo Mauragin, Lera Tzane when she hurried down from watch—they stood. So did Fesler, and one look from him stopped Mauragin when the young man went to sit on the edge of the bed.

Parnell cleared his throat. "All right—we're here, and the business is brief. Fesler, switch the intercom to record into ship's log." This done, Parnell said, "Control officers and Drive representative, the ship *Chanticleer,* in meeting. Ragir Parnell commanding and presiding. I have one item." He cleared his throat. "The shared ownership of this vessel is a matter of record." He paused, and Zelde thought, What was he up to?

Dopples said, "True, skipper. What's there to discuss?"

Parnell looked at him. "This much, Dopps. I'm going into surgery; I hope and expect to come out of it in good shape. But there are always risks—and I believe in providing for them."

He looked up at Zelde, then back to Dopples. "You're here to witness my last will and testament. When I die— today or years from now—all I own, which is mostly shares in *Chanticleer,* goes to Zelde M'tana."

She saw the shock hit—Dopples' look of resistance, Harger's puzzlement, Lera Tzane's accepting nod, and from Carlo Mauragin, sheer hate! *And I ain't told Parnell about that one, yet.*

She gripped Parnell's shoulder—he flinched, and briefly she thought she'd grabbed the bad one. No—just startled, probably. "Ragir, you don't need to do this. I—"

"Hush, Zelde." So quietly he said it, she barely heard him. But with her, the whole group went silent. Now Parnell's voice raised. "At Escape, Zelde saved my life; since then, it's been hers." He looked up. "Like it or not, Zelde, that's true." Now he turned back to the others. "And with it goes title to my possessions. You're all here to witness, and that's official."

He made to stand, but Dopples said, "A question or two, to be sure things are straight?" Parnell sat again. "Well, then—this isn't the way we handled the late Captain Czerner's holdings, is it? Or Terihew's, come to that. What's so different now?"

The captain shook his head. "Until we'd met, after Escape, and applied the Agowa formula, there were no such things as shares; you know that. UET owned the ship. Dopps—what's your real objection?"

The wrong time, this is. But for sure, there was no stopping him. Now Dopples said, "All right—here it is. Shares were assigned by rank, as shares of command, too. What I want to know is, are you saying it's the other way, too—that command goes with your shares?"

Two sick men throwing more force of will at each other than the rest, all together—including, Zelde realized, herself. No time for thinking—*just say something*. "My turn," and they listened. "Ragir—Captain, I mean—you're not for dying. Don't even think that." She heard a snort—Mauragin—and swung to face him; he shrank back. *Later I'll get to you!* And now, to Dopples: "Mr. Adopolous—"

He interrupted. "Parnell, are you seriously proposing that command go to this girl? Oh, she's become a good officer—but she never *saw* the inside of a ship, before this one."

"As I recall," Parnell said, "you're the one who suggested her for Third Hat. But I don't think Zelde was done talking."

"For certain, I'm not. Mr. A.—you're next in line and earned it. Shares or no shares, if you was in shape for the job—"

Again Dopples cut in. "I'll accept that—but even so, you're not next senior."

"No!" It was Lera Tzane. "Don't try to put command on *me*. Even temporarily—unless there's *no* one else, I don't want it."

"*You* don't," said Carlo Mauragin, "but M'tana sure does."

Now Tzane's face reddened. "But not you, I suppose! You and your little galley-politician games—and not even handling your Acting Third Hat properly. Zelde and I, covering for you—but not any longer! I promise you that."

It was all going to hell. Zelde said, "If Parnell wanted a hearing to chew the small stuff, he'd of called one." Seeing Lera's stricken look, she gave her a wink. "This is no kind of scene for a man going in surgery; let's stop it. Ragir—you say what you want and I'll stand by it." *And please don't stir this shit up any worse than it is.*

Breathing a little faster, Parnell showed no other sign of strain. His voice came mild. "I don't see the problem—why there should be one. We chose our course and destination in the approved fashion. Until *Chanticleer* reaches that destination, our agreed plans hold and it hardly matters who

nominally commands. As to the ship's good, I mean." He
looked around the group. "I *assume* that's what concerns
us all—and I hope so. Now, if there *is* a change of command, Mr. Adopolous, you will succeed me if physically
able. If not, then with Officer Tzane opting out of the succession, Officer M'tana will act in your stead."

Parnell shrugged. "Fair Ball's not too many weeks away.
And there, groundside, you can poll the ship by Agowa
formula, if need be, to determine your future course. As I
fully intend to do, peace willing, myself."

He stood; his gesture brushed away any try at argument.
"This meeting's at an end."

Carlo Mauragin muttered something. Parnell turned.
"Yes?"

At the door, Mauragin said, "Just agreeing with you,
sir."

"Do so aloud, please."

Carlo's face reddened; then he braced, chest out and
shoulders square. "That you don't understand the problem."

Quickly, to Parnell alone, Zelde said, "Forget it. I'll settle
this—and be back before you notice."

She ran to the door. Mauragin had scuttled out; at the
first cross-corridor she caught him and grabbed his arm.
To one side stood a storage cubby, empty. "In here,
Carlo—don't let's make a show." Sullen-faced, he followed
her.

"What do you want *now*?"

"For the cracks at me, nothing—yet. But twice in there,
it was Parnell you speared at. Do that again, and I'll have
your guts on the deck. Hear me?"

He looked puzzled. "You think you're ready to call me
out?"

"Not hardly. Just to *do* it—like I said. Saves time."

"Why—that's not regulation—the code doesn't provide—" He shook his head. "Ship's court would *crucify*
you. . . ."

"Sure." Deliberately, she rammed stiff fingers under his
breastbone. The jab rocked him back; before he could
catch his balance, she turned away. Over her shoulder she
said, "Keep saying that, Carlo—while you try to tuck yourself back together. Might help, some." Her knees shook a
little, but she walked good, anyway.

* * *

Going back to the meeting, it struck her that maybe her life as a Wild Kid hadn't been all waste. At the door she stopped; except for Dopples, everyone had left. "Where . . . ?"

"Surgery. But stay a minute here. You went after Mauragin. Why?"

"You heard him make snot at Ragir. He don't do that again."

Dopples raised up on his elbows. "What did you do?"

"Just told him—but I think he heard me."

Sighing, the First Hat lay back. "I wish I knew what the hell's going on. M'tana, I'm not your enemy."

"Never thought you was—or not lately." She started to leave.

"Wait—let's clear this." She stopped. "If Parnell . . . I'm not fit to take command, and may not be at all, during this trip. As for Tzane—command's no good in the hands of someone who's afraid of it. So that leaves you."

"And Carlo. He was Third before me. And seems to think—"

"*Seems* to—and I think that says it. M'tana—since lift-off, I don't like the feel of things. That Policebitch—"

"Not the problem, her. Leastways I don't think so. And Turk's looking it, there, so it's under control."

Silence, then Adopolous nodded. "I have to go along with you, M'tana. Until Ragir gets back to himself, there's no one else. So keep me informed, will you? And anything I can do for you—"

"Sure." *Because it's for the ship.* But it touched her, what he said. Grinning, she gave him the best salute she knew how.

Outside Surgery, Zelde squinted through the little window. Still an aide messing over Ragir, so all right to go in. The door swung shut behind her; she stopped and looked at him.

A tube in his arm; Fesler had said about that. His body was lathered from chest to thighs; the aide looked up, gestured with the razor in her hand. "The fancy gadget we have for this—it clunked out, naturally. So back to the Dark Ages."

Zelde smiled, and moved past to stand by Parnell's head. A little doped up, he looked, but not bad. "Ragir?"

He licked his lips. "Back, are you? Afraid you wouldn't be, before—" His headshake was slow. "What it was about, with Mauragin—tell me after. Can't think now—Fesler's drugs swinging my head on a string. But I thought—tried to fix everything simple, in case—and it all came up a fight. Zelde . . ."

To hear him, now, she had to bend down. She leaned all the way, and kissed him. "Don't worry. Stuff I got to tell you later, but—" What to say? Then she had it. "Rooster's upship, mounting our new insigne. And I just talked with Dopples, and he's solid on *our* side."

Lying back, his grin relaxed to slackness, Parnell sighed. "Ol' Dopps—*he's* with you, why thass' fine. He—"

Fesler's voice. "All right, Zelde—move back now, please?" As she did, Parnell's eyes closed, and Fesler made an injection. She moved farther away; from there she saw Parnell's lower torso—the aide was finished. She held back a giggle. *Never knew 'til now how big a man does look, not hiding in no bush!*

Masked and gloved, sorting through a tray of instruments, Fesler said, "It's time you left, Zelde."

"How so? I'll stay back, won't make a fuss. I—"

Emphatic headshake. "No. I have to do things, lifting and displacing, that you couldn't see without protesting." She tried to speak but he cut her off. "*No!* The captain needs all his best chances; I can't cope with distractions. So—"

She couldn't argue with that. "All right. Just do your best." She left without waiting for an answer—and heard her feet hit the deck as if daring someone to say they shouldn't.

Where to go—Control, galley, Turk's place? She went to quarters. But inside—no Parnell, and she couldn't go be with him. A drink? She poured whisky, tasted it. No, it needed ice, so she slugged off enough spirits to make room for a cube, and added it. She sat. She kicked off her shoes. She looked at the intercom—but who was there to call?

The swerving jar, when it came, threw her almost out of her chair. *What the living fuck?* She dropped the glass;

trying to get up, she fell to her knees. Drunk? No—under her, the ship had moved. Barefoot she scrambled to the intercom.

"Control? M'tana here. Report! What happened?"

No answer. "Goddamn you, up there! What's going on?"

There wasn't going to be an answer. All right—find the shoes, put them on; bare toes don't kick so good. She was outside before she thought of the gun. She paused, then shrugged. Who needed it?

Upship fast, and breathing deep on purpose, she went into Control. She stopped; everybody was just sitting like nothing happened. She looked around.

On watch was Mauragin—stop to think, she already knew that. Charvel on comm, and only one other. Two, then, on galley break.

Didn't matter—anybody pulling something, had to be Carlo. She went up beside him—a little back, so he had to look up and around to see her.

"What happened, Carlo? Tell it fast."

His face went stubborn. "A blip on the screen—close, and fast. I was lucky to dodge it, whatever it was."

"Pull back and run me the tape."

He shook his head. "No tape; something wasn't working."

"I didn't see any blip." It was Charvel who spoke, looking like he expected to get hit for it.

Carlo said, "If you'd been paying attention, you would have."

Well, now—maybe things were shaping up? But Charvel said, "Red light on the top airlock—what do I do about it?"

Mauragin hesitated. "Faulty alarm circuit. Cancel it."

Wait a minute! "Rooster Hogan—he still outside there?"

Charvel's face was blank, but Carlo's wasn't. No *time*, though. Zelde said, "You, Carlo—hold course *as is*—no matter what. That's an order, mister!" Then she turned and sprinted—fast as she could go, lungs burning her—to the topside airlock.

The outside light blinked; somebody wanted in. Through the inner port, Zelde squinted; the outer door wasn't opening, and it should be. The lights on the panel—she figured it out—Control held that door shut. All right. Manual over-

ride, here—she punched it, and that outer door moved. It
came wide enough; a suited figure came in. And then the
door wouldn't close!

Shit. Override again, it took, to shut space out. She
waited, while airlock pressure built up; then she undogged
the inner door. Rooster, grinning through his faceplate,
came inside.

Until she'd outwrestled Control to secure the airlock—
both doors—she couldn't help Rooster open the suit.
"Hey—you all right?"

"Just barely. How come somebody didn't want to let me
in?"

"Don't know yet—aim to find out, though. What happened?"

Rooster's story was simple enough. Outside, finished
with mounting the insigne—then came a fierce jolt. "Threw
me free of the ship, Zelde—I hung out there—it took a
time to pull myself in by my lifeline. And then I found the
lock was closed on it. I couldn't get in." His eyes widened.
"You think somebody did that on purpose?"

Think, hell—I know it! "We'll find out. Let's get you
free of that suit." One more problem, though. "You got no
kind of gun with you, I suppose?"

"For what? No, of course not."

It didn't matter; for now, Control and Mauragin had to
wait. "Never mind. Where we go first, we don't need one."

Downship, and fast—at the Surgery, Zelde peeked
through the small window, and knocked. Fesler—masked,
but who else moved the way he did?—looked up and signaled a wait. All right. "Let's sit down, Rooster—it may be
a while."

"I could use a coffee. You, too, maybe? I'd get it."

She thought. "No. Scout around here, find somebody's
not busy—send *them.* And not to say who they're getting it
for." He looked puzzled. "If somebody tried to kill you outside, why tell them where you are now? Got it?"

"Oh. Oh, *yeah.*" Now he looked as if he'd known it,
what she said, all along. He winked at her and left the
anteroom. Zelde sat, thinking. . . .

Rooster Hogan was no dummy. It was only—well, he
didn't realize how much of *everything* was out to kill you.

* * *

He brought back coffee and some tasty, buttered bread. She didn't ask how he got it; she thanked him, and ate. They waited a long time until Fesler, mask off, came to let them into Surgery. At first look, Zelde didn't like what he might say.

"Parnell—he all right?"

"I don't—I *hope* so. It was going well, easier than I expected, though I found some bad things—" The man shook his head. Zelde waited; for sure, there was more on his mind.

He craned his head from side to side—turning it, stretching the neck muscles. "I was doing the best I could, and then—what damned fool bucked the ship like that? And why? *Maybe two birds at once, Carlo had in mind to kill.* Fesler went on: "I was inside him—opened almost from navel to pubes, to make sure I didn't miss anything—I'd begun to cut, to separate an adhesion. Then the jar—it threw my *weight* onto that hand! I—"

"Not your fault, Fesler. Just tell the damage." In her own ears, her voice sounded dead.

"An artery—not the big one, peace be thanked—but he must have lost nearly two liters before I could find it in the mess and clamp it off. Then we got a transfusion going immediately—but still it took time to clear the blood out so I could find the other end and splice it back. And all the while, vital organs lacking for oxygen—though I detected no overt damage from that cause."

He sounded dazed, Fesler did. "A nerve bundle severed, too. It's butted back together—organic sealer—it *should* heal. I'm not even sure, though—with everything pulled off to the sides so I could get in where I had to—not sure which nerves they *are*."

Zelde's face, the tight muscles, hurt her; by effort she relaxed, some. "Any effects you noticed, from that?"

"No; the vital signs didn't change." He gave a nervous snicker. "The effect was on *me*. I'd been working pretty well, I thought—one thing at a time, being cautious. After that, though, I had no confidence—in myself, or the ship holding steady. Started working too fast—had to go back and do some things over again. Then I was afraid to *close* him, for fear I'd forgotten something. And I'm still not sure I was right to do so."

"You were. We *got* to believe that, for now." Between her hands Zelde took one of the man's clenched fists, kneading it until it loosened. "Now tell me the rest. What did you see wrong in him—and what did you do about it?" Some coffee was left—rank, by now, but better than nothing. She steered Fesler to a seat and poured him a cup.

He didn't seem to notice the taste, or that the cup had been used. He took one gulp. "As I'd thought—the liver's in bad shape. He simply has to stop drinking, any at all. Kidneys, I couldn't tell by looking—I don't know how. But the captain was right about adhesions—those were the worst of it."

"Could—did you fix all that?"

He nodded. "Pretty much, I think. One set of convolutions in the small intestine made almost a solid lump—I had to excise it completely, and resection. A wonder it hadn't closed off and killed him, months ago." He shook his head. "Another bad delay, there. I wasn't sure of the procedure, and had to stop everything while I looked it up."

He drained the cup; Zelde filled it again, but Fesler let it sit and cool. "But I cleaned up the adhesions, all right. As with Dopples—they won't grow together again, because the organic tape doesn't absorb before everything's healed."

"Then except for the . . . accident—"

"Except for that, I'd be fully optimistic. Nothing I can do about weakened organs, of course, but he won't be having that constant pain now. The mishap, though—having to keep him knocked out so much longer certainly didn't help his chances. I'll do the best I can; you know that."

"Sure. When's he due to come awake next?"

Headshake. "In his condition, I can't predict that. I'll call you." He looked up at the overhead, and said, "I still want to know who jumped the ship that way."

Zelde stood. "That's for me to take care of. And I think it's time I did."

As she went into Control, Rooster behind her, Mauragin turned and said, "You're late relieving me; do you know that?"

She looked around. Of Mauragin's watch, only he and Charvel remained; the others present were her own watchmates. "You're not exactly off duty yet, Carlo. I'm taking over, but you don't leave. You either, Charvel, if you don't mind."

Mauragin left his seat; Zelde went to it and stood, resting one buttock against an armrest. Carlo said, "What if *I* mind?"

"File a complaint. Then stuff it." Quickly she scanned back through the log. All it said, the part she wanted, was that watch-officer Mauragin spotted a fast incoming blip and swerved to avoid collision, then returned to proper course. She checked; yes, at least he'd done that much right. But no mention of his failure to have a confirming tape. She turned. "Tell it again, Carlo, why you jumped the ship around like that."

Same as before, he told it. She said, "Now you, Charvel. What you did see, I mean, this time—not what you didn't."

The short, redhaired man looked uncertain; he scratched his head. "Let me think a minute. Well, my panels were quiet. I was daydreaming, I guess—staring over past Carlo but not really seeing him, until he moved."

"Moved? How?"

"He was looking down at a screen"—down, so it would have to be interior view—"and he nodded. Then he looked up to the forward screen and yelled there was a blip. Then he reached, and the ship jumped." He spread his hands. "That's all I saw."

"Which inside screen was he watching? Could you tell?"

"Right side, I think."

She looked down. That one—it could cover the drive room, cargo holds, and—and, peace take it, all of Fesler's country! Including Surgery. To Charvel she said, "Thanks. I have what I need, and you're relieved." She tried to keep her face quiet. "Now then, Mauragin—"

"Now then, M'tana—" Even trying to mimic her, his voice came whiny. "Isn't it enough, you've kept me here past your proper relief time? I'm due back in my quarters—"

"Your little friend can wait. When you get the chance, explain to her. But for now—"

Red-faced, Mauragin shouted. "For now, have you logged yourself late on watch? You didn't give *me* time to do it. Or can the captain's pet come and go as she pleases? I *will* file a complaint! I—"

"You? You stinking turd, you're under arrest!" She left the control seat and moved toward him. He backed away.

"Under arrest? For *what?*"

"Attempted murder, two counts. That good enough?" Before he could answer: "Rooster—take him to his quarters; he stays there. Pick up a guard to see he does. Toss his girl friend out or leave her there—I don't care which. But either way, you and the guard search the place first, and bring me anything you think maybe I ought to see."

Nodding, Rooster took hold of Mauragin's arm. The man shook him off, and turned—and Zelde saw he was armed. His hand hung near the needle gun, not quite touching it. "M'tana? You want to think again?"

Don't wait—move! She walked to face him, one pace short of bumping. "You so much as touch the gun, you know what *that's* called. Give me it!" Could she take him, gun and all? Might have to try. "What's the matter? You need to ask, do you? Ask whoever's pulling your strings lately?" She bit her lip. *Damn! Why tell him everything I know?*

Whatever, it stopped him. "I was—well, defending myself."

"Defending? Against an order from me that ranks you? *You* think again—it won't lift." She held her hand out. "The gun. Now."

Other hand quivering, tense to chop, she watched him decide. Then, with thumb and first finger only, he brought the gun out and reached it toward her. She saw his face change, knew his mind was changing, too—but then, moving in no hurry, she had the gun.

She gave it to Rooster. "Just in case." She stepped back. "Take him along now. Like I said—remember?"

"Right." Hogan had the gun pointed a little away from Mauragin, down and to the side. Real polite, Zelde thought, but right there if he needed it. Then the two men left Control.

She took the watch seat and stared ahead, one hand tapping on its armrest. Something she should do—what was it? Her mind was fogging a little, and she knew she couldn't afford that.

"Officer M'tana?" The voice startled her. She shook her head.

She looked, and things started making sense again. "Charvel. What you still doing here?"

Head down, looking up through bushy brows, he seemed nervous. "It seems I started trouble; I still don't know how. But I felt I should stay and see it through." He cleared his throat. "Was it something I said, that decided you to arrest Carlo?"

Careful—don't tell all of it. "That what he saw, gave him the idea to jump us around like he did, was *inside* the ship. I know what it was. He goes to trial"—if he *lives* that long—"it'll all come out in the record. All right?"

"Sure, Officer M'tana—and thanks." He turned to leave.

Now she remembered what she had to do. "Stay a couple minutes, maybe?" He nodded; she switched the intercom to Dopples' room and picked up the hush-set. When the First Hat answered, she said, "Dopp—Mr. Adopolous, I mean—I just now done some things. Here's what, and here's why." She told it fast.

When she was done, he said, "For the most part, I can't fault your moves, M'tana—and I appreciate the report. However, you're short a watch officer. Do you have anyone in mind for the job?"

"That's what I'm asking *you.*" She hesitated. "You know a Charvel? Redheaded, short? Monitor tech, for one thing. You think he's qualified?" She explained her reasons.

After a pause, Dopples said, "Among the ratings—which doesn't give us a great field of qualifications—I'd say he's as good as most. Steady, as I recall—and would seem to be trustworthy, which is important just now. So if you wish, appoint him."

"Temporary," said Zelde. "Parnell to confirm later, if he agrees." For a moment she nearly choked. "Or—or you, Mr. A."

"Look on the bright side. Adopolous out." The circuit light died.

She turned to Charvel, still waiting. "You got a first name?"

"Why, yes—Gilman. Gil. But what . . . ?"

"Keep your same watch schedule, Gil Charvel. But from now, Mr. Adopolous says, you do it as Acting Third Hat."

For a moment he was still; then he shook his head. "Me? I don't know enough. I don't understand half the instruments."

"You've sat in for galley breaks? Sure you have."

"But then I can *call* someone—the watch officer, mostly."

Zelde thought about it. "I bet you know more than I did when Dopples handed *me* the job. Tell you what—if you got time now, sit down alongside and we'll go through a lot of this stuff for a while. And if you want to come in early, next watch, I'll tell Lera Tzane to expect you for more training. All right?"

"Well—" He shrugged. "Sure. And thanks, Officer M'tana."

"It's Zelde. Now set your ass down and let's start."

After two hours, Charvel sounded tired and Zelde sent him off. Then she logged the promotion—first, though, she entered Carlo Mauragin's arrest. Not the reasons—maybe this log could be tapped—but only the bare event.

After that, the watch was dull; she was glad when Lera Tzane arrived early, and briefly told the woman what had happened. No details on Parnell, of course—just the main how-and-why of arresting Mauragin, and then Charvel's promotion. "Seems to learn fast," she said. "If he comes in ahead of time, like we said, I expect you can fill him in on a lot I don't know."

Tzane kept pushing at her hair, where on one side it wasn't staying up so good. Maybe she was just stalling, because it was a while before she said, "Zelde? About Carlo—are you sure you didn't move too fast? Before you had all the facts?"

"Half-cocked, you mean? *'Course* I'm not sure I done right. Leaving that one alive could be the biggest mistake I ever made."

From the way Tzane looked, Zelde knew the two of them weren't seeing the same problem. She shook her head. "Lera—this is for the *ship*—and for Parnell. No way I dare take chances."

"But arresting Carlo—so abruptly, and without any real investigation—wasn't that taking a chance?"

"Not so bad as leaving him run loose. Lera, you got your ears turned off or something? He tried to kill Parnell—*and* Rooster, both at once. And came close to doing it. If I'd—"

With one last emphatic pat, Lera gave up on the hairdo.

"Zelde, you've made your move now, openly. But we have no idea who might be behind Carlo, still hidden."

Thinking about it, Zelde chuckled. "We got some idea how that one works, though. So, next time somebody moves wrong, we get a—what you call it?—a cross-sighting. And then we zero in."

Heading downship, Zelde felt better. What she'd said to Lera, she thought it made sense—at least, it sounded good.

She was hungry—but first, check on Parnell. Off duty, Fesler would be, by now—probably asleep. But she found a junior aide, his feet up on Fesler's desk. He gulped. "I was just—"

The small stuff, she didn't care about. Monitor instruments would call this man if anything went wrong with Parnell—or Dopples, for that matter. And he showed her his log, with hourly checkoffs on both of them. She nodded. "Parnell—can I see him yet?"

"Sure." He stood. "He may not be awake, or recognize you." She followed him, to the room next to Dopples'. Dim light—she couldn't tell about Parnell's coloring, but he breathed regular. She touched his forehead; his head moved and his eyes opened.

"Ragir—it's Zelde. You hear me?"

Nodding, he mumbled something. He knew her, she thought—but could he talk sense? "You'll be all right, Ragir. You got that?"

His brow wrinkled. "Zelde, I dreamed something. The ship—knocked off course—I *felt* it." His eyes closed again. ". . . means anything—I don't know. Careful. . . ." His lips moved, but there was nothing she could hear.

"Careful, yeah, Ragir. But now you rest up." She kissed him, then turned and left. *Even knocked out, he felt the ship jump!*

Outside, she thanked the aide. "Just watch out for him, will you?"

"Yes, of course." He turned back to Fesler's office. Zelde stood put—what needed doing next? Eat, maybe. Get some sleep—if she could, wound up like she was. No coffee, for sure, though mostly she could drink it by the pot and sleep like a rock. But now. . . .

In the galley she saw nobody she wanted to talk with.

Then she noticed two senior ratings, sitting together, watching her. Both, she knew, were pretty thick with Carlo. She thought, *Why the hell not?*—and carried her tray over, and sat down with them.

The skinny blond one, Paskow, pushed his longish hair back and stared at her. Staring back, she decided that without all those old pimple scars, he'd be good-looking.

But it was Bellarn—the pale, brown-haired woman— who spoke. "Evening, Acting Second. Care to join us?" Her voice was quiet, not showing the sarcasm of her words.

Zelde, with a straight face, said, "Thanks—don't mind if I do," and began eating. *Now let's see who makes the mistakes.*

It took a while, waiting. Then Paskow said, "Scuttlebutt has it that Acting Third Mauragin's been arrested."

Zelde took a big bite, and chewed it in no hurry, before answering. "That right? What else does it say?"

The two ratings looked at each other, then back to Zelde. "You haven't answered the question." Bellarn again.

"You didn't ask one."

Paskow leaned forward. "*Is* Carlo arrested? And if so, why?"

Zelde paused. Well, she'd started this; might as well go ahead. "Yeah. He is." She beat the next question. "By my orders, confirmed by Adopolous. New Acting Third is Gil Charvel—and the First Hat put his chop to that appointment, too."

Paskow licked his lips. "You haven't said *why*."

"That's right." She waited until Bellarn tried to speak, so that her own words cut the other off. "You'll get that answer when I do—when the court-martial brings in a verdict." Watching their faces, she purely hoped she had the jargon right!

Bellarn again. "How can you pull an officer from duty, put him under arrest, when you don't even have charges to prefer?"

Zelde was done eating. The others had coffee in front of them, but she didn't. She stood. "You got it wrong. There's charges, you bet your ass! It's only that until the trial, we can't be sure which ones fit the goddamn *facts*."

The two looked at her. She gave them time to come up with an answer. Then she turned away, walking just fast enough so she didn't look like running away from anything. And thinking, that setup hadn't worked so bad!

She went to quarters and found she was lonely. But after a bath—the unit's water-cycling quota was in good shape, so she soaked in a hot tub—it turned out she was close to sleepy. She had a short drink, bourbon over ice, and went to bed. She started to think about something—but lost track of it, and then was asleep.

She woke feeling good, came out of bed in one lunge, kicked high once and then ran tiptoe. Looking in the mirror she touched her breasts and ran her hands over her ribcage, and down along her sides and thighs. For a moment she shivered, grinning. Then it came back to her—all the troubles. She sighed, and got dressed.

She needed to talk; she checked the time, nodded, and called Turk's place. "You two ready to eat? Meet me in the galley?"

Some silence; then: "Rooster's working. You stay there; I'll bring breakfast." Before Zelde could answer, the circuit died.

After a time Zelde answered Turk's knock and let her in. Breakfast was mostly scrambled eggs—with a little meat, some juice, and a pot of coffee. "I hope you like it." Fine with Zelde, and she said so.

"Then let's shut up and eat." When they had cleaned their plates and were down to coffee, Turk said, "The reason we ate here—Zelde, this ship's ready to boil over. Right now, you shouldn't go *any*place without someone guarding your back. For that, I brought a gun." She showed it; then she told what she'd heard, including word from Torra Defose. At the end, Zelde nodded.

"All right, Turk—if you say so. But who's behind Carlo?"

Headshake. "No idea yet. Someone that's good at hiding."

Zelde tried to think about it, how it all fit. She couldn't find a handle. Well—"I'm going on watch now, early. If you think I need guarding, come with me—all right? There's nobody I trust more."

So when Zelde went to Control, Turk was right behind her.

* * *

Gilman Charvel had the watch. He wasn't doing much, though, because the man Paskow stood over him—and, by the looks of things, talking fast. The comm-panel seat was vacant; would that be Paskow's? She walked over, saying nothing until Paskow looked around, saw her, and shut up. She stopped behind Charvel's seat.

"Paskow—you on duty?" He nodded. "Where's your station?" He pointed to the communications console. "Then get your ass back to it."

He moved away. Zelde didn't look after him; if anything needed doing, that was Turk's job. She moved around so Charvel didn't have to crane his neck to see her. He looked nervous; she didn't want that, so she smiled. "How's your watch going, Acting Third?"

"All right, I suppose. Nothing I've needed to ask help for." His mouth twitched. "Paskow—I was about ready to send him back to station. But, you see—I'm not used to giving orders."

She had to chuckle. "Me either, until lately. You got to work at it." She nodded toward Paskow. "That one bothering you?"

"I—" He shook his head. "No, not really."

"See that he don't." She sat beside him, in the auxiliary control seat. "Now then—why don't you run me through what you been learning? That's why I'm here early."

Tense at first, Charvel loosened up as he talked. In her mind, Zelde checked off what he probably knew already, and what she'd told him herself. The rest of it had to be from Lera Tzane—and by the time he was done, Zelde was impressed. Toward the last she caught and corrected a couple of mistakes, but on the whole: "Not bad; not bad at all! I guess you did come on watch early, like we'd said."

"Yes. Officer Tzane stayed over with me, for more than an hour." Embarrassed, his laugh sounded. "I feel as if my head were so stuffed with facts that—" He stopped, pointing a finger. "There! On that screeen—a blip I don't understand. It happened once before, but didn't recur, so I—look! There it is again."

She saw the screen, and how the dials had set its function. *Uh-huh*—unless she had it wrong, that was another ship, out there.

*   *   *

She switched relay to Dopples' terminal. Turning to Charvel, she felt how tight her grin was. "This is one time I'm not too proud to get some advice, myself."

She hit the intercom switch. "Mr. Adopolous—you awake?"

Seconds seemed long; then his voice came. "I'm here, M'tana. What's this you're showing me?"

She told him. "At least, that's how it looked before, when we met the *Hoover*." He didn't answer; the blips increased.

Finally he said, "Can you get me the relative courses?"

She wasn't sure. Charvel touched her hand. "I can—that's one thing I learned on my old job, but never had occasion to use it." She nodded, and he began feeding data and sampling readouts. Watching, she thought she'd remember how it went, next time. When he was done, they both waited.

After a time, Dopples said, "I have it now, I think. Overhauling us at a slight angle from—oh, call it above and to your right. A close pass, but no intercept. Just a second, here." Then, in his voice, she heard satisfaction. "Yes. We're still accelerating, of course, short of turnover. The other ship's on decel, but hasn't been for long—since it still has some speed on us. So obviously it's on a considerably longer run." He paused. "Destination? Could be the same as ours, or possibly Johnson's Walk—from here, the angle between those two isn't all that big. There's not enough data, yet, to pin it closer."

Zelde cleared her throat. "Fine—but how you want me to *handle* this? You rather take it yourself, through this relay?"

No pause now. "You'll have to do it, M'tana—my screen only receives, and an off-screeen voice would seem fishy. And as to how—I think you know, don't you? From the last time?"

Oh, sure. "Yeah. Listen—but don't answer until we have to, to look right." Except, Paskow was on comm and she didn't trust Paskow. "Just a minute, Dopples." Too late, she realized what she'd called him—but Adopolous made no comment.

She turned. "Charvel, I'm taking Control; you take the comm. Paskow, you're relieved. Go get a meal or some sleep, or something."

"Why?" The blond man sounded peeved. Too bad, that was. . . .

"Because I'm feeling so kindly, you get off early. Now move it." When the man was gone and Charvel sat in his place, she watched him tune the comm for ships' signals. Then, on the intercom: "Mr. Adopolous? How I said—I didn't mean—it just came out, was all."

"M'tana! This situation's serious. Don't waste time on trivia." He gave instructions—full feed of offship signals to his terminal, but no return relay. "Anything I say to you stops in Control." A pause, and then: "Dopples out."

Charvel knew his business; soon Zelde heard the special hiss of ship-to-ship signal—but no modulation on it yet. She sat, watching the blips but not thinking. When Charvel spoke, she had to ask him to repeat.

"Officer M'tana—is anything wrong?"

"No. It's just—sometimes people surprise me."

The blips showed the other ship closing; now and then the channel hiss mumbled, but no words came through. Turk went to bring coffee and a midwatch snack, and Zelde took a minute to visit the off-Control latrine, while she had the chance.

Sooner or later it had to happen; the incoming signal came clear. ". . . can't ID your insigne yet, even on high mag, but it won't be long now. If you hear me —this is *Graf Spee,* Ilse Krueger commanding. Come in, please. . . ."

Then, under the ionic confluence of solar winds, the voice faded. Star shit, Parnell called it—*and how are you now, Ragir, love?*

Soon now, *Chanticleer* had to answer. Zelde used Parnell's trick—taping what she said and having Charvel distort it past understanding. Until on the intercom, Dopples said, "Next time, let them read you. Good luck, M'tana."

All right; Zelde braced for it. When *Graf Spee* next spoke, the woman's voice came deep and clear. "We have you close up on visual now. *Chanticleer,* is it? Come in, please."

A deep breath, then Zelde motioned Charvel to send her voice. *Do it like Parnell did with Bernardez.* "Chanticleer to *Graf Spee*—good meeting, out here in no place." What next? Don't tell any more than she had to. . . . "What news from Earth?"

She'd forgotten the distance lag; for a time, Ilse Krueger's questions continued. The woman paused, and said, "Earth? Twenty planets' years behind us, at least. You tell *us*, more likely." A cough. "But I've identified myself and you haven't. Who's there, for peace' sake? Anyone I know? Ilse Krueger here, as I've said."

Keep it simple; don't say too much. "Captain Ragir Parnell sends his respects and regards." She hoped she had that right. "If he can get up here before we lose signal, he will." True enough. "Speaking for him, this is Second Hat Zelde M'tana."

Even before she heard Dopples curse, she knew she'd said the wrong thing.

The ships were close now; on a side screen Charvel had an in-ship picture. Zelde saw a small blonde woman—and it worked both ways, for the woman said, "You're a big one, aren't you? But cut the shit! You're Escaped, the same as we are. So we have to talk fast, while we can."

Hardly any timelag now—when Zelde didn't answer, Krueger said, "Come *on*, will you? *Chanticleer* and *Graf Spee* aren't UET insignes—and neither of us put 'the' in front of them, and you called yourself Second Hat, not Second Officer." On the small face, her scowl looked grim. "Did you ever hear of a woman commanding a UET ship? Quit stalling, M'tana! There's no time!"

Dopples said, "Exchange all the information you can. Fast!"

No time to think. "All right, Krueger. What you want to know?"

The woman grinned. "More important is what *you* should know. Tape this next—it's on scramble, you can't read it—and punch it into the computer center of any Hidden World you reach. Ready?"

"Sure. Shoot it." Charvel flipped switches; Zelde hoped he knew what he was doing. For nearly a minute the screen went to chaos; then Ilse Krueger reappeared.

"I hope you got that. Now then—where are you headed?"

What to do? "Tell her!" Dopples said, so Zelde did.

"Good. So are we—but we'll have left before you can get

there. Here—record these computer access codes. They'll give you all the mail-drop info at Fair Ball—including the codes for any place you could reach in your next jump." Krueger smiled. "It's all part of the service. When you get the chance, pass it on."

When Charvel nodded that he had it all, Zelde said, "I—we do thank you. We're new, you see, and—"

"And can use some help to get oriented. I know, M'tana—we've been the same route and it's never easy." Signal lag was growing again. "One more thing—and it's important. In case the scramble tape I sent you doesn't reach all the proper places, log this—and enter it, *any* Hidden World you land on." A second's pause. "Here's the message. Ilse Krueger agrees to Tregare's terms and will try to meet his rendezvous. Place and time, both."

Tregare again? *Think quick.* "Might help if I knew what you mean."

Krueger's eyes widened. "Yes—it might, at that. Put it this way. On any Hidden World, use the codes I gave you and leave word of yourselves—and of me—for Bran Tregare. And if you ever happen to run into him, you *listen.*" Krueger spoke to someone out of view, then back to Zelde. "I think that's all of it, that we can do now. In case either of us thinks of anything more, let's keep the channels open until we fade out. All right?"

Zelde cut transmission, to ask, "Mr. Adopolous—anything else we should do here?"

"I can't think what. Dopples out."

Back to the offship channel. "Like you say, *Graf Spee,* it's been fine." How to say it, now? "Good speed and good landings."

Was that how Parnell had said? She couldn't remember. And after Krueger returned the wish, nothing more from *Graf Spee*; the blips got fewer and dimmer, and then just plain quit.

One thing, though. "Dopples out"—twice, he'd said that.

Her own relief crew was here; Charvel's watch left. Gil wanted to talk, but she had too much on her mind; he'd have to wait.

Turk came over and half sat on the armrest. "I think Charvel's worth trusting; I expect you already figured that." Zelde nodded. "That Paskow, you should lock up, since you don't have grounds to space him. The Bellarn woman, I don't know yet. There's more of them in on this, and I have one name that's not on ship's roster at all—first, last, or middle."

Zelde looked up; Turk shrugged. "It could be a code name, like in the Underground. But the person behind Mauragin—all the name I have is Franzel."

Zelde gripped Turk's hand. "All right. Thanks. We'll see about it later."

The rest of the watch, nothing much happened. When Lera Tzane came to relieve Zelde, she, too, agreed that Charvel would make a competent Acting Third. Lera didn't mention Carlo Mauragin, so neither did Zelde.

She and Turk started downship together. The older woman kept glancing at her but said nothing. Zelde frowned. "Something bothering you?"

"Mauragin. How long do you think you can keep him on ice this way? You'll have to do something, and fast."

Zelde thought, a moment. "When Parnell or Dopples is in shape for it, Carlo goes to trial. *I* can't sit as judge, that's sure. And Lera's not the type. So for now—we wait, I guess."

Turk made a face. "*We* do—but will Carlo's gang?"

To that, no answer; Zelde shrugged. "Maybe Parnell's up to talking, now. You coming along?"

Turk grinned. "How else?" They found Fesler at his desk, and the medic agreed that Zelde could see the captain. At the door to his room, Turk stopped. "I'll stay out here."

Zelde entered. The light was better this time, and Parnell was awake, and turned to see her. His face looked pale and pinched, but she smiled. "Hello, Zelde."

She went to him. He said, "Mind the plumbing, now"— as if she didn't know that! She made her embrace gentle, and her kiss. Then, carefully she sat on the bed's edge, where she could hold one hand.

"Ragir, love—how's it all go, now?"

His brows raised. "You'll have to ask Fesler. I'm still too full of dope to count my own legs and get the right answer."

Smiling, she pointed a finger once and then again. "Two,

I make it. But I mean, how you *feel*—tired or rested, wound up or relaxed? You got any good appetite yet?"

"Hmm. Tired, relaxed, not hurting—enjoying what food they give me, which for good reasons isn't much, yet."

Yeah—a length of *gut* cut out. Should he ought to be eating, at all? Well, she had to believe in Fesler or else give up on all of it. She said, "You feel like hearing about the ship? Nothing that can't wait, if you're too tired."

"Go ahead—lying here, I can *use* some new thoughts." So she told of the new insigne being placed, and then about passing in talk-range with *Graf Spee*. "You think we done right, Dopples and me?"

He pursed his lips, then nodded. "Yes. With the woman eager to give *us* information, she has to be straight." For a moment he drummed fingers against the bedside stand. "Krueger—yes, I know of her, by hearsay. Smallest person ever to survive the Slaughterhouse, all the way to officer grade. But—" Shaking his head, he scowled. "She shipped with my friend Doul Falconer; he was First and she was Second on—I forget the ship's name. But if they Escaped, where's Falconer? Off the ship by then, I hope. Otherwise I have to assume he was killed. . . ."

He seemed sunk in reverie. "Parnell? Something else to talk on, but not if you're too tired. I mean—"

His face took on the look of command. Too tired? Nonsense! So she began, about Carlo Mauragin. Not all—she didn't want him knowing he'd been cut more than Fesler intended—but most of it. "So—doped to sleep, Ragir, you *did* feel the jar, when that bastard tried to shake Rooster loose from the ship."

His expression changed. "So you've locked Mauragin up, waiting trial." He shook his head. "Dopples will have to preside—the situation won't hold together until *I'm* free of all this tubing, fit to be moved. You go see Dopps. Tell him, as soon as Fesler agrees he's ready, he's to try Mauragin. To convene a panel of his fellow Control officers, plus Harger. Now—what charges are you specifying?"

"*I* don't know that stuff, Ragir. I thought maybe *you*. . . ."

Weakly, he moved one hand. "Yes. Well—for a start, subversion. You have Tzane and Kestler as witnesses—and Defose, too. I assume they can find others. And for background you can use his lack of punctuality, and so forth,"

He coughed and fumbled at the bedside stand, but was lying too low among pillows to see what he reached for. "Water, Zelde?"

She got it for him, and held it while he sipped. "Thanks. Now then—maybe he tried to kill Rooster and maybe he didn't, but I don't think that charge is provable. Where's his motive?" And she couldn't tell him—that *he* was also a target.

"It's suspicious, certainly—no tape, for instance—but the court has to consider that he *could* have seen a threatening blip." He shook his head. "It might be best, Zelde, to settle for an Officers' hearing, and simply demote him for laxness and insubordination."

"And leave him loose to connive with this gang he's building? I'll call him out first. And maybe, I guess, I'll have to."

"Perhaps. But confer with me first, if that's at all possible."

She changed the subject then, trying to cheer him—but when she left she knew it hadn't really worked, much.

Zelde and Turk found Dopples awake. When Zelde brought him up to date, he said she should have told Parnell the whole story. "Then he'd agree to a full trial, not a mere hearing. And of course that's another reason for me to preside—not Ragir, even if he were fit. The victim of an attack can't sit as judge."

Through the covers, he rubbed his belly. "In another week, I should be up. Will the situation wait that long?"

Turk said, "Maybe it's better if that gang does try something. We'd learn a lot that we haven't been able to find out."

"Assuming we won." But from Dopples' expression, Zelde guessed that he liked Turk's thinking. He raised a finger. "If we're in a hurry, there's another way. Harger has the rank to convene a court."

Startled, Zelde frowned. "Rank, yeah—but does he know how?"

"His training, at the Slaughterhouse, was the same as ours—and probably just as rusty by now. M'tana, even Parnell would have to bone up on that procedure." He squinted at her. "The information's all in the computer, if you're curious."

He yawned. "I'm tired again; that still comes too easily. But before you go—what do you intend to do next?"

The decision didn't take long. "Go have a talk with Carlo Mauragin. It's about time I did that."

As they approached Mauragin's guarded door, that door opened. A woman came out—short, a little chubby but well shaped. Fluffy blonde hair, blue eyes in a face that owed some of its roundness to fat. She said something to the guard; he nodded, and she turned to leave. Zelde moved, caught her arm and spun her around.

"Hold it a minute. What's all this?"

The blonde licked her lips. "I was just visiting Carlo. I'm—"

"I know who you are. Except your name."

"Vanny Hackter." Turk said it.

Zelde nodded. "All right, Vanny—what's this *visiting*?"

"They told me—I could go or stay—you didn't care. So . . ."

Peace make a puddle! She hadn't said—yes, she had, too. "All right—my fault. I meant you could go *or* stay—not both. You've been in and out, just as you please?"

"Yes. I thought—"

"No blame. Except now you go in and you stay there."

"But I'm supposed to—" She stopped, gulped; a hand went to her mouth.

Zelde's grip tightened. "Say it." The girl shook her head.

Turk said, "If you want answers, Zelde, I can get them." Again Vanny shook her head. "Oh, yes, I can, missy—no trouble at all." Turk put a hand to Vanny's neck, and squeezed once.

While Zelde tried to decide—did she want this kind of thing, right now?—Vanny started crying. "I was just to tell—someone—Carlo's tired of waiting. That's all. And I don't know what it means—I really don't."

I do, maybe. She nodded to Turk. "All right. Let's go in."

Hackter squirmed and tried to pull away. "My things—I don't have much of anything at Carlo's."

"Make out a list. Somebody'll take care of it for you." And to the guard: "From now on, this one stays here. She and Mauragin, they don't talk to nobody without I say they can. Anything anybody brings here, you or your relief inspect it before you hand it in. Same with stuff coming out. Got it?"

The man nodded. "That's how we've done it—except that *she* could go in and out. I—"

"My mistake, not yours. Forget it."

The three went inside. Carlo Mauragin, wearing a pair of shorts, sat drinking beer. He had better muscles than Zelde expected, but the way he looked and smelled, it had been a while since he combed his hair, or washed. And by his flushed face and reddened eyes, he'd been drinking most of that time.

He squinted up at her. "Well! A visit from the jailer." His voice didn't sound drunk. "When do I get a hearing? You can't coop me up here forever, M'tana. Regulations say—"

"UET Regs, Carlo?" She shook her head. "You get a trial—not a hearing—when I say you do."

"You?" His laugh, now, showed the drink he'd had. "Same as outside, just now, about letting people talk to me. Not the skipper, huh—or Dopples, or even Tzane. Who put *you* on the throne?"

Getting mad, not wanting to show it, she said, "Parnell and Dopples—while they're off duty status the rest of us act for them. Consult with them, too, if you was wondering. And Tzane leaves you to me because she wants no part of you!" She caught her breath. "You got any more smart-ass questions?"

No answer; for a moment he looked like a hurt child. Not thinking, Zelde said, "Carlo—what the hell's got *into* you? You fucked up your first promotion and was set back—and took it good, I thought. Then next time you started better, but pretty soon—well, you got like a spoiled brat. And now worse—a *lot* worse."

He sat, blinking; he drained his beer and snapped fingers at Vanny Hackter. She scurried to bring him another. Zelde shook her head. "Still got you somebody to boss, right? Damn it, Carlo—what's wrong? You been acting like the biggest dumbass ever was—but I know you're *not* dumb. So who's been at you, Carlo? And what the hell they been selling you?"

She thought he wasn't going to answer, but finally he did. "Nobody had to sell me anything. As you said, I'm not stupid; I can figure things out. Like the way, ever since

Escape, I've never had a fair chance on this ship—and whose fault *that* is!"

Straight at her, he was staring. *Try a shot.* "Is that what Franzel's been telling you?"

His face went blank. "I never heard of her."

Abruptly, Zelde motioned to Turk, and the two walked out.

"But why leave *then*?" Turk sounded puzzled. "He was just—"

"Just *what*?" Zelde thumped fist into palm. "You heard him—but was it a slip or a plant? I wanted out fast, to look at it, think on it—before anything more happened." She stopped walking. "Think back—before he said that, how long did he wait? A little slowed with the drink, keep in mind. But did he give something away, before he thought, or did he say that on purpose?"

Turk shrugged. "I don't know him well enough to tell."

Again, Zelde started walking. "Me either." Eyes half-closed, she thought back—timing Mauragin's pause, then recalling his face when he spoke. She nodded. "He wasn't faking—not on such short notice, and drunk to boot."

"So?"

"So pass it to Torra Defose that Franzel's a woman, like as not." Her eyes burned; she blinked. "I'm going to catch some sleep."

"I'll see you to quarters." And more than that—Turk came in and made sure the place was empty. Zelde grinned. *Tough deal, if I was having somebody in just now.*

At the door, Turk said, "Call me when you're ready to go out next. I expect I'll be home by then."

"Sure." Turk left. Zelde showered, had a beer and some crackers, and went to bed.

Noise, not loud, woke her. At the door, someone rapping—two knocks, three, two more—pause and repeat. It didn't mean anything—was it supposed to? Squinting in dim light she fumbled for her robe and didn't find it. She shrugged and got up.

At the door, she said, "Yeah? What is it?"

"Message." She didn't know the voice.

"Who from? And what's wrong with the intercom?" Now she was coming awake better.

232 F. M. Busby

"I was told you'd know. And the intercom's not secure."
From Defose, maybe? Zelde drew the bolt—and opened
the door, only a little, to look out.

One glimpse she got—somebody small. And something
shiny—then a gesture, and light exploded to blind her.

Something stung her side; the door banged against her.
She gasped; eyes streaming while she saw only flashing
glare, she braced herself and slammed back at the door. It
didn't shut all the way—she heard a *thunk* on the deck,
and pulled back and slammed again. A cry—pain, or anger? A third slam, and this time the door closed solidly.
She found the bolt and set it, then felt around on the deck
until she found what had fallen there.

A knife, it was—and where her side burned, blood ran.
Still she couldn't see, but felt for the switch and turned up
the lighting. Waiting, after a while she had some sight, and
then more. Meanwhile she tried to rerun the one quick
look she'd had at the knife artist.

Small, sure. Skinny? Maybe. Hair ragged—flat to the
head with a few wisps outlined against the light. And—not
clear—something funny about the face. Lopsided? No clue
to coloring—hair or face, either one. No point in putting
out any kind of alert, on what she had. But the voice—
yeah—a woman's.

With only dim floating lights now, in the way of seeing,
she looked at her side. A long cut, through the fatty layer
at deepest, and nicking the muscle—with her fingers she
spread it wider, to see, to make sure it wasn't deeper.
Bleeding enough to wash the wound clean—and mess up
the deck, pretty soon—but nothing to worry about.

She used paper tissues to mop off the blood running
down her hip, then blotted at the cut itself. She found the
first-aid kit and got out dressings already coated with anti-
infectant. It took two of those to close the cut all its length,
and she pulled them up tight before pressing the upper
halves to her skin. Yes—that should hold the edges together. She moved, flexing her body—it hurt, but not
enough to bother. She washed off the rest of the blood, and
got dressed.

Now she was hungry. The time? Too early to call
Turk—so Zelde made do with more crackers, a packet of
cheese, and a can of meat broth—the kind that heated itself
when you opened it.

Only two hours sleep, she'd had—but no hope of sleeping now. She lay down anyway—but then the intercom sounded. She answered and listened—then she gasped. "I'll be right there!"

Ragir was alive! The place was wrecked—most of the complicated equipment smashed and scattered—but with Fesler working over him, Parnell raised a hand to greet her. The medic waved her back, and she saw tubes still protruding from her man's arm. All right—she could wait. But: "What the *hell* . . . ?"

Fesler shook his head; it was Parnell who answered. "I heard something, looked up." Somebody bending over him, holding a hypo. Told him to shut up—a woman's voice, it was. He tried to move away, but couldn't—and for an instant, in light from the doorway, he saw the intruder. Now he coughed. "Water?"

His was spilled; Zelde brought some from the next room. Parnell sipped, then spoke again. "That face I won't forget. Slabsided—the nose bent to one side. No one I'd ever seen before—which, here on the ship, puzzles me."

Same one came after me—it has to be!

Fesler pulled a tube from Parnell's arm; the captain winced. "Is that the last of it?" The medic nodded, and Parnell went on with his story. The woman had tripped over a cable and knocked down part of his support system—he yelled, and swung the water pitcher at her head. "My bad shoulder, I had to use—it could stand a shot, Fesler, when you have time."

"Sure, skipper—but first I had to patch the leaks."

"Yes." The woman had pulled back, hands empty now, and scrabbled on the deck—for the hypo, probably. Parnell heard someone coming—Fesler, as it turned out. "She did, too, I suppose—she got up and began tearing the apparatus apart. Tried to hit me with part of it, but a cable snubbed it and she missed."

"And that's about the time," said Fesler, "that I came in one door, just in time to see the other one slam in my face."

"Right," said Parnell. "Very welcome you were, too." He frowned. "One thing I just remembered. She favored her right hand—used the left one almost entirely."

Zelde's laugh surprised her; Parnell stared. "It's—well,

the right hand, I slammed the door on it a couple of times. When she tried for *me* a few minutes ago." She told it fast—how she'd been caught half asleep—and shook her head. "Busy bitch, that one is."

Parnell tried to raise his head. *"Are you all right?"*

"Oh, sure." She gestured. "Caught me along the side with her knife—*my* knife now—but not deep." Fesler looked worried. "No, really—I looked close and washed it out careful, and bandaged it shut, good. You can look later if you want, Fesler—but I been cut worse with *no* help, and healed up okay."

"If you say so." Fesler checked a final dressing on Parnell's arm, and straightened up. "Skipper—given the choice, I'd have left you on the plumbing another day or two. I'll dig out replacements for the equipment, of course, but I think you're stable. And for now, safer in your quarters than you were here."

Zelde snorted. "Like *I* was?"

"You were off guard," said Parnell. "From now on—until that creature is caught—we'll both know better."

"That one? And maybe more." But Zelde nodded. "All right. Fesler, you putting an aide on duty with Parnell? Or can he and I take care of him, yet?"

"I'll assign someone—you can manage, I think, until I get schedules rearranged." He left the room briefly, and came back with a tray of bottles—pills and liquids, both— and a clipboard. "Captain, the galley has your prescribed meal chart. Order food when you want it—and try to eat hearty; you've lost weight." Then to Zelde: "Here's the medication schedule. You see that it's followed."

"Hear that, Ragir?" Parnell nodded. "Then all right."

"There's one thing," said Fesler. "Changing from IV drugs to pills, for pain. There's a lot of that stuff in your blood right now, skipper—so take *no* pain pills until, say, ten hundred hours tomorrow. And then only half-dosage for that day. Clear?"

"Very," said Parnell. He cleared his throat. "There was something said, though, about a shot for my shoulder." And Zelde saw the beads of sweat on his upper lip and forehead.

"Of course," and Fesler gave the injection. "Now, I think, you're ready to go. I'll get a stretcher, and we'll move you."

"Not by ourselves," said Zelde. "Not now." And a little later, as she and Fesler carried the stretcher, Turk and Rooster and Torra Defose—all armed—marched escort. How *easy* the carrying was, though—that near broke her heart.

Inside quarters, with Parnell bedded as comfortable as might be, Turk and Rooster left to set up guards for the door. "Same as for Mauragin," Zelde said, "but not quite the same idea." Turk grinned and closed the door; not long after, the first guard reported for duty.

Torra Defose stayed, so that Zelde—and Parnell, though he was getting sleepy—could tell her their stories. At the end she said, "All right; back to the files. If I find anything, I'll call you," and left.

Parnell dozed off. Looking at him, seeing how much less he was than what he had been, briefly Zelde put her face in her hands. After a while she poured herself a whiskey. Sipping on it, she thought about what she should do next. Should—or *could*? Or maybe "had to"? Did she have any peace-kicking *choice*?

She managed an hour's nap; then the intercom sounded. Torra Defose: "I have to see you. I can't find Turk, and there's no time for this go-between stuff now, anyway."

Now what? "Come here, then. I'll tell the guard to pass you. But we talk soft—Parnell's sleeping."

She called Lera Tzane in Control. "We got us some problems—I'll be late for watch, likely, if I make it at all. Can you . . . ?"

"Charvel and I can split that watch, if necessary." Zelde thanked her, and sat, waiting for Torra Defose.

When the woman entered, Zelde saw excitement in her face, and said, "Let's sit around the corner here, in the snack cubby." She poured coffee, then said, "You got something?"

"I've got Franzel." The set of the lean jaw showed determination; Defose gestured. "Oh, not my hands on her—not yet. But I know who she is." Zelde waited. "Not on the roster, no. But Parnell said he didn't recognize his assailant, so I looked further." Torra pushed both hands back through tousled hair. "In the cargo—that's where I found her!"

Cargo? "But all those was put on the roster, after Escape."

Defose shook her head. "Not those who were killed in that fighting. There's no current listing at all. And this one—"

Frowning, Zelde protested. "But how—you mean, somebody *hiding out* all this time? I don't believe it."

Against Zelde's headshake, Defose nodded. "You'll have to. Look—here's the description." She read from a paper. "Tessi Franzel. Forty-two bio-years, as of Earth liftoff. One-sixty centis tall, and masses fifty-two kaygees. Hair and eyes, brown. Scars—umm, bla bla—yes, *this* one! Nose broken, flattened to the left side." Wide-eyed, she looked at Zelde. "Isn't that what you saw—you and Parnell both?"

Trying to recall the cargo hold, Zelde caught a glimpse of past-seeing but couldn't hold it. It was enough, though. "Yeah. But how could anybody—what kind of person . . . ?"

Gently, Torra's palm thumped the table. "Hide out, unlisted, on this ship? I've thought, and it's not as hard as you might expect. *I* could do it—manage to eat and sleep and have all the time in the world for my—I mean, Tessi Franzel's—real business."

Zelde sighed. "You caught me where I'm dumb, I think. Explain, a little bit?"

"Surely. Every group you're with, you say you're from some *other* working outfit. In the galley you're usually Lower Drive, so you can wear the hood and goggles—and as much as possible, come in to eat when the real Lower Drive people aren't there. If anyone asks questions, talk with your mouth full and mention a provisional transfer. Zelde, it wouldn't be so difficult."

"But—*who?*"

"Yes." Defose didn't look happy. "Only one kind of person, with one kind of training. Zelde—whatever else Tessi Franzel is, she's a UET plant. All the way, from the time she came aboard."

There was more. Why hadn't Franzel gone to the Police on Terranova? Ship's routine—no ID to show the main ramp or cargo hatch guards, and unrated crew didn't leave ship singly. Torra grinned. "Franzel must have been one frustrated little Utie!" And suddenly, hearing Defose use that term as if she'd said it all her life, Zelde lost the last of her mistrust.

On impulse she reached and squeezed the other's hand. At Torra's questioning look, she said, "Never mind. You just said something I liked, was all."

Defose smiled, and went on with it. Franzel's timing— the ship was understaffed, unsettled, Captain and First Hat both out of action. On Fair Ball, Parnell would recruit up to strength and there wouldn't be a Utie in the lot! Meanwhile, the Hidden World's coordinates were in the computer. A big haul, really big—if Franzel could bring it off!

"Yeah." Zelde saw it. "And Carlo—he expects command?"

"That's the bait, yes—and they'd give him the rank, certainly. But not even UET would let that fool keep a ship. The first place he landed, he'd be transferred groundside, to a desk."

It made sense. Carlo was the only handle the Uties had—and no good until he'd been given Acting Third again. Kill Parnell and Dopples—Zelde, too, probably. And to get the ship landed safely, offer Lera Tzane a choice—UET's amnesty, or death. Unless Franzel herself could land a ship. . . .

"It's a solid case," said Torra. She stood, ready to leave. "But proving it—that's another matter."

Late for watch, Zelde stopped to look at Parnell. He lay on his side; in his throat, his breath rattled phlegm. Hell— she couldn't leave him alone here! Fesler didn't answer the intercom; well, he couldn't stay at his desk all the time. She'd stop by on her way to Control, and have him send someone.

Turk's quarters didn't answer, either. Zelde shook her head—she couldn't wait around here forever. If a gun and knife weren't enough—she checked the gun for full load— the hell with it. At the door she told the guard to expect a medic soon; then she went to Fesler's area.

She found him and explained her problem. "All right, Zelde. I'll locate someone right away, to send to your quarters."

She thanked him and headed upship, stopping by the galley for a sandwich and eating it as she climbed farther.

One landing below Control, she met Rooster. The man was crying.

"What—"

"They got *Turk!*"

This needed sitting down—right on the steps, pulling Rooster down beside her and holding him. "Who? What happened?"

He shook his head like he wanted to get rid of it. "I don't *know*. Our quarters, nobody there—the place a mess, and blood. . . ." He wiped his eyes. "Then, the intercom—it's Turk."

Not dead, then. "Go on."

"Saying, 'Rooster, help me,' and all. That she's locked up. And then 'Nowhere, nowhere soon'—voice sounding tinny and high-pitched, and sort of leaving the middle out of 'nowhere.' Then it cut off—I went to Control, they didn't know anything. Zelde, I—"

"Hold it." Nowhere, without the middle. Nowhere— no'ere—and high-pitched. "No *air!*" She jumped up and pulled at him. "The airlock, Rooster! Topside—same one they tried to kill *you* with! Come on!"

She didn't wait, but drove herself upship as hard as she could go—panting, legs aching, she climbed. And when she reached the right deck—pausing, the deck level with her waist—at the airlock door were two hooded figures. And one of them shot at her.

The first shots hit wide. She ducked, and now the stairs gave cover. When the firing stopped, she brought her own gun up—hand raised first, shooting before her head topped the step—and sprayed the area with vicious, glancing pellets. One enemy was down, gun lying free of the outstretched hand. The other, running now, fell once and then scrambled around a corner, out of sight. Up on the deck, sprinting for the airlock, Zelde heard a door creak. Down the hullside stairs, that one was going.

All right—that could wait. The airlock—she looked inside. Turk lay writhing, hands to her throat, pink froth bubbling from nose and mouth. But the high whistling noise—what was it?

The airlock control lights read "Open to space"—but the lock *wasn't* open. Pressure down to—*oh my God! She'll be dead!*—and now Zelde heard the exhaust pump throbbing, and turned it off. The door wouldn't open—not with that much pressure difference. She pulled the handle once, anyway, then looked for another answer.

Now she saw what made the whistling. Her own shooting—two holes in the heavy airlock window, and air screaming through them. All right—pointblank she shot a pattern, a rough circle, hoping the needles wouldn't ricochet to find Turk. Then she wrapped her jacket around one fist, stepped back, and lunged to hit with her full weight. And the tough plastic shattered.

Vacuum took the jacket—by luck she got her hand back out without laying the wrist open on the jagged edges. Explosively, air filled the lock. And as Rooster finally joined her, she got the door open.

They went in together. On her knees, Zelde wiped bloody foam from her friend's face. Was she breathing? Not to notice. . . . Zelde put her mouth to the other's and—once, and again, and another time, for luck—blew in, as hard as she could. Then she pulled back and looked. Yes—blood still came, but now Turk was breathing on her own.

Zelde got up. Rooster sat, and cradled Turk's head in his lap. "Is she going to make it?"

"She's got a chance—let me get Fesler." But the intercom terminal was dead. "Rooster—I got to find me a call box; they wrecked this one." She looked at Turk, and made the best guess she could. "Shouldn't hurt to move her. Why don't you start bringing her downship?" He nodded; she turned toward the landing.

Then she thought, and went to the hullside stairs door. It was open—looking down, she saw no one. Just in case, though, that's the route she took—gun out and ready—until she got to where people were. Then she called Fesler.

Fine. He'd come topside right away—and not alone.

All right—long enough, she'd been running around like a chicken with its head cut off. Time she got to Control and found out what was going on. In a hurry, she went there.

The place was full of smoke—she couldn't see very far, and she heard a lot of coughing. Holding a sleeve across her face, she headed for the watch-officer's station.

Somebody said, "Hold it right there! Who are you?" She

didn't know the voice, for sure, so she hunkered down behind a readout console. *Could be one of them!*

But when she said who she was, the other said, "Good. Then we're both in safe country," and she stood again.

Three more steps and she could see Lera Tzane. Zelde spoke first. "What *is* this?"

Tzane's hair straggled across a bruised cheek. "I—don't know. I tried to call you. But *this*—" She gestured toward the rest of the room. "It must have been the messenger. He—"

"What messenger? Start from scratch, will you?"

After a deep, shuddering breath—and at least the air was clearing—Tzane said, "I didn't see him come in. I was checking a blip that didn't repeat. Someone tapped my shoulder and I turned to see—saw this man—they say he came in as a messenger—and he hit me. Then the smoke bomb went off, and I—"

"Tzane! You got *anything* that makes sense?"

The woman shook her head. "Not really, Zelde. I suppose the same man had the bomb, set it down—no one would notice a box—"

"Why'd he hit you? And stop with that, I mean?"

"How could I know? He had something in his hand—I dodged the blow, a little—and when the bomb went, a gun fired, too. Then the man ran, back through the smoke."

Tzane looked like apologizing; Zelde touched the bruised cheek and said, "Not your fault, Lera. Those peacefucking Uties—they're hitting us every place all to once! Tried to kill me—then Parnell, and Turk—we're lucky, I guess, that whatever they were after, here, they didn't get it."

Tzane looked unhappy. "I hope you're right. But a sheaf of readouts is missing—it was right here beside me."

"Important?"

"I don't know, Zelde. I'd had no chance to look through it."

Damn all!—more to worry on? She shook her head—forget it! Right fast now, either she'd have their ass or they'd have hers—and the rest went with it.

She said, "Full alert, we go on! Lera, roust up guards for all of it. In pairs. The usual scutwork can wait." Something else? Yes. "First thing, special—get Dopples protected!" Tzane nodded, and Zelde turned to go. She nearly bumped into Gil Charvel; he carried a crumpled stack of paper. "What's that?"

"A man running out of here," said Charvel. "He dropped these."

"The readouts!" said Lera.

"Then that's one thing," Zelde said, "we don't have to worry about."

She was nearly to the door when someone called, "Officer M'tana—emergency!" At the comm-panel, she heard one of Fesler's aides.

It was too much. When she could answer, she said, "I'll be right there."

But when she got to quarters, Parnell was dead. And for a time, there, she didn't know where she was or what she did.

She was still hugging him, crying, trying to breathe life into him again, when Fesler made her stop. "It's no use, Zelde. My aide—" Zelde looked at the frightened woman, as Fesler said, "She called me immediately, when she found him like this—and then applied all the resuscitation techniques. No time wasted; she did everything she could. And so did I—another adrenalin shot, all of it." He spread his hands. "There was no chance, Zelde."

Holding his head in her lap, she sat up. "What—what did it?"

He pointed. The glass had a little whiskey in the bottom; the bottle—it hadn't been open, last she'd seen—was down maybe five centimeters. "He drank all that?"

Looking pained, Fesler nodded. "And he *knew*, with so much drug in his bloodstream, he shouldn't drink at all. I can only think—waking up groggy, and paining, he went for it automatically."

She noticed she was shaking her head, and stopped. "How he even got up and *found* it. . . ." Gently she let Parnell's head down onto the bed, and stood. "What I'm going to do now, Fesler—without Ragir—I don't know. But right now I got to. This mess won't wait."

The aide touched Zelde's arm. "Officer M'tana—I *tried*."

Zelde pressed the woman's shoulder. " 'Course you did. Don't blame yourself—just peace-be-damned bad luck." But *she*—what could *she* have done different? So Parnell wouldn't be left alone, so this couldn't happen? Step by step, she thought back.

No—the way things went, nothing she could do. Except, now—eat the pain. And go ahead. . . .

Guard and aide helped Fesler take the body out. Zelde needed a drink. She looked at the bottle. Not out of *that* one, she didn't.

It was time she got back to Control; Zelde reloaded her gun, fully. Her stomach cramped on emptiness, but she couldn't think of anything that might stay down if she did eat it. She paused—*got to get my head working better, or no chance at all!*

She started for the door, but the intercom sounded so she went to it. The other voice came low. "Torra here, Zelde. Mauragin's loose—shot the guard and joined up with part of his gang. Headed upship. I'm stuck here, hiding in a cubby—two of his guards covering the corridor outside. I'll try—"

The all-ship broadcast circuit, hissing with distortion, drowned her voice. "Now hear this! The captain speaking—Captain Carlo Mauragin. Parnell's dead. Adopolous will be in custody soon. Tzane and Charvel already are. M'tana—you have ten minutes to turn yourself in. After that you'll be shot on sight."

He paused; Zelde could hear someone talking to him, but no words. "Yes," he said. "All personnel not assigned by *me*, stay put—out of the corridors. Anyone moving around and not cleared, you *may* have time to surrender—but don't count on it."

The hiss ended. Zelde called Torra's name, but the circuit was dead.

I'm on my own. And threats or no threats, that left her only one choice.

Mauragin's guards weren't out yet in force; Zelde was three landings down before she met the first pair. They weren't fast enough, and died for it. Then, without further resistance she reached the level just above the drive room and headed for the equipment staging area. The only question was—had Carlo beat her to it?

He hadn't. The top half of the power suit lay back across a workbench; the rest of it trailed to the deck. She locked the door; it wasn't the only one into the general area, but she didn't know where the others were, so maybe Carlo didn't, either. She went over to the suit, thinking through what she'd learned—how to get in it, close it secure, and then put the power on. She nodded—yes, she remembered. But with no help, it wouldn't be easy. . . .

The bottom half was all right—like climbing into stiff, bulky trousers. Then it got tougher. Standing, she couldn't reach back for a solid grip on the arms or shoulders. Finally she squatted—slowly, the framework hard to move without power—until the upper section came partway off the bench. Then—slow again, and a lot of work to it—she stood again, and now could reach where she had to. Awkward as hell—but first she got the shoulder harness, then the arms, and finally the headpiece. Panting, she forced herself through the rest of it—closing the suit, putting power to it and running systems checkouts. Too bad the suit's projector wouldn't plug in and work—but she saw it was gone from here, anyway. From a locker she took a standard, two-handed energy gun—except that in the suit, she could cradle and shoot it with one hand. She checked it—full charge, all right—and did a few quick exercises to get the feel of the suit. All right—it would have to do. She opened the door, and started upship.

She had no choice of routes. The hullside stairs, that she'd stormed up during Escape, would be cramped passage for the bulky suit. Easy to block, too—push a desk onto a landing and weld it in place. She'd play hell clearing such a barricade, under fire. And the bypass from Drive to Control—the access was down one level, and Mauragin's people probably held Drive, by now. Anyway, she'd climbed two decks before she thought of it! So, too late now. . . .

She got more than halfway before anybody shot at her— Carlo didn't have the ship covered so good, after all. *Keeping his troops to protect his own skin?* Two, again—one with bullets and the other with a projector like her own. She stopped and steadied, and cut them both in half. Damn—burned through the bulkhead behind them—*short* bursts, remember?

At Fesler's deck she heard shooting and took a side-track—down the corridor and around a corner she found a siege in progress. Three gunners attacking the medical area, and not many shots fighting back. The three had no chance to turn around; she chopped them down and went to pick up their guns. The hospital door had its window blown out; the gun, that pointed through it, wavered. She yelled, "M'tana here! The ones shooting at you, they're dead. Have some guns, Fesler. Is Dopples all right?"

"We're okay, mostly—two wounded but no dead." Fesler sounded more mad than scared. "They barged in, the first bunch, and it was tight for a while. Dopples tried to fight, and caught a smash in the head—he's out cold, but breathing. Torra Defose got here and made the difference; those attackers are dead or captured. Then this new batch came. You got them all?"

"Like I said, yeah." The medic was burn-smudged, but as he took the three guns he had a fighting grin. Behind him, Torra waved a hand; Zelde waved back. Fesler said, "What else is happening?"

She was already turning away. "Tell you after I get up to Control. Just hold the fort." He said something more—but charging up the next stairs, she didn't hear the words.

Now at each landing she met firing. How many left?— she'd lost track. But this job was turning into a real piss-cutter!

After her first fire fight above the medical area, she thought of another way to do it. The suit made noise—no chance of sneaking up on anybody. So at each landing she barged right on up until her head showed above the deck, then ducked down. When shooting came, she waited until it stopped—then she eased the heavy energy gun up over, to point along the deck, and cut loose with a quick, swinging blast. And then came up and took care of what was left.

Twice, that meant killing. One time, all she saw was people running away, leaving guns on the deck. And three times there were men or women nursing seared legs, not interested in the guns they'd dropped. She tossed the weapons down the stairwell, and didn't bother asking anybody to surrender.

Up to the next level—at the galley entrance stood an armed guard. Inside, she saw people sitting, not moving.

The guard's gun sank to point down at the deck; he stared at Zelde like he wished he didn't have to.

Past him, at a table, Zelde saw Rooster Hogan. She said, "Guard! How you stay alive is, I call somebody out from the galley and you give him that gun." She waited; the man gave a short, jerky nod. "All right—Rooster, the man wants you to have his gun." And a minute later, Rooster had the guard's job—but from inside, behind a barricade.

As Zelde left, he shouted after her, "Turk's still hurting, but she's going to make it!" She waved back to him.

Now, she knew, none of it would be easy. From the next level, before she got up there, a grenade bounced down the steps. Her energy gun caught it, and it blew like a steam kettle, not a bomb. Then she ran straight up into the lot of them, and caught them flatfooted, not expecting what they saw. One died and two gave up.

Coming to the next deck, it sounded too quiet, so she looked hard and saw something—a trip-thread, stretched straight across. She reached up and pulled it—and projector fire washed the deck above. When it died out—and she figured that what was left wouldn't get her, through the suit—she went on up. She passed that charred area and saw no one, dead or alive.

One deck below Control, she ran into trouble. When she did her routine of pop up and duck back, the return fire didn't stop. And at a quick guess, she'd seen at least six armed people.

Waiting would make it worse—they could get more troops from upstairs, and pinpoint her. Down two levels—*fast*—she picked up the corpse, and its needlegun. Then, back up again.

She shoved the dead one up to take the fire—and that fire came. With her left hand—the dead arm hung over it—she sprayed bullets, counting the seconds. At ten, she screamed and let the body sag down onto her, below deck-level; her last shot took out the overhead light. Then she waited.

First, only one looked down at the corpse sprawled over her—then two, then a third. She threw the body at them, and stood, looking across the deck, and fired short projector bursts until nothing lived to stop her.

One more climb, to Control. They'd be warned—the

fight below hadn't been quiet. But she found the landing clear, and turned toward the control room itself.

The door was open—blown partly off its hinges and sagging to one side. A direct approach was too dangerous; she came at an angle and risked a quick look inside. Before she could see much, she got what she expected—a burst of energy fire. But it was heavier than her own gun could give. *What the hell?*

She dropped flat—the suit's gyros made the move slower than she liked—and peered around the door edge.

It wasn't good—before the crash of energy fire came, over her head but only a little, she saw that much. A barricade—everything loose must have been piled up to make it. And somebody in a helmet—Carlo? probably—aiming a gun over it. And now she saw where the big projector, designed as part of the suit, had gone. Carlo had it.

The one good part was the *way* he had it, lying across a cabinet. He couldn't point it down to reach her—his blasts came dead flat across.

But he wasn't the only one shooting—energy and needle weapons, both. She hitched her own gun up and sprayed at the lot—fast, so as not to wreck Control but maybe get their heads down and the guns quiet. The suit was tough—but repeated hits in one place could get through and kill her.

In sudden quiet she came to her feet—running stooped-down, she charged. She swung her gun in quick bursts—*keep down, you peacefuckers!*—but the bigger weapon on the barricade was reaching for her, flaring. She wasn't close enough—she threw her own gun and knocked the other out of line.

Firing from the sides distracted her; she ignored it and hit the piled-up barrier with the suit's full power. As she crashed through, falling, a gun came close against her head. She grabbed it and threw it down—and saw she'd also torn away the hand that held it.

One of the suit's knees jammed. She pivoted on the other leg and saw Mauragin, face pale through the helmet's visor, backing away. One lurching step, and she had him by the shoulder. He shrieked; she picked him up, one-handed, and threw him at two who shot at her.

Off balance, she fell. Scrambling up—the knee worked again but the suit was slow now, its gyro clutches chatter-

ing—she swung a heavy chair first against one gun-wielder
and then the other. She dropped it and picked up the big
projector Carlo had used—wired, with untidy cabling, to
draw ship's power. She moved, so that no Control functions
were in her line of fire—and blasted everything that stood.
Smoke billowed—and the *stink.* . . .

Gasping, she turned to see if anybody was running the
ship. Gil Charvel, handcuffed to an armrest, sat in one
Control Seat. Two seats away, both hands bound, was Lera
Tzane—and bending over her, facing away from Zelde, was
a short, skinny woman. Lera screamed; Zelde made the
crippled suit move, and caught the woman's arm.

Carefully, so as not to tear the arm off, she turned that
one to face her. She hardly noticed the hypo-ampoule the
woman dropped. What she saw was the face—the nose,
flattened to one side. And now, from Hold, Portside Upper, she remembered it.

Harder than she meant to, Zelde shook the woman; she
heard bone snap. "Tessi Franzel, you'd be. I think you owe
me more than your whole life's got in it, to pay. But we'll
have us one real good talk, finding out."

Sorting things out—that took some time. Dazed now, in
reaction—not feeling real at all—Zelde sat on an over-
turned cabinet. Still in the suit, but she had the headpiece
off.

Torra Defose seemed to know what she was doing; Zelde
just sat and watched, and listened. She ate something—
Lera Tzane made her do that—but she didn't taste it. *What
a peace-bedamned mess!* Torra had a crew cleaning Control up, dead bodies and all—but that was the least of it.

Lera wasn't hurt, or Charvel—they'd been taken at gun-
point, no chance to fight. Dopples was still out cold. Turk
would be all right, but not soon. *And Ragir—he's dead!*

Carlo—he could be patched up, if there was any point to
it. Tessi Franzel—Torra brought the woman, one arm dan-
gling limp, to face Zelde. "I'll question this one for you. Is
there anything special, besides names, that we need to
know?"

Franzel made a tight, one-sided grin. "Whatever you
want to know, you won't hear it from me."

With her fingers, Torra made a sign. Franzel's eyes went
wide, and she tried to whisper to the taller woman. Defose

shook her head. "No. But I *was* Police—so now you know you'll talk."

Zelde said, "Maybe I should come, help ask questions."

"No." Torra's face was a mask. "You don't want to see it." And she took Franzel away. When she came back, alone, she said, "Eighteen others, besides herself and Mauragin. Ten secret Uties—and the rest just plain scared into going along. I wouldn't bother punishing those last—the two left alive—if I were you."

"How about the rest—the Uties? And where's Franzel?"

No expression on Torra's lean face. "I spaced her."

Zelde tried to stand. The suit, power off now as Henty Monteil worked on the damaged knee, didn't budge. "Torra—wasn't that *my* place, to decide?"

Defose paused. "Making that one talk wasn't easy. I told you, you didn't want to see it—you wouldn't like the result, either. By the time she told it all, she was better off dead. So after I finished throwing up, I gave her to the airlock."

There wasn't much way to answer that, so Zelde didn't.

Five of the closest Uties still lived. No time, now—Zelde had them locked up. She was giving a lot of orders in a hurry—and paused once, wondering why Lera wasn't doing any of it. Then she shrugged—some folks do things and some don't. It wouldn't look good in the log, but who was going to argue?

Monteil finished with the knee joint. "It should work—but don't put much strain on it."

Zelde restored power and—leaving the headpiece back—tried the suit's action. Not as strong as before, but she could move around. "Thanks, Henty," and the small woman smiled and took her tools away.

Carlo, now. She went—slow, getting the new feel of the suit—over to where he lay, head pillowed on a rolled-up jacket.

Seeing her, his eyes turned up nearly out of sight. She said, "This won't take long." Not hard, just barely, she touched his crushed shoulder. "Don't bother fainting—I'll just wake you back up." He did faint twice, but his story fit what Defose got from Franzel. "All right, Carlo. We're done now."

Pale-faced, sweating, he said, "What—what happens to me?"

She had to think. "You got Parnell killed—in a half-assed way, but you managed it. Tried to kill me, too—and Dopples. Tried to give us back to UET—*that's* the worst." She shook her head. "I'm spacing you, Carlo."

All the way—while she carried him downship and put him in the main airlock, and finally opened it to space—not once did he stop screaming.

When she got to the equipment staging area, to take the suit off—as tired, she thought, as if she had to move it without power—she found that Torra Defose was with her. "How . . . ?"

"I followed you, Zelde. And I admired how you forced yourself to hear Carlo, all that way. Me—I'd have put him unconscious. But you—"

"Shit. Didn't think of it, was all." She leaned against the workbench and fumbled at the suit's fastenings.

Defose moved forward. "Let me help you."

"You know how?"

The woman shrugged. "If you'll point to where things work, I think I can figure it out." So, feeling thankful, Zelde let her help get the suit off. Free of it, she turned and straightened the joints, looking for damage. No, nothing that showed—Henty should probably check closer, though. She turned to Defose.

"I guess I better—" Try to sleep, she meant to say. But—"Who's got the watch?"

"Charvel, then Tzane. After that—if you're not up to it, Zelde, Rooster Hogan's ready to sit in. Or I can, myself." Zelde's surprise must have showed; Defose said, "All the watch has to do, just now, is call someone if anything changes. So don't worry. And now, let's get you upship and lying down."

Not thinking too well—and she knew it—Zelde went up-ship. She didn't lean on Defose—not exactly. In quarters she lay down, too tired to take her clothes off. Torra did that for her, and pulled the covers up. Zelde couldn't think, couldn't talk—couldn't even cry. The last she remembered, the woman was still holding her, so she didn't shake quite so much.

When she woke, Torra was gone. Zelde showered and dressed. Either her head was working again, or fooling her—it would have to do. Nearly time for her regular watch; she decided she might as well stand it. For a moment she paused—the trouble was over now, wasn't it? But just the same, she wore her knife and the needle gun.

Passing the galley, she found she had an appetite again, and took time for breakfast—but only one cup of coffee, and she drank it fast. Then she went to Control.

Most of the wreckage was cleared away, but the seared deck and bulkheads still showed the effects of the fire fight. Lera Tzane, with three technicians, had the watch; talking to Lera was Torra Defose. Zelde walked over and greeted them.

Tzane looked around. "Zelde, are you all right?"

Zelde shrugged. "No. But ready to work. Situation report?"

"I've logged the mutiny attempt, the best I could—you'll probably need to add to it. Casualties—thirteen mutineers dead and spaced, seven confined. We lost eight dead and several injured. Dopples is still unconscious; Fesler's worried." *That makes two of us!*

"And the ship. Course? Position sightings?"

"All on sked, Zelde."

"Then I'll take over; you're relieved. I expect you can use some rest."

Lera nodded, but Torra Defose spoke. "Zelde—hadn't you better settle first, who's running this ship?" When Zelde didn't answer, the other said, "I mean, call a meeting—as Parnell did, I understand, under similar circumstances—and make sure the situation is clear to everyone."

Lera touched Zelde's arm. "With Parnell gone and Dopples in a coma, we're all that's left. Well, Gil, of course. This ship's jumpy—ask Torra—and I think you have to set the new officers' roster and announce it officially. In meeting—that's best."

"Go ahead, Zelde," Defose said. "I'll sit in for you here."

Not sure of her ground, Zelde said, "Just a minute. Lera, *you're* Acting First. I—"

"No. It's the way Parnell said. You own Captain's shares, you're in Captain's quarters—and I don't *want* command."

"All right." But it'd still be dicey; Zelde knew that.

* * *

In quarters—all hers now, damn it!—she faced the group. Lera, Charvel, Harger and two of his Engineering officers, and six senior ratings—the rest of those were dead or locked up. She offered drinks around; Harger and Juvier took beer; the others passed the offer. She sat, then, and said, "Meeting in council of officers and senior ratings, the ship *Chanticleer*." And that was something else needed changing—she couldn't stand it, in her mind seeing Parnell when he'd given that name. She thought of another one, but for now she shook her head. "First order of business—I'm in command now. Mr. Adopolous isn't fit, and Acting First Hat Lera Tzane passes it."

Harger gestured toward the two who had come with him. "M'tana—my people are armed, and so am I."

"What's that supposed to mean?"

"Only that some questions need answering—and don't fly off the handle when I ask them."

Eyes narrowed, she watched the plump man. "Ask away."

He coughed into his hand. "The trouble is that *Mauragin* predicted this—Parnell dead, then Dopples, probably—and you running the show. You have to admit it looks bad. But maybe you can explain. I hope so."

Furious, she fought the urge to call him out and have done. "When *Parnell* set the succession this way, I didn't notice you bucking him none. And anybody bother to tell you yet, Harger—the woman that gave Mauragin his lines was a Utie plant? That the whole idea was he'd of given us back to UET—and got himself a Captain's rank for it? And even more than that for Franzel, likely."

She'd slowed the man down; now she gave him the story. She saw some of the others fidget, looking uncomfortable—and guessed they'd been braced, too, by Franzel. Harger asked questions, but after a time he nodded. "All right, I believe you. One thing, though—about your command, spell it out. Acting, or permanent?"

Zelde poured herself a drink. Only after she'd sipped the whiskey did she realize it was the same bottle that had killed Parnell. *Well, he wouldn't want it wasted!* She said, "That's between me and Dopples—when he's awake again, and talking. I own Parnell's shares and I'm acting on them—since Fesler can't say when Dopples might be fit for duty. We're close onto turnover—and course change, if that's needed. So—" She made up her mind. "From here to groundside, on Fair Ball, I'm captain—and there's no Acting about it."

In several faces she saw objections forming; she went ahead. "Second item. It's Captain's right to rename a ship, and—" For a moment, she choked. "—personal reasons—I propose this ship be *Kilimanjaro*." A mountain, that was, in Africa where her folks was from. And Parnell wouldn't mind—would he? "Vote?"

They passed it. "All right. My officers, here to Fair Ball. Lera Tzane, First Hat, Gilman Charvel, Second, and—" Who *was* there? All at once, she decided. "For Third, Torra Defose."

Harger's brows went up. "Now wait a minute. M'tana, I came on this ship as Chief Engineer working under certified officers. And, no offense—but Tzane was a rating and *you* came aboard as *cargo*. And now you ask me to accept a Policebitch as Third Hat?"

Zelde's surge of rage surprised her; she held it back. "It was Torra figured who was behind Carlo—who it had to be, and why. And told us about Refuge being a UET trap. I'm vouching for her, Harger."

The man shrugged. "All right—I can't argue with your results, to date, given the circumstances. Defose you say, and Defose it is."

Nobody else commented. Zelde wondered how to close this thing off. "Any more questions?"

Lera Tzane said, "What do you intend to do about the surviving mutineers?"

"Haven't decided—but I will." Zelde stared at all of them. "I earned the right. On that, there won't be no vote."

When nobody answered, she said, "Meeting closed, then. I thank you all for coming." And the lot of them filed out, leaving her to wonder what she could have done better.

She called Rooster. Turk was going to make it, Fesler'd told him, but not fast. Yes, Rooster could relieve Torra on watch. "That's good, Rooster—and thanks. I need her for something, just now."

And a few minutes later, Torra Defose followed Zelde down to Hold, Portside Upper, where the seven living mutineers waited.

* * *

Outside the hold, a guard sat—and inside, another. The second gestured with her gun, toward two prisoners who sat apart from the others. "If you'd move those somewhere else, I wouldn't be needed. The rest aren't too fond of them."

One of the two was Bellarn, her brown hair mussed and one pale cheek bruised. The other was a young black man, short and stocky. Zelde said, "What's it about?"

Behind her, Torra Defose whispered. "Those two were coerced into joining Mauragin. The other five are out-and-out Uties."

One of those was Paskow, the thin blond man had blood on his jacket. His voice came shrill. "You're not going to win, you know! Where's Carlo? And—" He stopped.

Zelde grinned. "Franzel, you're asking about? Spaced—and so's Mauragin. You here, you're all that's left." She walked toward him and he stepped back. "Paskow—what's it you love so much about UET, you want to get back to it?"

He shook his head. Bellarn said, "We'd all be officers, Carlo told us. I didn't care about that—didn't want UET again at any price. But then it was stick with him and Franzel, or get killed."

Paskow spat at her. "You filthy traitor!" He started toward her, and Bellarn cringed. Zelde caught him and pushed him back.

"Traitor, huh, Paskow? How about *you*—going back on your word you gave Parnell, right after Escape?"

Jaw set, he shouted. "That doesn't apply! Renegades, faithless men—what right could *they* have to my loyalty? I—"

She'd had enough; with one move she slapped him silent. "But Franzel bought it, easy enough." She paused. "Doesn't matter, I guess—except what do I do with you?" Torra whispered again; Zelde nodded. To Bellarn and black man she said, "Defose vouches for you two; you can go out of here with us. Not your ratings, though—from here on you work in the unrated gangs. And your earned shares over and above unrated pay are forfeit into the pot."

Bellarn nodded, and the other didn't protest. Zelde turned back to Paskow's group. "I already made up my mind about you five—you got anything to say, might change it?"

The blond man shook his head. *Figures to die brave, that one.* A middle-aged woman—lean-faced, with one arm in a sling, said, "It's as Paskow said. We went along with your mutiny—your Escape—because after the fact there was no other choice. Then Franzel, organizing us, made our odds sound better than they turned out to be. Being an officer—" The woman shrugged. "That didn't matter, to me. What I really wanted was to see Earth again. I have grandchildren growing up there."

And likely Welfared by now. But Zelde didn't say it. "Anybody else?" None spoke. "All right. Only sensible thing is to space the lot of you—alive, you're more trouble than you're worth. And you cost me the best man I ever knew." Defose tugged at her sleeve, but Zelde shook free. "This once, though, I'll be stupid. 'Til we land, you stay locked up here. Then, groundside, I'll ask. You can't be the first leftover Uties ever turned up on a Hidden World. If they got ways to keep you out of trouble, you go free— with your personal stuff, but *no* share money."

She stared at them. "If Fair Ball don't want you running loose, that's time enough to make you dead." Nobody answered; she turned to leave, and told the guard, "Bring those two along with you. Then, like you said, you're relieved here."

Now Paskow spoke. "I don't get it—I'd have sworn you'd kill us. Or don't you have the authority? You say *you're* deciding—but who are you really speaking for?"

At the door now, Zelde paused. "Never did see a man try so hard, to get himself killed. But you get an answer. I speak for *me*—Zelde M'tana, captain of *Kilimanjaro.* And why I don't space you—I ever figure that out, I'll send somebody down to tell you."

Now they did leave, and the door closed. Zelde told the guard from inside to take Bellarn and the black man up-ship, and have their new status logged in the computer. Zelde and Torra took another route, and after a time Defose said, "*I* thought you'd kill them, too. I wanted to talk you out of it."

"I knew that."

"But you really don't know why you decided as you did?"

A shrug. "Maybe—I might need a break myself, some-time. Or maybe I paid back some I got already—who knows? And those poopers—by themselves, wouldn't have been anything at all."

Torra hugged Zelde's arm. "The main point—you mustn't ever let killing become the automatic answer to things. And you didn't."

Then, thinking how close she'd come to doing just that, Zelde shuddered.

They stopped to see Turk; she couldn't talk much, but wanted to hear what had happened. With nods, she agreed with Torra's listing of Uties and victims in the mutiny group. And said, finally, "You did good, Zelde—you *both* did."

Walking upship, then, Zelde remembered to tell Torra about her promotion. "So go take the rest of my watch, will you?"

The dark lean face went solemn. "You really want me for Third?"

Still moving, Zelde shrugged. "Who else?"

"And the others agreed?"

"Harger pissed a little but he took it."

Defose nodded. "Then I'll take it, too."

"Good. On watch, anything you need to ask, call me. If I don't answer right away, I'm asleep—so call Lera Tzane."

At the next landing they separated and Zelde went to quarters. She kicked off her shoes and sat at Parnell's work desk. There stood the bottle that had killed him.

"You sonofabitch—I'm going to drink you!"

She didn't finish it, though; she got too much too fast and threw up, barely making it to the toilet in time. Bleary, staggering, she rinsed her sour mouth and washed her face. Then, shedding clothes, she made her clumsy way to bed and felt sleep coming.

At least, she didn't dream.

The intercom woke her. Remembering the booze bout, she braced herself for hangover, but felt only thirst—and hunger. To the intercom she said, "M'tana here."

"Defose. I'm just off watch and ready to eat. Do you feel like having breakfast?"

"I do, yeah."

"Shall we meet in the galley? Or could I bring you a tray?"

"I'd thank you kindly if you brought it. Eggs and such." Torra agreed. While Zelde waited, she had a quick shower; when she answered the door, towel in one hand, she was still dripping from it. Carrying two trays, Torra Defose came in.

She looked Zelde up and down. "That's what I should have done, but I was too hungry." She put the trays down, and the two sat.

"Clean up here, if you want. Eat first, though." Zelde had good appetite herself; she finished the food and sipped coffee.

When Torra was done, she said, "You mean that? I can shower here?"

"Why not?" So the other went into the bathroom, then came out toweling herself. Full-bodied, the woman was, but firm; she looked nearly as hard-muscled as Zelde. She stood, the two of them looking at each other, and set the towel aside. She came to where Zelde sat. Standing close, she reached to hug the younger woman, and held Zelde's head to her chest. She stroked the maimed ear.

After a long silence, Torra spoke. "Zelde—maybe— would you?"

Quietly, not breaking away, Zelde stood. "Hell, yes!" Then they were kissing, holding each other; they stumbled over to the bed.

It was a long time since Tillya—and where that fragile girl had been timid, almost withdrawn sometimes, Torra Defose was vigorous and positive. Not harsh, but fiercely demanding, both in giving and taking. When they were done, lying in loose embrace, Zelde said, "I guess we need another shower."

That one, they took together. And when Zelde, for no reason she knew, started shaking, Torra held onto her until she was all right again. And then said, "What was *that* about?"

"Dunno." But then Zelde nodded. "Yeah, I do. Didn't see how hard I been bracing, me, to keep going—with Parnell gone for always and nobody by me. I guess it hit me, just now, I don't *have* to brace no more, for that. On account of there's you."

* * *

Coffee was a little stale but still hot; dressed now, they sat and drank it while they talked. Torra said, "Asking you, Zelde—I was really frightened. Not that you'd be cruel, but that maybe you didn't like things this way, or just wouldn't want *me*." She smiled. "And when I came in, Zelde, and saw you—I—"

She shook her head. "Then—suddenly it was all right. Wasn't it?"

Zelde reached and squeezed her hand. "You know that." She paused. "Torra—are you all for women?"

"Does it matter?"

"No—I wondered, was all."

Torra laughed. "Now you, I didn't have to wonder about—not on that score." Zelde's thought of Parnell must have showed in her face, for Torra said, "I'm sorry—I didn't mean to—but anyway, the answer's no. To come onto this ship, I left a male lover. More than lover, really— we were married, freestyle."

"Couldn't you of brought him along?"

"Double negative. He's not Police; there was no valid excuse to bring him on my fake mission. And he's solid UET, I'm afraid—and ambitious. He's in Administration, and trying to wangle transfer to Summit Bay, where the promotions are." She sighed. "In many ways, a good man—and not only in bed. But we didn't want the same things."

"And what's it you want now, Torra? To stay on the ship?"

"Yes. My training—overall, not just Police—is more valuable here than on groundside, I think. And *you're* on the ship."

Zelde thought. "You want to move in here, then? I'd like it, if you would." Torra frowned, and Zelde said, "If you don't, it's all right. I just thought—"

Defose shook her head. "I do want to—but it might cause trouble. You being Captain, I mean. And if you find a man you like, I don't want to be in the way. I don't expect to own my lovers—you or any other, past or future."

Zelde drained her cup and poured again; at half-full the flow stopped. "No man on this ship I want, that I know of. If there was—for either of us—it's like you say; nobody owns anybody. Though with Parnell I didn't look around;

didn't want to." She felt her mouth go tight. "No two ways; I'll miss that man."

"I know," and Defose had a sad look to her. "For that matter, I miss mine, too. And, well—rationally I know I've done the right thing, and certainly I can't regret strangling that hyena Cort Verrane, but still. . . ." Past Zelde, she stared. "All the years of loyalty I gave UET, I realize it wasn't deserved. I mean, four *years* ago I got fed up and began the slow process of feeling my way with the Underground. And worked with them, ever since I managed to make the connection. But perhaps I was kidding myself, thinking I was only bucking UET for its own greater good."

"Huh? What you mean?"

"Not sure, Zelde. But now that I've made the irrevocable plunge, I find all my training, all my upbringing from earliest childhood, back there nagging at me. 'Torra, you're being a *bad* girl.' Any time I let my guard down; it's worst when I'm tired."

Switching back, this one? Squinting at her, Zelde decided, *Hell, no!* She said, "Give yourself a little time; it'll wear off." And time now to change the subject. "Hey. We was talking about you moving in here. Now then—you're my Third Hat and Security Chief and—and bodyguard, for peace' sakes! So if I want you close to hand. . . ."

"All right." Now Torra smiled. "I'll guard your body."

Zelde felt stirrings but put them back. "Sure. But not right now. We got to be seeing about some business, on this ship!"

With three officers appointed, Zelde didn't need to stand regular watch. Torra left to collect her things—not much of those, only what she'd worn and carried aboard, and clothing and such from ship's issue. Quickly, trying not to think what it meant, Zelde arranged Parnell's belongings to make room. Then she went to talk with Fesler.

Dopples was awake some now, he told her, and improving slowly. "He has trouble talking, Zelde, as if he'd had a stroke. It was a *bad* concussion; maybe some bleeding, inside the skull, that caused pressure. Not for long, though, or he'd be dead."

She began to speak, but he waved a hand. "Yes, I know—a real doctor would operate to relieve it. But I

don't know enough—and the proper tools aren't here, anyway. If it were life or death—but he *is* coming back,
though slowly—so I prefer the risk of inaction."

Zelde had to agree. Fesler went out, and came back to
say that Dopples was awake now; they went to his room.

Looking up, blinking slowly, Adopolous mumbled something. Zelde shook her head; Fesler said, "I've had more
practice. He wants a briefing on ship's status. I've told him
what I know, but probably there's a lot I don't."

Zelde thought, and told of Tessi Franzel's part in the
mutiny—and of that woman's death, and Carlo Mauragin's. She gave the casualty list—on both sides—and what
she'd done about the surviving Uties. At that, the man's
head moved, a feeble nod.

She told of taking command, and of her other appoint-
ments. Again the faint nod, and she said, "I'm glad you
think I done right."

One more thing on her mind. "Mr. Adopolous—for
turnover, I hope you can be there, and talking good. I
think we can do it, Lera and me—but I'll feel better with
you to check us."

The corners of his mouth moved—a smile, almost—and
his right hand moved a little. She reached and shook it.
"All right, Mr. Adopolous. I'll be looking in again, for
sure."

As she and Fesler left, the ailing man muttered something. She looked back, but the medic moved her along.
Outside, he turned to her. "What he said, there at the last,
was 'Dopples.' "

In Control, other business waited. First, Lera Tzane.
"Zelde, this ship's running crazy with rumors. You have to
get on the intercom, and straighten things out."

"All right." Zelde checked the log—no problems there—
and opened the broadcast circuit. "Now hear this. Zelde
M'tana here. You probably know Parnell's dead—and Mr.
Adopolous hurt bad but getting better now. From here to
Fair Ball, I'm in command—and the ship's name is *Kili-
manjaro*." She named the other officers, then said, "Carlo
Mauragin's mutiny was organized by a UET agent called
Tessi Franzel; those two are dead—spaced." She listed the
other dead, and the Uties she'd locked up, but didn't men-

tion Bellarn or the black man—if she did, somebody'd be wanting their hides.

She paused. "That's the size of it. Anybody got more questions, leave them with the watch officer—and best I can, you'll get answers." Anything more? No. "M'tana out."

She turned to Lera. "Think that covers it?" The woman nodded. "What else, then, I need to do?"

Tzane looked down, then again up to Zelde. "The arrangements for Captain Parnell—Henty Monteil has him ready. But the honor guard—the choosing for it, and rehearsing. . . ."

Zelde's sight blurred; she shook her head. "I don't—I never heard—what's it all about?"

Lera explained. Wearing his dress uniform, Parnell lay in the topside airlock; it was open to vacuum. "In the book," Lera said, an honor guard in suits performed a ceremony before a ship's captain was given to space. "So we should get started if—"

Zelde shook her head. "A Utie ceremony? Parnell don't need it. But—I hadn't thought—*something*, I ought to do. What you think?" She couldn't get it straight. What had she expected? Parnell already spaced? "I guess," mostly to herself, she said it, "I just didn't want to know."

She thought, then nodded. "No guard. No suits, no words set down by UET. I'll do it myself."

Lera touched Zelde's arm. "Shouldn't someone be with you? And shouldn't you announce it, so that if others want to pay their respects . . . ?"

Not used to this stuff. Who should she have there? Turk couldn't, or Dopples. Rooster, though. Fesler. Torra—she'd done her best to help him. Lera had the watch. All right—Zelde called the others to meet her at the airlock—eighteen hundred hours. Then: "You announce it, Lera. So's anyone who wants to, can—oh, *I* don't know!"

"How about one minute's silence throughout the ship? That's a traditional way of expressing respect—from long before UET."

"Fine—do it like that." She patted the other's shoulder. "And thanks, Lera."

She got there early, and closed the lock to let air fill it. When she went in, she could feel the cold. Parnell lay centered, feet toward the outside door. She'd never seen the fancy uniform he wore—and in a way she hated it, for it was UET's. But what else, what better, could he have on? She shrugged, and bent to look closer.

Cold and vacuum had shrunk his skin; he looked like a hungry boy, but the shrinking showed his beard stubble. She touched his cheek, and felt the cold pull at her finger— if she kissed him, her lips would freeze at the surface, and tear when she pulled away. She rubbed them dry with a finger and gave him a quick peck, anyway—and when she got away with that, a longer one. This time a small spot did stick—when she freed herself, she tasted blood.

Behind her, sounds; she turned and saw Rooster coming toward her—and with him, Torra and Fesler. She checked the time—three minutes, yet. They came up to her and stood, looking uncomfortable.

She said, "I don't know how to do this. Come inside here, for now—and, I guess, anybody wants to say something, do it."

In the airlock, Torra leaned down toward the body. "I hardly knew you, Captain—but enough to be glad I was on your side."

Standing back, Fesler said, "Parnell forgave me a serious wrong I did him. I tried, the best I could, to repay that."

Rooster cleared his throat. "Skipper—anything I could do to help, I'd do it. You know that. I'm not sure about religions, and all—but peace take you, sir!"

Blinking tears back, Zelde couldn't see much. "I think— what I tell him, I want to say just alone. If it's all right. . . ."

They left her and she knelt beside him. In her mind, words were everything and nothing. She touched his shoulder—the bad one, it was, so that frozen stiff or not, habit made her touch gentle. And finally she said, "Parnell— Ragir, love—I tried to do you right. You're the best man I ever knew. I find another—I know you wouldn't grudge me—I'll cherish him, too. And for now—peace let me do your *ship* right!"

She moved to him—it was awkward, but she wanted to do it all herself—and lifted and stood him against the door to outside. Erect, leaning back just enough to balance there. She stared, wanting to be able to remember—*but this isn't him!* Then she left the airlock, fast, looked back once and closed the door.

The time—past eighteen hundred, but only by a few seconds. She pushed the other switch. The outer door opened, and the rush of air took Ragir Parnell like a feather; he turned a little and seemed to vanish instantly, leaving no sign of him.

Zelde's hands went to her face. Arms held her; she didn't know whose. After a time, when she raised her head and could see again, she found herself in the middle of all three of them.

Somehow that last good-bye to Parnell cleared Zelde's mind, and let her accept her life as it was. She began to put things together; running the ship settled into routine. Turk Kestler, up and around on a part-time basis, made an insigne for *Kilimanjaro*—a snowy peak against blue sky, with the name in big letters slashing down across it. Rooster went outside to place the sheet—and this time, with Torra Defose on watch, had no trouble getting back in.

Torra, now. Zelde found herself totally interested in talking—almost trading lives, in talk—with the other woman. When Torra asked her age—and, close as she could guess, Zelde gave it—Torra sighed. "Zelde, compared to me, you're a baby. Half my age, give or take a little. And here's *Kilimanjaro*, an Escaped ship, and you by full right commanding it." She shook her head. "No, don't think I'm jealous—command isn't one of my twistups. But now that the guilt's wearing off, as you said it would, I wonder—why did it take *me* so long to cut loose from UET?"

Stroking Torra's neck—Zelde wasn't sure whether the loving was done with, for now—she said, "You ever have the *chance*, before?"

Eyes closed, Torra lay back. "I'm not sure. The ship just before you, at Parleyvoo—it wasn't Escaped yet; I'm certain of that. But the signs were right; that ship was a powder keg if ever I saw one. The captain didn't seem to know it, and I didn't tell him. And Cort Verrane—" She laughed. "His wife Amzella sensed something, but he never listened to her if he could help it. So I handed Verrane my objective report—no inferences, which I'd usually add in such cases—and he gave his smug smile, and congratulated me for clearing the ship so quickly. How that man could be so paranoid and at the same time so gullible, I'll never know."

Zelde thought back. "Hey—that's the ship, left a message for Parnell?"

Torra nodded. "Not officially. From the Irishman, Malloy—First Officer. I tried to talk with that one; being Police, I got nowhere. But I know a hungry man when I see one—and my guess is that Malloy has an Escaped ship for himself. Or soon will."

"Pig in the Parlor."

"I don't understand."

"What he'll name the ship. Parnell told me."

Torra laughed. Her hand moved; ticklish, Zelde turned like a cat. But the intercom sounded; the call was routine, but it broke the mood. Zelde shrugged. "Probably time I got upship and did some work, anyway."

Well ahead of turnover, Dopples was up and moving some. Two canes he needed, to walk with, and help on stairs. But he'd be in Control when the time came, and could talk some, too—but slow. He moved back into his quarters—and if Hilde and Helga missed the young ratings who'd been hanging around, Zelde hoped they knew better than to let on.

She spent more time in Control now, checking star sightings against ship's time and feeding the results to Dopples' portable screen terminal. He agreed with her—everything was on the money, and turnover-warning sounded almost exactly when they expected it. So far, so good.

Nearly midway in Lera's next watch, then, the blondes brought Dopples in. After helping him into the backup seat, they moved to sit well back, out of the way. To Lera's other side, Zelde had the primary screens and computer readout; duplicate tapes went to Dopples' position. Time shortened; no one talked much.

At five minutes, Tzane broadcast the free-fall warning. To the side, Zelde saw Hilde glance at Helga or maybe the other way around. Both made pouting faces, and Zelde guessed what they'd rather be doing.

As before—*except then, Parnell was here!*—the numbers came, the count, the relays to Harger and his responses. Once Dopples began to speak; then he looked again at the tape and shook his head. "It's . . . all right."

At signal, gravity eased off and vanished. Again Zelde felt the ship turn—so slow, like forever. And then the drive

started, began to push—*it coughed!*—and once again, and
then caught hold solidly. And Harger laughed.

Zelde let out her held breath. "Harger! We all right?"

"Just fine. Pardon my little joke—did I scare anyone?"

If you was up here! But she said, "Good job—no harm
done."

Now decel needed setting. Lera said, "Point-seven max,
as before, gives about eighty-five days to our coordinates
for Fair Ball." It sounded right to Zelde, but Dopples
cleared his throat.

They looked at him. In his new, slow way he said, "I'd
use point-seven-five. A little leeway." So that's how Zelde
relayed it down to Harger.

Four days later, Henty Monteil called, saying that Zelde
was hard to find lately. Well, she'd been exploring parts of
the ship she didn't know, trying to learn as much as she
could. The rest of Henty's message was that the power suit
was fixed. "I had to replace the effectors in that knee and
thigh—I think you caught projector crossfire there while
using max effort, and the circuits overheated." But the
thing was, Zelde should come down and run the suit
through a full set of operating tests.

All right—but that gave her another idea. As officers,
Gil Charvel and Torra should know the suit. So after she'd
checked it out, she put both of them through some quick
training. She knew she'd forgot some that Parnell had
shown her, and she didn't have time to study through the
whole manual—not that all of it still applied now. She left
them that part to do, on their own. And before long the
two could handle the thing well enough, and Zelde put her
mind to other matters.

It wasn't a happy ship she had—and Zelde wasn't sure
why. One day, scanning a maintenance log, she found several entries missing—and the chief of that crew, when she
located him, was in his quarters playing cards. The big,
dark-haired man looked up, frowning. "Something you
want?" Like talking to an errand boy. The other three—
two men and a woman—after one glance, they acted as if
Zelde wasn't there.

The man's name?—oh, yeah. "First you stand up, Sam
Dargan." She waited, and he did. "Now say me how come
you're here in duty hours, with your logs a week behind."

Some heavier than she was, but no taller, he shrugged. "Forgot to make the little pencil marks, I guess."

"How about the *work*, Dargan? You forget that, too?"

Again he shrugged; maybe that was what he did best. "UET schedules? Who pays attention now? Parnell didn't. So now all of a sudden, M'tana—"

"*Captain* Parnell—could be he got too sick to wipe your nose for you all the time. And it's Captain M'tana, too. Remember?"

"Ten twelve weeks, maybe—until we land, you're Captain. That much, we've all heard."

Wants trouble, this one. All right. . . . "And this happens to *be* one of those ten–twelve weeks, Dargan."

"So?"

"So get your ass up on the job—double shifts until you catch your logs up. And I don't mean pencil marks—you do the *work*."

Now he laughed. "Who'd know? You're not even trained."

"I'm working on it—and I got people that are." Angered to the killing point, she still tried to reason. "If *you're* trained at all, you know the ship's our life—we take care of it so it takes care of *us*. You don't know that much, you're unrated where you stand!"

He shuffled forward a little. "Unrated? Come to think of it, I don't see *you* wearing any rank—not so it shows." And at that, the other three began moving. *Gang up!*

She made her voice harsh. "Feel like calling me out, do you, Dargan? You three, there—you're witness!"

And the formula, the code, sat them back and out of action. Dargan saw it happen, looked startled, then turned back to Zelde. "I might—I just might. What if I did?"

Close now, she laughed in his face. "When I got done with you, nobody *else* would." Could she back the bluff? Tensed, she breathed up as much oxygen as she could but tried not to show it.

Then he lost his juice—without moving, he seemed to shrink. "I didn't mean—a few drinks, you know—" He spread his hands. "Can't we just forget it—uh, Captain?"

"One more thing, and we can."

"Well, sure—if you want an apology—"

"Don't waste my time with that shit! What I want is, you get the hell to *work!*"

The others left. When Dargan got his tools together, and moved off toward his first check-station, Zelde left, too.

Turk was still working only part-time; Zelde found her in quarters, resting, and told the story. Sipping an odd-smelling tea that Zelde recognized from Terranova, Turk made her guesses. *Not* another mutiny building, but plain jealousy from ratings Zelde had leapfrogged. "Cargo to Captain—that's what they find hard to swallow. You can't expect—"

"Maybe not." Zelde stood. "But they're stuck with me for now—and sure's hell they're going to do their work. Thanks."

"Any old time. I'll help where I can."

"Yeah, I know. I *said,* thanks."

And later, over dinner, Torra told her much the same. "Though with me, since I moved in here, it's more what they don't say than what they do. You see?"

"Sure." Zelde touched the other's cheek. "Hey—you mind, we just sleep tonight?" Seeing Torra's look, she added, "It's just—my thinking won't go that good way, right now."

Likely the grapevine helped—after Dargan, nobody bothered her any, straight out. In the next weeks the work improved, and the ship even felt more cheerful to her. Part of it, she guessed, was the sulkers hanging together to gripe at her—it gave them something to talk on.

Hell with it—she had her job; they could damn well do theirs!

She looked through Parnell's notes on Fair Ball. Not much there—star type, bigger and whiter than Earth's sun. The planet, farther out than Earth, had a longer year. Tilted orbit—all right, she got that—and more eccentric. Off-center, yeah. Not much axial tilt; moving in and out made the seasons.

Small planet, heavy for its size—gravity about like Earth's. Only one main settlement, far as Terranova knew—and how many years out of date was *that* report? At least twenty, Parnell had guessed—by the time the ship could get there.

Which—by ship's clocks—wouldn't be long, now.

* * *

The day they spotted Fair Ball's sun—ninety percent definite and two weeks out, was the guess—Zelde called quarters and told Torra. "Ten hours 'til your watch. Let's celebrate!"

"I'm in favor of that. When will you be down?"

Zelde looked at the main clock. "About an hour. All right?"

"Fine. I have to check some things with Dopples, from my last night's watch. It shouldn't take long."

But Zelde found their quarters empty. Putting a bottle of jash to cool, then having a shower, she didn't notice the time. After that, though, Torra didn't show up for another hour.

She looked flustered, and her hair was mussed. Zelde said, "Anything wrong?"

Torra pushed at the hair, getting it off her forehead. Longer now—uncut since she joined the ship—it tended to flop around. "I—I'm not sure. It depends on you."

Zelde frowned. She'd started to pick up the bottle; now she nestled it back into the ice again. "What does?"

Torra started to smile, but didn't make it stay. "I told you I had things to check with Dopples. I didn't expect to end up in bed with him."

Zelde's thought, then, almost made her laugh. "All of you?"

"What—oh, you mean Hilde and Helga. No—he threw them out. That's what—"

If this was going to take time, Zelde was thirsty. Now she opened the jash, and poured. "Sit down, Torra, and have some. And start from scratch, will you?"

Well. Torra had found Dopples in process of clearing the two blondes out of his quarters. "Clothes all over the place—Dopples pacing back and forth, kicking them across the floor." And the women, half dressed, making little shrieks when Dopples slapped whatever part he could reach. "They each had red marks—but no real bruises, that I saw."

Torra swallowed some jash; Zelde sipped hers. Did this business bother her any? No—not unless it churned Torra a lot. "Anybody say what started it?"

Dopples hadn't minded the women playing around while he was out of action—he had sense enough to expect that.

"But they were too public about it—they didn't save face for him at all. And since he's back they've kept it up, on the side. Finally he had too much, that's all, and he was giving them the heave-ho."

"You already said that. Where's *your* part come in?"

From under lowered brows Torra looked at her, then nodded. "When they were out the door. Dopples found a blouse on the deck and went to throw it after them. I saw something else, before he shut the door, and handed it to him. And he threw that, too, and then made the slam. He came back—I had my report in one hand—and he was laughing. Then he was crying, and fell against me, and the report is what hit the deck next."

"And you two, the bed? Just like that?"

Headshake. Maybe in another month or two the hair would be long enough to comb good. "No. He had to talk." Zelde's brows raised. "Oh, about everything, nearly. That Parnell's dead, and Dopples would have died for him. How it still hurts that he'll never see Earth again—he had some family there, the last he knew. How he regrets being hard on *you* earlier." Her forehead wrinkled. "Something odd about that—he started to say more, and then didn't. But the last straw, I guess, was those two dumb mattress-bouncers. First, being unable to keep them in line—and then the two of them thinking they were *fooling* him."

She paused. "Can you understand that?"

Zelde nodded. "Sure. Parnell—" Wait—would this be disloyal? She decided not. "He was a long time getting sicker—and sometimes he could and sometimes he couldn't. It bothered him." She shook her head. "His pride—I sure tried to be easy on it. And I never had somebody else, either." She thought about it. "Parnell would of agreed, if I'd wanted. But there wasn't anybody. Not until you."

For seconds, Torra's lips clamped tight. "It was when Dopples said he felt betrayed—that all he'd needed was a little time and patience, but now it was too late. I told him it wasn't, either, too late."

Now she raised her head. "And then I showed him."

She waited, and Zelde said, "Have some more jash; let's drink to that. And then, like I said earlier, let's celebrate."

"You mean, you don't mind?"

"Dopples? That man took a *knife* for me."

So they celebrated. After that, sometimes Torra stayed over with Dopples. She always asked Zelde first, and Zelde always said yes, and that she didn't *have* to ask. But she did ask, anyway.

Coming in toward Fair Ball—crawling now, compared to light—*Kilimanjaro* was hailed. Zelde went to Control. The signal was a loop tape; before answering, Zelde heard it through twice, to make sure she had everything straight. For one thing, the voice said nothing about Fair Ball being a Hidden World. Going by the words, it could have been a colony—except that unless the Utics had found and taken it, it wasn't.

All right—play it straight. She spoke her own tape, heard it once and then sent it out. "*Kilimanjaro*, calling Fair Ball. *Kilimanjaro*, Zelde M'tana commanding. We're last from Terranova—where we wore another insigne and their brass never heard of you." At that point on the tape, a pause, while she'd thought hard. "You want references? We got some. Malloy and Ilse Krueger, for starters—more, when we have some from you. Anybody groundside now, we might know?"

Another pause, then her voice again. "All for now; we're tuned for you and homing." Oh, yeah—they'd asked for estimated time of landing. "ETL, approx ninety hours. Greetings to you, from *Kilimanjaro*. M'tana out."

Beside her, in the backup seat, Dopples smiled. "Just right, I'd say." His speech was getting better, fast. "We'll have a wait now. Give me a hand downship to the galley?"

No canes now—just a little help on ladders. They had coffee and snacks, and were back in Control when Fair Ball answered.

Not a standard tape this time; the woman's voice sounded immediate. "Baseline Port to *Kilimanjaro*—Fair Ball settlement calling Captain Zelde M'tana. One of your credentials suits us; that's better than some can give, who turn out to be all right. So welcome here." Somebody coughed; the sound came loud. "Our local admiral wants to ask some questions." And Zelde was *sure* this wasn't UET.

A different voice said, "You cite Krueger and Malloy. Do the following names mean anything to you?" Another cough. "Sten Norden. Bernardez. Quinlan. Limmer. Jargy

Hoad. Tregare. Rasmussen." Only a slight pause, then: "And some ships—*Nonstop, Deuces Wild, Inconnu, Carcharodon, Red Dog.* And the *Hoover.* Think back, and let us know. Baseline Port out, and listening."

Dopples touched Zelde's arm. "Now we know—Bernardez *is* Escaped. But UET doesn't know it yet."

"Right. Dopples—help me figure what's next." And he told her the names he recognized.

Her next tape was short. "M'tana here. We passed close—talking distance—with Kickem Bernardez, farside of Terranova. Neither of us admitted we was Escaped. The rest you said—Tregare and his armed ship *Inconnu,* yes. And Norden, and Quinlan. Not the others. We're new, is what." No more to say. "M'tana out."

This time, a shorter wait. Timing it, Dopples told what it meant in terms of ship's speed and distance.. "Only approx, Zelde—but it fits our sightings." He called Harger. "Cut decel to point-six of max—so we don't come to dead stop before we get there." Sure—that'd be the leeway he'd mentioned.

They listened. "Baseline to *Kilimanjaro.*" The man's voice again. "You're saying that we're your first Hidden World. Then—no offense, but we'd like more confirmation. Because we have a quite extensive list of ships' officers—and, M'tana, your name's not on it. If you'd tell us your ship's former name, and those of its officers—alive or dead—for correlation, we'd be reassured. Thank you—and Baseline out."

Dopples said, "Let me take this one." Zelde nodded. "Cyras Adopolous speaking. I should be listed for the *Great Khan*—also Ragir Parnell and Cleotis Terihew, who have not survived. Zelde M'tana was promoted after Escape; she commands now because I've been disabled for a time." He looked at Zelde, and his expression puzzled her. "That tells most of it, I think. Now—Baseline, is there anyone groundside now that *we* might know? Adopolous out."

He went silent. Something on his mind, for sure—about *her?* She cleared her throat. "Dopples—what happens, groundside? With me, I mean. Back to Second Hat, I guess?" Shares or no shares, that was fair—she'd feel odd, but she could do it.

Between his brows the wrinkles deepened. "I hope it's

that easy." Then he motioned for someone to help him down to his quarters.

The closer to Fair Ball, the easier things got; even the little hassles stopped. Everybody excited, Zelde guessed—waiting to see what it was like, a Hidden World that UET didn't even know about. And except for wondering how *she* stood, Zelde felt the same way, too.

Two ships sitting groundside, Baseline had said—*Red Dog* under Pell Quinlan, and *Cut Loose Charlie*, no captain named. When Zelde asked, Baseline said, "Cade Moaker brought *Charlie* in on his drive's last legs; it'll never lift again, not without new components we don't have and can't make, yet. That's ten years ago, and Moaker's been dead for five. The officers incorporated under our rules here, and run it as Board of Directors. But it's a business now, not a ship."

Business? Yes—the Nielson cube was bad, but not the power systems. So *Charlie* sold power to the Port. Cargo was good for starting up a trading post. The ship's repair shops—machine tools, instruments—did a good business. And more—listening, Zelde realized how complex, compared to most groundside enterprises, a ship really was.

Fair Ball was near enough now—magged-up, it filled the screen—that Zelde could study it on visual. More water than land, she saw—though Tzane told her the proportion of land was higher than Earth's. Two fair-sized continents—one in the "northern" half and the other, the bigger one, almost straight opposite. Connecting those, completing a sort of girdle, were strings of islands—peaks of sunken mountain chains. Scattered islands, too, she saw—but was told that none of those were settled. All this she saw on frequencies outside visual range—Fair Ball's air lay thick and full of clouds.

In the northern continent sat Baseline Port—about midway east to west, and several hundred kilos from the southern shore. On a big river, Parnell had said, and in the middle of plains. Not far south of it a desert began, and continued to the sea. "And that's why," Dopples said, "the colonists didn't try the usual river-mouth type of settlement. The fertile belt on the coast isn't wide enough to support more than a village culture."

Thirty hours out, Zelde still couldn't spot Baseline Port. She knew where it was, pretty well—but she couldn't *see* it.

Two watches ahead of ETL, Dopples called a meeting. "Control and Engineering officers, in my quarters. I'm not on active duty, so this is a request, not an order." But everybody got there on time.

All nine of them had chairs; Dopples had seen to that. Zelde looked around. Of Harger's people she knew only Juvier, the light-skinned black. That group sat facing Dopples. Torra and Zelde were to his right, Gil Charvel and Lera Tzane on the other side. Dopples said, "Let's get to it."

Nobody answered; he nodded. "Before we land and get busy dealing with groundside, let's settle our command situation." He cleared his throat. "The problem is that I have Slaughterhouse training, and seniority, but Zelde M'tana owns command shares."

"I never asked for those—I didn't know Parnell was going to do what he did. You know—you was there."

"But you own the shares." Dopples smiled. "Zelde, I don't begrudge you. And without formal training you've handled command well, in a very difficult time. I appreciate this and I thank you—but it doesn't change matters."

Zelde leaned forward. "*What* matters? You want command back? You earned it, you got it—I already said that. I go back to Second. What more you need?"

Plump Harger's smile looked more like a sneer. "There's a joke going around, M'tana—on paper. The idea is, it's your application for the job of Captain on this ship."

He stopped. Zelde said, "Tell it or don't!"

High-pitched, he spoke. "Having studied under Captain Parnell for some months, I am now ready to assume his position." Then he laughed, and two of his officers followed suit.

With no memory of getting up, Zelde stood over the man. "Talk shit about *me* all you want, Harger. But put any more onto Ragir Parnell, you better have your knife out! You'll need it."

Dopples motioned at her, but before he could speak she was back in her chair. Torra reached both hands to squeeze one of Zelde's. Dopples slapped his chair arm.

"Harger—in my own quarters I'll see courtesy, or you leave. Is that clear?"

Red-faced, Harger said, "I didn't mean——"

"Then the matter is dropped. Zelde?" She nodded. Not that she was forgetting the insult—but this was Dopples' show. He said, "Harger illustrated the problem, though. Zelde M'tana is fit to be officer or Captain of any ship—except this one."

Zelde looked to him. "You don't say that because I'm any kind of threat to you. So why *do* you?"

Like a schoolchild, Lera Tzane raised a hand. Dopples nodded, and she said, "It's because you came out of cargo and advanced past ratings who wanted promotion. And they *do* think it's because you were with Parnell. When you were Third Hat, and Acting Second, they could take it. Captain, they can't."

Zelde shook her head. "You was in line—you turned it down. If you hadn't of done that——"

Again, Dopples' palm slapped down. "We're not talking blame—I'm not, at least—we're talking about *now*. You've agreed that, ship's shares or not, I'm better qualified to command." She nodded. "And since you *were* Captain—and still are, until landing—I don't think you can revert to Second. Because a lot of people won't let you."

She thought of Sam Dargan. "Because I've had to use authority I won't have, then—I'll get pushed at. That what you mean?" She shrugged. "I can take it, Dopples."

The man shook his head; he looked unhappy. "You can, yes. But the *ship* can't. There's been too much trouble already."

She felt her face go stiff, like wood. "What you want me to do—go unrated? Or back to cargo, maybe? I——"

His hand moved to push the words away. "Nothing like that, Zelde. I propose that we—the whole ship—buy out your command shares. And you get off at Fair Ball, holding enough wealth to buy a good berth on some other ship, when it comes there. A fresh start." He smiled. "I'll write you one hell of a good reference—because that's the kind of job you've done."

Others argued; in the shock of it, Zelde couldn't keep track. Dopples called a vote. She didn't notice who voted which way—she was looking down at the deck, but not seeing it. She heard him say, "Then it's five to three in favor, M'tana abstaining as indicated." And Lera's voice: "I'm sorry, Zelde—but he's *right*."

Dopples again. "There's a problem." *Is that right?* "Your shares, Zelde—buying you out will leave the ship about fifty thousand Weltmarks short, dealing for fuel and cargo. I—"

She found herself standing, not sure who to face. So she faced the door and moved toward it. "Why don't you pass your fucking hat? I need to piss, anyway."

She would have slammed the door, but her hand missed it.

She locked herself in quarters and poured bourbon to her glass's brim—but after one swallow and another sip, she sat and looked at it. Could have used some ice, but too much work, getting it. When the knock came, she first ignored it and then shouted, "Stay the hell out!" Whoever. . . .

"Zelde—it's Torra. Please—"

Oh, what the hell? She let Torra in, and got hugged—not kissed, though, because she turned her face away—and then was sitting while Torra held her. "Zelde?"

"Oh, *Utie*-shit!"

"He's really trying to do what's best, Zelde—Dopples, I mean."

With a shudder, Zelde sighed. "Yeah, I know. But—"

"Come back, won't you? And give him a chance?"

"What for? He's got it all working. I don't need it."

Torra tightened her hug. "He needs *you*."

"To chop my own head off? Why should I?"

Gently, Torra Defose shook her. "Not that—not at all. It's to set the terms—which does have to be done before we land."

"He can do it himself—like the rest of it."

A hand under Zelde's chin brought her head up. "He won't, though." Serious, Torra's face was. "Unless you agree—and understand what you're agreeing to—Dopples will let the whole thing go hang. And the ship can't afford that."

So, She took a swallow—and one more—of bourbon, then went and filled the glass with ice. "All right. Let's go."

* * *

Going into Dopples' quarters, Zelde looked straight ahead—not at any face. "You throw a lousy party, Dopps, when I got to go get my own drink." Where she'd sat before, she sat again. "Now where was we? Something about fifty thousand Weltmarks?" How much of her shares that was, she didn't know. But damned if she'd ask—not if it put her off the ship bareass.

"Well—" Before, Dopples had been right on top of stuff; now he didn't sound sure of himself. "That amount is what's giving us trouble, buying you out. And I know how you feel. I—"

"No such a thing, do you know!" Her voice grated. "I come back on account of Defose says I should. So get to what counts."

"Yes." She didn't look up, but she knew how his face would be—and mostly, she quit being mad. "Forget the fifty thousand, Zelde—you'll get your full due. The only place we can short ourselves is fuel, but with a judicious choice of destination—"

Without intending, she threw her glass. Missed him, but not by much. "Cut the shit!" Surprised, she saw him grinning. She said, "How much of my shares is that fifty thousand?" Then, trying not to let on how much she didn't know, "Nearest percent, I mean."

Going by Dopples' face, she hadn't fooled him any. "Twelve, a little under. A considerable portion, I grant you."

She thought fast. "But I can afford it. I'll *give* you the fifty thousand."

She saw Harger smile; he tipped up his belt-hung figure machine and punched buttons. "By the Agowa formula—"

"Stuff your formula in your ear, Harger! *You* don't get any. This is my free gift—right?" Dopples nodded. "Then it goes where I say." She looked around, at all of them. "I take care of my own. Four thousand, each, to Turk Kestler and Rooster Hogan. Then, by the Agowa ratios—you figure that part, will you, Dopples?—the rest to the Control Hats, only. Lera Tzane, Gilman Charvel, and Torra Defose." She looked at Dopples. "They're short on shares for their rank—you're not. You see?"

The man nodded. Harger tried to argue—and Zelde saw Juvier make his boss shut up—but Dopples adjourned the meeting. Soon—but not soon enough for Zelde—the others left. Except Torra; looking uncomfortable, she stood to one side.

Zelde went to her. "Torra, where you stay tonight is your business. But right now I got to talk to Dopples. Alone."

When the woman had left, Cyras Adopolous sat like a statue. "Something more on your mind, M'tana?"

"One question. You wanting me off the ship. Anything about Torra, would that be?"

The way his face went, she knew she'd guessed wrong. He said, "I expect that she'll probably go with you. But you realize—Zelde, the ship comes first."

That instant, she loved him all the way. But, except to reach out a handshake, she didn't move. "I should of known, Dopps. Had to ask, though. Well—" A lot she'd like to say, but no way to say it; she shrugged. "Good luck to you—and to the ship."

She let go of his hand; time to leave. Then she turned back. "You decide yet, what you'll name it? None of my business, but I'd like to know."

At first he didn't look like talking; then he said, "I have a name in mind, yes. *Strike Three*." He touched her shoulder. "If you don't understand, it's too long a story." She stood, puzzled. He said, "This much, then. Three turnovers of command. And now the ship is out—out free."

"If you say so." She made a salute-wave and got out of there.

In quarters, she saw Torra sprawled naked across the bed. She had a glass of whiskey—dark, no ice in it. Half full, it sat. Her eyelids twitched once—the only sign that she might have heard Zelde come in.

Zelde cleared her throat. "How come you're the boozer around here?"

Squinting, picking up the glass, Torra sat up. "Why should you have the monopoly? Maybe things hurt me, too."

Might's well be drunk, as the way I am. Zelde poured a glass for herself and took a good slug, and began getting out of her clothes, laying them across a chair. "All right. Let's talk."

Torra said nothing. Zelde sniffed. "Lots of help, aren't

you? It's *my* ass that got bounced off the ship. You didn't listen?"

Torra sat her glass down—too hard; it sloshed over, a little. She curled one arm over her face. "Zelde, I—"

And of a sudden, Zelde knew. "You're staying on with Dopples." Silence. "Can't blame you, I guess. It's just that—oh, *piss on it!*" She ran into the bathroom, slammed the door hard, locked it. *Lose everybody, all at once!*

But, like it or not, that's how it was. So she came out to where Torra Defose lay, curled up facing the wall, and said, "So I wasn't fair. But turn over and talk now, or get your ass the hell out."

Eyes wide, Torra looked up. "You do understand?"

"Like hell I do."

Torra reached to grip Zelde's shoulders. "Do you think I want to lose you?" No answer to that; Zelde waited. "You went up this ship like a squirrel up a tree. There'll be other ships for you—and other people." Shuddering, she sighed. "Dopples *needs* me—just as Parnell needed you. He has no one else."

And me? She began to pull away, but Torra sat up and leaned to hold her close, cuddling her head against her chest. "It'll be all right, Zelde. You'll see. I—"

Things blurred for Zelde; she felt her mind closing down—and she fought it. She tore loose from the older woman and stood, panting. *No! Not this time!* She shook her head until her vision cleared, and managed to say, "No, don't—" She backed away, seeing Torra look hurt and puzzled. When she could talk, she said, "Not mad at you. Don't give me comfort, is all." And not sure why she said it—except, seemed like she had to.

Quiet-voiced, Defose said, "Everyone needs comfort sometimes, Zelde. It's nothing to be ashamed of."

Headshake. "Not that, either. It's just—I—" But she couldn't explain; she didn't know. Zelde put a grin on her face and hoped it worked; she was breathing better now, anyway.

Now she went to Torra and pulled her up standing and hugged her; *she* did the hugging, so that was all right. "All right, Torra. I'll take that, what you said about you and Dopps, for later. This minute, though—any reason why we got to let *now* go to waste?"

Maybe it was their last time, Zelde thought—maybe not. Either way, though—for sure, they weren't wasting it.

As at Terranova, Lera Tzane landed the ship. Dopples was sitting backup; on Lera's other side, Zelde played figurehead and no more. Nobody had announced anything, but she felt that everyone knew she wasn't really Captain now—or even part of the ship. When the landing checkout was done, she got up to leave.

Dopples said, "If you're not in a hurry—"

"Happens I am, that."

"The local bigwigs will be boarding, to greet us. Stay and get introduced. There's no point in your debarking like a tourist, not knowing any of the people who can be of use to you."

Against hurt and anger she thought, *He's trying to help.* She tried to smile, couldn't, and shook her head. Then she said, "All right—I guess I can stand it if you can. How soon?"

He told her. She had time to visit quarters first. There, she looked at what she'd planned to take with her—twice as much as she could carry, and for this she wouldn't ask help. So she unpacked, and sorted through again. Souvenirs of Parnell—how many had to do with *her*? They'd never exchanged gifts; all that his things could mean to her was that in her memory he mustn't die. Looking through all of it, trying to decide, she hardly noticed that she had to wipe her eyes a lot.

At the end she kept a few pictures, a blazoned scarf—things like that. She'd already set aside what could revert to the ship, and she added to that lot. The rest of it—valuable, maybe, to his family if he had one—but no chance in time or space that it could ever reach them. Crying openly now and not bothering to hide it, she put all that was left over into the disposal bin.

Ragir, love, I'm sorry—here, there's not a way to do you right.

One last look around quarters, then she carried her gear to the galley—a good place to leave it while she met the groundhogs.

Hungry, of a sudden, she picked up a tray and went to the service counter. But from behind her, Lera Tzane called. "Don't bother. Dopples is putting on a spread for the locals; we can eat there."

Why not? She followed Lera to Dopples' place. The group was smaller than she expected—from Engineering, only Harger, and neither Charvel nor Defose were there. Just the four of them, plus groundsiders.

The "local admiral" was older than his voice sounded, either on-screen or in person. He'd been tall once; now he stooped. Captain Gannes, his name was—but captain of what, nobody said.

Marisa Hanen, Gannes' assistant, stood as tall as Zelde and bulked wider—but not much of her size looked like fat. She had blue eyes in a round face, and wispy blonde hair above a very high forehead. She spoke in a soft, clear voice and shook hands firmly.

Dopples saw everybody fed, all right, and added three bottles of Terranovan wine. He and the visitors carried most of the talk; Zelde didn't much put her mind to it, until he said, "Zelde M'tana, over here—she's leaving the ship, so we're buying out her shares. Captain Gannes, do you have any particular advice for her, while she's on Fair Ball?"

Fingers worrying his fringe of white hair, the old man looked at her. "Between ships, will you be? Or planning to stay? I began here myself, that way, some years back. Decided I was getting too old to play tag with UET any longer, and set up here with the proceeds from my ship's shares. But—if you don't mind my saying so—you seem a little young, yet, to do that."

I like this one. "I'm between ships, if I can find one to buy into." He looked puzzled; she said, "Captain Adopolous told you, over the screen, I caught command at a troubled time—him down hurt, and all. Put some noses out of joint, I guess. Now he's up to it again, *I'd* be trouble, staying on. So I'm not."

He asked what her shares came to; the answer made him whistle. "We have to credit Weltmarks at standard—only sound basis for trade. But three hundred and fifty thousand—strictly on paper, bringing no real wealth to back it—you splash that into our local economy all at once, and *we'll* have problems."

She didn't know what to say. Dopples cleared his throat. "It's buying into a new ship that Zelde wants to do. But I was hoping you might advise her on short-term investments—very liquid—to provide living expenses while she's here."

Captain Gannes' expression relaxed. "Oh, surely. The most convenient, likely, would be short-term loans to the Port Authority itself—payable on demand if you'd accept, partially, commodities in lieu of credits. Since fuel's a commodity and the Port controls it, you'd have no problem in dealing with any ship. Not that we get many here. You could be in for quite a wait."

Marisa Hanen leaned forward. "Ms. M'tana—what sort of accommodations, living arrangements, did you have in mind?"

She didn't know! Except on the ship, she'd never lived anyplace at all, on her own. Just with the Kids. What . . . ?

She saw Dopples cover a smile. He said, "Ship's people aren't used to thinking in groundside terms. What would you recommend?"

Scratching at her hairline, the big woman made a pout—for a moment, she looked like a fat baby. "There's an inn, a little this side of town and toward Main River. It serves meals—and has a few small units behind the main building, complete for cooking. Either doing your own or paying the help to do for you." Now she smiled. "Or would you like to stay with me for a few days, while you look around and decide?"

Woulln't know how to act! "I do thank you, Ms. Hanen—but I expect I better start right out on my own. You see?"

"Of course." *She's pissed some, though.* "Well, when you're ready to move groundside, call Port Control and ask for a car to take you to River House."

Again, Zelde thanked her. Then Dopples turned the talk. "Going from personal concerns to general," he said, "when can you fill us in on things we need to know? Such as coordinates of other Hidden Worlds, and news of Escaped ships we might be able to make rendezvous with?"

"Ha!" It was Captain Gannes and now he laughed. "Always in a hurry, you people. But it doesn't come that easy, Mr. Adopolous. Because although your bona fides appear sound, you *still* might be a UET plant. So you get your information in small doses, as you need them to carry out your next trade mission. Then after a time . . . you understand?"

Dopples looked flustered; then he got his face working again. "I hadn't thought of that aspect. But I see your point. All right; you're saying you'll tell *us* where to go, and what cargo to carry. So let's get to that."

Startled at first, Zelde didn't stay that way long; Dopples would work it out and she was off the ship anyway. Its trade with the Port was none of her business so she didn't listen close. But when it was all over, and the others left, Dopples motioned her to stay.

He handed her two envelopes, and touched the top one. "Letter of recommendation—remember? Three copies. Read it, if you like."

She did, and was interested. ". . . joined the ship at Earth . . ." and the date. ". . . chosen for training . . ." with a list of her learned skills—communications, navigation, weapons and other combat work, the power suit—and her test marks as scored by Dopples or Parnell. "Appointed Third Hat, then Acting Second; assumed command in emergency and so functioned for the duration of the trip. Under trying circumstances, performed all duties effectively."

She looked up from the paper. "You didn't say I was cargo first. Or that I got to be trouble, on here. Nothing about making my way in bed, either."

He shook his head. "The first doesn't apply to what you are *now*. I was wrong about the last, I've told you that before—and I regret ever saying it. The trouble—it wasn't your fault; we both know that." He paused. "Aren't you going to look at your shares certificates?"

"All right." The fancy paper looked good, but all she understood of it was the numbers. There was a packet of plastic wafers, too, stamped as yea-many Weltmarks each. "That's a lot of Weltmarks." As if she knew what a Weltmark was worth. . . .

"Yes." Briefly, Dopples grinned. "Some might begrudge you, taking so much of the ship's wealth groundside. I don't." She waited, and he said, "Twice, Zelde—*twice*, if not for you, UET had this ship back. And I know—a little, anyway—how much you meant to Ragir Parnell. And he was *my* friend, too."

However it came about, she was hugging Cyras Adopolous. *Who'd of thought it?* Then, stepping back, she said, "I better go now—groundside, I mean. Two–three people to say good-bye first, and then—"

"A few more than that, Zelde." He smiled. "There's a party at Turk and Rooster's, and you're late for it."

She blinked. "Then aren't you, too?"

"No. This was our party. Good luck, Zelde."

"You too, Dopples—good landings."

He walked beside her to the door. "We'll be here a few weeks. Come visit." She thanked him—but she didn't figure to be back.

The party wasn't all that big, but it crowded the place some. Turk and Rooster, Lera and Gil and Torra—some rating holding down the watch, must be. And Fesler, and Henty Monteil, and Juvier from Engineering. Zelde looked around, and nodded to people.

Jash and trair were the drinks—she took jash. After shaking hands a lot, she had time to drink some of it. Between Fesler and Juvier she found a place to sit. She saw Torra looking at her—but that was done with.

She said to Fesler, "You got a spare contraceptive implant handy? I think mine's about due to run out."

The medic gave a chuckle. "Do you have someone in mind already, groundside?"

"Hell, no—but there could be."

Turk was halfway drunk, singing a song Zelde hadn't heard—something about ". . . only one latrine in all of U!E!T!" Stopping on a hiccup, she said, "Underground fight song, from the Slaughterhouse—the Space Academy."

Zelde nodded. "I know. Parnell said about it, once. Couldn't remember the words, though."

"Rooster did. Heard it—aw, that doesn't matter." Turk shook her head, hard. "Want to say, Zelde—shitty damn shame, bumping you off the ship. For two centum I'd shuck it and go with you. Rooster, too—right?" And Rooster nodded.

"Just say the word, Zelde—just say it."

No. *This shouldn't happen.* "Thanks for how you feel, Turk—but it's *right,* I go groundside. Didn't seem like it, at first, but—oh, well. You and Rooster, though—you got your places, here on the ship. And good ones. So you stay." As she said it, she watched Torra—and after a pause the woman nodded.

Good—then I don't have to tell her, special.

Juvier tapped her knee. "Wanted to say—Harger's sniping—he was talking just for himself, not for me."

"I hadn't thought any different. Why you need to say it?"

When the man smiled, his bony face looked better. Holding a bottle of jash, he poured Zelde's glass full again. "My boss—a good engineer but hell to work for. Gets on me a lot—wants everyone to agree with him. Well, I don't."

He set the bottle down, stood, and offered a handshake. Then he left, not walking too steady, drunker than he'd seemed. Still, Zelde thought, not tracking so bad!

With all of them she talked and listened. She saw that Torra wanted to see her alone—but how many times can you say good-bye? She joked with Henty about the leftover gold ring, and with Turk about having to paint up a third new insigne—"And Rooster, you got to go out again and put it on. But this time you won't need a suit—just a good strong line on you." He laughed, and explained to her what *Strike Three* meant.

When Fesler left, she went with him. To his own digs, not his working space. "For reasons of my own," he said, "I keep a few implants on hand here." She knew he didn't mean anything personal right now, so she pulled her lower clothes down around her knees and waited while he swabbed her bare thigh and jabbed the thing in. It never hurt much, and not this time, either.

She tugged the clothes back up in place. "Thanks, Fesler." She turned to go, but he had a hand on her shoulder. "What . . . ?"

When she looked at him, he was serious. "Zelde. You're going."

"Sure am. Got to. I guess you heard."

"Yes. But—" His face changed; she couldn't tell what he felt. He said, "All that happened on here. Zelde—"

Now she knew what he meant. Her hands on his shoulders now, she moved like to shake him, but just a little, so she really didn't. "Fesler, you don't got to say nothing; not to me. All that first stuff, it don't mean shit anymore. After the good you done for Parnell. Up to you, I mean, and Ragir'd be living. I know that."

Never thought to see that pale man cry, but he was. Never thought to kiss him, either, but she did. Then she went to the galley, to pick up her things.

* * *

Dopples was there, and a tall man—thin, with a tawny beard. "Zelde? Come meet Pell Quinlan. He's Captain of *Red Dog.*"

She got a cup of coffee first, then shook hands and sat down. Quinlan said, "Looking for a ship, I hear. Well, I have all my Hats, and satisfied with them. Supercargo space, now—I charge reasonably, and if you fill in some watches now and then when we need it, I'll credit that against your fare." He spread his arms and stretched. "I'm here another week or so—you don't have to make your mind up immediately."

A new idea, this. "Where you headed, captain?"

Grinning, he shook his head. "Oh, no—except for those of us who voted on it, not even my own crew knows that, until we lift. No offense, I hope."

" 'Course not." But she didn't like it—was this how Escaped ships treated each other? She said, "I'll think on it."

As if something was important, Quinlan squinted at her. "Not too long, I hope. I have one really good cabin open. A lady thinks maybe she'll take passage or maybe not. Speak up fast and it's yours."

Zelde drained her cup. "Thanks, but I'll have to take my chances. Haven't seen groundside yet, and I want to do that."

She stood; so did Dopples. Quinlan said, "When you decide, let me know." She nodded and picked up her luggage; when she turned toward the door, Dopples was following her.

Outside, he said, "I have nothing against Quinlan, but—"

She touched his arm. "Don't worry, Dopps—I pick my own; they don't pick me." His knuckles tapped her shoulder; then he went back inside.

At the airlock Torra waited. "Zelde, don't you have any time for me at all?"

Only one answer to that. "Not now. You're set up—and I need to start me all over again, *off* this ship. Give me a couple days—then, if you want, come see me at River House." And not waiting to hear what Torra might say, Zelde walked down the ramp and stood, groundside, on Fair Ball.

* * *

She'd forgot to call the Port about a car, so she started walking. Ahead, a fair-sized building looked like it might be Admin. The warm air smelled good—whatever the trees or brush was, growing green to the left of her, upwind, she liked it. Heavy, though, that air—took some getting used to. Like before—*when?* Yeah—real little, she'd been, not long with the Kids, and two nights they hid *deep* in the ground. A dead mine, and climbing down at least an hour—coming back up, maybe twice that. This air here—even heavier, but sure smelled better. She felt her face making a smile. *What's so wrong with starting fresh again?*

Pale sky, hazed over, only a hint of blue. Bright, though—glare narrowed her eyes. *Good,* to walk outside again. On ships was where she belonged—but not *all* the time. And right now, her business at the Port could wait; getting settled, in town, came first.

The first building she came to—wood and stone, three levels—wasn't Admin, but a woman there made a call for her, and a car came. Zelde said, "Thanks," and went out to it. She told the young driver that she wanted to go to River House, then put her things in back and sat beside him.

He sat looking at her, so she looked back. A cap hid his hair; what she saw, mostly, was wide grin and snub nose and a lot of freckles. He said, "You're off the ship there?"

"That's right."

"Welcome to Fair Ball. Uh—is it all right to ask where you've come from?"

"I guess so. What you say we move it, though? We can talk on the way." And as the car turned past a larger building—Administration, the sign read, so that's where she should have gone in the first place—she said, "Terranova, most lately. Before that, Earth."

The car veered, but he didn't look around to her. "Earth? Really? What's it like there? Tell me about it."

"I can't."

"They won't let you? I thought—"

He was so *young.* Her own age, likely, but still. . . . She said, "That's not it." The thing was, what he was asking, wasn't anything *she* knew. How to say it? "I left there real young, is all."

He swallowed. "All your life in space. What's *that* like?"

She didn't want to talk, really; her mind was on her own
purposes; but this kid was so friendly—like the puppies,
sometimes, at camps with the Kids. "What's it like, living
here? Y'see—what's your name?—if I could, I'd tell you.
But to know where it is, you got to live it."

The car hit a rough stretch—bumpy, and a tight corner.
Past that, he said, "Sure—I see it. My name's Casey
Rohrvach. What's yours, and what did you do on the
ship?"

"Zelde M'tana. At the last, I was Captain. They bought
me out." As soon as she said it, she knew he didn't believe
her. The hell with it—until they came to River House she
didn't talk again. Then she thanked him and got out.

The inn was wood-built, with heavy beams showing. The
owner, a small elderly woman named Lynne, took Zelde to
see one of the separate cabins, but Zelde settled for a two-
room setup—plus bath—in the main building. The larger
room looked north, toward the mountains. Snow on them,
whatever time of year this was—and they were mostly
rounded, with only two sharp peaks she could see. The
land between—rising toward foothills—was hazed over, but
in and past the town she saw groves of trees.

The rooms weren't fancy but they were clean; the lights
and plumbing worked, and she didn't need a lot of furniture, anyway. She followed Lynne downstairs and signed
the book. The woman said, "In the dining room, have them
put your meals on the tab. Residents eat cheaper than if
you came in off the street." Street? Well, if that's what she
wanted to call the unpaved road. . . .

Which reminded Zelde—"What's the name of the town?
And how many people does it have?"

The question brought her almost the total history of Fair
Ball, from the time a UET ship discovered it but became
an Escaped ship just after landing. Before Lynne's time
here, that was; she'd come most lately from Number One,
the first and best-populated Hidden World. And before
that, from Earth, by way of the Twin Worlds.

Finally Zelde got her answers. The *city* of First Base—
not town, mind you—had about ten thousand people, and
the planet several times that. "Hidden Worlders breed
fast—a matter of need. I had two kids myself, though I was
past the best age for it, on Number One." Boys, she said,

and nearly grown now—one working a fishing barge on Main River and the other herding highland cattle in the foothills. Not Earth-type cattle—Fair Ball's "buffhides" weren't mammals, even, and the "fish" weren't especially fishlike, either. "But," said Lynne, "they're both good eating."

Thanking the woman, Zelde got loose from the talk and went up—two flights of stairs—to her room. She started to unpack, but suddenly didn't feel like making this place so permanent. She looked out at the mountains, and at the town—buildings of wood, red brick, or tan stone, all three levels or less except for a tower rising from a building she couldn't see.

In five minutes she was bored. She had a shower—there were plenty of towels, at least. Then, though it was early yet, she went down to the dining room.

The menu, most of it, didn't mean much to her; she ordered the roast buffhide special. At first she didn't like it; she expected it to taste like beef and it didn't, quite. But after a few bites she got used to it, and enjoyed the green, tart fruit and a mix of pan-fried vegetables she couldn't recognize at all. She finished off with coffee and a deep pink liqueur; it looked to be sweet, but had a heavy, smoky aroma and a taste to match.

Lynne was on the pay-desk when Zelde signed her dinner tab. "How far is it, about, to the middle of town—I mean, the city?"

"A little over a kilo. You're going in to have a look around?" Lynne squinted out the window. "You have about an hour until sunset, and then another or two of twilight, this time of year."

"Fine. I think I'll walk over, then."

She was turning away. Lynne said, "You're new; I should tell you—people here, we're friendly. If you make a mistake, not knowing customs, just be polite about it and nobody'll call you out. But don't expect any leeway for being a woman—it doesn't work that way."

Zelde grinned. "It don't on the ship, either." Then: "How's it after dark, here?" She fingered the scar where her earlobe had been. "In Parleyvoo—that's on Terranova—walking around alone could get you knifed for what you carried."

Lynne's eyes widened. "Nothing like that around *here*.

People caught robbing and thieving don't live to do it twice. Why, the Council hasn't had to hang one up on hooks, to dry there, for—oh, it must be nearly five years now."

So, were there Police? No—Lynne said that *anybody* had Police authority if it was needed. Zelde didn't see how that would work, but Lynne said it did, so Zelde left without asking anything more.

Outside, walking, she felt the late-afternoon breeze—hot, off the southern desert—and took off her jacket to hang it over one arm. She met a few people coming the other way; about half of them smiled or nodded or said hello. Keeping her own pace, she passed several going in her own direction, and one—a young boy, moving at a trot—passed her. Two groundcars came by, raising dust that made her hold her breath until it blew aside. Then a car passed her and stopped just ahead. The driver—one man alone—looked back to her. "You want a ride?"

The heat had her sweating; she moved quickly and climbed in. "Thanks," and the car moved again. The man—thin, and probably in his bio-thirties—liked to ask questions, so Zelde told the bare facts about her stay on Fair Ball. ". . . and so I'm at River House until another ship comes along."

He gave his own name: "Jady Trevaile—that's from J. D., my initials," and told her he was a Chief Mechanic at the Port. They were on pavement now, between blocks of buildings, not separate houses. He pointed out City Hall, a brick front showing four rows of windows; the lower one, so near the ground, had to be a half-basement floor. "If you're here a while, they like you to register with Immigration. No big fuss, but in case you run into any problems, it's as well to be on record." In front of the building, he stopped.

"Here we are. Anything else I can do for you?" So she asked him about transportation to the Port, and learned that a bus made that trip three times a day and would pick her up at River House if she called the depot in time. "Or I could, for that matter, if you reach me before seven hundred hours when I leave for work. Jady Trevaile—got it?"

"Yeah—and thanks." She stepped down now, and he drove away.

City Hall meant Authority; Zelde looked at it a while, reminding herself that this was a Hidden World, not one of UET's. Then she tipped her chin up a little and climbed the steps, and walked in. Two doors back, along the corridor behind the lobby, the sign read, "Department of Fisheries, Mines, Fuel Refining & Immigration."

Inside, three desks—two were vacant. At the third, a young Oriental woman looked up. She pushed at the coil of hair on top of her head, and spoke. "Can I help you? And which hat do I wear?"

"Immigration, sort of. I'm off *Kilimanjaro* —the ship just in today—staying a while but not for keeps. Fella gave me a ride, said I should ought to check in with you people."

"Surely. Just a moment." Moving to another desk, the woman brought out some papers. "Now, then—"

There weren't many questions. Name? Zelde gave it. Age? "Bio or chrono?" The woman wasn't sure; Zelde gave her best guess at both. Occupation? Ship's officer. Reason for coming to Fair Ball?

That one took some thinking; ship's business wasn't hers to tell. Finally, "It was the closest Hidden World we knew of. Why *I'm* stopping over—just looking for a new berth, is all."

Skills? The woman smiled. "We have no openings for ships' officers, of course—but if you run short of money while you're waiting, perhaps we could help you find work."

"Don't expect I'll need to, but thanks anyway."

The woman set the completed forms aside, but she wasn't done talking. Was Zelde interested in traveling? The freighters on Main River took passengers, up to the edge of the Outfield Mountains or down-current to the ocean. Or aircar passage could sometimes be arranged—and there were overland convoys to the mines and their small settlements. "Keep us advised where you'll be, if you leave the city for any length of time. That's so we can get word to you, if a ship arrives."

"Well, thanks." Zelde paused, then said, "This here, it's my first Hidden World. The idea, coming in to register—I almost didn't. But you sure's hell run things different from UET."

The woman smiled. "I'd hope so. Though if you'd found Elzie Kretchlein here instead of me, you might wonder. She acts like a judge sentencing a thief. But of course no one has to take her seriously!"

Zelde laughed, and reached to shake hands. "Glad to meet you."

"You haven't, quite. I'm Sandra Wing."

Well, all right. Leaving the building, Zelde felt fine.

No sun now, but twilight was holding up good. She walked the town, sorting out where things were, until the sky began to darken. Then, passing a small tavern, she smelled food and decided she could use a snack.

Inside, she liked the place—low look-over partitions of woven reed, with the same kind of patterns covering the walls. Seated, she asked the waitress—a blonde girl with short frizzled hair—to recommend something. "Try the twenty-year soup. The kettle's been hot that long, and every day they add to it, it gets better. Over bread—that is, a slice at the bottom—it's best." So Zelde ordered the twenty-year soup and a big mug of beer.

The soup lived up to the story and the cold beer was good, too. Zelde cut her lip once—and cussed a little, under her breath—before she saw the spoon had a sharp edge on one side. Yeah—it was made to double as a table knife. All right; after that, she was more careful.

When the soup was gone she had another beer, and a short whiskey alongside. The whiskey wasn't much—it tasted a little *off*—so she didn't finish it. She paid, in plastic wafers, and left.

Outside, until her eyes got used to it, was dark for real— hardly any street lights, and not much light from buildings. No moon showing, or stars as such—a couple of bright spots in the haze, and a vague patch of lighter sky to the south. Big star cluster, she guessed—one of the Magellanics, maybe? But looking along the street now, she could see well enough to walk it.

Back at River House she showered again and had some real whiskey from the ship, and went to bed early.

* * *

Light woke her—red sun just pulling free of the horizon. Rested and hungry, she dressed and went downstairs. A skinny young man in the office showed her how to find Jady Trevaile's phonecode—voice only, no screen here—so she called him.

Another man answered—voice deeper than she'd expected—but then Jady came on. Sure, he'd pick her up. Half an hour? So she had time for a quick breakfast in the dining room, and met him outside. The air was cool yet— the sky a little bluer than yesterday but not much. She got in the car and they started off, he asking how she liked the city and she finding not much to say about it. "Safe to walk around in, anyway." And she told him about Parleyvoo on Terranova.

Then it was his turn to talk. The man who'd first answered her call was his wife's other husband. Lots more men than women on Fair Ball, so that's the way it worked, for many. One neighbor woman had five men all her own, and raised hell when they wanted another woman in the marriage. "It takes all kinds, I guess."

Uphill now, the road slanted through scattered bushes— no real trees here—with broad, blue-green leaves. Timber for construction, he said, came from up Main River a way—no clearing off the trees in and around town until some logged-off areas regrew.

At the Port's main building, with instructions how to reach him for a ride back in the afternoon, he let her off and drove away.

Admin was concrete—orange, with green trim around the windows. Ugly as hell, first look—but then Zelde decided she liked it. Inside, she found that Captain Gannes wasn't in, but Marisa Hanen—up one floor—saw her right away. Friendly enough—smiling, shaking hands—the woman showed Zelde the short-term investment program Gannes had set up for her. Not too hard to figure—her shares in safekeeping to back what she bought and sold, with expense money on hand to draw from Baseline Trading, in town. Good enough; for starters she put half her shares on general loan to the Port.

Checking the computer terminal further, Zelde made sure the ship's true log was entered, and Ilse Krueger's message for Tregare. She thought. "Can I add something here myself?" Hanen nodded.

More thinking, then Zelde keyed her entry to the log—*Strike Three*, the ship was now. She punched in, then, the Hat jobs she'd held—including command for a time—and her offer to buy up a berth, or depending on ships' customs, just work one on shares.

What else? Yeah—that she had recommendations from Dopples. And an offer to ride supercargo, maybe—work odd watches and pay for the rest of it—to get to someplace that got more traffic.

Satisfied, she turned to Hanen. "I think that does it."

"Quite welcome. Courtesies of the Port." Then: "Oh, yes—your ship called here, after failing to reach you at River House. Someone named Kestler. The message was merely to call back."

So Zelde called. Turk wanted to see her on the ship. All right—Zelde thanked Marisa Hanen, went outside and started walking.

The ramp guard greeted her. "How do you like the place so far?"

She grinned. "It'll do, for now. All right I go upship?"

"Sure." And going up the ramp and inside, she thought of when the Utie woman had first brought her aboard. *But then, Parnell was here!* She passed the corridor that led off to Hold, Portside Upper—and farther up, peered into the galley and returned waves from people who happened to see her. By habit, she went on to Control—but stopped, just inside. *I got no business here now.*

The watch officer looked around—Torra Defose. "Zelde! I'm glad you're back." The woman came to her, hands reaching out, and would have embraced. But Zelde caught the hands and held them.

"Just not thinking, I come up here. I shouldn't of—"

Torra shook her head. "I can't stand it, your hating me. Can't we—"

"I don't—" But *was* she taking her own grotch out on Torra? All right. "When you get off watch?" Afternoon, was the answer. "Good. Can you come in town with me then? If you want to, I mean."

"Yes, and *yes!*" So now they hugged, and Zelde said where she'd be, and left and went down to Turk's place.

* * *

Rooster was just leaving—cheerful as ever, he gripped her arm and shook hands. Then Turk took hold of her shoulders, and said, "You're not easy to locate—but I'm glad you're here."

"Sure. Glad to be here, too. But—anything on your mind, special?"

"Have a drink first." Real bourbon again, with ice—and again Zelde realized how bad the local whiskey was. Then Turk said, "Rooster and me—we can get you back on this ship!"

Swallowing, Zelde choked— coughing, sneezing the raw booze out of her nose. "Turk—that's crazy!"

"Wait and hear—and forget about share-votes. We've lined up enough people who'd walk off this ship—and *stay* off—that Dopples and Harger would have to knuckle un der. How's that?"

Tears came, but Zelde made the effort and laughed instead. Quickly, she hugged Turk; then she sat. "I—I may have friends as good as you, but none better. But now *you* hear—Dopples is *right*. At the party I said that, you may be too boozed to hear me straight." Turk tried to talk but Zelde wouldn't stop. "There's too many, pissed that I come out of cargo and passed them to wear Hats—and then be Captain. Skipper's whore, I've heard whispered. And *would* I of got a Hat, hadn't been I was with Ragir?" She shrugged. "No way to know—but it's best I'm off here. I do thank you and Rooster, though—peace knows I do." She drained her glass. "We got time for one more?"

Breathing hard, Turk took a minute to calm; then she could smile a little. "All day, if we want to. And—all right, Zelde—if you say so, we'll drop it. It's a shame, though. We wanted to do something for you. . . ."

Pulling at her hair over one ear, Zelde grinned. "You could give me a haircut. This is bushed out way too much." That stopped the argument; Turk took her time, cutting. Zelde looked at the result—like a tight cap of thick felt—and said, "Thanks—for everything."

Early for lunch, it was, but Zelde and Turk went to the galley. Rooster was there, having coffee, and Gil Charvel joined the group. The two men looked worried, until Turk said, "She'll have nothing to do with it, and convinced me she's right. So forget it—and pass the word."

Rooster left; Charvel said, "I'd have walked off, Zelde—believe that. But I knew what it would cost me to do it."

Sure—his shares and experience wouldn't buy him a Hat on another ship. "So it's good you don't need to. Just the same, thanks." He'd eaten fast; now he shook hands and left. Zelde turned to Turk. "Thank the rest for me, will you? Hey—if I'm nosy, say so. But who all else was there?"

Some of the names Zelde hardly knew. Henty Monteil, sure—and, yeah—then it hit her. Not Lera Tzane or Torra Defose, on the list. Well, 'course not. They'd be stupid; too much to lose. Still she felt—no, not angry, not with *them*, but a little sad. Then she told herself *she* was being stupid, and said only, "So many? I wouldn't of thought it."

They got up to leave; just outside the galley they met Dopples. "Zelde! Turk, can I borrow this one for a few minutes? A little talk?" Turk nodded; Zelde followed Dopples to his quarters.

Inside, there, she realized something. "How come you're not in captain's digs? I mean—"

He smiled. "No hurry. And I wasn't sure you were done, there. You took hardly any of the booze—and you know I don't drink much bourbon."

Well. She hadn't wanted to be greedy, even if she'd been able to carry much more when she left. But when he offered to send a load to River House, she took him up on it. Bourbon, and some jash and trair, too. "And I thank you."

Serious now, he leaned forward. "And I want to thank *you*—for heading off Turk Kestler's plan."

"What?"

A wry grin. "Torra spotted it—so Turk's intercom sends whether she knows it or not, lately. I was pleased to hear you—"

"Wait a minute!" Zelde stood. "You was spying—right? Just like UET! I ought to—"

His arms came up. "Zelde! I had to know what those people intended to do to this ship. So that I could—"

"So's you could *what?* Shoot somebody?"

He looked surprised. "You know me better than that! No—so that if Turk's group left, I'd be ready to start recruiting in town, and training people to replace them. And one reason I'm glad it won't happen is that *Turk's* very valuable to this ship."

When Zelde couldn't find an answer, he said, "About Torra—she couldn't join the plan, of course, or even let on that she knew about it. But she's torn, Zelde—she's unhappy. I think if you asked her to go with you, to stay groundside—" He sighed. "I think she'd probably do it."

Why was he saying this? She cleared her throat. "And how about you? How do *you* feel?"

Dopples shrugged. "How do you suppose? I want to keep Torra—of course I do! But only by her own choice." He clasped his hands together, fingers working, and looked down at them.

After a time, Zelde said, "I won't be asking her, Dopps. Not handing out any free gifts, me. It's just—she wouldn't get half the chance for herself off this ship, as on it." His head was still down; she said, "What if I did want to take her off here? What thing would you say then? And do?"

Showing no expression, he looked up. "I'd get on with running this ship—as I must, anyway. If you mean my personal life—well, Hilde and Helga don't care much for ratings' quarters. They keep whining about coming back." He stretched his arms wide, and yawned. "The trouble is, whining bores me—makes me wonder why I ever put up with those two in the first place."

No answer to that, so she said, "Just lucky, I guess." She turned, and Dopples stood and showed her out.

She looked around, here and there, and talked with a few people—Henty, Rooster, a quick chat with Turk: "Dopples was onto you all the time. There's no kickback, though—he's glad to keep you, is all." She didn't locate Lera Tzane, and left word for Torra that she'd be back to pick her up, late in the afternoon.

She went down the ramp, exchanged jokes with the new guard, and walked to Admin. Getting more exercise now, she was, than the brief routines she'd done aboard ship. It felt good.

This time she didn't bother Gannes or Hanen; all she needed was the use of a readout-only computer terminal. No problem; she got it, and began punching for everything she could find out about Fair Ball, other Hidden Worlds—

she knew better than to expect coordinates for those—and Escaped ships. She got a sheetpad out of her bag, and what she didn't already know, she made notes on—places like Franklin's Jump and Target Place. She did find coordinates for Stronghold, UET's fortress setup where they sent so many armed ships—farside of Earth from any UET colony *or* any Hidden World. Somebody'd added a comment: "Rumor is, UET didn't invent stardrive at all. Stole it from aliens, and killed them. That's what Stronghold's all about." So Turk wasn't the only one who had that idea.

Escaped ships, then. Sten Norden and *Valkyrie*, she'd heard of. Quinlan's *Red Dog* was still here—would she go out on it? Likely not, she thought. Now, then—

She wanted to know about Tregare and his *armed* ship—the only one ever to Escape—but didn't find much. Just that he'd done things that sounded bad, and nobody trusted him much. Except, Ilse Krueger had—or talked like it, anyway.

Tregare either had or hadn't taken another Escaped ship by main force, groundside someplace. The report said, "It's thought that the ship is now *Lefthand Thread*, commanded by Derek Limmer." And then, just when Zelde expected to learn something, the item ended.

The only other solid thing was that Raoul Vanois in *Carcharadon* had raided UET on Iron Hat. Zelde closed her notepad. She still didn't know much—but she wasn't done looking.

She'd used a lot of time; afternoon was into late hours. She called Jady Trevaile; when he got off work he picked Zelde up at Admin and Torra Defose at *Strike Three*. On the way to town, not much talk. Getting out at River House, Zelde thanked Jady. Then she and Torra went inside the inn.

Before dinner—not talking at all—they made love. Then in the dining room, during the meal and after—coffee and a liqueur—nobody said much. Zelde asked if Torra wanted to go see the town; Torra didn't, so they went back to Zelde's rooms.

Torra reached to embrace; Zelde pulled back. "Not just yet. Don't you want to talk any?"

"I'd rather pretend—that there's nothing that needs saying."

"There is, though." She sat in a chair; after a moment Torra went to the couch. Seated, she looked only at Zelde, eyes wide.

Zelde shook her head. "Then *I'll* say it. You need to stay on the ship. With Dopples."

Torra's mouth twisted. "How about what *you* need?" And then Zelde realized something she hadn't known. *I don't need anybody. Maybe I did, all along, without knowing it. But I don't now.*

When had the change happened? And how? Suddenly she knew; part of it, anyway. It was when she'd been offered the chance to get back on *Strike Three*, and had the good sense to turn it down.

She didn't say any of it. Instead: "I need a new ship—a Hat berth on it. Wouldn't be one for you, likely, so you're best off where you are. Think a little, you'll know that."

Blinking back tears, Torra nodded. Zelde went to her. "All right, then. And for now—this is going to be one great night."

Nuzzling Zelde's cheek, Torra said, "It has to be—because it's the last. Once more is all I can stand, to say good-bye."

"I know. I got the same trouble." But Zelde lied. She was free now, whether Torra was or not.

They finished breakfast next morning too late to ride with Jady Trevaile; the morning bus was gone, too. At the office, Zelde asked Lynne about transportation. The old woman pursed her lips "For a Weltmark you can use my groundcar—drive it yourself." Zelde signed a tab for the amount, and she and Torra went to the car.

"You drive, Torra—and show me how, so I can bring it back." Seeing Torra's look, she added, "I've watched folks drive—I could manage, probably. This is just to be sure." So as Torra started up, and drove, she explained just what she was doing. About halfway to the Port, she stopped.

"Maybe you should try it now, while I'm still with you."

"Sure." They changed seats and Zelde began—jerky, at first, but soon she caught the hang. Torra had her do some things she didn't need to, just then, so she'd know how when she had to. Then they came to the Port and to *Strike Three*, and Zelde cut the power.

She reached to Torra and kissed her. "Now look—we

been *good* together. So have a lot of luck for yourself, will you? And take care of Dopples."

Torra's eyes were wet. Zelde felt no tears—not now. "You take care of *you*, Zelde. Be careful. I—"

"Don't worry on me, none. I come a long way since Earth—and I don't mean only the distance. Not figuring to stop now."

One more hug, and Torra got out and walked toward the ship. Zelde didn't wait to see her aboard; she started the car and drove away. She knew Torra would stop, going in, and look back—and Zelde didn't want to see her do it.

The car was easy. When she got back to River House, Zelde stopped it where she'd found it, and once more ran through all the controls. Especially the ones she hadn't needed—lights, backup shift, wheels-lock for staying stopped on hills, even the compartment heater. Then she nodded. All right—now she could drive one of these things!

When she went in to tell Lynne she had her car back, she asked about some of the travel ideas the waitress, two nights ago, had mentioned. Lynne lit a thin cigar—to Zelde, it stunk like somebody set a chicken on fire—and squinted through the smoke.

"Downriver to the ocean—nothing to see there. You'd be bored silly, and bitten bloody by desert gnats. Cross-country, now—to the mines and their crummy little villages—there's not much to interest anyone." Ash fell from her cigar; she ignored it. "Upriver, to the mountains' edge—that's what's worth seeing. The mountains up closer, the herds and the herders' camps—some of the lakes, the lower ones, aren't too hard to reach, hiking." She nodded. "Yes. In your place, with a little time to spare, that's what I'd do."

Lynne knew some freightboat people; she could arrange the trip, on commission. Fine; Zelde shook hands on the deal.

Nothing happened right away, though. Restless, Zelde spent time nosing around town, getting the feel of the place. She liked it, mostly—but it wasn't a *ship*, with work to do, and new planets to see, and the years rolling up the way they did. . . .

It took her a while to see how different it was, here, with no UET on top of everybody. City Hall and the Port ran things, sure—but nobody was *scared* of anything. If you had a gripe with the brass, you might win it or lose it, but that's *all* you lost.

Maybe the ship still had more UET stuck to it than she'd thought. Then she thought again—the ship had to run tight because if somebody screwed up it could be everybody's ass. Here, groundside, that stuff didn't matter so much. All right. . . .

She caught her share of attention—especially if she had a drink in town—from men on the loose. Some she liked, some she didn't—but for now, she plain couldn't get interested.

One man, though, was different. Not to look at—middle-sized, maybe thirty bio-years, red-faced and sandy-haired. But Niels Jarding was a teacher.

That's how Zelde, one day, stood in front of a couple of dozen boys and girls maybe ten to fourteen years old, while Jarding told them she'd explain all about living on starships.

A long time since she'd done anything like this. Not since working for Honcho, talking to groups of the younger Kids—how to dodge the Welfare catchers, stuff like that. These, now—a lot different. Not just cleaner—*these got nothing to be scared of.*

Then Jarding was done; it was her turn. *Living* on a ship—so she left out UET, and the hell of killings at Escape, and that turd Mauragin—none of those things fit, here. The work, the jobs, how a ship hung together—the best she could put it straight, that's what she told. And pretty soon, seeing their faces, enjoyed the telling.

And then the questions. One girl—twelve, maybe, and chubby—asked, "How did *you* get into space? I mean, you haven't said."

Zelde was stopped. Then, finally: "That don't figure, here. Because you're not starting—none of you, for sure—from where I did." She grinned. "What you mean is, how *you* might get off groundside?" From the girl's nod and Jarding's smile, she took her cue.

What there was of it. "I'm sorry—I don't have you an answer." She thought. "Try to get work at the Port, when you can. Anything—scutwork, running errands, whatever.

When you think you know a little something, ask can you put word into—well, it's a kind of bulletin-board circuit for ships, in the Port's computer. That you want on a ship— and tell what you can do. It could work. Then if you do get on, learn *everything* you can. Just in case."

A lanky boy, bony-faced, stood. "We heard you were *Captain* on your ship. How old are you?"

She looked at him—eager grin, awkward stance. "I lost track—chrono and bio both. Yeah, though—I wound up with command, a time there. Because—" She swallowed bile. "Because the real Captain died, and the First Hat hurt too bad for duty. And—" No, she couldn't say it—not behind Lera Tzane's back. "And the Second Hat had her own reasons to pass it."

They dropped the matter, and she told shipboard stories —the kind kids would like. Spoof tricks in the galley, Parnell jockeying talk with Kickem Bernardez of the *Hoover*, neither letting on they were Escaped, but Bernardez dropping a veiled clue about the Underground. When she came to what Ilse Krueger had said, several youngsters clapped their hands. Pirate or no pirate, to these kids Tregare was a hero.

Not to Niels Jarding, though. Over lunch, later—his treat, to repay Zelde for her time—he explained why killing and violence were no answer to human problems. Then he asked her to spend the night with him. She shook her head.

"But why, Zelde? Don't you feel you know me well enough?"

"Know you fine—can't figure you, though. But you don't know *me*, is what." She leaned forward. "Niels, I been a fighter since I was maybe twelve. I mean, that was my *job*. And killing—in a big fight, you can't even keep count." She saw his face change. "Don't mean I *like* it— but sometimes you got to."

"Well—self-defense, I suppose. . . ."

"Not always." *Carlo Mauragin, screaming.* "Niels—I said I couldn't figure somebody, won't fight when it's got to be. You're all right where you are, I guess. Hope it stays that way." Through the rest of the meal they didn't talk. When they shook hands afterward, Zelde ready to leave, Jarding still looked puzzled. Zelde grinned, patted his shoulder, and walked out.

* * *

Restless—the town was beginning to bore her—Zelde went back to River House. In her room she found a note from Lynne: the freighter *Mainliner*, leaving for upriver in two days, had one passenger space vacant—did Zelde want it? Zelde did, and Lynne made the arrangements.

The ship *Mainliner*—and it struck Zelde funny, calling a water-barge a ship—was about fifty meters long and fifteen wide. Built low, except for a sort of building in the middle—two levels high, most of it—covering a space maybe thirty meters by eight. The captain, Chais Geddeke, was an ex-spacer grounded by injuries; she had a metal hand, no front teeth, and was half-bald from radiation damage. Mostly she wore a cap.

Zelde's cabinmate was Bailey Poindecker, a herd rancher—tall as Zelde, red-haired, with a scarred left cheek. At first, not liking the man, she figured him to push her for screwing, and was set to stop that idea, fast. But the problem, when it came up, was different; the first afternoon, she found herself locked out of the cabin. An hour later, when Poindecker came out with a young crewman, he didn't pay much attention to her complaint; he'd do as he damned well wanted to.

"Fine," said Zelde. "Next time you do, though, and I want in, I'll shoot the lock off." After that, when he wanted the private use of the cabin, he asked first.

A little less than six days, the trip took. There'd be a ten-day stay, Geddeke had said, and then about four days for the downstream run. By the second day on *Mainliner*, Zelde found herself missing First Base. Town or city, at least there was more of it.

Nobody to talk to, much. Geddeke wasn't unfriendly, but her mind brooded on tumors cut out of her body—and maybe more growing in there right now. That's all she could talk about, for long. Zelde watched the passing riverbanks—different kinds of trees and bushes, sometimes animals but not often, or close enough to see very well. She sat in on a card game for a while, in the deckhouse. The game was new to her but the rules were simple. So was the dealing—she'd never seen such clumsy cheating. For the stakes involved—centums, not Weltmarks—the crookery wasn't worth calling. But she did, anyway—and the others laughed instead of fighting, and after that, played straight cards. Maybe she'd passed some kind of test, there.

That night, not sleepy, she sat a while on top of the deckhouse, watching dim outlines of trees and hills pass by, and once looking back to see the bright patch of sky that might be a Magellanic.

From behind, there, came a rumble like soft thunder; through the haze a blue glow lanced upward. Only for seconds—then it was gone. Zelde shrugged. Too soon for *Strike Three* to lift; it had to be Quinlan's *Red Dog*.

The third day, *Mainliner* was pulled up through swirling rapids—with a lot of thumping and grinding on rocks—by winched cables. Then the ship went up a long narrow lake, past the gap through foothills, winding along a broad valley. Half a day along that lake, then the river narrowed and the current was stronger, slowing *Mainliner*. For two more days the land flattened—Zelde could see it stayed that way to the edge of the second foothills where they rose steep. The morning of the sixth day, the ship docked. Less than two kilos away, the hills began.

Not much of a town. Carrying her travel case, Zelde walked along a rutted lane deep with loose dust; at the sides and up the middle, weeds grew. She came to a low sheet-metal building with radio dishes on top; the sign read, "Message Center. Information."

She took a closer look—the dishes pointed north, toward the hills. Squinting, through the high haze she saw three towers on the nearest summit. Sure—get the signal up a ways, *then* beam it south. She turned and walked inside.

Lots of comm-gear—it all looked pretty much alike to her. She asked at the counter, and a young woman found two messages for her—forwarded from River House at a quarter-Weltmark each. Cheap enough; she paid, and unfolded the first paper.

It said *Strike Three* was leaving the next day—which, now, was yesterday—and that Quinlan had already gone. Another ship was on its way in—signal detected, but not good enough to read or identify. The message ended with two signoffs: "Best of luck, Dopples," and "Love, Torra."

The second one was shorter. "Good knowing you, Zelde. Hope we meet again. Turk and Rooster."

Before leaving, Zelde rented a talker. "To keep in touch

here," the woman said. "Half a Weltmark per day, and the
range is better than a hundred kilos." Zelde paid a deposit,
and followed through the instructions the woman gave her.
All right. She left and headed on into town. She was getting
hungry.

She got lucky. The small place with the sign "Eats and
Drinks" served good food—and the big blond man sitting
next to her, Ole Rolvaag, ran an aircar service. Zelde decided she could use an air tour; they were shaking hands
on the deal when the waiter brought their coffee. A little
later, they walked to Ole's office.

The office was a tarpaper shack; the car didn't look
much better. Ole said, "She runs good. A couple of my
night-flying instruments don't work—so I don't fly at night.
The looks of her, though—pretty, I can't afford." They got
in, and the propulsion unit started up, smooth enough. He
listened to its hum and nodded; the car moved forward.
Then he shoved the power lever full-forward and pulled up
on his control wheel, and they were up—turning toward
the mountains, climbing fast. When they were high enough
that the buildings behind were only dots, he said, "Do you
fly these things?"

Zelde touched the duplicate wheel in front of her.
"Never had a chance to learn." Or groundcars, either, until
here. . . .

"Watch what I do. Then you try it." He made the car
dip and rise, turn and straighten, speed up and slow down.
"All right—do everything very gently. And if I tell you, let
go the controls."

"Right." She expected to overcontrol at first, and she
did; the car dipped and swung. On a hunch she let go the
wheel for a moment—sure enough, the car leveled off and
flew straight. Then she took hold again, careful not to
move anything in the taking, and now made very slight
moves until she got the feel of it. When she'd done the
same maneuvers Ole showed her, she was sweating. "Want
it back now, Ole? How'd I do?"

"Not bad. If you knew how to land this thing, you could
solo." He grinned. "Landing, though, takes more learning.
I'll show you."

* * *

Crossing the foothills she saw the herding ranches—groups of the odd-looking cattle, buildings, people in open groundcars tending the herds. Ole said, "Like to set down and see it close?"

"No. Rather see the mountains—lakes and things." So he turned north again and climbed higher, then leveled off. Oxygen equipment not working, he explained. "So this is as high as we go."

It was high enough; they passed between two mountains, and below, in a rounded valley, she saw a deep-blue lake. That's where Zelde wanted to go, and Ole brought the car down, explaining everything he did as he landed the car. Yeah, Zelde thought—she could do it, maybe, if she had to.

She got out and walked the few meters to the lakeshore, through loose sand that grew tan-colored tufts of something that wasn't exactly grass. She dipped a hand in the water. "Really cold."

"Off the mountain ice," Ole said. "This is one source of Main River."

Breathing deep, she looked up and around. More blue to the sky here—altitude, or just contrast with the white peaks? And the lower slopes—first, some kind of trees, though not here in the valley, and then tan ground-cover flecked with green. "I'm glad I saw this place."

But now she was restless—ready to go again but with no place in mind. Back in the car he let her try takeoff; she did it well enough, if a little jerkiness didn't count. She didn't let it give her a swelled head—these things were *built* to handle easy. And now, getting used to the controls, she wasn't nervous—*I could fly it all day*. Except that when they passed the foothills and had line-of-sight to the settlement, her rented talk-set bleeped.

She looked to Ole; he took control and she switched the set on. "Message Center calling Zelde M'tana. The Port wants to talk with you."

Signal from the Port, relayed, wasn't good; Zelde got maybe half the words. Enough, though. "I'll be there soon as I can," she said, and repeated until she got a Roger. "M'tana out."

She turned to Ole. "Can you fly me to Baseline Port?"

"Not today—we don't have enough daylight. I told you my night-flying instruments are out of business."

Damn! She thought. "This is important—a starship in Port, and not staying long. Look—can't you follow Main River? I came up it; at night, it reflects skylight good. And at the far end you got the town lights, and the Port's. You see?"

He hesitated. "I'd need to refuel first. And the cost—round-trip fare, because coming back is deadhead." He named a figure. "You have that much?"

"Not with me. On deposit with Baseline Trading, though. You can call and check it."

"All right. As soon as we're close enough to hear better."

Baseline confirmed Zelde's money status; when he heard the amount, Ole whistled. He landed in the settlement; again, she kept close watch on how he did it. "I'll be a little while, refueling," he said, "and I'd like to get a meal and maybe a drink before we leave. If you—"

Zelde motioned toward her traveling case. "There's drinks in there, you need one." A little whiskey left, and some trail. "I'll get some takeout food; we can eat while we're moving."

He didn't argue, so she left him to his work. Walking fast, she went to the Message Center and asked for a circuit to the Port. "I'm sorry; they're all busy now." Zelde waited for a time, then gave it up. Where she'd eaten before, she bought a bag of wrapped snacks. When she got back to the aircar, Ole Rolvaag was in his seat, leaning back, sipping from a cup.

She climbed in. "We ready to go?" He nodded. "Then let's move—and the fastest you figure to be safe. But no faster."

He rammed power to the car so that it literally jumped off the ground, then kept the indicator just under redline until they hit top cruising speed. Then he filled his cup again, putting the bottle under the seat when Zelde didn't want any—and sat back, only the fingers of one hand resting on the control wheel. Zelde watched the river, and the light retreating up the mountains behind.

Just before dark, they ate. She thought they might land then, for a couple of minutes, because later wouldn't be so good—but the car had a toilet setup in the back, so they didn't need to. Then it got dark. She was right—below, Main River showed clearly.

*   *   *

It might have been an hour later—she'd dozed some—
that the car wobbled. Zelde looked over; Ole had the bottle
to his face. "Hey! Watch what's happening, will you?"

He reached the bottle to her. "C'mon—have some. Almost half full, still." But the whiskey bottle had been less
than that—*lots* less. The other—the trair—*it* had been
nearly full.

She took the bottle, and sniffed it. Trair, all right. "Ole?
You drink all this?"

"Sure. *Great* stuff. Usually, wouldn't have more'n a
drink or two. But this—more I drink, more alert I feel.
Except—"

She found the cap on the instrument shelf and sealed the
bottle. "Ole, give me the controls. You go in back and stick
your finger down your throat and puke, all you can. Drink
water and do it again. Move!"

"Whatcha mean? I'm—oops—all right." The car almost
fell off to one side; Zelde took hold of her own set of controls and pulled it steady.

"That's *trair* you drank. Yeah—it keeps you sober for a
while. But when that part wears off—Ole, get your ass back
there and puke!"

"Can you . . . ?"

"I got to. Move it!"

And he did. Wobbly now, he climbed out of the seat and
felt his way toward the back. Zelde couldn't spare a look to
see how he was doing, but heard him gag. Then nothing—
so she got the controls set dead neutral, where they'd hold
steady, and stood up to see.

He'd started forward again, but he was sprawled flat,
snoring.

She sat. Stupid, *stupid*—saying sure, go ahead and have
a drink, and not warning him what trair did. *I can land this
thing*, she'd thought. Now, the way it looked, she'd damn
well have to.

For a time the car ran itself and she let it. Then the river
curved to the right and the car didn't; updraft from the
hills tilted it. She took the wheel and turned, seeing how
fast the river's light dimmed with a little distance.

Just follow the river; stay right over the middle of it.
Should be easy. Couldn't tell how high she was, though—

that instrument read a thousand meters, no matter what, and the haze was worse now. There were cliffs along here somewhere, she remembered. She squinted to the sides— but wasn't sure she really saw anything out there, except darker patches of haze. And she had no idea how far it was—in hours—to Baseline Port. But the river would be getting wider. So if she kept it looking about the same, to her, she'd be sure to stay high and safe.

Holding the wheel, her muscles ached and her hands sweated. Every chance she had, she got the car running straight and level so she could let go and flex her fingers She got out another snack and ate it—she was thirsty, but the water was in back. So she took a swallow from the trair bottle, and the stuff relaxed her. She checked the time— one shot every hour wouldn't get her drunk, and it sure helped!

By the time she had her third jolt of trair, she was used to where she was and what she was doing. A little later she saw lights ahead, and tightened up again—she still had to land this thing! And then she heard a noise behind her. "Ole?"

"Whass happ'nin'? Y'awright? Lemme have it now." He had his hand on the back of his seat and was trying to stagger around into it. She checked that the controls were neutral and turned to face him. He fell against her and she pushed him.

"Ole! Stay away—you can't hit the floor with your hat!" He kept coming—too drunk, still, to listen. So she brought her knife out. "Hear me! You touch those controls, I'll cut your head off!" He didn't stop, so she jammed the knife's point into his shoulder, and hit bone. Not much blood came.

The shock sobered him. "That hurts!"

"I figured." The car was tilting; she straightened it. "Sorry. You want to sit down; all right. But keep your hands off the controls." She watched him as he climbed around into the seat. "Have yourself something to eat, why don't you?"

As he did that, she watched the lights ahead as they appeared to expand and then separate into two groups—the town and the Port. No hills here, so she left the river and turned directly toward her goal. Sooner than she expected, she was past the town—and higher than she'd thought, too. Ahead she spotted the Admin building, and past it, two ships—*Cut Loose Charlie*, sitting dead, and another. She had to go beyond the Port and circle back, to get down where she could judge how to land. And now there was nothing in her mind at all, except light and shadow and distance.

With rigid hands she moved the wheel. Now, away from the river's guidance, she felt less sure of her control—the car seemed to weave and drift, and when she tried to correct for its movements, she overcontrolled. On her left, something went past the edge of her vision—*too low! It's a building!* She pulled up then, made a slow turn and found she'd lost orientation—she didn't know which way things were. Shaking her head for a moment, she looked until she found the river; then in her mind she set how the port must lie, and eye-searched until she found the place she needed.

"Pro'lem?" said Ole. "Want me to take her down?" He didn't sound very good yet; Zelde shook her head, then told him aloud. "Wha'ever you say," he mumbled, and she guessed he was shrugging.

How high was she? From this angle the light was wrong; she couldn't get a good sighting. All right—up again, just in case—make a turn, keeping track of where she was, and come back the other way. Then start down again—faster, because the place wasn't as big as she'd thought—but close to the ground, *cut power.*

And then the wheels touched, and bounced and came down solid—but *damn it! Where's the brakes?* She swerved to miss a groundcar, ran out of space and dodged between two buildings and steered to a stop.

Then she saw where she was, and laughed. She'd ended up right where she wanted to be—behind Admin, where other aircars sat.

She cut power entirely now, and flexed her hands. Ole said, "You did very well—you know that?" He sounded sober.

Zelde grinned. The pressure was off, all the way, and she felt *good.* "In one piece we got here, anyway." She was in a hurry, but needed to finish this deal. "Let's go into Admin; I'll get your money. Where you going to stay tonight?"

"Here in the car. A bed folds out; I use it sometimes." So he followed her out of the car, toward the building. As she walked, something stuck in her mind. The new ship, the quick look she'd had—it was different. Yeah—at the top, things sticking out. Projector turrets, like she'd seen once, on Earth?

She squinted past the corner of the building, up at that ship. Above the open ramp, a copy of its insigne was spotlighted.

Inconnu. Tregare's ship, this was. The one with guns.

Zelde walked into the building. Nothing happening downstairs, so she went up. As she turned a corner she saw closed doors, darkened—but light came from one that stood ajar. It was where she'd talked with Marisa Hanen. Well, might as well try it.

Going toward that office she heard a man's voice—raised, harsh—and a thumping sound. "Peace take you, you *will* refuel me! Just as the Compact states. Or I'll orbit a beacon, blacklisting you with every ship that comes into signal range."

She looked inside. The man standing, beating a fist on Marisa Hanen's desk, was as tall as Zelde. His sallow, bony face held a taut scowl; over a high forehead, his curly black hair looked rumpled. On his left cheek, reddened with anger, she saw the full-circle tattoo of a UET captain. *Tregare? Must be.*

Hanen sat back in her chair; seated near her were two men Zelde hadn't seen before. One, heavy and red-faced, said, "Sure we'll refuel you; I never said otherwise. It's only a matter of price, the same as with the food. Now, if you'll undertake our mission—"

The tall man sat down hard, and leaned forward. "Your *stupid* mission! My ship to take Far Corner, you say, and hold it against UET? And then what? Think *ahead* once, Fairgrave. We couldn't hold it, anyway, except by keeping the ship there—and then, only until UET found out and brought more force against us. You think I'll waste my life on that mudball?"

Fairgrave looked pretty mad himself. "I've told you—UET ships land, unsuspecting, and we take them. Soon we have—"

"You have a hatful of shit, Fairgrave! If you don't know that, I do. It's not worth the trying—and that's final. Now let's talk about the fuel you have to sell me."

The other nodded. "Of course. A matter of price, as I said."

"You said, yeah. Twice the usual, you're asking."

"Do our mission, and you can have it free. But—"

"But you're asking a hundred and twenty thousand Welt-marks to fill my tanks, where sixty's a good normal price."

"I'm sorry—but taking Far Corner, that's *important*, Tregare."

"You wouldn't know important if it bit you on the leg. I—" Looking up, he saw Zelde. "You! Who are you? What's your business here?"

Now everyone looked toward her; she stepped inside. "Zelde M'tana. My business, it's with the computer terminal over there. Go right on yelling—it won't bother me none." Nobody said not to, so she walked past the group and sat down at the terminal.

She punched to see how much of her money was tied up—and in what—and how much was free. Checking a few price quotations, she grinned—yes, she could do it. She bought and sold, shifting her own holdings—then a little more, for safeties—and put the readout tape in her jacket pocket. *First move.* Then she remembered to punch payment for Ole Rolvaag—with ten percent extra, for luck.

The talk was more quiet now—and she hadn't been listening. She stood and turned back to the group. Tregare frowned at her. "You get done what you wanted—M'tana, is it?"

"Some part of it, yeah."

Marisa Hanen said, "Zelde—no offense, but you *are* interrupting a very important meeting. Could you—"

Tregare cut in. "What else do you need, M'tana?"

"To talk with you." His brows raised; she said, "Stay all night here, you still get no place—and you know it. And I bet nobody's had dinner, though it's late for that. Tregare—buy me a drink on your ship, and a meal with it. We need to talk."

Lips tightened, he began to shake his head. Fairgrave said, "That's the most arrogant, ridiculous thing—you walk in here and—"

Grinning, Tregare slapped the desk, and stood. "If *you* don't like it, Fairgrave, then it has to make sense. This meeting's recessed for two hours—or *I* am, at least. Come on, M'tana—you just bought yourself some drinks, and dinner."

"*And* talk."

As she walked past him, he touched her shoulder. "Yeah—that, too."

At the door, Zelde gave Ole the readout tape that Baseline Traders would redeem in cash, and shook hands with him. "Thanks, Ole. You'll be all right?"

"Sure. Sorry I screwed up with your booze."

"No problem. Just be careful with what's left." Following Tregare outside, she motioned him to wait while she detoured to the aircar and got her travel case. Then they went to *Inconnu*—the ramp guard's wave was hardly a salute—and upship. Not to the galley, but to captain's quarters—and all the way she noticed that the layout was some different from what she knew. Not too much, though.

Inside, he pointed where she should sit, and went to the intercom. "Tregare. Dinner for two, here in quarters. The best that's quick and handy—but not slapdash." He turned to Zelde. "About your booze—are you particular?"

This one gets right to it. "Spirits with ice—nothing sweet. Bourbon's fine, if you got it."

"Bourbon it is." When he sat facing her, and they'd clinked glasses and sipped, he said, "First, now—tell me who you are."

She handed him the papers Dopples had given her. He read them, handed them back and nodded. "Yes. I've skimmed the bulletin-board circuit. So you're the one who wants a Hat berth." With one eyebrow slanting up, he grinned. "Worked up from cargo, did you—all the way to Captain, for a while—by way of the skipper's bed?"

How . . . ? Dopples wouldn't have crossed her this way! Not smiling now, Tregare said, "The abstract of your ship's log. Your name and a lot of others aren't on the roster until after Escape; then, there you all are, and coded with quarters' assignments. You see?"

She shook her head. "It wasn't like you think. Tell you sometime, maybe. For now, I'll stand on what Dopples wrote."

The doorchime sounded. He went, and came back with two trays. "Eat now, M'tana. Talk later."

*   *   *

When they finished, he brought out and poured some wine that had a stinging aftertaste. "All right—you said we need to talk. You start."

She swallowed. "Like you said first, I'm the one wants a Hat berth. You got one open?"

"Two. Second and Third—and only one good prospect to promote from the ratings." She waited. "First I had to put a cadre on another ship—left me short of talent. Then my new Second got pregnant by my new Third—on purpose, they did that—and hearing my plans, they decided to get off here. I bought them out fairly, of course." Not looking angry, he frowned at her. "Now before we even start to dicker—just to pay for your meal and drinks—start telling me all I don't know about you and the ship you came off of, and any ships you had contact with."

Then he grinned, and it looked friendly enough. "Because what I'm planning, I need to know more than I'll ever find out."

She began with herself and what she'd learned of ships. Yes, *Inconnu*'s controls might be some different, and she didn't know ships' weapons, only portables. And she hadn't lifted off or landed, real, but her simulation tests showed she could if she had to. So far, Tregare didn't say much.

Some things, important just to her, she skipped. Anyway, he knew about her being cargo and then living with Parnell—*before* that, was what he asked about. All right— the Wild Kids, and getting caught by the Committee Police their own damned selves. And again, not all of it—just what fit with where she was right now.

They finished the wine; he opened another bottle. "So. I wondered what training you had, before you got shuffled into cargo. Now I know—from UET, nothing. But out there on the loose, you learned command before you were fourteen." He nodded. "It starts to make sense. Go on."

Escape, she told of. He interrupted. "If Parnell hadn't logged it, that you by yourself took out an armed man in a power suit—"

She explained how it happened, then cut to the contacts with other ships. Each time, he had comments. On Bernardez: "He's Escaped, all right—but keeping cover with UET ships and colonies. That's smart—but then, he always was. And at a message drop he left me something—the whole basis for my new plans." He had to be a little drunk now, Tregare did; he leaned closer to her. "Fairgrave's idea—he has the wrong place, is all. Stronghold! That's the key." Stronghold, yeah—Zelde remembered now. Except she couldn't figure Tregare's angle on the place. . . .

He shut up then; she went along, telling. About Malloy, he said, "*Pig in the Parlor,* huh? Well, I've left coded word for him; maybe he'll find it someday." Krueger: "Tell me more on that." Best she could remember, Zelde did. "Yeah. If Ilse gets word in time, she'll bring *Graf Spee.*"

Quinlan: "Pell's a loner. No point in coding anything for him here, anyway—he'll hardly be back. A general note, though, to all Escaped ships—that could reach him second-hand somewhere, same as anyone else." Tregare straightened up. "One thing more, M'tana—how did you get up to Captain? Tell it all."

All right. "Ragir's hurts brought him down." Nothing to say of her own pain. "And Dopples out flat, so long." Like telling something she'd only heard, not lived, she explained. Then Carlo Mauragin, and Franzel—just bare fact on that, too. "But I got to the power suit—it worked good enough, except no way to use the projector that went with it, and—"

That's when Tregare laughed. She looked at him; before he answered, he filled her glass. "M'tana—in a way we're twins, you and I. After Escape, *I* scotched a UET takeover using a suit. Wrecked mine, though—no parts left to fix it, afterward."

Squinting at her, he sat back. Waiting for something more? She said, "So we had the ship again—but nobody except me, to run it. And I'd had to kick so much ass, and me up from cargo—too many couldn't live with all that. So—" She shrugged. "I had to sell off, was all. You see it?"

To answer, took him a time. He'd been looking down; now he stared at her directly. "On *Inconnu* you wouldn't have that problem. All I'd log, for record, is what Adopolous gave you to show around." He nodded. "I could use you on here, M'tana. But the question is, can I afford you?"

"What's that mean?"

"Weltmarks—I need a lot, maybe you gathered, and I have only the Hat berths to peddle for them." She tried to talk but he cut in. "Don't offer to come aboard as a rating—I'd never ship an ex-officer in a pride-hurting job. Too risky; you people found that out with—what's his name?"

"Mauragin. But I—"

"So if you can't afford to buy a berth, you're out. I'm sorry."

"Sorry, yeah. What kind of figure you got, on Second Hat?"

His eyes narrowed. "Two hundred thousand—Second or Third, either one; makes no difference. Do you have it?"

Zelde shook her head. "What I got, or what I don't—seems you're pricing kind of high, though."

One hand he put out to the side, fingers spread. "You heard what they're trying to do to me here! I *need*—"

This one, I can't be easy on—not ever! She thought fast. "One forty, I'll go. Out of that, I'll see you fueled."

"No." Gulping from his wineglass, shaking his head. "It leaves me only twenty thousand fluid credit from the deal. I need more than that—a lot more."

She laughed. "You *got* more." She showed him the read-out tape. "See? I *own* that fuel—bought it at regular price, and you get it the same way. Leaves you—"

"Eighty thousand clear, yeah! And—you bought a fair load of food, too." Now he scanned the tape closer. "You—the time code on this tape—"

"That's right." Zelde felt good; she smiled at him. "Heard the argument, you see, and—"

He slammed his glass down so hard it broke, and leaned back laughing. "*That's* what you were doing on the computer? Buying up fuel before Fairgrave changed the price officially?"

"Yeah." She nodded. "Seemed like a good move."

Grinning wider than she'd seen him do, Tregare pumped his right fist twice, up and out. He stood; at the intercom he said, "Watch officer—that you, Gonnelsen? Right. Call Port Admin—Gannes or Hanen, whoever you reach—tell them we're adjourned until tomorrow. Mid-morning should be soon enough. Tregare out."

He came back and sat down. "All right. Second Hat M'tana—and when I have the fuel and the eighty thousand, that's who you are on this ship, long as you can hack it—let's have a drink."

* * *

Waiting until he'd poured—bourbon again, now—she was going to thank him, but he spoke first. "Now then—you want to stay here tonight? Or do you have things to take care of, in town?"

Her shoulders moved, not quite a shrug. "Some stuff to pick up at River House—I can do that tomorrow, or whenever. No—Second Hat quarters on here sounds fine."

"That's not quite what I meant. My Second and Third haven't cleared out yet. What I had in mind, M'tana, was right here."

Get this part straight, fast! Groundside, either way it wouldn't matter. But she'd be *living* on this ship. . . .

She tried to think it out. He was starting to talk when she cut in on him. "You said you was shorthanded—means you got space. Some kind of place I can be, for now." She waved a hand at him, didn't want him to say before she did. "One thing you should know, Tregare."

He waited. "My men—*I'm* the one as does the picking." He didn't answer. "This change anything? I mean—you want some other Second Hat—and get your fuel someplace else, too?"

Don't push him too far!

Tightened, gradually his face relaxed. "No problem. You're right—there's space." He gripped her arm and then let go. "There's time, too." Either he laughed, then, or cleared his throat.

"Wasn't out to mad you up. Just had to say it."

Now he did laugh. "If you couldn't stand up to me, M'tana, how could you stand up *for* me?" He grabbed her by the arms, held her face to face with him. The bottom quarter of his tattoo didn't match the rest, quite. No—it had to be the other way—he'd been only Third Hat at Escape, with the top three-quarters added later. Not a good job—Henty, she'd done Parnell and Dopples a lot better.

He reached to touch the ear with no lobe. "Tell me about that sometime, will you?"

"Sure. It wasn't so much."

"I'll bet." He gripped her shoulders—tense, shaking her, but not hard. "Stick with me, M'tana, you'll have your own ship again someday. And maybe more."

For the night he gave her a rating's cabin—empty for a while, it looked—and went with her to draw bedding and the rest. Alone in the place, she didn't bother to unpack. Tomorrow she'd get her things from River House, and close accounts with the Port. Any trouble about that? No—not with her and Tregare backing each other.

Tregare. She might be with him a while sometime, at that. The way of the man—not like Parnell, but he made her *feel* something. Parnell she'd *had* to have—and come to think on it, Honcho, too. This one she didn't—if she needed him at all, it was for what he was and where he was going. And maybe that's why he needed her.

The main thing, she decided—just short of sleep—was keeping it straight. Like always.

Magnificent Fantasy From Dell

Each of these novels first appeared in the famous magazine of fantasy, *Unknown*—each is recognized as a landmark in the field—and each is illustrated by the acknowledged master of fantasy art, Edd Cartier.